CEDAR COVE
16 Lighthouse Road
204 Rosewood Lane
311 Pelican Court
44 Cranberry Point
50 Harbor Street
6 Rainier Drive
74 Seaside Avenue
8 Sandpiper Way
92 Pacific Boulevard

BLOSSOM STREET
The Shop on Blossom Street
A Good Yarn
Susannah's Garden
(previously published as Old Boyfriends)
Back on Blossom Street
(previously published as Wednesdays at Four)
Twenty Wishes
Summer on Blossom Street
Hannah's List

Thursdays at Eight

Christmas in Seattle
Falling for Christmas
A Mother's Gift

Debbie Macomber

A Mother's Gift

MIRA

Published in Great Britain 2011
MIRA Books, an imprint of Harlequin (UK) Limited,
Eton House, 18-24 Paradise Road,
Richmond, Surrey, TW9 1SR

A Mother's Gift © Harlequin Books S.A. 2011

The publisher acknowledges the copyright holder of the individual works as follows:

The Matchmakers © Debbie Macomber 1986
The Courtship of Carol Sommars © Debbie Macomber 1990

ISBN 978 0 7783 0440 1

55-0411

MIRA's policy is to use papers that are natural, renewable and recyclable products and made from wood grown in sustainable forests. The logging and manufacturing processes conform to the legal environmental regulations of the country of origin.

Printed and bound by
CPI Group (UK) Ltd, Croydon, CR0 4YY

Debbie Macomber is a number one *New York Times* bestselling author. Her recent books include *44 Cranberry Point, 50 Harbor Way, 6 Rainier Drive* and *Hannah's List*. She has become a leading voice in women's fiction worldwide and her work has appeared on every major bestseller list. There are more than a hundred million copies of her books in print. For more information on Debbie and her books, visit www.Debbie Macomber.com.

The Matchmakers

Chapter One

"Danny, hurry up and eat your cereal," Dori Robertson pleaded as she rushed from the bathroom to the bedroom. Quickly pulling on a tweed skirt and a sweater, she slipped her feet into black leather pumps and went back into the kitchen.

"Aren't you going to eat, Mom?"

"No time." As fast as her fingers would cooperate, Dori spread peanut butter and jelly across two pieces of bread for a sandwich, then opened the refrigerator and took out an orange. She stuffed both in a brown paper sack with a cartoon cat on the front. Lifting the lid of the cookie jar, she dug around and came up with only a handful of crumbs. Graham crackers would have to do.

"How come we're always so rushed in the mornings?" eleven-year-old Danny wanted to know.

Dori laughed. There'd been a time in her life when everything had fit into place, but not anymore. "Because your mother has trouble getting out of bed."

"Were you always late when Dad was still alive?"

Turning, Dori leaned against the kitchen counter and crossed her arms. "No. Your father used to bring me a cup of coffee in bed." Brad had had his own special way of waking her with coffee and kisses. But now Brad was gone and, except for their son, she faced the world alone. Still, the rushed mornings were easier to accept than the long lonely nights.

"Want me to bring you coffee? I could," Danny offered. "I've seen you make it lots of times."

A surge of love for her son constricted the muscles of her throat, and Dori tried to swallow. Every day Danny grew more like his father. Tenderly she looked down at his sparkling blue eyes and the freckles that danced across his nose. Brad's eyes had been exactly that shade of bottomless blue, though the freckles were all hers. Pinching her lips together, she turned back to the counter, picked up a cup and took her first sip of lukewarm coffee. "That's very thoughtful of you," she said.

"Then I can?"

"Sure. It might help." Anything would be better than this insane rush every morning. "Now brush your teeth and get your coat."

When Danny moved down the hallway, Dori carried his empty cereal bowl to the sink. The morning paper was open, and she folded it and set it aside. Danny used to pore over the sports section, but recently he'd been reading the want ads. He hadn't asked for anything in particular lately, and she couldn't imagine what he found so fascinating in the classified section. Kids! At his age, she remembered, her only interest in the paper had been the comics and Dear Abby. Come to think of it, she didn't read much more than that now.

Danny joined her in the kitchen and together they went out the door and into the garage. While Dori backed the Dodge onto the narrow driveway, Danny stood by and waited to pull the garage door shut.

"One of these days," she grumbled as her son climbed into the front seat, "I'm going to get an automatic garage-door opener."

Danny gave her a curious look. "Why? You've got me."

A smile worked its way across Dori's face. "Why, indeed?"

Several minutes followed while Danny said nothing. That was unusual, and twice Dori's eyes sought his. Danny's expression was troubled, but she didn't pry, knowing her son would speak when he was ready.

"Mom, I've been wanting to ask you something," he began haltingly, then paused.

"What?" Dori said, thinking the Seattle traffic got worse every morning. Or maybe it wasn't that the traffic got heavier, just that she got later.

"I've been thinking."

"Did it hurt?" That was an old joke of theirs, but Danny didn't have an immediate comeback the way he usually did.

"Hey, kid, this is serious, isn't it?"

Danny shrugged one shoulder in an offhand manner. "Well, I know you loved Dad and everything, but I think it's time you found me another dad."

Dori slammed on her brakes. The car came to a screeching halt at the red light as she turned to her son, eyes wide with shock. "Time I did *what?*" she asked incredulously.

"It's been five years, Mom. Dad wouldn't have wanted you to mope for the rest of your life. Next year I'm going to junior high and a kid needs a dad at that age."

Dori opened her mouth, searching for words of wisdom that didn't come.

"I can make coffee in the morning, but that's not enough. You need a husband. And I need a dad."

"This is all rather…sudden, isn't it?" Her voice was little more than a husky murmur.

"No, I've been thinking about it for a long time." Danny swiveled his head and pointed behind him. "Hey, Mom, you just missed the school."

"Darn." She flipped on her turn signal and moved into the right lane with only a fleeting glance in her rearview mirror.

"Mom…watch out!" Danny shrieked just as her rear bumper barely missed the front end of an expensive foreign car. Dori swerved out of its path, narrowly avoiding a collision.

The driver of the other car blared his horn angrily and followed her when she pulled into a side street that would lead her back to the grade school.

"The guy you almost hit is following you, Mom, and, boy, does he look mad."

"Great." Dori's fingers tightened around the steering wheel. This day was going from bad to worse.

Still looking behind him, Danny continued his commentary. "Now he's writing down your license plate number."

"Wonderful. What does he plan to do? Make a citizen's arrest?"

"He can do that?" Danny returned his attention to his flustered mother.

"Yup, and he looks like the type who would." Judging by the hard, uncompromising face that briefly met hers in the rearview mirror… The deep-set dark eyes had narrowed, and

the thick, equally dark hair was styled away from his face, revealing the harsh contours of his craggy features. He wasn't
what could be called handsome, but his masculinity was blatant and forceful. "A man's man" was the term that came to
mind.

"I recognize him," Danny said thoughtfully. "At least I
think I do."

"Who is he?" Dori took a right-hand turn and eased to a
stop in front of Cascade View Elementary. The man in the
BMW pulled to a stop directly behind her and got out of his
car.

"He looks familiar," Danny commented a second time, his
wide brow furrowed in concentration, "but I don't know from
where."

Squaring her shoulders, Dori reluctantly opened the car
door and climbed out. She brushed a thick swatch of auburn
hair off her shoulder as she walked back to meet the tall for-
midable man waiting for her. His impeccable suit and expensive leather shoes made him all the more intimidating.
His eyes tracked her movements. They were interesting and
arresting eyes in a face that looked capable of forging an
empire—or slicing her to ribbons—with one arch of a brow.
Dori was determined not to let him unnerve her. Although
she indicated with her hand that Danny should stay by the
car, he seemed to think she'd need him for protection. She
didn't have time to argue.

"I don't appreciate being followed." She decided taking the
offensive was her best defense.

"And I don't appreciate being driven off the road."

"I apologize for that, but you were in my blind spot and
when I went to change lanes—"

"You didn't even look."

"I most certainly did," Dori said, her voice gaining volume. For the first time she noticed a large brown stain on his suit jacket. The beginnings of a smile edged up the corners of her mouth.

"Just what do you find so amusing?" he demanded harshly.

Dori cast her eyes to the pavement. "I'm sorry. I didn't mean to be rude."

"The most polite thing you can do is stay off the road."

Hands on her hips, Dori advanced one step. "In case you weren't aware of it, there's a law in Washington state against drinking any beverage while driving. You can't blame me if you spilled your coffee. You shouldn't have had it in the car in the first place." She prayed the righteous indignation in her tone would be enough to assure him she knew what she was talking about.

"You nearly caused an accident." He, too, advanced a step and a tremor ran through her at the stark anger in his eyes.

"I've already apologized for that," Dori said, knowing that if this confrontation continued she'd come out the loser. Discretion was the better part of valor—at least that was what her father always claimed, and for once Dori was willing to follow his advice. "If it'll smooth your ruffled feathers, I'll pay to have your suit cleaned."

The school bell rang, and Danny hurried back to the car for his books and his lunch. "I've got to go, Mom."

Dori was digging around the bottom of her purse for a business card. "Okay, have a good day, hon." She hoped one of them would; hers certainly didn't look promising.

"Don't forget I've got soccer practice after school," he reminded her, walking backward toward the steps of the school.

"I won't."

"And, Mom?"

"Yes, Danny?" she said irritably, the tight rein on her patience slackening.

"Do you promise to think about what I said?"

Dori glanced at him blankly.

"You know, about getting me another dad?"

Dori could feel the hot color creep up her neck and invade her face. Diverting her gaze from the unpleasant man standing beside her, she expelled her breath in a low groan. "I'll think about it."

A boyish grin brightened Danny's face as he turned and ran toward his classmates.

Searching for a business card helped lessen some of Dori's acute embarrassment. Another man might have said something to ease her chagrin, but not this one. "I'm sure I've got a card in here someplace."

"Forget it," the man said gruffly.

"No," she argued. "I'm responsible, so I'll pay." Unable to find the card, after all, Dori wrote her name and address on the back of her grocery list. "Here," she said, handing him the slip of paper.

He examined it briefly and stuck it in his suit pocket. "Thank you, Mrs. Robertson."

"It was my fault."

"I believe you've already admitted as much." Nothing seemed likely to crack this man's granite facade.

"I'll be waiting for the bill, Mr...?"

"Parker," he said grudgingly. "Gavin Parker." He retreated toward his car.

The name was strangely familiar to Dori, but she couldn't recall where she'd heard it. Odd. Danny had recognized him, too.

"Mr. Parker," Dori called out.

"Yes?" Irritably he turned to face her again.

"Excuse me, but I wonder if I could have another look at the paper I gave you."

His mouth tightened into an impatient line as he removed the slip from his pocket and handed it back.

She scanned the grocery list, hoping to commit it to memory. "Thanks. I just wanted to make sure I remembered everything."

He looked at her coldly, and by the time Dori was in her car and heading for the insurance office, she'd forgotten every item. Just the memory of his eyes caused a chill to race up her spine. His mouth had been interesting, though. Not that she usually noticed men's mouths. But his had been firm with that chiseled effect so many women liked. There was a hard-muscled grace to him— Dori reined in her thoughts. How ridiculous she was being. She refused to spend one extra minute on that unpleasant character.

The employee parking lot was full when she arrived and she was forced to look for a place on the street, which was nearly impossible at this hour of the morning. Luckily, she found a narrow space three blocks from the insurance company where she was employed as an underwriter for home-owner policies.

By the time she got to her desk, she was irritated, exhausted and ten minutes late.

"You're late." Sandy Champoux announced as Dori rolled back her chair.

"I hadn't noticed," Dori returned sarcastically, dropping her purse in a bottom drawer and pretending an all-consuming interest in the file on her desk as her boss, Mr. Sandstrom, sauntered past.

"You always seem to make it to your desk on time," Sandy said, ignoring the sarcasm. "What happened this morning?"

"You mean other than a near-accident with a nasty man in an expensive suit or Danny telling me I should find him a new father?"

"He's right, you know."

Purposely being obtuse, Dori batted her thick lashes at her friend and smiled coyly. "Who's right? Danny or the man in the suit?"

"Danny! You *should* think about getting married again. It's time you joined the world of the living."

"Ah—" Dori pointed her index finger at the ceiling "—you misunderstand the problem. Danny wants a father the same way he wanted a new bike. He's not interested in a husband for me...." She paused and bit her bottom lip as a thought flashed into her mind. "That's it." Her eyes lit up.

"What's it?" Sandy demanded.

"The bike."

"You're going to bribe your son so he'll forget his need for a father?" Sandy was giving Dori the look she usually reserved for people showing off pictures of their children.

"No, Sandy." Dori groaned, slowly shaking her head. "You don't want to know."

Frowning, Sandy reached for a new policy from her basket. "If you say so."

Despite its troubled beginnings, the day passed quickly and without further incident. Dori was prepared to speak to her son when he stomped into the house at five-thirty, his soccer shoes looped around his neck.

"Hi, Mom, what's there to eat?"

"Dinner. Soon."

"But I'm starved *now*."

"Good, set the table." Dori waited until Danny had washed his hands and placed two dinner plates on the round oak table before she spoke. "I've been thinking about what you said this morning."

"Did it hurt?" Danny asked and gave her a roguish grin, creating twin dimples in his freckled face. "What did you decide?"

"Well…" Dori paid an inordinate amount of attention to the cube steak she was frying, then said, "I'll admit I wasn't exactly thrilled with the idea. At least not right away."

"And now?" Danny stood at the table, watching her keenly.

She paused, gathering her resolve. "The more I thought about it," she said at last, "the more I realized you may have a valid point."

"Then we can start looking?" His voice vibrated with eagerness. "I've had my eye on lots of neat guys. There's Jason—he helps the coach with the soccer team. He'd be real good, but I don't think he's old enough. Is nineteen too young?"

This was worse than Dori had thought. "Not so fast," she said, stalling for time. "We need to go about this methodically."

"Oh, great," Danny mumbled. He heaved a disgusted sigh. "I know what that means."

"It means we'll wait until the dinner dishes are done and make up a list, just like we did when we got your bike."

Danny brightened. "Hey, that's a great idea."

Dori wasn't as sure of that as Danny was. He bolted down his dinner, and the minute the dishes were washed and put away, he produced a large writing tablet.

"You ready?" he asked, pausing to chew on the tip of the eraser.

"Sure."

"First we should get someone as old as you."

"At least thirty-three," Dori agreed, pulling out a chair.

"And tall, because Dad was tall and it'd look funny if we got a short guy. I don't want to end up being taller than my new dad."

"That makes sense." Again Dori was impressed by how seriously her son was taking this.

"He should like sports 'cause I like sports. You try, Mom, but I'd like someone who can throw a football better than you."

That was one duty Dori would relinquish gladly. "I think that's a good idea."

"And it'd be neat if he knew karate."

"Why not?" Dori agreed amicably.

Danny's pencil moved furiously over the paper as he added this latest requirement to the growing list. "And most important—" the blues eyes grew sober "—my new dad should love you."

"That would be nice," Dori murmured in a quavering voice. Brad had loved her. So much that for a while she'd thought she might die without him. Even after all these years, the capacity to love another man with such intensity seemed beyond her.

"Now what?" Danny looked up at her expectantly.

"Now," she said, taking a giant breath. "Now that we know what we're looking for, all we need to do is wait for the right man to come along."

Danny seemed doubtful. "That could take a long time."

"Not with both of us looking." She took Danny's list and attached it to the refrigerator with a large strawberry magnet. "Isn't it time for your bath, young man?"

Danny shoved the pad and pencil into the kitchen drawer and headed down the hall that led to his bedroom.

Dori retired to the living room, took out her knitting and turned on the television. Maybe Danny was right. There had to be more to life than work, cooking and knitting. It wasn't that she hadn't tried to date; she had. Sandy had fixed her up with a friend of a friend at the beginning of summer. The evening had turned out to be a disaster, and Dori had refused her friend's attempts to match her up again. Besides, there hadn't been any reason to date. She was fairly content and suffered only occasionally from bouts of loneliness, usually late at night. Danny filled her life. He loved sports and she loved watching him play.

But Danny did need a father figure, especially now as he reached adolescence. Dori didn't see how any other man could replace Brad. Danny had been too young to remember much about his father, since Brad had died when Danny was just six. Her own memories of that age were vague and distant, and she wondered how much she would have remembered of her father if she'd been in Danny's place.

The house was unusually quiet. Danny was normally in and out of the bath so quickly that she often suspected he didn't get completely wet.

Just as she was about to investigate, Danny ran into the room, clutching a handful of sports cards. "Mom, that was Gavin Parker you nearly ran into today!"

Dori glanced up from her knitting. "I know."

"Mom—" his voice was filled with awe "—why didn't you *say* something? I want his autograph."

"His autograph?" Suddenly things were beginning to add up. "Why would you want that?"

"Why?" Danny gasped. "He's only the greatest athlete in the whole world."

Dori decided to ignore her son's exaggeration. Gavin Parker might be a talented sportsman of some kind, but he was also rude and arrogant. He was one man she instinctively wanted to avoid.

"Here, look." Danny shoved a football card under her nose.

Indeed, the name was the same, but the features were younger, smoother, more subdued somehow. The dark piercing eyes in the picture merely hinted at the capacity for aggression. Gavin Parker's appearance had altered over the years and the changes in him were due to more than age. The photo that stared back at her was of an intense young man, full of enthusiasm and energy for life. The man she'd met today was angry and bitter, disillusioned. Of course, the circumstances of their meeting hadn't exactly been conducive to a friendly conversation.

The back of the card listed his height, weight and position—quarterback. According to the information, Gavin had played for the Raiders, leading his team to two Super Bowl championships. In the year he'd retired, Gavin had received the Most Valuable Player award.

"How did you know who he was?" Dori asked in a tone of surprise. "It says here that he quit playing football six years ago."

"Mom, Gavin Parker was one of the greatest players to ever throw a football. *Everyone* knows about him. Besides, he does the commentary for the Vikings' games on Sundays."

Every Sunday afternoon, Dori and Danny joined her parents for dinner. Vaguely, Dori recalled the football games that had captured the attention of the two men in her life:

her father and her son. It was a sport that had never interested her very much.

"Can we ask him for his autograph?" Danny asked hopefully.

"Danny," Dori said with a sigh, yanking hard on the wool, "I sincerely doubt we'll ever see Mr. Parker again."

His shoulders sagged with defeat. "Darn. Now the guys won't believe me when I tell 'em my mom nearly ran Gavin Parker off the road."

"You may find this hard to believe," Dori admitted softly, "but I'd rather not have the world know about our little mishap this morning, anyway."

"Aw, Mom."

"Haven't you got homework?"

"Aw, Mom."

She felt her lips curve and her resolve not to smile vanished. "The room seems to have developed an echo."

Head drooping, Danny returned to his bedroom.

The following morning, in the early dawn light, Dori was awakened by a loud knock on her bedroom door. Struggling to lift herself up on one elbow, she brushed the wild array of springy auburn curls from her face.

"Yes?" The one word was all she could manage.

Already dressed in jeans, Danny entered the bedroom, a steaming cup of coffee in his hand.

"Morning, Mom."

"My eyes are deceiving me," she mumbled, leaning back against the pillow. "I thought I saw an angel bearing me tidings of joy and a cup of java."

"Nope," Danny said with a smile. "This is coffee."

"Bless you, my child."

"Mom?"

"Hmm?" Still fighting off the urge to bury her face in the pillow and sleep, Dori forced her eyes open.

"Do…I mean, do you always look like this when you wake up?"

Dori blinked self-consciously and again smoothed the unruly mass of curls. "Why?"

Clearly uneasy, Danny shuffled his feet and stared at the top of his tennis shoes. "If someone saw you with your hair sticking out like that, I might never get a new dad."

"I'll try to do better," she grumbled.

"Thanks." Appeased, Danny left, giving Dori the opportunity to pout in private. Muttering to herself, she threw back the sheets and climbed out of bed. A glance in the bathroom mirror confirmed what Danny had said. And her hair wasn't the only thing that needed improvement.

By the time Dori arrived in the kitchen, she'd managed to transform herself from the Wicked Witch of the West to something presentably feminine.

One look at his mother, and Danny beamed her a radiant smile of approval. "You're really pretty now."

"Thanks." She refilled her cup with coffee and tried to hide her grimace at its bitterness. Later, with the utmost tact and diplomacy, she'd show Danny exactly how much ground coffee to use. Any more of this brew, she thought, would straighten her naturally curly hair.

"Do you think we might see Gavin Parker on the way to school?" her son asked brightly as they pulled out of the driveway.

"I doubt it," Dori answered. "In fact, I doubt Mr. Parker lives in Seattle. He was probably just visiting."

"Darn. Do you really think so?"

"Well, keep your eyes peeled. You never know."

For the remainder of the ride to the school, Danny was subdued, studying the traffic. Dori was grateful he didn't catch a glimpse of Gavin Parker. If he had, she wasn't sure what Danny would've expected her to do. Running him off the road again was out of the question. She felt lucky to have come away unscathed after yesterday's encounter.

Danny didn't mention Gavin again that day or the next, and Dori was convinced she'd heard the last about "the world's greatest athlete." But the following Monday a cleaning bill arrived in the mail.

The envelope was typed, and fleetingly Dori wondered if Mr. Gavin Parker had instructed his secretary to mail the bill. In addition to the receipt from a downtown dry cleaner, Gavin had sent back her grocery list. Hot color blossomed in Dori's cheeks as she turned it over and saw the bold handwriting. At the bottom of her list Gavin had added "Driving lessons." Dori crumpled the paper and tossed it into the garbage.

The sooner she ended her dealings with this rude man the better. She'd just finished writing the check when Danny wandered into the room.

"What can I have for a snack?" he asked as he looked over her shoulder.

"An apple."

"Can I have some cookies, too?"

"All right, as long as you promise to eat a decent dinner." Not that there was much worry. Danny had developed a perpetual appetite of late. The refrigerator door opened behind her.

"Hey, Mom, what's this?"

Dori glanced over her shoulder at the yellow nylon bag Danny was holding up, pinched between forefinger and thumb. "Tulip bulbs. For heaven's sake, don't eat one."

He ignored her attempt at humor. "How long are they going to be in here?"

Dori flushed slightly, recalling that she'd bought them on special six weeks earlier. "I'll plant them soon," she said.

Loudly crunching a crisp red apple, Danny pulled up the chair across from her. "What are you doing?"

"Paying a bill." Guiltily she looked down at her checkbook, deciding to leave well enough alone and not mention *whose* bill she was paying. Another one of her discretion-and-valor decisions.

Saturday morning, Dori came out of her bedroom, sleepily tying the sash of her housecoat. The sound of cartoons blaring from the living room assured her that Danny was already up. An empty cereal bowl on the table was further testimony. The coffee was made, and with a soft smile she poured a cup and diluted it with milk.

"You're up." Danny came into the kitchen and grinned approvingly when he saw she'd combed her hair.

"Don't get hooked on those cartoons," she warned. "I want us to get some yard work done today."

Danny's protest was immediate. "I've got a soccer game."

"Not until eleven-thirty."

"Aw, Mom, I hate yard work."

"So do I," she said, although planting the tulip bulbs was a matter of pride to her. Otherwise they'd sit in the vegetable bin for another year.

Twenty minutes later, dressed in washed-out jeans and a faded sweatshirt that had seen better days, Dori got the hand trowel from the garage.

The day was glorious. The sun had broken through and splashed the earth with golden light. The weather was unseasonably warm for October; the last days of an Indian summer graced Seattle.

Danny was content to rake the leaves that had fallen from the giant maple tree onto the sidewalk, and Dori was surprised to hear herself humming. The scarf that held her hair away from her face slipped down and she pushed it back with one hand, smearing mud on her cheek.

She was muttering in annoyance when Danny went into peals of excitement.

"You came, you came!" Danny cried enthusiastically.

Who came? Stripping off her gloves, Dori rose to find Gavin Parker staring at her from across the yard.

"This had better be important," he said as he advanced toward her.

Chapter Two

"Important?" Dori repeated, not understanding. "What?"

"This." Impatiently Gavin shoved a slip of paper under her nose.

Not bothering to read the message, Dori shrugged. "I didn't send you anything other than the check."

His face reddening, Danny stepped forward, the bamboo rake in his hand. "You didn't, Mom, but I...I did."

Dori's response was instinctive and instant. "What?" She jerked the paper from Gavin's fingers. "I MUST TALK TO YOU AT ONCE—D. ROBERTSON" was typed in perfect capital letters. "In person" was written beneath.

"You see," Danny went on to explain in a rushed voice, "Mom said we'd probably never see you again and I want your autograph. So when Mom put the envelope on the counter to go in the mail, I opened it and stuck the note inside. I *really* want your autograph, Mr. Parker. You were the greatest quarterback ever!"

If Gavin felt any pleasure in Danny's profession of undying loyalty, none was revealed in the uncompromising line of his mouth. From the corner of her eye, Dori glimpsed a blonde fidgeting in the front seat of his car, which was parked in the street. Obviously Gavin Parker had other things on his mind.

Placing a protective arm around her son's shoulders, Dori met Gavin's unflinching gaze. "I apologize for any inconvenience my son has caused you. I can assure you it won't happen again."

Taking his cue from the barely restrained anger vibrating in his mother's voice, Danny dropped his head and kicked at the fallen leaves with the toe of his tennis shoe. "I'm sorry, too. I just wanted your autograph to prove to the guys that Mom really did almost drive you off the road."

A car door slammed and Dori looked up. Shock mingled with disbelief. It wasn't a woman with Gavin Parker, but a young girl. No more than thirteen and quite pretty, but desperately trying to hide her femininity.

"What's taking so long?" The girl strolled up in faded blue jeans and a Seahawks football jersey. The long blond hair was pulled tightly away from her face and tied at her nape. A few curls had worked themselves free and she raised a disgruntled hand to her head, obviously displeased with the way they'd sprung loose.

A smile lit her eyes as she noticed that Danny was wearing a football jersey identical to her own. "Hey, do you like the Seahawks?"

"You bet. We're gonna make it to the play-offs this year," Danny boasted confidently.

"I think so, too. My dad used to play pro ball and he says the Hawks have a good chance."

Dimples appeared on Danny's freckled face as he smiled, nodding happily.

"Get back in the car, Melissa." Gavin's tone brooked no argument.

"But, Dad, it's hot in there and I'm thirsty."

"Would you like a glass of orange juice?" Danny offered enthusiastically. "Gosh, I didn't think girls liked football."

"I know everything there is to know about it and I throw a good pass, too. Just ask my dad."

Before either Gavin or Dori could object, Melissa and Danny were walking toward the house.

Dori raised her brows in question. "I'll trade you one cup of coffee for an autograph," she said resignedly. A cup of Danny's coffee was poetic justice, and a smile hovered at the corners of her mouth.

For the first time since their dubious beginning, Gavin smiled. The change that simple movement made in his austere expression was remarkable. Deep lines fanned out from his eyes and grooves that suggested smiles and even laughter bracketed his mouth. But the transformation didn't stop with his face. Somehow, in some way, the armor he wore had cracked as she was given a rare dazzling smile.

Unfortunately his good humor didn't last long, and by the time he'd followed her into the house the facade was back in place.

Melissa and Danny were at the kitchen table, sipping from tall glasses filled with orange juice.

"Dad—" Melissa looked up eagerly "—can Danny go to the Puyallup Fair with us? It's no fun to go on the rides by myself and you hate that kind of stuff."

"I'm afraid Danny's got a soccer game this afternoon," Dori said.

"I'm the center striker," Danny inserted proudly. "Would you like to come and watch me play?"

"Could we, Dad? You know I love soccer. When the game's over we could go to the fair." Melissa immediately worked out their scheduling.

It was all happening so fast that Dori didn't know what to think.

"Mrs. Robertson?" Gavin deferred to her for a decision.

"What time would Danny be home tonight?" Dori asked, stalling for time. Gavin Parker might be a famous football player, but he was a stranger and she wasn't about to release her child to someone she didn't know. If she had to come up with an excuse, she could always use church the following morning and their weekly dinner with her parents.

"You have to come, too," Melissa insisted. "Dad would be bored to tears with Danny and me going on all the rides."

"Could we? Oh, Mom, could we?"

Needing some kind of confirmation, Dori sought Gavin's eyes.

Gavin said quietly, "It would make Melissa happy."

But not him. It didn't take much for Dori to tell that Gavin wasn't pleased with this turn of events. Not that she blamed him. The idea of spending an afternoon with two children and a dirt-smudged mom wouldn't thrill her, either.

Apparently seeing the indecision in her eyes, Gavin added, "It would solve several problems for me."

"Oh, Mom, could we?" repeated Danny, who seemed to have become a human pogo stick, bouncing around the kitchen.

"Who could refuse, faced with such unabashed enthusiasm?" Dori surrendered, wondering what she was letting herself in for. She gave Gavin the address of the nearby park where the game was to be played and arranged to meet him and Melissa there.

Granted a new audience, Danny was in top form for his soccer game. With boundless energy he ran up and down the field while Dori answered a multitude of questions from Melissa. No, Dori explained patiently, she wasn't divorced. Yes, her husband was dead. Yes, she and Danny lived alone. Danny was eleven and in the sixth grade.

Then Melissa said that her parents were divorced and her dad had custody. She boarded at a private school in Seattle because her dad traveled so much. As the vice president in charge of sales in the whole northwest for a large computer company, her dad was really busy. In addition, he did some television commentaries for pro football games on Sunday afternoons, and she couldn't always go with him.

Standing on the other side of his daughter, Gavin flashed her a look that silenced the girl immediately. But her father's censure didn't intimidate Melissa for long, and a few minutes later she was prodding Dori with more questions.

Danny kicked two of his team's three goals and beamed proudly when Gavin complimented him on a fine game. A couple of the boys followed the small group back to the car, obviously hoping one or the other would get up enough courage to ask Gavin for his autograph. Since even the discouraging look he gave them wasn't enough to dissuade the boys, Gavin spent the next five minutes scribbling his name across a variety of slips of paper, hurriedly scrounged from jacket pockets.

The party of four stopped at the house so Danny could take another of his world-record-speed baths and change clothes. While they were waiting, Melissa watched Dori freshen her makeup. When Dori asked the girl if she'd like to use her cologne, Melissa looked at her as though she'd suggested dabbing car grease behind her ears.

"Not on your life. No one's going to get me to use that garbage. That's for sissies."

"Thanks, anyway," Gavin murmured on the way out to the car.

"For what?"

"I've been trying for months to turn this kid into a girl. She's got the strongest will of any female I've yet to meet."

Dori couldn't imagine Gavin losing any argument and was quick to conceal her surprise that his daughter had won this battle.

The Puyallup Fair was the largest agricultural fair in Washington state. Situated in a small farming community thirty miles southwest of Seattle, the fair attracted visitors from all over western Washington and presented top Hollywood entertainment.

As a native Seattleite, Dori had been to the fair many times in the past and loved the thrill and excitement of the midway. The exhibits were some of the best in the country. And the food was fabulous. Since Gavin had paid for their gate tickets, Dori treated everyone to hush puppies and cotton candy.

"Can we go to the rides now?" Melissa asked eagerly, her arms swinging at her side.

The crowds were thick, especially around the midway, giving Dori reason for concern.

"I think I'd rather look at some of the exhibits before you two run loose," she said, turning to Gavin. His stoic expression told her he didn't care either way.

If Melissa was disappointed at having to wait, she didn't show it. Spiritedly she ran ahead, pointing out the displays she and Danny wanted to see first.

Together they viewed the rabbits, goats and pigs. Despite

herself, Dori laughed as Melissa and Danny ran through the cow barn holding their noses. Gavin, too, seemed to be loosening up a little, and his comments regarding Melissa's and Danny's behavior were quite amusing, to Dori's surprise.

"Dad, look." Melissa grabbed her father's arm as they entered the chicken area and led him to an incubator where a dozen eggs were set under a warm light. A tiny beak was pecking its way through the white shell, enthralling everyone who watched.

The bee farm, its queen bee marked with a blue dot, was another hit. Fascinated, Danny and Melissa studied the inner workings of a hive for several minutes. As they left, Dori stopped to hear a ten-minute lecture from a wildlife group. Gavin and the kids weren't nearly as interested, but they all stood and listened to the plight of the American bald eagle.

From the animal barns, they drifted to the 4-H displays and finally to the agricultural center.

Two hours later, Dori and Gavin sat drinking coffee at a picnic table on the outskirts of the midway while the two kids lined up for rides.

"You don't like me much, do you?" Gavin's direct approach shocked her a little.

It wasn't that she actually disliked him. In fact, she'd discovered she enjoyed his sharp wit. But Dori didn't try to fool herself with the belief that Gavin had actively sought her company. Having her and Danny along today simply made this time with his daughter less complicated.

"I haven't made up my mind yet." She decided to answer as straightforwardly as he'd asked.

"At least you're honest."

"I can give you a lot more honesty if you want."

A slow smile crinkled around his eyes. "I have a feeling my ears would burn for a week."

"You're right."

A wariness was reflected on Gavin's face. "I've attracted a lot of gold diggers in my day. I want you to understand that I have no intention of remarrying."

What incredible conceit! The blood pounded angrily through Dori's veins. "I don't recall proposing marriage," she snapped.

"I didn't want you to get the wrong idea. You're a nice lady and you're doing a good job of raising your son. But he's looking for a father, or so he's said, and you're looking for a husband. Just don't try to include me in your rosy little future."

Dori's hand tightened around the cup of coffee as she fought back the urge to empty the contents over his head.

She noticed the beginnings of a smile. "You have the most expressive eyes," he said. "There's no doubt when you're angry."

"You wouldn't be smiling if you knew what I was thinking."

"Temper, temper, Mrs. Robertson."

"Far be it from me to force myself on you, Mr. Parker." The derision in her voice was restrained to a minimum. Dori was astonished that she'd managed this much control. Standing, she deposited her half-full coffee cup in a nearby bin. "Shall we synchronize our watches?"

He stared at her blankly.

"Three hours. I'll meet you back here then."

With his attitude, she'd enjoy herself more alone. There were still a lot of exhibits to see. Staying with Gavin was out of the question now. Undoubtedly he'd spend the entire time worrying that she was going to slip a wedding ring on his finger.

Standing hastily, Gavin followed her, confusion narrowing his eyes. "Where are you going?"

"To enjoy myself. And that's any place you're not."

Stopping in his tracks, Gavin looked stunned. "Wait a minute."

Dori jerked the strap of her purse over her shoulder. "Forget it." Rarely had a man evoked so much emotion in her. The worst part, Dori thought, was that given the slightest encouragement, she could come to like Gavin Parker. He was a mystery—and she always enjoyed a mystery. Melissa was an impressionable young girl, desperately in need of some female guidance. It was obvious the girl was more than Gavin could handle. From their conversation during Danny's soccer game, Dori had learned that Melissa spent very few weekends with her father. Dori could only speculate as to the whereabouts of the girl's mother, since Melissa hadn't mentioned her. And Dori didn't want to pry openly.

"You know what your problem is, Gavin Parker?" Dori stormed, causing several people to turn and stare curiously.

Gavin cleared his throat and glanced around self-consciously. "No, but I have a feeling you're going to tell me."

Having worked herself up to a fever pitch, Dori hardly heard him. "You've got a chip on your shoulder the size of a California redwood."

"Would it help if I apologized?"

"It might."

"All right, I'm sorry I said anything. I thought it was important that you understand my position. I don't want you to go home smelling orange blossoms and humming 'The Wedding March.'"

"That's an apology?" Dori yelped.

People were edging around them as they stood, hands on their hips, facing each other, their eyes locked in a fierce duel.

"It's the best I can do!" Gavin shouted, losing his composure for the first time.

A vendor who was selling trinkets from a nearby stand apparently didn't appreciate their arguing in his vicinity. "Hey, you two, kiss and make up. You're driving away business."

Gavin tucked her arm in his and led her away from the milling crowd. "Come on," he said, then took a deep breath. "Let's start over." He held out his hand for her to shake. "Hello, Dori, my name is Gavin."

"I prefer Mrs. Robertson." She accepted his hand with reluctance.

"You're making this difficult."

"Now you know how I feel." She bestowed her most chilling glare on him. "I hope you realize I have no designs on your single status."

"As long as we understand each other."

Dori was incredulous. If he wasn't so insulting, she would have laughed.

"Well?" He was waiting for some kind of response.

"I'm going to look at the farm equipment. You're welcome to join me if you like. Otherwise, I'll meet you back here in three hours." It simply wasn't a real fair to Dori if she didn't take the time to check out the latest in farm gear. She supposed that was a throwback to her heritage. Her grandfather had owned an apple orchard in the fertile Yakima Valley—often called the apple capital of the world.

Gavin rubbed the side of his clean-shaven face and a fleeting smile touched his mouth. "Farm equipment?"

"Right." If she told him why, he'd probably laugh and she wasn't making herself vulnerable to any more of his attacks.

As it turned out, they walked from one end of the grounds to the other, admiring a variety of exhibits as they went. Several times people stopped to stare curiously at Gavin. If he was aware of their scrutiny, he gave no indication. But no one approached him and they continued their leisurely stroll undisturbed. Dori assumed the reason was that no one would expect the great Gavin Parker to be with someone as ordinary as she. Someone over thirty, yet.

At the arcade, Dori made a serious effort to restrain her smile, which hovered on the edge of laughter, as Gavin tried to pitch a ball and knock over three milk bottles. With his pride on the line, the ex-football hero was determined to win the stuffed lion. An appropriate prize, Dori felt, although he could've purchased two for the amount he spent to win one.

"You find this humorous, do you?" he muttered, carrying the huge stuffed beast under his arm.

"Hilarious," she admitted.

"Well, here." He handed the lion to her. "It's yours. I feel ridiculous carrying this around."

Feigning shock, Dori placed a hand over her heart. "My dear Mr. Parker, what could this mean?"

"Just take the stupid thing, will you?"

"One would assume," Dori said as she stroked the orange mane, "that an ex-quarterback could aim a little better than that."

"Ouch." He put out his hands and batted off invisible barbs. "That, Mrs. Robertson, hit below the belt."

She bought some cotton candy, sharing its sticky pink

sweetness with him. "Now you know what 'smelling orange blossoms and humming "The Wedding March"' felt like."

Masculine fingers curved around the back of her neck as his eyes smiled into hers. "I guess that did sound a little arrogant, didn't it?"

Smiling up at him, Dori chuckled. "Only a little."

The sky was alight with stars and a crescent moon in full display before they left the fairgrounds and drove back to Seattle. The BMW's cushioned seats bore a number of accumulated prizes, hats and other goodies. By the time they located the freeway, both Danny and Melissa were asleep, exhausted from eight solid hours of recreation.

Forty minutes later, Gavin parked in front of Dori's small house. Suppressing a yawn, she offered him a warm smile. "Thank you for today."

Their eyes met above the stuffed lion's mane. He released her gaze by looking down at her softly parted lips, then quickly glancing up.

Flushed and a little self-conscious, Dori directed her attention to her purse, taking out her house keys.

"I had fun." Gavin's voice was low and relaxed.

"Don't act so surprised."

At the sound of their voices, Danny stirred. Sitting upright, he rubbed his eyes. "Are we home?" Not waiting for an answer, he began gathering up his treasures: a mirrored image of his favorite pop star and the multicolored sand sculpture he'd built with Melissa.

Undisturbed, Gavin's daughter slept on.

"I had a great time, Mr. Parker." The sleepy edge remained in Danny's voice.

Gavin came around to open her door. With her keys in one hand and the stuffed lion in the other, Dori climbed out.

Then she helped Danny from the backseat. "Thanks again," she whispered. "Tell Melissa goodbye for me."

"I will." Gavin placed a hand on Danny's shoulder. "Good night, Danny."

"Night." The boy turned and waved, but was unsuccessful in his attempt to hold back a huge yawn.

Dori noted that Gavin didn't pull away until they were safely inside the house. Danny went directly into his bedroom. Setting the lion on the carpet, Dori moved to the window to watch the taillights fade as Gavin disappeared into the night. She doubted she'd ever see him again. Which was just as well. At least that was what she told herself.

"Time to get up, Mom." A loud knock at her bedroom door was followed by Danny's cheerful voice.

Dori groaned and propped open one eye to give her son a desultory glance. Mondays were always the worst. "It can't be morning already," she moaned, blindly reaching out to turn off the alarm before she realized it wasn't ringing.

"I brought your coffee."

"Thanks." Danny's coffee could raise the dead. "Set it on my nightstand."

Danny carefully put down the mug, but instead of leaving as he usually did, he sat on the edge of the bed. "You know, I've been thinking."

"Oh, no." Dori wasn't ready for any more of Danny's insights. "Now what?"

"It's been a whole week and we still haven't found me a new dad."

After spending Sunday afternoon arguing that Gavin Parker wasn't husband material, Dori couldn't handle another such conversation. Besides, someone like her wasn't going to interest Gavin. In addition, he'd made his views on marriage quite plain.

"These things take time," she murmured, struggling into a sitting position. "Give me a minute to wake up before we do battle. Okay?"

"Okay."

Dori grimaced at her first sip of strong coffee, but the jolt of caffeine started her heart pumping again. She rubbed a hand over her weary eyes.

"Can we talk now?" Danny asked.

"Now?" Whatever was troubling her son appeared to be important. She sighed. "All right."

"It's been a week and other than Mr. Parker we haven't met any guys."

"Danny." Dori reached over to rest a hand on his shoulder. "This is serious business. We can't rush something as important as a new father."

"But I thought we should add bait."

"Bait?"

"Yeah, like when Grandpa and I go fishing."

Another sip of coffee confirmed that she was indeed awake and not in the middle of a nightmare. "And what exactly did you have in mind?"

"You."

"Me?" Now she knew what the worm felt like.

"You're a neat mom, but you don't look like the moms on TV."

Falling back against the pillows, Dori shook her head. "I've heard enough of this conversation."

"Mom."

"I'm going to take a shower. Scoot."

"But there's more." Danny looked crestfallen.

"Not this morning, there's not."

His face sagged with discouragement as he got off the bed. "Will you think about exercising?"

"Exercising? What for? I'm in great shape." She patted her flat stomach as proof. She could afford to lose a few pounds, but she wouldn't be ashamed to be seen in a bikini. Well, maybe a one-piece.

Huge doubting eyes raked her from head to foot. "If you're sure…"

After scrutiny like that, Dori was anything but sure. Still, she was never at her best in the mornings; Danny knew that and had attacked when she was weakest.

By the time Dori arrived at the office, her mood hadn't improved. She'd begun to attack the latest files when Sandy walked in, holding a white sack.

"Good morning," her friend greeted her cheerfully.

"What's good about Mondays?" Dori demanded, not meaning to sound as abrupt as she did. When she glanced up to apologize, Sandy was at her side, setting a cup of coffee and a Danish on her desk. "What's this?"

"A reason to face the day," Sandy replied.

"Thanks, but I'll skip the Danish. Danny informed me this morning that I don't look like a TV star."

"Who does?" Sandy laughed and sat on the edge of Dori's desk, one foot dangling. "There are the beautiful people of this world and then there are the rest of us."

"Try telling Danny that." Dori pushed back her chair and peeled the protective lid from the cup. "I'm telling you, Sandy, I don't think I've ever seen this child more serious. He wants a father and he's driving me crazy with these ideas of his."

A smile lifted the corners of Sandy's mouth. "What's the little monster want now?"

"Danny's not a monster." Dori felt obliged to defend her son.

"All kids are monsters."

Sandy's dislike of children was well-known. More than once she'd stated emphatically that the last thing she ever wanted was a baby. Dori couldn't understand her attitude, but Sandy and her husband were entitled to their own feelings.

"Danny's decided I need to start an exercise program to get into shape," she said, her hands circling the coffee cup as she leaned back in her chair. A slow smile grew on her face. "I believe his exact words were that I'm to be the *bait*."

"That kid's smarter than I gave him credit for." Sandy finished off her Danish and reached for Dori's.

Dori had yet to figure out how anyone could eat so much and stay so thin. Sandy had an enormous appetite, but managed to remain svelte no matter how much she ate.

"I suppose you're going to give in?" Sandy asked, wiping the crumbs from her mouth.

"I suppose," Dori muttered. "In some ways he's right. I couldn't run a mile to save my soul. But what jogging has to do with finding him a father is beyond me."

"Are you honestly going to do it?"

"What?"

"Remarry to satisfy your kid?"

Dori's fingers toyed nervously with the rim of the coffee cup. "I don't know. But if I do marry again it won't just be for Danny. It'll be for both of us."

"Jeff's brother is going to be in town next weekend. We can make arrangements to get together, if you want."

Dori had met Greg once before. Divorced and bitter, Greg didn't make for stimulating company. As she recalled, the entire time had been spent discussing the mercenary inclinations of lawyers and the antifather prejudices of the court. But Dori was willing to listen to another episode of *Divorce Court* if it would help. Danny would see that she was at least making an effort, which should appease him for a while, anyway.

"Sure," Dori said with a nod of her head. "Let's get together."

Sandy didn't bother to hide her surprise. "Danny may be serious about this, but so are you. It's about time."

Dori regretted agreeing to the date almost from the minute the words left her lips. No one was more shocked than she was that she'd fallen in with Sandy's latest scheme.

That afternoon when Dori returned home, her mood had not improved.

"Hi, Mom." Danny kissed her on the cheek. "I put the casserole in the oven like you asked."

In a few more years, Danny would be reluctant to demonstrate his affection with a kiss. The thought produced a twinge of regret. All too soon, Danny would be gone and she'd be alone. The twinge became an ache. *Alone*. The word seemed to echo around her.

"Are you tired?" Danny asked, following her into the bedroom where she kicked off her shoes.

"No more than usual."

"Oh." Danny stood in the doorway.

"But I've got enough energy to go jogging before dinner."

"Really, Mom?" His blue eyes lit up like sparklers.

"As long as you're willing to go with me. I'll need a coach." She wasn't about to tackle the streets of Seattle without him. No doubt Danny could run circles around her, but so what? She wasn't competing with him.

Dori changed out of her blue linen business suit and dug out an old pair of jeans and a faded T-shirt.

Danny was running in place when she came into the kitchen. Dori groaned inwardly at her son's display of energy.

As soon as he noticed her appearance, Danny stopped. "You're not going like that, are you?"

"What's wrong now?" Dori added a sweatband.

"Those are *old* clothes."

"Danny," she groaned. "I'm not going to jog in a dress." No doubt he'd envisioned her in a skintight leotard and multicolored leg warmers.

"All right," he mumbled, but he didn't look pleased.

The first two blocks were murder. Danny set the pace, his knobby knees lifting with lightning speed as he sprinted down the sidewalk. With her pride at stake, Dori managed to meet his stride. Her lungs hurt almost immediately. The muscles at the back of her calves protested such vigorous exercise, but she succeeded in moving one foot in front of the other without too much difficulty. However, by the end of the sixth block, Dori realized she was either going to have to give up or collapse and play dead.

"Danny," she gasped, stumbling to a halt. Her breath was coming in huge gulps that made talking impossible. Leaning forward, she rested her hands on her knees and drew in deep breaths. "I don't…think…I…should…overdo it…the first…day."

"You're not tired, are you?"

She felt close to dying. "Just…a little." Straightening, she murmured, "I think I have a blister on my heel." She was silently begging God for an excuse to stop. The last time she'd breathed this deeply, she'd been in labor.

Perspiration ran down her back. It took all the energy she had to wipe the moisture from her face. Women weren't supposed to sweat like this, were they? On second thought, maybe those were tears of agony on her cheeks. "I think we should walk back."

"Yeah, the coach always makes us cool down."

Dori made a mental note to give Danny's soccer coach a rum cake for Christmas.

Still eager to show off his agility, Danny continued to jog backward in front of Dori. For good measure she decided to add a slight limp to her gait.

"I'm positive I've got a blister," she said, shaking her head for emphasis. "These tennis shoes are my new ones. I haven't broken 'em in yet." In all honesty she couldn't tell whether she had a blister or not. Her feet didn't ache any more than her legs did, or her lungs.

The closer they came to the house, the more real her limp became.

"Are you sure you're all right, Mom?" Danny had the grace to show a little concern.

"I'm fine." She offered him a feeble smile. The sweatband slipped loose and fell across one eye, but Dori didn't have the energy to secure it.

"Let me help you, Mom." Danny came to her side and placed an arm around her waist. He stared at her flushed and burning face, his brows knit. "You don't look so good."

Dori didn't know what she looked like, but she felt on the verge of throwing up. She'd been a complete idiot to try to maintain Danny's pace. Those six blocks might as well have been six miles.

They were within a half block of the house when Danny hesitated. "Hey, Mom, look. It's Mr. Parker."

Before Dori could stop him, Danny shouted and waved.

Standing in the middle of the sidewalk, hands on his hips, stood Gavin Parker. He didn't bother to hide his amusement, either.

Chapter Three

"Are you okay?" Gavin inquired with mock solicitude.

"Get that smirk off your face," Dori warned. She was in no mood to exchange witticisms with him. Not when every muscle in her body was screaming for mercy.

"It's my fault," Danny confessed, concerned now. "I thought she'd attract more men if they could see how athletic she is."

"The only thing I'm attracting is flies." She ripped the sweatband from her hair; the disobedient curls sprang out from her head. "What can I do for you, Mr. Parker?"

"My, my, she gets a bit testy now and then, doesn't she?" Gavin directed his question to Danny.

"Only sometimes." At least Danny made a halfhearted attempt to be loyal.

There was no need for Gavin to look so smug. His grin resembled that of a cat with a defenseless mouse trapped under its paws.

"Aren't you going to invite me in?" he asked dryly.

Clenching her jaw, Dori gave him a chilly stare. "Don't

press your luck, Parker," she whispered for his ears only. Hobbling to the front door, she struggled to retrieve her house key from the tight pocket of her jeans.

"Need help?" Gavin asked.

The glare she flashed him informed him she didn't.

With a mocking smile he raised his arms. "Hey, just asking."

The front door clicked open and Danny forged ahead, running to the kitchen and opening the refrigerator. He stood at the entrance, waiting for Dori to limp in—closely followed by Gavin—and handed her a cold can of root beer.

With a hand massaging her lower back, Dori led the way to the kitchen table.

"Do you want one, Mr. Parker?" Danny held up another can of soda.

"No, thanks," Gavin said, pulling out a chair for Dori. "You might want to soak out some of those aches and pains in a hot bath."

It was on the tip of her tongue to remind him that good manners wouldn't let her seek comfort in a hot bath while he still sat at her kitchen table.

Danny snapped open a can and guzzled down a long swig. Dori restrained herself to a ladylike sip, although her throat felt parched and scratchy.

"I found Danny's jacket in the backseat of the car the other day and thought he might need it," Gavin said, explaining the reason for his visit. He handed Danny the keys. "Would you bring it in for me?"

"Sure." Danny was off like a rocket, eager to obey.

The front screen slammed and Gavin turned his attention

to Dori. "What's this business about jogging to make you more attractive to men?"

Some of the numbness was beginning to leave Dori's limbs and her heartbeat had finally returned to normal. "Just that bee Danny's got in his bonnet about me remarrying. Rest assured you're out of the running."

"I'm glad to hear it. I'm rotten husband material."

A laughing sigh escaped as Dori's eyes met his. "I'd already determined that."

"I hung the jacket in my room," Danny told his mother, obviously wanting to please her. "It was nice of you to bring it back, Mr. Parker."

For the first time, Dori wondered if the jacket had been left intentionally so Gavin would have an excuse to return. She wouldn't put it past her son.

Gavin held out his palm to collect the keys.

"How come Melissa isn't here?" Danny wanted to know. "She's all right for a girl. She wasn't afraid to go on any of the rides. She even went on the Hammer with me. Mom never would." A thoughtful look came over Danny as if he was weighing the pros and cons of being friends with a girl. "She did scream a lot, though."

"She's at school." Gavin stood up to leave, the scrape of his chair loud in the quiet kitchen. "She thought you were all right, too…for a boy." He exchanged teasing smiles with Danny.

"Can we do something together again?" Danny asked as he trailed Gavin into the living room. Dori hobbled a safe distance behind them, pressing her hand to the ache at the small of her back. Who would've believed a little run could be this incapacitating?

"Perhaps." Gavin paused in front of the television and

lifted an ornate wooden frame that held a family portrait taken a year before Brad's death. It was the only picture of Brad that Dori kept out. After a silent study, he replaced the portrait and stooped to pat the stuffed lion, now guarding the window. "I'll get Melissa to give you a call the next weekend she's not at school."

"Not at school?" Danny repeated incredulously. "You mean she has to go to school on Saturdays, too?"

"No," Gavin said. "She boards at the girls' school she attends and spends the weekends with me if I'm not broadcasting a game. Things get hectic this time of year, though. I'll have her give you a call."

"Danny would like that," Dori said, smiling sweetly, assured that Gavin had understood her subtle message. Having Melissa call Danny was fine, but Dori didn't want anything to do with Gavin.

As Gavin had suggested, a leisurely soak in hot water went a long way toward relieving her aching muscles. Her parting shot had been childish, and Dori regretted it. She drew in a deep breath and eased down farther in the steaming water. It felt sinful to be so lazy, so relaxed.

"The table's set and the timer for the oven rang," Danny called.

With her hair pinned up and her lithe—but abused—body draped in a cozy housecoat, Dori ambled into the kitchen. Danny was standing by the refrigerator, rereading the list of prerequisites for a new father.

"Dinner smells good. I'll bet you're hungry after all that exercise."

Danny ignored her obvious attempt to divert his attention. That kid was getting wise to her ways.

"Did you realize Mr. Parker knows karate? I asked him about it."

"That's nice." Dori hoped to play down the information. "I'll take out the casserole and we should be ready to eat."

"He's tall and athletic and Melissa said he's thirty-six—"

"Danny," she snapped, "no! We went over this yesterday. I have veto power, remember?"

"Mr. Parker would make a great dad," he argued.

Her glass made a sharp clang as it hit the table. "But not yours."

To his credit Danny didn't bring up Gavin Parker's name again. Apparently the message had sunk in, although Dori knew her son genuinely liked Gavin and Melissa. As for herself, she still hadn't made up her mind about Gavin. Melissa was a sweet child but her father was another matter. No one exasperated Dori more than he did. Gavin Parker was arrogant, conceited and altogether maddening.

Another week passed and Danny marked off the days on their calendar, reminding her daily of his need for a new dad. Even the promise of a puppy wasn't enough to dissuade him. Twice he interrupted her while they did the weekly shopping to point out men in the grocery store. He actually wanted her to introduce herself.

The date with Sandy's brother-in-law, Greg, did more harm than good. Not only was she forced to listen to an updated version of *Divorce Court*, but Danny drilled her with questions the next morning until she threatened to drop the new father issue entirely.

The next few days, her son was unusually subdued. But Dori knew him well enough to suspect that although she'd won this first battle, he was out to win the war. The situation was weighing on her so heavily that she had a nightmare about waking up and discovering a stranger in her bed who claimed Danny had sent him.

Monday evening, when Danny was supposed to be doing homework, she found him shaking money from his piggy bank onto his bed. She'd purposely given him a bank that wouldn't open so he'd learn to save his money. He dodged her questions about the need to rob it, telling her he was planning a surprise.

"That kid's got something up his sleeve," Dori told Sandy the following day.

"Didn't you ask?"

"He said he was buying me a present." This morning Dori had brought in the coffee and Danishes, and she set a paper sack on Sandy's desk.

"Knowing Danny, I'd say it's probably a jar of wrinkle cream."

"Probably," she murmured and took a bite of the Danish.

"I thought you were on a diet."

"Are you kidding? With all the aerobics and jogging Danny's got me doing, I'm practically wasting away."

Sandy crossed one shapely leg over the other. "And people wonder why I don't want kids."

The phone was ringing when Dori let herself into the house that evening. She tossed her purse on the kitchen table and hurried to answer it, thinking the caller was most likely her mother.

"Hello."

"I'm calling about your ad in the paper."

Dori frowned. "I'm sorry, but you've got a wrong number." The man on the other end of the line wanted to argue, but Dori replaced the receiver, cutting him off. He sounded quite unpleasant, and as far as she was concerned, there was nothing more to discuss.

Danny was at soccer practice at the local park, six blocks from the house. The days were growing shorter, the sun setting at just about the time practice was over. On impulse, Dori decided to bicycle to the field and ride home with him. Of course, she wouldn't let him know the reason she'd come. He'd hate it if he thought his mother was there to escort him home.

When they entered the house twenty minutes later, the phone was ringing again.

"I'll get it," Danny shouted, racing across the kitchen.

Dori didn't pay much attention when he stretched the cord around the corner and walked into the hall closet, seeking privacy. He did that sometimes when he didn't want her to listen in on his conversation. The last time that had happened, it was because a girl from school had phoned.

Feeling lazy and not in a mood to fuss with dinner, Dori opened a package of fish sticks and dumped them on a cookie sheet, shoving them under the broiler with some French fries. She was chopping a head of cabbage for cole slaw when Danny reappeared. He gave her a sheepish look as he hung up the phone.

"Was that Erica again?"

Danny ignored her question. "Are you going to keep on wearing those old clothes?"

Dori glanced down at her washed-out jeans and Irish cable-knit sweater. "What's wrong with them?" Actually, this was one of her better pairs of jeans.

"I just thought you'd like to wear a dress for dinner or something."

"Danny—" she released an exasperated sigh "—we're having fish sticks, not filet mignon."

"Oh." He stuck his hands in his pockets and yanked them out again as the phone rang. "I'll get it."

Before Dori knew what was happening, he was back in the closet, the phone cord stretched to its farthest. Within minutes, he was out again.

"What's going on?"

"Nothin'."

The phone rang and the doorbell chimed simultaneously. "I'll get it," Danny hollered, jerking his head from one direction to the other.

Drying her hands on a dish towel, Dori gestured toward the living room. "I'll get the door."

Gavin Parker stood on the other side of screen, the morning paper tucked under his arm.

"Gavin." Dori was too surprised to utter more than his name.

Laugh lines fanned out from his eyes, and he had that cat-with-the-trapped-mouse look again. "Phone been ringing a lot lately?"

"Yes. How'd you know? It's been driving me crazy." Unlatching the screen door, she opened it, silently inviting him inside. What a strange man Gavin was. She hadn't expected to see him again and here he was on her doorstep, looking inexplicably amused.

Gavin sauntered in and sat on the sofa. "I don't suppose you've read the morning paper?"

Dori had, at least the sections she always did. Dear Abby, the comics, a trivia column and the front page, in that order. "Yes. Why?"

Making a show of it, Gavin pulled out the classified section and folded it open, laying it across the coffee table. Idly, he moved his index finger down the column of personal ads until he located what he wanted. "I was checking out cars in today's paper and I found something else that was pretty interesting...."

A sick feeling attacked the pit of Dori's stomach, weakening her knees so that she had to lower herself into the maple rocking chair across from him.

"Are you in any way related to the person who ran this ad? 'Need dad. Tall, athletic, knows karate. Mom pretty. 555-5818.'"

It was worse, far worse, than anything Dori would ever have dreamed. Mortified and angry, she supported her elbows on the arms of the rocker and buried her face in the palms of her hands. A low husky sound slipped from her throat as hot color invaded her neck, her cheeks, her ears, not stopping until her eyes brimmed with tears of embarrassment.

"Daniel Bradley Robertson, get in here this minute!" Rarely did she use that tone with her son. Whenever she did, Danny came running.

The closet door opened a crack and Danny's head appeared. "Just a minute, Mom, I'm on the phone." He paused, noticing Gavin for the first time. "Oh, hi, Mr. Parker."

"Hello, Daniel Bradley Robertson." Gavin stood up and took the receiver out of the boy's hand. "I think your mother would like to talk to you. I'll take care of whoever's on the phone."

"Yeah, Mom?" A picture of innocence, Danny met Dori's fierce gaze without wavering. "Is something wrong?"

Her scheming son became a watery blur as Dori shook her head, not knowing how to explain the embarrassment he'd caused her.

"Mom?" Danny knelt in front of her. "What's the matter? Why are you crying?"

Her answer was a sniffle and a finger pointed in the direction of the bathroom. Danny seemed to understand her watery charade and leaped to his feet, returning with a box of tissues.

"Do you people always use the hall closet to talk on the phone?"

Gavin was back and Danny gave his visitor a searching look. "What's the matter with Mom? All she does is cry."

The phone pealed again and Dori gave a hysterical sob that sounded more like a strangled cry of pain.

"I'll get it," Gavin assured her, quickly taking control. "Danny, come with me into the kitchen. Your mother needs a few minutes alone."

For a moment it looked as though Danny didn't know what to do. Indecision played across his face. His mother was crying and there was a man with an authoritative voice barking orders at him. With a weak gesture of her hand, Dori dismissed her son.

In the next hour the phone rang another twenty times. With every ring, Dori flinched. Gavin and Danny remained in the kitchen and dealt with each call. Dori didn't move. The gentle sway of the rocker was her only solace. Danny ventured into the living room just once, to announce that dinner was ready if she wanted to eat. Wordlessly shaking her head, she let him know she didn't.

After a while her panic abated somewhat and she decided not to sell the house, pack up her belongings and seek refuge at the other end of the world. A less drastic approach gradually came to mind. The first thing she had to do was get that horrible ad out of the personals. Then she'd have her phone number changed.

More composed now, Dori blew her nose and washed her tear-streaked face in the bathroom off the hall. When she walked into the kitchen, she was shocked to discover Gavin and Danny busy with the dinner dishes. Gavin stood at the sink, the sleeves of his expensive business shirt rolled up past his elbows. Danny was standing beside him, a dish towel in his hand.

"Hi, Mom." His chagrined eyes didn't quite meet hers. "Mr. Parker told me that what I did wasn't a very good idea."

"No, it wasn't." The high-pitched sound that issued from her throat barely resembled her voice.

"Would you like some dinner now? Mr. Parker and I saved you some."

She shook her head, then asked, "What's been happening in here?"

In response the phone rang, its jangle almost deafening—or so it seemed to Dori, who immediately cringed.

Not hesitating at all, Gavin dried his hands and went to the wall phone.

"Listen to him," Danny whispered with a giggle. "Mr. Parker figured out a way to answer the phone without having to argue. He's really smart."

Catching Dori's eye, Gavin winked reassuringly and picked up the receiver. After a momentary pause, he mocked the phone company recording. "The number you have reached has been disconnected," he droned in a falsetto voice.

For the first time that evening, the tight line of Dori's mouth cracked with the hint of a smile. Once again, she was forced to admire the cleverness of Gavin Parker.

Grinning, he hung up the phone and sat in the chair next to Dori's. "Are you feeling okay now?"

"I'm fine." She managed a nod. The confusion and anger

she'd experienced earlier had only been made worse by Gavin's gloating. But now she felt grateful that he'd stepped in and taken charge of a very awkward situation. Dori wasn't sure what would have happened otherwise.

A finger under her chin tilted her face upward. "I don't believe you're fine at all. You're as pale as a sheet." A rush of unexpected pleasure shot through her at the contact, impersonal though it was.

His finger ventured over the smooth line of her jaw in an exploratory caress. The action was meant to soothe and reassure, but his touch was oddly sensual and highly arousing. Bewildered, Dori raised her eyes to his. They stared at each other as his hand slipped to her neck, his fingers tangling with her shoulder-length hair. Dori could see the rise and fall of his chest and noted that the movement increased slightly, as if he too had been caught unawares by these emotions. His eyes narrowed as he withdrew his hand. "You need a drink. Where…?"

With a limp arm, Dori motioned toward the cupboard that held her small stock of liquor. As he poured a shot of brandy into a glass, Gavin said quietly, "Danny, haven't you got some homework that needs to be done?"

"No." Danny shook his head, then hurriedly placed his fingers over his mouth. "Oh…I get it. You want to talk to my mom alone."

"Right." Gavin exchanged a conspiratorial wink with the boy.

As Danny left the room, Gavin deposited the brandy in front of Dori and sat beside her again. "No arguments. Drink."

"You like giving orders, don't you?" Whatever had passed between them was gone as quickly as it had come.

Gavin ignored the censure in her voice. "I have an idea that could benefit both of us."

Dori took a swallow of the brandy, which burned her throat and brought fresh tears to her eyes. "What?" was all she could manage.

"It's obvious that Danny's serious about this new father business and to be truthful, Melissa would like me to remarry so she won't have to board at the school anymore. She hates all the restrictions."

Dori sympathized with the young girl. Melissa was at an age when she should be testing her wings and that included experimenting with makeup and wearing the latest fashions.

"You're not humming 'The Wedding March,' are you?" Dori asked.

Gavin sent her a look that threatened bodily harm, and she couldn't contain a soft laugh. She loved turning the tables on this impudent man.

"I've already explained that I have no intention of remarrying. Once was enough to cure me for a lifetime. But I am willing to compromise if it means Melissa will let up on the pressure."

"How do Danny and I fit into this picture?"

Eager now, Gavin shifted to the edge of his seat and leaned forward. "If the two of us were to start going out on a steady basis, Melissa and Danny would assume we're involved with each other."

Dori drew in a slow trembling breath. Much as she hated to admit it, the idea had promise. Melissa needed a woman's influence, and all Danny really cared about was having a man who'd participate in the things she couldn't. Dori realized her son was already worried about the father-son soccer game scheduled for the end of the season. For years his grandfather had volunteered for such events, but her dad was close to retirement and these days playing soccer would put a strain on him.

"We could start this weekend. We'll go to dinner Friday night and then on Sunday I'll take Danny to the Seahawks game if you'll take Melissa shopping." His mouth slanted in a coaxing smile.

Dori recognized the crooked grin as the one he probably used on gullible young women whenever he wanted his own way. Nibbling her lower lip, Dori refused to play that game. She wasn't stupid; he was willing to tie up Friday and Sunday, but he wanted Saturday night free. Why not? She didn't care what he did. As long as he didn't embarrass her in front of Danny and Melissa.

"Well?" Gavin didn't look nearly as confident as he had earlier, and that pleased Dori. There was no need for him to assume she'd fall in with his plans so easily.

"I think you may have stumbled on to something."

His smile returned. "Which, translated, means you doubt I have more than an occasional original thought."

"Perhaps." He'd been kind and helpful tonight. The least she could do was be a little more accommodating in exchange. "All right, I agree."

"Great." A boyish grin not unlike Danny's lit up his face. "I'll see you Friday night about seven."

"Fine." Standing, she clasped her hands behind her back. "And, Gavin, thank you for stepping in and helping tonight. I do appreciate it. I'll phone the paper first thing in the morning to make sure the ad doesn't appear again and contact the phone company to have my number changed."

"You know how to handle any more calls that come in tonight?"

Dori plugged her nose and imitated the telephone company recording.

The laugh lines around his eyes became prominent as he grinned. "We can have a good time, Dori. Just don't fall in love with me."

So he was back on that theme. "Believe me, there's no chance of that," she snapped. "If you want the truth, I think you may be the—"

She wasn't allowed to finish as he suddenly hauled her into his arms and kissed her soundly, stealing her breath and tipping her off balance. With her hands pushing against his chest, Dori was able to break off the unexpected attack.

"Shh," Gavin whispered in her ear. "Danny's right outside the door."

"So?" She still wasn't free from his embrace.

"I didn't want him to hear you. If we're going to convince either of those kids, we've got to make this look real."

She felt herself blush. "Give me some warning next time."

Gavin eased her away, studying the heightened color of her face. "I didn't hurt you, did I?"

"No," she assured him, thinking the worst thing about being a redhead was her pale coloring, which meant the slightest sign of embarrassment was more pronounced.

"Well, how'd I do?"

"On what?"

"The kiss." He shook his head as though he expected her to know what he was talking about. "How would you rate the kiss?"

This, Dori was going to enjoy. "On a scale of one to ten?" She let a lengthy pause follow as she folded her arms and quirked her head thoughtfully at the ceiling. The time had come for someone to put this overconfident male in his place. "If I take into consideration that you're an ex-quarterback, I'd say a low five."

His mouth twitched briefly. "I was expecting you to be a little less cruel."

"And from everything you say," she went on, "I don't expect your technique to improve."

"It might," he chuckled, "but I doubt it."

Danny chose that moment to wander into the kitchen. "I'm not interrupting anything, am I?"

"You don't mind if I take your mom out for dinner on Friday night, do you?"

"Really, Mom?"

Dori would willingly have given her son double his allowance not to have sounded quite so eager.

"I guess," she said dryly. Gavin ignored her lack of enthusiasm.

"But I thought you said Mr. Parker was a—"

"Never mind that now," she whispered pointedly, as another flood of color cascaded into her cheeks.

"I'll see you at seven on Friday." Gavin rolled down the sleeves of his shirt and rebuttoned them at the wrist.

"It's a date."

Dori had hardly ever seen Danny happier about anything. He quizzed her on Friday from the moment she walked in the door after work. As she drove him to her parents' place—they were delighted to have their grandson for the night—he wanted to know what she was going to wear, what kind of perfume, which earrings, which shoes. He gave her advice and bombarded her with football statistics.

"Danny," she said irritably, "I don't think Gavin Parker expects me to know that much about football."

"But, Mom, it'll impress him," he pleaded in a singsong voice.

"But, Danny." Her twangy voice echoed his.

Back at her own house, an exhausted Dori soaked in the tub, then hurriedly dried herself, applied some makeup—why was she doing it with such care? she wondered—and dressed. She wasn't surprised that Gavin was fifteen minutes late, nor did she take offense. The extra time was well spent adding a last coat of pale pink polish to her nails.

Gavin looked rushed and slightly out of breath as he climbed the porch steps. Dori saw him coming and opened the front door, careful not to smear her polish. "Hi." She didn't mention the fact that he was late.

Gavin's smile was wry. "Where's Danny?"

"My mom and dad's."

"Oh." He paused and raked his fingers through his hair, mussing the carefully styled effect. "Listen, tonight isn't going exactly the way I planned. I promised to do a favor for a friend. It shouldn't interfere with our date."

"That's okay," Dori murmured and cautiously slipped her arms into the coat Gavin held for her. She hadn't the faintest idea what he had in mind, but knowing Gavin Parker, it wasn't moonlight and roses.

"Do you mean that?" Already he had his car keys out and was fiddling with them, his gaze lowered. "I ran into some complications at the office so I'm a bit late."

"Don't worry about it, Gavin. It's not like we're madly in love." She couldn't restrain a bit of sarcasm. Thank goodness Danny wasn't there to witness her "date."

While she locked the front door, Gavin sprinted down the

porch steps and started the engine. Dori released an exasperated sigh as he leaned across the seat and opened the passenger door. With a forced smile on her lips, she slid inside. So much for any pretense of gallantry and romance.

It wouldn't have shocked her if there was another woman waiting for him somewhere. What did surprise her was that he pulled into a local fast-food place, helped her out of the car and seated her, then asked what she wanted to eat. She told him, and he lined up with the schoolkids and young parents to order their meals. She didn't know what he had up his sleeve or if he expected some kind of reaction to the choice of restaurant, but she didn't so much as blink.

"I did promise you dinner," he said, handing her a wrapped cheeseburger, fries and a chocolate shake.

"That you did," she returned sweetly.

"Whatever else happens tonight, just remember I fed you."

"And I'm grateful." Not for the first time, she had difficulty keeping the sarcasm out of her voice. Good grief, where could he be taking her?

"The thing is, when I asked you to dinner I forgot about a…previous commitment."

"Gavin, it's fine. For that matter you can take me back to my house—it's not that big a deal. In fact, if there's another woman involved it would save us both a lot of embarrassment." Not him, but the two women.

Gavin polished off the last of his hamburger and crumpled the paper. "There isn't another woman." He looked horrified that she'd even suggest such a thing. "If you don't mind coming, I don't mind bringing you. As it is, I had a heck of a time getting an extra ticket."

"I'm game for just about anything." Fleetingly Dori wondered what she was letting herself in for, but learning that it involved a ticket was encouraging. A concert, maybe? A play?

"Is it a performance?" she asked brightly.

"You could say that," he replied. "Sometimes these things can go on quite late."

"Not to worry. Danny's staying the night with my parents."

"Great." He flashed her a brilliant smile. "As Danny would say, for a girl, you're all right."

He made it sound exactly like her son. "I'm glad you think so."

After dumping their leftovers in the garbage, Gavin escorted her to the car and drove out of the parking space. He took the freeway toward Tacoma. Dori still wasn't sure precisely where they were going, but she wasn't turning back now.

Several other cars were parked outside a dimly lit part of downtown Tacoma. Gavin stepped out of the car and glanced at his wristwatch. He hurried around the front of the car to help her out. His hand grasped her elbow as he led her toward a square gray building. The streetlight was too dim for Dori to read the sign over the door, not that Gavin would have given her time. They were obviously late.

They entered a large hall and were greeted by shouts and cheers. As Dori scanned the audience, the automatic smile died on her lips and she turned furiously to Gavin.

"I promised a friend I'd take a look at his latest prodigy," he explained, studying her reaction.

"You mean to tell me that you brought me to the Friday-night fights?"

Chapter Four

"Is that a problem?" Gavin asked defensively, his gaze chal lenging hers.

Dori couldn't believe this was her "date" with the handsome and popular Gavin Parker. She'd never gone to a boxing match in her life, nor had she ever wanted to. But then, sports in general didn't interest her much—unless they were her son's soccer games. Despite that, her "No, I guess not," was spoken with a certain amount of honesty. Danny would be thrilled. Little else would convince the eleven-year-old that Gavin was serious about her.

Following Gavin into the auditorium and down the wide aisle, Dori was a little hesitant when he ushered her into a seat only a few rows from the ring. Whatever was about to happen she would see in graphic detail.

Apparently Gavin was a familiar patron at these matches. He introduced Dori to several men whose names floated past her so quickly that she could never hope to remember them. Glancing around, Dori noted that there were only a few other women present. In her little black dress and wool coat, she was decidedly overdressed. Cringing, Dori huddled down in her seat while Gavin carried on a friendly conversation with the man in the row ahead of them.

"You want some peanuts?" He bent his head close to hers as he asked.

"No, thanks." Her hands lay in her lap, clutching her purse and an unread program she'd received at the door. People didn't eat while they watched this kind of thing, did they?

Gavin shrugged and stood up, reaching for some loose change in his pocket. He turned back to her. "You're not mad, are you?"

Dori was convinced that was exactly what he'd expected her to be. Perhaps it was even what he wanted. Her anger would be just the proof he needed that all women were alike. Based on everything that had occurred between them, Dori realized Gavin didn't particularly *want* to like her. Any real relationship would be dangerous to him, she suspected—even one founded on friendship and mutual respect.

"No." She gave him a forced but cheerful smile. "This should be very interesting." Already she was fashioning a subtle revenge. Next time they went out, she'd have Gavin take her to an opera.

"I'll be back in a minute." He left his seat and clambered over the two men closest to the aisle.

Feeling completely out of her element, Dori sat with her shoulders stiff and squared against the back of the folding wooden seat. She was mentally bracing herself for the ordeal.

"So you're Dori." The man who'd been talking to Gavin turned to her.

They'd been introduced, but she couldn't recall his name. "Yes." Her smile was shy as she searched her memory.

"This is the first time Gavin's ever brought a woman to the fights."

Dori guessed that was a compliment. "I'm honored."

"He was seeing that gorgeous blonde for a while. A lot of the guys were worried he was going to marry her."

A blonde! Dori's curiosity was piqued. "Is that so?" Gavin hadn't mentioned any blonde to her. If he was going to see someone else regularly it would ruin their agreement. Gavin took her to the Friday-night fights, while he probably wined and dined this blonde on the sly. Terrific.

"Yeah," the nameless man continued. "He was seeing her pretty regularly. For a while he wasn't even coming to the fights."

Obviously Gavin and the blond woman had a serious relationship going. "She must've been really something for Gavin to miss the fights." Smiling encouragingly, Dori hoped the man would tell her more.

"He doesn't come every week, you understand."

Dori nodded, pretending she did.

"Fact is, during football season we're lucky to see him once a month."

Dori was beginning to wonder just how "lucky" she was. The man grinned and glanced toward the aisle. Dori's gaze followed his and she saw Gavin coming down the crowded center aisle, carrying a large bag of peanuts.

As soon as he sat down, Dori absently helped herself to a handful.

"I thought you said you didn't want any," Gavin said, giving her the bag.

"I don't," she mumbled, cracking one open with her teeth. "I don't even like peanuts."

"Then why did you grab them out of my hand the minute I sat down?"

"I did?" When she was agitated or upset, the first thing she usually did was reach for something to eat. "Sorry," she said, returning the paper sack. "I didn't realize what I was doing."

"Is anything bothering you?" Gavin asked. His eyes darkened as though he was expecting an argument.

Dori hated being so easy to read. She'd thought that sometime during the evening she'd casually bring up his liaison with this...this other woman who was jeopardizing their tentative agreement.

"Nothing's bothering me," she answered. "Not really."

His glittering eyes mocked her.

"It's just that your friend—" she gestured with her hand toward the row in front of them "—was saying that you were seeing a blonde and..."

"And you jumped to conclusions?"

"Yes, well...it isn't exactly in our agreement." What upset Dori the most was that it mattered to her if Gavin was seeing another woman. She had no right to feel anything for him—except as far as their agreement was concerned. But if Danny heard about this other woman, she might slip in her son's estimation, she told herself. He might decide that Gavin wasn't interested in her and redouble his search for a new husband-and-father candidate.

"Well, you needn't worry. I'm not seeing her anymore."

"What's the problem," Dori taunted in a low whisper, "was she unfortunate enough to smell orange blossoms?"

"No." He pursed his lips and reached for a peanut, cracking it open with a vengeance. "Every time she opened her mouth, her brain leaked."

Dori successfully hid a smile. "I'd have thought that type

of girlfriend was the best kind." *For someone like you,* she added mentally.

"I'm beginning to have the same feeling myself," he said dryly, his gaze inscrutable.

Feeling a growing sense of triumph, Dori relaxed and didn't say another word.

Soon cheers and loud hoots rose from the auditorium as the young boxers paraded into the room with an entourage of managers and assistants.

The announcer waited until the two men had parted the ropes and positioned themselves in their appropriate corners. Glancing at her program, Dori read that these first two were in the lightweight division.

Pulling down a microphone that seemed to come from nowhere, the announcer shouted, "Ladies and gentlemen, welcome to the Tacoma Friday-night fights. Wearing white trunks and weighing 130 awesome pounds is Boom Boom Bronson."

The sound echoed around the room. Cheers and whistles followed. Boom Boom hopped into the middle of the ring and punched at a few shadows, to the delight of the audience, before he returned to his corner. Even when he was in a stationary position, his hands braced against the ropes, Boom Boom's feet refused to stop moving.

Then the other boxer, Tucker Wallace, was introduced. Tucker hopped in and out of the middle ring, punching all the way. The crowd went crazy. The man beside Dori stormed to his feet, placed two fingers in his mouth and pierced the air with a shrill whistle. Dori grabbed another handful of peanuts.

The two fighters met briefly with the announcer and spoke with the referee before returning to their respective corners.

The entourages formed around each fighter again. Probably to decide a strategy, Dori mused.

The bell clanged and the two men came out swinging. Dori blinked twice, stunned at the fierce aggression between the men. They might have been listed in the lightweight division, but their corded muscles told her that their stature had little to do with their strength or determination.

Gavin had shifted to the edge of his seat by the end of round one. The bell brought a humming silence to the room.

Dori knew next to nothing about boxing. She hated fighting, but the competition between Boom Boom and Tucker seemed exaggerated and somehow theatrical. Despite her dislike of violence, Dori found herself cheering for Boom Boom. When he was slammed to the ground by Tucker's powerful right hand, Dori jumped to her feet to see if he was hurt.

"Oh, goodness," she wailed, covering her forehead with one hand as she sank back into her seat. "He's bleeding."

Gavin was looking at her, his compelling dark eyes studying her flushed, excited face as if he couldn't quite believe what he saw.

"Is something wrong?" Boldly her gaze met his and a shiver of sensual awareness danced over her skin. "I'm cheering too loud?" She'd become so engrossed in what was happening between the two boxers that she must have embarrassed him with her vocal enthusiasm.

"No," he muttered, shaking his head. "I guess I'm surprised you like it."

"Well, to be honest," she admitted. "I didn't think I would. But these guys are good."

"Yes." He gave her a dazzling smile. "They are."

The adrenaline pumped through Dori's limbs as Boom Boom fought on to win the match in a unanimous decision.

At the end of three bouts the evening was over and Gavin helped her on with her coat. The night had turned rainy and cold, and Dori shivered as they walked to the car.

The moment they were settled, Gavin turned on the heater. "You'll be warm in a minute."

Dori stuck her bare hands deep in her pockets. "If it gets much colder, it'll probably snow."

"It won't," Gavin stated confidently. "It was hot in the auditorium, that's all." He paused to snap his seat belt into place. Dori averted her face to check the heavy flow of traffic. They wouldn't be able to get out of their parking spot for several minutes, but there wasn't any rush. Although she was reluctant to admit it, she'd enjoyed the evening. Being taken to the fights was the last thing she'd expected, but Dori was quickly learning that Gavin was a man of surprises.

"Here," Gavin said, half leaning across her. "Buckle up." Before Dori could free her hand to reach for the seat belt, Gavin had pulled it across her waist. He hesitated, his eyes meeting hers. Their mouths were close, so close. Dori swallowed convulsively. Her heart skipped a beat, then hammered wildly. She stared at him, hardly able to believe what she saw in his eyes or the feelings that stirred in her own breast. A strange, inexplicable sensation came over her. At that moment, she felt as if she and Gavin were good friends, two people who shared a special bond of companionship. She liked him, respected him, enjoyed his company.

She knew when he lowered his head that he was going to kiss her, but instead of drawing away, she met him halfway, shocked at how much she wanted him to do exactly this. His mouth fit easily, expertly, over hers in a tender, undemanding caress. One hand smoothed the hair from her temple as he lifted his mouth from hers and brushed his lips over her brow.

"Feeling warmer?" he asked in a husky murmur.

Her body was suffused by an unexpected rush of heat, her blood vigorously pounding through her veins. Unable to find her voice, she nodded.

"Good." He clicked her seat belt into place, and with utter nonchalance, checked the rearview mirror before pulling onto the street.

Silently Dori thanked God for the cover of night. Her face burned at her own imprudence. Gavin had kissed her and she'd let him. Worse, she'd enjoyed it. Enjoyed it so much that she'd been sorry when he'd stopped.

"I give you a six, maybe a low seven," she challenged, struggling to disguise his effect on her.

"What?"

"The kiss," she returned coolly, but there was a brittle edge to her airy reply. Her greatest fear was that he might be secretly amused by the ardor of her response.

"I'm pleased to know I'm improving. As I recall, the last kiss was a mere five." He merged with the moving traffic that led to the main arterial, halted at a stoplight and chuckled. "A seven," he repeated. "I'd have rated it more of an eight."

"Maybe." Dori relaxed and a light laugh tickled her throat. "No, it was definitely a seven."

"You're a hard woman, Dori Robertson."

Her laugh would no longer be denied. "So I've been told."

Instead of heading for the freeway as she expected, Gavin took several turns that led indirectly to the waterfront.

"Where are we going?"

"For something to eat. I thought you might be hungry."

Dori had to stop and think about it before deciding that yes, she probably could eat. "One thing."

"Yeah?" Gavin's eyes momentarily left the road.

"Not another hamburger. That's all Danny ever wants when we go out."

"Don't worry, I have something else in mind."

Gavin's "something else" turned out to be The Lobster Shop, an elegant restaurant overlooking the busy Tacoma harbor. Dori had often heard about the restaurant but had never been there. It was the kind of place where reservations were required days in advance.

"You were planning this all along," she said as he drove into the parking lot in front of the restaurant. She studied the strong, broad face and thick dark hair with silver wings fanning out from the temples.

"I thought I might have to appease you after taking you to the fights."

"I enjoyed myself."

His soft chuckle filled the car. "I know. You really surprised me, especially when you flew to your feet and kissed Boom Boom."

"It's so different from seeing it on television. And I blew him a kiss," she said on a note of righteous indignation. "That's entirely different from flying to my feet and kissing him. I was happy he won the bout, that's all."

"I could tell. However, next time you feel like kissing an athlete, you might want to try me."

"You must be joking!" She brought her hand to her heart and feigned a look of shock. "What if you rated me?"

Gavin was still chuckling when he left the car and came around to her side. There was a glint of admiration in his eyes as he escorted her into the restaurant.

The food was as good as Dori had expected. They both had lobster and an excellent white wine; after their meal, they sat and talked over cups of coffee.

"To be truthful," Dori said, staring into the depths of her drink, "I didn't have much hope for our 'date.'"

"You didn't?" A crooked smile slid across Gavin's mouth.

"But to my utter amazement, I've enjoyed myself. The best thing about this evening is not having to worry about making any real commitment or analyzing our relationship. So we can just enjoy spending this time together. We both know where we stand and that's comfortable. I like it."

"I do, too," Gavin agreed, finishing his coffee. He smiled absently at the waitress as he paid their bill.

Dori knew they should think about leaving, but she felt content and surprisingly at ease. When another waitress refilled their cups, neither objected.

"How long have you been a widow?" Gavin asked.

"Five years." Dori's fingers curved around the cup as she lowered her gaze. "Even after all this time I still have trouble accepting that Brad's gone. It seems so…unreal. Maybe if he'd had a lingering illness, it would've been easier to accept. It happened so fast. He went to work one morning and was gone the next. A year later I was still reeling from the shock. I've thought about that day a thousand times. Had I known it was going to be our last morning together, there would've been so many things to say. As it was, I didn't even get a chance to thank him for the wonderful years we shared."

"What happened?" Gavin reached for her hand. "Listen, if this is painful, we can drop it."

"No," she whispered and offered him a reassuring smile. "It's only natural for you to be curious. It was a freak accident. To this day I'm not sure exactly what happened. Brad was a bricklayer and he was working on a project downtown. The scaffolding gave way and a half ton of bricks fell on him. He was gone by the time they could free his body." She swallowed to relieve the tightness in her throat. "I was three months pregnant with our second child. We'd planned this baby so carefully, building up our savings so I could quit my job. Everything seemed to fall apart at once. A week after Brad's funeral, I lost the baby."

Gavin's fingers tightened on hers. "You're a strong woman to have survived those years."

Dori felt her throat muscles constrict and she nodded sadly. "I didn't have any choice. There was Danny, and his world had been turned upside down along with mine. We clung to each other, and after a while we were able to pick up the pieces of our lives. I'm not saying it was easy, but there really wasn't any choice. We were alive, and we couldn't stay buried with Brad."

"When Danny asked for a new father it really must've thrown you."

"It certainly came out of left field." Her eyes sparkled with silent laughter. "That boy thinks up the craziest ideas sometimes."

"You mean like the want ad?"

Dori groaned. "That has to be the most embarrassing moment of my life. You'll never know how grateful I am that you stepped in when you did."

"If you can persuade Melissa to buy a dress, I'll be forever in your debt."

"Consider it done."

Strangely, her answer didn't seem to please him. He gulped down the last of his coffee, then pushed back his chair and rose. "You women have ways of getting exactly what you want, don't you?"

Dori bit back an angry retort. She didn't understand his reaction; she hadn't done anything to deserve this attack. But fine, let him act like that. She didn't care.

As he held open her car door, he hesitated. "I didn't mean to snap at you back there. I apologize."

An apology! From Gavin Parker! Dori stared at him. "Accepted," she murmured, hiding her astonishment as she concentrated on getting into the car.

On the return drive to Seattle, Dori rested her head against the seat and closed her eyes. It had been a long, difficult week and she was tired. When Gavin stopped in front of her house, she straightened and tried unsuccessfully to hide a yawn.

"Thank you, Gavin. I had a good time. Really."

"Thank *you*." He didn't turn off the engine as he came around to her side of the car. Dori experienced an odd mixture of regret and relief. She'd toyed with the idea of inviting him in for a nightcap or a final cup of coffee. But knowing Gavin, he'd probably assume the invitation meant more. In any case, he'd left the engine running, so he was ready to be on his way. Dori found she was disappointed that their time together was coming to an end.

With a guiding hand at her elbow, Gavin walked her to the front porch. She fumbled in her purse for her key, wondering if she should say anything. It hadn't slipped her notice that he'd asked about Brad yet hadn't offered any information regarding his ex-wife. Dori was filled with questions she didn't want to ask.

She hesitated, the key in her hand. "Thanks again." She didn't think he was going to kiss her, but she wouldn't object if he tried. The kiss they'd shared earlier had been pleasant, more than pleasant—exciting and stirring. Even now the taste of his mouth clung to hers. Oh, no! Why was she feeling like this? Dori's mind whirled. It must be the wine that had caused this lightheaded feeling, she decided frantically. It couldn't have been his kiss. Not Gavin Parker. Oh, please, don't let it be Gavin.

He was standing so close that all she had to do was sway slightly and she'd be in his arms. Stubbornly, Dori stood rigid, staying exactly where she was. His finger traced the delicate line of her chin as his eyes met hers in the dim glow of her porch light. Dori's smile was weak and trembling as she realized that he *wanted* to kiss her but wouldn't. It was almost as though he was challenging her to make the first move—so he could blame her for enticing him.

Dori lowered her eyes. She wouldn't play his game. "Good night," she said softly.

"Good night, Dori." But neither of them moved. "I'll pick up Danny about noon on Sunday," he added.

"Fine." Her voice was low and slightly breathless. "He'll be ready." Knowing Danny, he was ready now. Her quavering smile was touched by her amusement at the thought.

"I'll bring Melissa at the same time," Gavin murmured, and his gaze shifted from the key clenched in her hand to her upturned face.

"That'll be fine."

He took a step in retreat. "I'll see you on Sunday then."

"Sunday," she repeated, purposefully turning around and inserting the key in her lock. When the door opened, she looked back at him over her shoulder. "Good night, Gavin."

"Good night." His voice was deep and smooth. She recognized the message in his eyes, and her heart responded while her nerve endings screamed a warning. Hurrying now, Dori walked into the house and closed the door. He hadn't kissed her, but the look he'd given her as he stepped off the porch was far more powerful than a mere kiss.

The next morning the front door slammed shut as Danny burst into the house. "Mom! How did it go? Did Mr. Parker ask you any football questions? Did he try to kiss you good-night? Did you let him?"

Dori sat at the kitchen table, dressed in her old bathrobe with the ragged hem; her feet rested on the opposite chair. Glancing up from the morning paper, she held out her arms for Danny's hug. "Where's Grandma?"

"She has a meeting with her garden club. She wanted me to tell you she'd talk to you later." Pulling out a chair, Danny straddled it backward, like a cowboy riding a wild bronco. "Well, how'd it go?"

"Fine."

Danny cocked his head to one side. "Just fine? Nothing *happened?*" Disappointment made his voice fall dramatically.

"What did you think we were going to do?" Amusement twitched at the edges of her mouth, and her eyes twinkled. "Honey, it was just a date. Our first one, at that. These things take time."

"But how long?" he demanded. "I thought I'd have a new dad by Christmas, and Thanksgiving will be here soon."

Dori set the paper aside. "Danny, listen to me. We're dealing with some important issues here. Remember when we got your bike? We shopped around and got the best price possible. We need to be even more careful with a new father."

"Yeah, but I remember that we went back and bought my bike at the very first store we looked at. Mom, Mr. Parker will make a perfect dad." His arm curled around the back of the chair. "I like him a lot."

"I like him, too," Dori admitted, "but that doesn't mean we're ready for marriage. Understand?"

Danny's mouth drooped and his shoulders hunched forward. "I bet you looked pretty last night."

"Thank you."

"Did Mr. Parker see how pretty you looked?"

Dori had to think that one over. To be honest, she wasn't sure Gavin was the type to be impressed by a new dress or the fact that she was wearing an expensive perfume. "Do you want to hear what we did?"

"Yeah." Danny's spirits were instantly buoyed and he didn't seem to notice that she hadn't answered his question.

"First we had hamburgers and fries."

"Wow."

Dori knew that would carry weight with her son. "But it wasn't even the best part. Later we went to a boxing match in Tacoma."

Danny's eyes rounded with excitement.

"If you bring me my purse, I'll show you the program."

He bounded into the other room and grabbed her handbag. "Mom—" he hesitated before passing it to her, staring pointedly at her feet "—you didn't let Mr. Parker know that you sometimes sleep with socks on, did you?"

Dori could feel the frustration building inside her. "No," she said, keeping her eyes on her purse as she pulled out the program. "The subject never came up."

"Good." The relief in his voice was evident.

"Gavin wants you to be ready tomorrow at noon. He's taking you to the Seahawks football game."

"Really?" Danny's eyes grew to saucer size. "Wow! Will I get to meet any players?"

"I don't know, but don't ask him about it. All right? That would be impolite."

"I won't, Mom. I promise."

Danny was dressed and ready for the game hours before Gavin arrived on Sunday morning. He stood waiting at the living room window, fidgeting anxiously. But the minute he spotted the car, Danny was galvanized into action, leaping out the front door and down the steps.

Dori followed and stood on the porch steps, her arms around her middle to ward off the early-November chill. She watched as Melissa and Gavin climbed out of the car, then smiled at the way Danny and Melissa greeted each other. Like conquering heroes on a playing field, they ran to the middle of the lawn, then jumped up and slapped their raised hands in midair in a gesture of triumph.

"What's with those two?" Gavin asked, walking toward Dori.

"I think they're pleased about…you know, our agreement."

"Ah, yes." A frown puckered his brow as he gave her a disgruntled look and stepped past her into the house.

Dori's good mood did a nosedive, but she turned and followed him inside. "Listen, if this is too much of an inconvenience we can do it another week." Somehow she'd have to find a way to appease Danny. The last thing she wanted was for Gavin to view his agreement to spend time with her son as an annoying obligation. For that matter, she could easily take Danny and Melissa to a movie if Gavin preferred it. She was about to suggest doing just that when Danny and Melissa entered the house.

"Hi, Mr. Parker," Danny greeted him cheerfully. "Boy, I'm really excited about you taking me to the game. It's the neatest thing that's ever happened to me."

Gavin's austere expression relaxed. "Hi, Danny."

"Mom packed us a lunch."

"That was nice of your mom." Briefly, Gavin's gaze slid to Dori. Although he offered her a quick smile, she wasn't fooled. Something was bothering him.

"Yeah, and she's a really great cook. I bet she's probably one of the best cooks in the world."

"Danny," Dori warned in a low voice, sending him an admonishing look.

"Want a chocolate chip cookie?" Danny switched his attention to Melissa instead. "Mom baked them yesterday."

"Sure." Gavin's daughter accompanied Danny into the kitchen.

Dori turned to Gavin. "You know, you don't have to do this. I'll take Danny and Melissa to a movie or something. You look worn out."

"I am." He jammed his hands deep inside his pockets and marched to the other side of the room.

"What's wrong?"

"Women."

Dori recognized the low murmuring that drifted out from the kitchen as the sound of Melissa talking nonstop and with great urgency. Whatever was wrong involved Gavin's daughter.

"In the plural?" Dori couldn't hide a knowing grin as she glanced toward the children.

"These are the very best cookies I've ever had in my whole life," Melissa's voice sang out from the kitchen.

Shaking her head, Dori broke into a soft laugh. "Those two couldn't be any more obvious if they tried."

"No, I suppose not." Gavin shifted his gaze and frowned again. "Melissa and I had an argument last night. She hasn't spoken to me since. I'd appreciate it if you could smooth things over for me."

"Sure, I'll be happy to try."

Gavin lapsed into a pensive silence, then stooped to pat the stuffed lion he'd won for her at the fair. "Aren't you going to ask what we fought about?"

"I already know."

As he straightened, Gavin's dark eyes lit with amused speculation. "Is that a fact?"

"Yes."

"All right, Ms. Know-It-All, you tell me."

Dori crossed the living room and stopped an inch away from him. "The next time you go out with another woman, you might want to be a bit more discreet." Deftly she lifted a long blond hair from his shoulder.

Chapter Five

"It wasn't my fault," Gavin declared righteously. "Lainey showed up last night uninvited."

Dori's eyebrows arched expressively. How like a man to blame the woman. From the beginning of time, this was the way it had been. It had started in the Garden of Eden when Adam blamed Eve for enticing him to partake of the forbidden fruit, Dori thought, and it was still going on. "Uninvited, but apparently not unwelcome," she murmured, doing her best to hide a smile.

Gavin rubbed the back of his neck in an agitated movement. "Don't you start on me, too." His angry response cut through the air.

"Me!" It was all she could do to keep from laughing outright.

"No doubt I'm sentenced to a fifteen-minute lecture from you, as well."

Feigning utter nonchalance, Dori moved to the other side of the room and sat on the sofa arm. With relaxed grace she crossed her legs. "It wouldn't be fair for me to lecture you. Besides, I have a pretty good idea of what happened."

"You do?" He eyed her speculatively.

"Sure. This gorgeous blonde showed up.…" She paused to stroke her chin as if giving the matter deep thought. "Probably with two tickets to something she knew you really wanted to see."

"Not tickets but—" He stopped abruptly. "Okay. You're right, but I was only gone an hour and Melissa acted like I'd just committed adultery or worse." His defensiveness returned. Stalking over to stand by the television set, he whirled around, asking, "Are you mad at me, too?"

"No." Amused was more the word.

Gavin expelled his breath and looked visibly relieved. "Good. I swear this arrangement is almost as bad as being married."

"Even if I was upset, Melissa's scolded you far more effectively than I ever could."

A smile touched his eyes, revealing tiny lines of laughter at their outer corners. "That girl's got more of her mother in her than I realized."

"One thing, Gavin."

"Yes?" His gaze met hers.

"Is this Lainey the one whose brain leaks?"

"Yeah, she's the one."

"So you went out with her again although you claimed you weren't going to?" She wanted to prove to him that he wasn't as stouthearted or strong-willed as he'd wanted her to believe.

He surveyed her calmly. "That's right."

"Then what does that make you?" Dori hated to admit how much she was enjoying this.

His eyes were locked on her face. "I knew you'd get back at me one way or another."

Blinking her lashes wickedly, Dori gave him her brightest smile. It was obvious that Gavin was angrier with himself than with anyone else and that he didn't like his susceptibility to the charms of this blonde. And to be honest, Dori wasn't exactly pleased by it, either, although she'd rather have choked than let him know.

"Don't worry, all is forgiven," she said with a heavy tone of martyrhood. "I'll be generous and overlook your faults. It's easy, since I have so few of my own."

"I hadn't asked for your forgiveness," he returned dryly.

"Not to worry, I saved you the trouble."

A barely suppressed smile crossed his face. "I can't remember Melissa ever being so angry."

"Don't worry, I'll talk to her."

"What are you going to say?"

Not for the first time, Dori noticed how resonant his voice was. She shrugged one shoulder and glanced out the window. "I'm not sure, but I'll think of something," she assured him.

"I know what'll help."

"What?" She raised her eyes to his.

He strode over to her and glanced into the kitchen. "Danny, are you about ready?" Before Danny had a chance to answer, Gavin pulled Dori to her feet, enfolded her in his arms and drew her so close that the outline of his body was imprinted on hers.

"Ready, Mr. Parker," Danny said as he flew into the living room with Melissa following sluggishly behind. Before Dori could say anything, Gavin's warm mouth claimed hers, moving sensuously over her lips, robbing her of thought. Instinctively her arms circled his neck as his fiery kiss burned away her objections.

"Gavin!" The word vibrated from her throat. Somehow she managed to break the contact and, bracing her hands against his chest, separated her body from his. She was too stunned to say more than his name. The kiss had been so unexpected—so good—that she could only stare up at him with wide disturbed eyes.

"Danny and I should be back about five. If you like, we can all go to dinner afterward."

Mutely, Dori nodded. If he'd asked her to swim across Puget Sound naked, she would have agreed. Her mind was befuddled, her senses numb.

"Good." Gavin buried his mouth in the curve of her neck and Dori's bewildered eyes again widened with shock. As he released her, she caught a glimpse of Melissa and Danny smiling proudly at each other. Dori had to smother an angry groan.

"See you at five." With a thoughtful frown, Gavin ran his index finger down the side of her face.

"Bye, Mom," Danny interrupted.

"Bye." Dori shook her head to clear her muddled thoughts and calm her reactions. "Have a good time."

"We will," Gavin promised. He hesitated, studying his daughter. "Be good, Melissa."

The brilliant smile she gave him forced Dori and Gavin to hide a tiny, shared laugh.

"Okay, Dad, see you later."

Gavin's astonished eyes sought Dori's and he winked boldly. Parents had their own forms of manipulating. Again, Dori had difficulty concealing her laughter.

The front door closed and Melissa plopped down on

the sofa and crossed her arms. "Dad told you about *her*, didn't he?"

"He mentioned Lainey, if that's who you mean."

"And you're not mad?" The young girl leaned forward and cupped her face in her hands, supporting her elbows on her knees. "I thought you'd be furious. I was. I didn't know Dad could be so dumb. Even I could see that she's a real phony. Ms. Bleached Blonde was so gushy last night I almost threw up."

Dori sat beside the girl and took the same pose as Melissa, placing her bent elbows on her knees. "Your dad doesn't need either of us to be angry with him."

"But..." Melissa turned to scrutinize Dori, her smooth brow furrowed in confusion. "I think we should both be mad. He shouldn't have gone out with her. Not when he's seeing you."

Throwing an arm around the girl's shoulders, Dori searched for the right words. Explaining his actions could get her into trouble. "Your father was angrier at himself than either of us could be. Let's show him that we can overlook his weaknesses and...love him in spite of them." Dori knew immediately that she'd used the wrong word.

"You love Dad?"

A shudder trembled through Dori. "Well, that might have been a little too strong."

"I think he's falling in love with you," Melissa said fervently. "He hardly talks about you, and that's a sure sign."

Dori was unconvinced. If he didn't talk about her, it was because he wasn't thinking about her—which was just as well. She wasn't going to fool herself with any unwarranted emotions. She and Gavin had a dating agreement and she wasn't looking for anything more than a way of satisfying

Danny's sudden need for a father. Just as Gavin was hoping to appease his daughter.

"That's nice," Dori said, reaching for the Sunday paper. "What would you like to do today?" Absently she flipped the pages of the sales tabloids that came with the paper.

The girl shrugged and reclined against the back of the sofa. "I don't know. What would you like to do?"

"Well." Dori eased herself into a comfortable position and pretended to consider the possibilities. "I could do some shopping, but I don't want to drag you along if you'd find it boring."

"What are you going to buy?"

Remembering the way Melissa had watched her put on makeup sparked an idea. "I thought I'd stop in at Northgage plaza and sample a few perfumes at Macy's. You can help me decide which one your father would like best."

"Yeah, let's do that."

Two hours later, before she was even aware of Dori's scheme, Melissa owned her first cosmetics, a new dress and shoes. Once Dori had persuaded the girl that it was okay to experiment with some light makeup, progressing to a dress and shoes had been relatively easy.

Back at the house Melissa used Dori's bedroom to try on the new outfit. Shyly she paraded before Dori, her intense eyes lowered to the carpet as she walked. The dress was a lovely pink floral print with a calf-length skirt that swung as she moved. The ballet-style shoes were white and Melissa was wearing her first pair of nylons. Self-consciously she held out her leg to Dori. "Did I put them on right?"

"Perfect." Dori smiled with pride. Folding her hands together, she said softly, "Oh, Melissa, you're so pretty."

"Really?" Disbelief made her voice rise half an octave.

"Really!" The transformation was astonishing. The girl standing before her was no longer a defiant tomboy but a budding young woman. Dori's heart swelled with emotion. Gavin would hardly recognize his own daughter. "Come and look." Dori led her into the bathroom and closed the door so Melissa could see for herself in the full-length mirror.

The girl breathed a long sigh. "It's beautiful," she said in a shaking voice. "Thank you." Impulsively she gave Dori a hug. "Oh, I wish you were my mother. I really, really wish you were."

Dori hugged her back, surprised at the emotion that surged through her. "I'd consider myself very lucky to have you for a daughter."

Melissa stepped back for another look at herself. "You know, at first I was really hoping Dad would marry Lainey." She pursed her lips and tilted her head mockingly. "That's how desperate I am to get out of that school. It's not that the teachers are mean or anything. Everyone's been really nice. But I really want a family and a regular, ordinary life."

Dori hid a smile. *Really* was obviously Melissa's word for the day.

"But the more I thought about it, the more I realized Lainey would probably keep me in that stupid school until I was twenty-nine. She doesn't want me hanging around. If Dad marries her, I don't know what I'd do."

"Your father isn't going to marry anyone…" Dori faltered momentarily. "Not someone you don't like, anyway."

"I hope not," Melissa said heatedly. Turning sideways, she viewed her profile. "You know what else I'd really like to do?"

"Name it." The day had gone so well that Dori was ready to be obliging.

"Can I bake something?"

"Anything you like."

The spicy aroma of fresh-baked apple pie filled the house by the time Danny burst in the front door. "Mom!" he screamed as if the very demons of hell were in pursuit. "The Seahawks won. The score was 14 to 7."

Dori had been so busy it hadn't occurred to her to turn on the television. "Did you have a good time?"

"Mr. Parker bought me a hot dog and a soda pop and some peanuts."

Dori cast an accusing glare at Gavin, who shrugged, then grinned sheepishly.

"What about the lunch I packed you?"

"We couldn't bring it into the stadium. Mr. Parker says it's more fun to buy stuff at the game, anyway."

"Oh, he did, did he?" Amused, Dori found her laughing eyes meeting Gavin's.

The bedroom door opened a crack. "Can I come out yet?"

Guiltily Dori glanced at the hallway. "Oh, goodness, I nearly forgot. Sit down, you two. Melissa and I have a surprise."

Gavin and Danny obediently took a seat. "Ready," Dori called over her shoulder. The bedroom door opened wide and Melissa started down the hallway. Halting her progress for a moment, Dori announced, "While you two were at the game, Melissa and I were just as busy shopping."

Confident now, none of her earlier coyness evident, Melissa strolled into the room and gracefully modeled the dress, turning as she came to a stop in front of the sofa. Smiling, she curtsied and demurely lowered her lashes. Then she rose, folding her hands in front of her, ready to receive their lavish praise.

"You look like a girl," Danny said, unable to disguise his lack of enthusiasm. At the disapproving look Dori flashed him, he quickly amended his hastily spoken words. "You look real pretty, though."

Dori studied Gavin's reaction. A myriad of emotions were revealed in the strong, often stern features. "This can't be my little girl. Not Melissa Jane Parker, my daughter."

Melissa giggled happily. "Really, Dad, who else could it be?"

Gavin shook his head. "I don't know who's wearing that dress, but I can hardly believe I've got a daughter this pretty."

"I made you a surprise, too," Melissa said eagerly. "Something to eat."

"Something to eat?" He echoed her words and looked at Dori, who smiled innocently.

Tugging at his hand, Melissa urged her father off the couch and led him into the kitchen. "Dori helped me."

"Not that much. She did most of the work herself."

"A pie?" Gavin's gaze fell to the cooling masterpiece that rested on the kitchen countertop.

"Apple," Melissa boasted proudly. "Your favorite."

Later that night, Dori lay in bed gazing up at the darkened ceiling, her clasped hands supporting the back of her head. The day had been wonderful. There was no other word to describe it. She'd enjoyed shopping with Melissa, particularly because the girl had been so responsive to Dori's suggestions. Dori didn't like to think about the baby she'd lost after Brad's death. She'd so hoped for a daughter. Today it was almost as if Melissa had been hers. Dori felt such enthusiasm, such joy, in sharing little things, like shopping with Melissa. She loved Danny beyond reason, but there were certain things he'd never appreciate. Shopping was one. But Melissa had enjoyed it as much as Dori had.

Danny's day had been wonderful, too. All evening he'd talked nonstop about the football game and had obviously had the time of his life. Long after Gavin and Melissa had left, Danny continued to recount the highlights of the game, recalling different plays with a vivid memory for detail. Either the two children had superlative—and hitherto unsuspected—acting abilities, or their reactions had been genuine. Dori found it difficult to believe this had all been a charade. She'd had her suspicions when Gavin first suggested their arrangement, but now she thought it might be the best thing to have happened to her in a long time—the best thing for all of them.

The next morning Sandy looked up from her work when Dori entered the office.

"Hi," Dori said absently as she pulled out the bottom drawer of her desk and deposited her purse. When Sandy didn't immediately respond, Dori glanced up. Sandy was studying her, head slightly cocked. "What's with the funny, bug-eyed look?" Dori demanded.

"There's something different about you."

"Me?"

"Yeah. You and this football hero went out Friday night, didn't you?"

Dori couldn't help chuckling. "Yes. To the fights, if you can believe it."

"I don't."

"Well, do, because it's the truth. But first he took me out for a four-star meal of hamburgers, French fries and a chocolate shake."

"And he's alive to tell about it?"

Dori relaxed in her chair and crossed her arms, letting the memory of that night amuse her anew. "Yup."

"From that dreamy look in your eyes I'd say you had a good time."

Dreamy look! Dori stiffened and reached for her pen. "Oh, hardly. You just like to tease, that's all."

Sandy raised her eyebrows in response, then returned to the file she was working on. "If you say so, but you might want to watch where you walk, what with all those stars blinding your eyes."

At about eleven o'clock the phone buzzed. Usually Sandy and Dori took turns answering, but Sandy was away from her desk and Dori automatically reached for the receiver.

"Underwriting," she announced.

"Dori?"

"Gavin?" Her heart began to pound like a jackhammer gone wild. "Hi."

"What time are you free for lunch?" he asked without preamble.

"Noon." From the sound of his voice, he was concerned about something. "Is anything wrong?" Dori probed.

"Not really. I just think we need to talk."

They agreed on an attractive seafood restaurant beside Lake Union. Gavin was already seated at one of the linen-covered tables when Dori arrived an hour later. She noticed that his eyes were thoughtful as he watched the maître d' lead her to his table.

"This is a nice surprise," she said to Gavin, smiling appreciatively at the waiter who held out her chair.

"Yes, although I don't usually take this kind of lunch break." There seemed to be a hidden meaning in his statement.

Gavin always managed to throw her off course one way

or another. Whenever she felt she understood him, he'd say or do something that made her realize she hardly knew this man. Her intuition told her it was about to happen again. Mentally she braced herself, and a small sigh of dread quivered in her throat.

To mask her fears, Dori lifted the menu and studied it with unseeing eyes. The restaurant was known for its seafood, and Dori was toying with the idea of ordering a Crab Louis when Gavin spoke. "Melissa had a good time yesterday."

"I did, too. She's a wonderful child, Gavin." Dori set the menu aside, having decided on a shrimp salad.

"Once we got off the subject of you, Danny and I had a great time ourselves," Gavin murmured.

Dori groaned inwardly at the thought of Danny endlessly extolling her virtues. Gavin must have been thoroughly sick of hearing about her. She'd make a point of speaking to Danny later.

"Danny certainly enjoyed himself."

Gavin laid the menu alongside his plate and stared at her in nerve-racking silence.

Instinctively, Dori stiffened. "But there's a problem, right?" she asked with deliberate softness, fighting off a sense of unease.

"Yes. I think you might have laid on this motherhood bit a little too thick, don't you? Melissa drove me crazy last night. First Danny and now my own daughter."

Anger raged within Dori and it was all she could do not to bolt out of the restaurant. To Gavin's twisted way of thinking, she had intentionally set out to convince his daughter that she'd be the perfect wife and mother. On the basis of nothing more than her visit with Melissa the day before, Gavin had cynically concluded that she was already checking out engagement rings and choosing a china pattern. "You know, I was thinking the same thing myself," she said casually, surprised at how unemotional she sounded.

Gavin studied her with amused indifference. "I thought you might be."

His sarcastic tone was her undoing. "Yes, the more I think about it, the more I realize that our well-plotted scheme may be working all *too* well. If you're tired of listening to my praises, then you should hear it from my end."

"Yes, I imagine—"

"That's exactly your problem, Gavin Parker," she cut in, her voice sharp. "The reason Melissa responded to me yesterday was because that child has a heart full of love and no one who seems to want it." Dori fixed her gaze on the water glass as she fought back a rising swell of anger. "I feel sorry for you. Your thinking is so twisted that you don't know what's genuine and what isn't. You're so afraid of revealing your emotions that…that your heart's become like granite."

"And I suppose you think you're just the woman to free me from these despicable shackles?" he taunted.

Dori ignored the derision and the question. "For Melissa's sake I hope you find what you're looking for." She tilted her head back and raised her eyes, meeting his with haughty disdain. "For my part, I want out." She had to go before she became so attached to Melissa that severing the relationship would harm them both. And before she made the fatal mistake of falling for Gavin Parker.

His eyes glittered as cold and dark as the Arctic Sea. "Are you saying you want to cancel our agreement?"

Calmly, Dori placed the linen napkin on her unused plate and stood. "I swear the man's a marvel," she murmured. "It was nice knowing you, Gavin Parker. You have a delightful daughter. Thank you for giving Danny the thrill of his life."

"Sit down," he hissed under his breath. "Please. Let's discuss this like adults."

Still standing, Dori boldly met Gavin's angry eyes. Sick at heart and so miserable that with any provocation at all she would have cried, she slowly shook her head. "I'm sorry, Gavin, but even a phony arrangement can't work with us. We're too different."

"We're not different at all," he argued, then paused to glower at the people whose attention his raised voice had attracted.

"Careful, Gavin," she mocked, "someone might think you're coming on a bit too—"

"Melissa's mother phoned me this morning," he said starkly, and for the first time Dori noticed the deep lines of worry that marred his face.

"What?" she breathed, her pulse accelerating at an alarming rate. She sat down again, her eyes wide and fearful at the apprehension on Gavin's face.

"Our conversation was less than congenial. I need to talk to someone. I apologize if I came at you like a kamikaze pilot."

If, Dori mused flippantly. He'd invited her because he wanted someone to talk to and then he'd tried to sabotage their lunch. "What happened?"

"The usual. Deirdre's in New York and is divorcing her third or fourth husband, I forget which, and wants Melissa to come and live with her."

Dori gasped. She knew nothing about this woman. Until today she hadn't even known her name. But Dori was aware of the pain this woman had inflicted on Gavin's life. "Does she have a chance of getting her?" Already her heart was pounding at the thought of Gavin losing his daughter to a woman he so obviously detested.

Gavin's laugh was bitter. "Hardly, but that won't stop her from trying. She does this at the end of every marriage. She has an attack of guilt and wants to play mommy for a while."

"How does Melissa feel about Deirdre? Does she ever see her mother?" She didn't mean to pry and she didn't want him to reveal anything he wasn't comfortable sharing. But the thought of this young girl being forced into such a difficult situation tore at her heart.

"Melissa spends a month with her every summer. Last year she phoned me three days after she arrived and begged me to let her come home. At the time Deirdre was just as glad to be rid of her. I don't know what happened, but Melissa made me promise that I wouldn't send her there by herself again."

"I realize you're upset, but the courts aren't going to listen to your—"

"I know," Gavin interrupted. "I just needed to vent my frustration and anger on someone. Melissa and I have gone through this before and we can weather another of Deirdre's whims." Gavin's hand gently touched hers. "I owe you an apology for the way I behaved earlier."

"It's forgotten." What wasn't forgotten was that he'd sought her out. Somehow, she'd reached Gavin Parker—and now they were on dangerous ground. This charade became more real every time they saw each other. They'd been convinced they could keep their emotions detached—but they were failing. More and more, Gavin dominated her thoughts, and despite herself, she found excuses to imagine them together. It wasn't supposed to work like this.

"You told me about Brad. I think it's only fair to let you know about Deirdre."

A feeling of gladness raced through Dori. Not because Gavin was telling her about his ex-wife. To be truthful, Dori wasn't even sure she wanted to hear the gory details of his marriage breakdown. But the fact that Gavin was telling her was a measure of his trust. He felt safe enough with her to divulge his deepest pain—as she had with him. "It isn't necessary," she said softly.

"It's only fair that you know." He gripped the icy water glass, apparently oblivious to the cold that must be seeping up his arm. "I don't know where to begin. We got married young, too young I suppose. We were in our last year of college and I was on top of the world. The pros were already scouting me. I'd been seeing Deirdre, but so had a lot of other guys. She came from a wealthy family and had been spoiled by an indulgent father. I liked him. He was a terrific guy, even if he did cater too much to his daughter—but he loved her. When she told me she was pregnant and I was the baby's father, I offered to marry her. I have no difficulty believing that if I hadn't, she would've had an abortion. I went into the marriage with a lot of expectations. I think I was even glad she was pregnant. The idea of being a father pleased me—proof of my manhood and all that garbage." He paused and focused his gaze on the tabletop.

Dori realized how hard this must be for him, and her first instinct was to tell him to stop. It wasn't necessary for him to reveal this pain. But even stronger was her sense that he needed to talk—to get this out of his system.

"Usually people can say when they felt their marriage going bad. Ours went bad on the wedding day. Deirdre hated being pregnant, but worse, I believe she hated me.

From the moment Melissa was born, she didn't want anything to do with her. Later I learned that she hated being pregnant so much that she had her tubes tied so there'd never be any more children. She didn't bother to tell me. Melissa was handed over to a nanny and within weeks Deirdre was making the rounds, if you know what I mean. I don't think I need to be any more explicit."

"No." Dori's voice was low and trembling. She'd never known anyone like that and found it impossible to imagine a woman who could put such selfish, shallow pleasures ahead of her own child's needs.

"I tried to make the marriage work. More for her father's sake than Deirdre's. But after he died I couldn't pretend anymore. She didn't want custody of Melissa then, and I'm not about to give up my daughter now."

"How long ago was that?"

"Melissa was three when we got divorced."

Three! Dori's heart ached for this child who'd never experienced a mother's love.

"I thought you should know," he concluded.

"Thank you for telling me." Instinctively Gavin had come to her with his doubts and worries. He was reaching out to her, however reluctantly he'd done so at first. But he'd made a beginning, and Dori was convinced it was the right one for them.

That same week, Dori saw Gavin two more times. They went to a movie Wednesday evening, sat in the back row and argued over the popcorn. Telling Dori about Deirdre seemed to have freed him. On Friday he phoned her at the office again, and they met for lunch at the same restaurant they'd gone to the previous Monday. He told her he was going to be away for the weekend, broadcasting a game.

By the following Monday, Dori was worried. She had so much difficulty keeping her mind on her work, she wondered if she was falling in love with Gavin. It didn't seem possible that this could happen so quickly. Her physical response to his touch was a pleasant surprise. But it had been years since a man had held her the way he did, so Dori had more or less expected and compensated for the physical impact. The emotional response was what overwhelmed her. She cared about him. Worried about him. Thought about him to the exclusion of all else. They were in trouble, deep trouble. But Gavin had failed to recognize it. If they were going to react sensibly, the impetus would have to come from her.

Dori's thoughts were still confused when she stopped at the soccer field to pick up Danny after work that Monday night. She pulled into the parking lot and walked across the lawn to the field. The boys were playing a scrimmage game and she stood on the sidelines, smiling as she watched Danny weave his way through the defenders.

"You're Danny's mother, aren't you?"

Dori switched her attention to the thin, lanky man standing next to her. She recognized him as Jon Schaeffer's dad. Jon and Danny had recently become the best of friends and had spent the night at each other's houses two or three times since the beginning of the school year. From what she understood, Jon's parents were separated. "Yes, you're Jon's father, right?"

"Right." He crossed his arms and nodded at the boys running back and forth across the field. "Danny's a good player."

"Thank you. So is Jon."

"Yeah, I'm real proud of him." The conversation was stilted and Dori felt a little uneasy.

"I hope you won't think I'm being too bold, but did you put an ad in the paper?"

Dori felt waves of color flood her face. "Well, actually Danny did."

"I thought he might have." He chuckled and held out his hand. "My name's Tom, by the way."

Less embarrassed, Dori shook it. "Dori," she introduced herself.

"I read the ad and thought about calling. Despite what I'd hoped, it doesn't look like Paula and I are going to get back together and I was so lonely, I thought about giving you a call."

"How'd you know the number was mine?"

"I didn't," he was quick to explain. "I wrote it down on a slip of paper and set it by the phone. Jon spent last weekend with me and saw it and wanted to know how come I had Danny's phone number."

"Oh." Color blossomed anew. "I've had the number changed since."

"I think Jon mentioned that. So Danny put the ad in the paper?"

"All on his own. It's the first time I've ever regretted being a mother." Involuntarily her voice rose with remembered embarrassment.

"Did you get many responses?"

He was so serious that Dori was forced to conceal a smile. "You wouldn't believe the number of calls that came the first night."

"That's what I figured."

They lapsed into a companionable silence. "You and your husband split up?"

Tom had a clear-cut view of life, it seemed, and a blunt manner. The question came out of nowhere. "No, I'm a widow."

"Hey, listen, I'm sorry. I didn't mean to be nosy. It's none of my business."

"Don't worry about it," Dori told him softly.

Tom wasn't like most of the men she'd known. He was obviously a hard worker, frank, a little rough around the edges. Dori could tell that he was still in love with his wife and she hoped they'd get back together.

"Jon and Danny are good friends, aren't they?"

"They certainly see enough of each other."

"Could you tolerate a little more togetherness?" His gaze didn't leave the field.

"How do you mean?"

"Could I take you and Danny to dinner with Jon and me?" He looked as awkward as a teenager asking a girl out for the first time.

Dori's immediate inclination was to refuse politely. The last thing she wanted to do was alienate Jon's mother. On the other hand, Dori needed to sort through her own feelings for Gavin, and seeing someone else was bound to help.

"Yes, we'd enjoy that. Thank you."

The smile he beamed at her was bright enough to rival the streetlight. "The pleasure's all mine."

Chapter Six

"Mom," Danny pleaded, following her into the bathroom and frantically waving his hand in front of his face while she deftly applied hair spray.

"What?" Dori asked irritably. She'd been arguing with Danny from the minute he'd learned she was going out with Tom Schaeffer.

"Mr. Parker could phone."

"I know, but it's unlikely." Gavin hadn't been in touch with her since their Monday lunch. If he expected her to sit around and wait for his calls, then he was in for a surprise.

Danny's disgruntled look and defiantly crossed arms made her hesitate. "If he does phone, tell him I'm out for the evening and I'll return his call when I get home."

"But I thought you and Mr. Parker were good friends... *real* good friends. You even kissed him!"

"We are friends," she said, feigning indifference as she tucked in a stray hair and examined her profile in the mirror. With a sigh of disgust she tightened her stomach and wondered how long she could go without breathing.

"Mom," Danny protested again, "I don't like this and I don't think Mr. Parker will, either."

"He won't care," she said with more aplomb than she was feeling. Danny assumed that because she was going out on a weeknight, this must be a "hot date." It wasn't. Tom had invited her out after their dinner with the boys and Dori had accepted because she realized that what he really wanted was a sympathetic ear. He was lonely and still in love with his wife. She couldn't have picked a safer date, but Danny wouldn't understand that and she didn't try to explain.

"If you're such good friends with Mr. Parker, how come you're wearing perfume for Jon's dad?"

"Moms sometimes do that for no special reason."

"But you're acting like tonight *is* special. You're going out with Mr. Schaeffer."

Dori placed her hands on her son's shoulders and studied him closely. His face was pinched, his blue eyes intense. "Don't you like Mr. Schaeffer?"

"He's all right, I guess."

"But I thought you had a good time when we went out to dinner Monday night."

"That was different. Jon and I were with you."

Dori knew that Danny wasn't terribly pleased that a high school girl from the neighborhood was coming to baby-sit. He was at that awkward age—too young to be left completely alone, especially for an evening, but old enough to resent a babysitter, particularly when she was one of his own neighbors.

"I'll be home early—probably before your bedtime," Dori promised, ruffling his hair.

Danny impatiently brushed her hand aside. "But why are you going, Mom? That's what I don't get."

Dori didn't know how she could explain something she didn't completely understand herself. She was worried that her emotions were becoming too involved with Gavin. Tom was insurance. With Tom there wasn't any fear of falling in love or being hurt. But every time she saw Gavin her emotions became more entangled; she cared about him and Melissa. As far as Gavin was concerned, though, the minute he knew she'd fallen for him would be the end of their relationship. He'd made it abundantly clear that he didn't want any kind of real involvement. He had no plans to remarry, and if she revealed any emotional commitment he wouldn't hesitate to reject her as he'd rejected others. Oh, she might hold on to him for a time, the way Lainey was trying to. But Gavin wasn't a man easily fooled—and Dori wasn't a fool.

The doorbell chimed and the sixteen-year-old who lived across the street came in with an armful of books.

"Hello, Mrs. Robertson."

"Hi, Jody." Out of the corner of her eye Dori saw that Danny was sitting down in front of the television. She wasn't deceived by his indifference. Her son was not happy that she was dating Tom Schaeffer, as he'd informed her in no uncertain terms. Dori ignored him and continued her instructions to the sitter. "The phone number for the restaurant is in the kitchen. I shouldn't be much later than nine-thirty, maybe ten." The doorbell chimed again and Danny answered it this time, opening the door for Tom, who smiled appreciatively when he saw Dori.

"Be good," Dori whispered and kissed Danny on the cheek.

He rubbed the place she'd kissed and examined the palm of his hand for any lipstick. "Okay," he agreed with a sad little smile calculated to tug at a mother's heart. "But I'm waiting up for you." He gave her the soulful look of a lost puppy, his eyes crying out at the injustice of being left at the fickle mercy of a sixteen-year-old girl. The emphasis, of course, being on the word *girl*.

If Dori didn't leave soon, he might well win this unspoken battle and she couldn't allow that. "We'll talk when I get back," she promised.

Tom, dressed in a suit, placed a guiding hand at the small of her back as they left the house. "Is there a problem with Danny?"

Dori cast a speculative glance over her shoulder. She felt guilty and depressed, although there was no reason she should. Now she realized how Melissa had made Gavin feel when he'd gone out with Lainey that Saturday night. No wonder he'd been upset on Sunday. Neither of them was accustomed to this type of adolescent censorship. And she didn't like it any more than Gavin had.

"Danny's unhappy about having a baby-sitter," she answered Tom half-truthfully.

With such an ominous beginning, Dori suspected the evening was doomed before it had even begun. They shared a quiet dinner and talked over coffee, but the conversation was sporadic and when the clock struck nine, Dori fought not to look at her watch every five minutes.

On the drive home, she felt obliged to apologize. "I'm *really* sorry..." She paused, then remembered how often Melissa used that word and, in spite of herself, broke into a full laugh.

Tom's bewildered gaze met hers. "What's so amusing?"

"It's a long story. A friend of mine has a daughter who alternates *really* with every other word. I caught myself saying it just now and..."

"It suddenly seemed funny."

"Exactly." She was still smiling when Tom turned into her street. Her face tightened and her smile disappeared when she saw a car parked in front. Gavin's car. She clenched her fists and drew several deep breaths to calm her nerves. There was no telling what kind of confrontation awaited her.

As politely as possible, Dori thanked Tom for the dinner and apologized for not inviting him in for coffee.

When she opened the door a pair of accusing male eyes met hers. "Hello, Gavin," Dori said cheerfully, "this is a nice surprise."

"Dori." The glittering harshness of his gaze told her he wasn't pleased. "Did you have a good time?"

"Wonderful," she lied. "We went to a Greek restaurant and naturally everything was Greek to me." She forced a laugh. "I finally ordered exactly what the waiter suggested." Dori hated the way she was rambling like a guilty schoolgirl. Her mouth felt dry and her throat scratchy.

Danny faked a wide yawn. "I think I'll go to bed now."

"Not so fast, young man." Dori stopped him. Her son had played a part in this uncomfortable showdown with Gavin. The least he could do was explain. "Is there something you want to tell me?"

Danny eyed the carpet with unusual interest while his cheeks flushed a telltale red. "No."

Dori was convinced that Danny had called Gavin, but she'd handle that later with a week's grounding. "I'll talk to you in the morning."

"Night, Mr. Parker." Like a rabbit unexpectedly freed from a trap, Danny bolted down the hallway to his bedroom.

It didn't escape Dori's notice that he hadn't wished her good-night. Hanging her coat in the hall closet gave her a moment to collect her thoughts and resolve to ignore the distressing heat that warmed her blood. When she turned to face Gavin, she saw that a cynical smile had quirked up the corners of his stern mouth.

"Don't look so guilty," he muttered.

Dori's cheeks burned, but she boldly met his eyes. "I'm not." She walked into the kitchen and prepared a pot of coffee. Gavin followed her and she automatically took two mugs from the cupboard. Turning, her back pressed against the counter, Dori confronted him squarely. "What happened? Did Danny phone you?"

"I thought we had an agreement."

Involuntarily, Dori flinched at the harshness of his voice. "We do," she said calmly, watching the coffee drip into the glass pot.

"Then what were you doing out with a man? A married one, at that."

"Exactly what has Danny been telling you? Tom and his wife are separated. For heaven's sake, we didn't even hold hands." She studiously avoided meeting his fiery glare, angry now that she'd bothered to explain. "Good grief, you went out with Lainey. I don't see the difference."

"At least I *felt* guilty."

"So did I! Does that make it any better?"

"Yes!" he shouted.

She whirled around, tired of playing mouse to his cat. Her hand shook as she poured hot coffee into the mugs.

"Are we going to fight about it?" she asked as she set his mug on the kitchen table.

"That depends on whether you plan to see him again." His face was impassive, as if the question were of no importance. Dori marveled at his self-control. The hard eyes that stared back dared her to say that she'd be seeing Tom again.

"I don't know." She sat in the chair opposite him. "Does it matter?"

His mouth twisted in a faintly ironic smile. "It could. I don't particularly relish another frantic phone call from your son informing me that I'd better do something quick."

"Believe me, that won't happen again," Dori said, furious with Danny and more furious with herself. She should've known Danny would do something like this and taken measures to avoid it.

"So you felt guilty." His low, drawling voice was tinged with amused mockery.

"I didn't like it any more than you did." She expelled her breath and folded her arms in a defensive gesture. "I don't know, Gavin. Maybe our agreement is working too well." She reached impatiently for the sugar bowl in the middle of the table and stirred a teaspoon into her coffee. "Before we know it, those two kids are going to have us married and living in a house with a white picket fence."

"Don't worry about that."

"Oh, no—" she waved her hands in the air helplessly "—of course that wouldn't concern you. Mr. Football Hero can handle everything, right? Well, you admitted that Melissa made you miserable when you saw Lainey. Danny did the same thing to me. I think we should bow gracefully out of this agreement while we can." Although Dori offered the suggestion, she hoped Gavin would refuse; she needed to know that the attraction was mutual.

"Is that what you want?" Deftly he turned the tables on her.

In a flash of irritation, Dori pushed back her chair and walked quickly to the sink, where she deposited her mug. She sighed with frustration and returned to the table. "No, unfortunately I don't. Darn it, Parker, in spite of your arrogant ways, I've discovered I like you. That's what scares me."

"Don't sound so shocked. I'm a great guy. Just ask Danny. Of course, it could be my virility that you find so alluring, in which case we're in trouble." Chuckling, he rolled lazily to his feet and took his empty cup to the sink.

"Don't *you* worry," she muttered sarcastically, "your masculinity hasn't overpowered me yet."

"That's probably the best thing we've got going for us. Don't fall in love with me, Dori," he warned, the amusement gone from his eyes. "I'd only end up hurting you."

Her pulse rocketed with alarm. He was right. The problem was that she was already halfway there. And she was standing on dangerous ground, struggling to hold back her feelings.

"I think you've got things twisted here," she told him dryly. "I'm more concerned about you falling for me. I'm not your usual type, Gavin. So the risk could well be of your own making."

Her appraisal didn't appear to please him. "There's little chance of that. One woman's already brought me to my knees and I'm not about to let that happen again."

Dori forced back the words of protest, the assertion that a real woman didn't want a man on his knees. She wanted him at her side as friend, lover and confidant.

"There's another problem coming up, and I think we should discuss it," he continued.

"What?"

He ignored her worried look and leaned casually against the counter. "Melissa and I are going to San Francisco over Thanksgiving weekend. I'm doing the play-by-play of the

49ers game that Saturday. Melissa's been asking me for weeks if you and Danny can come with us."

"But why? This should be a special time for the two of you."

"Unfortunately, that isn't how Melissa sees it. She'll be in the hotel room alone on the Saturday because I'll be in the broadcast booth and I don't want her attending the game by herself. It *is* Thanksgiving weekend, as Melissa keeps pointing out. But I hate to admit that my daughter knows exactly which buttons to push to make me feel guilty."

"I'm not sure, Gavin," Dori hedged. She'd planned to spend the holiday with her parents, but she loved San Francisco. She'd visited the Bay area as a teenager and had always wanted to return. This would be like a vacation, and she hadn't taken one in years.

"The way I see it," Gavin went on, "this may even suit our needs. The kids are likely to overdose on each other if they spend that much time together. Maybe after three or four days in each other's company, they'll face a few truths about this whole thing."

Dori was skeptical. "It could backfire."

"I doubt it. What do you say?"

The temptation was so strong that she had to close her eyes to fight back an immediate *yes.* "Let…let me think about it."

"Fine," he said calmly.

Dori pulled out a chair and sat down. "Have you heard anything more from Deirdre?"

"No, and I won't."

"How can you be so sure?"

The hard line of his mouth curved upward in a mirthless smile. "Trust me on this."

The manner in which he said it made Dori's blood run

cold. Undoubtedly Gavin knew Deirdre's weaknesses and knew how to attack his ex-wife.

"There's no way on this earth I'll hand my daughter over to *her*."

Dori had never seen a man's eyes look more frigid or harsh. "If there's anything I can do…" She let the rest fade. Gavin wouldn't need anything from her.

"As a matter of fact, there is," he said, contradicting her thoughts. "I'm broadcasting a game this Sunday in Kansas City, which means Melissa has to spend the weekend at school. Being there on Saturday and Sunday is the worst, or so she claims."

"She could stay with us. I'd like that immensely." There wasn't anything special planned. Saturday she'd be doing errands and buying the week's groceries, and Danny had a soccer game in the afternoon, but Melissa would enjoy that.

"I was thinking more like one day," Gavin told her. "As it is, you'll hear all about my many virtues for twenty-four hours. Why ask for more?"

"Let her stay the whole weekend," Dori said. "Didn't you just say we should try to 'overdose' the kids?"

Gavin's warning proved to be prophetic. From the moment Dori picked Melissa up at the Eastside Boarding School on Mercer Island, the girl chattered nonstop, extolling her father's apparently limitless virtues—just as he'd predicted.

"Did you know that my father has a whole room full of trophies he won playing sports?"

"Wow," Danny answered, his voice unnaturally high. "Remember our list, Mom? I think it's important that my new dad be athletic."

"What else was on the list?" Melissa asked, then listened attentively as Danny explained each requirement. She launched into a litany of praise for Gavin, presenting him as the ideal father and husband in every respect. However, it hadn't escaped Dori's notice that Melissa didn't mention the last stipulation, that Danny's new father love Dori. Instinctively Melissa recognized that would be overstepping the bounds. Dori appreciated the girl's honesty.

As Melissa continued her bragging about Gavin, Dori had to bite her tongue to keep from laughing. Given the chance, she'd teach those two something about subtlety—later. For now, they were far too amusing. In an effort to restrain her merriment, she concentrated on the heavy traffic that moved slowly over the floating bridge. Friday afternoons were a nightmare for commuters.

The chatter stopped and judging by the sounds she heard from the backseat, Dori guessed that Danny and Melissa were having a heated discussion under their breaths. Dori thought she heard Tom's name but let it pass. With all the problems her date with him had caused, she doubted she'd be seeing Tom again. For his part, he was hoping to settle things with his wife and move back home in time for the holidays. Dori knew that Jon would be thrilled to have his father back, and she prayed Tom's wife would be as willing.

Following the Saturday expedition to the grocery store, the three of them attended Danny's soccer game. To Melissa's delight, Danny scored two goals and was cheered as a hero when he ran off the field at the end of the game. Luckily they arrived back home before it started to rain. Dori made popcorn and the two children watched a late-afternoon movie on television.

The phone rang just as Dori was finishing the dinner dishes.

She reached for it and glanced at Danny and Melissa, who were playing a game of Risk in the living room.

"Hello," she answered absently.

"Dori, it's Gavin. How are things going?"

"Fine," she said, unreasonably pleased that he'd phoned. "They've had their first spat but rebounded remarkably well."

"What happened?"

"Melissa wanted to try on some of my makeup and Danny was thoroughly disgusted to see her behaving like a girl."

"Did you tell him the time will come when he'll appreciate girls?"

"No." Her hand tightened on the receiver. Gavin was a thousand miles from Seattle. The sudden warmth she felt at hearing his voice made her thankful he wasn't there to witness the effect he had on her. "He wouldn't have believed it, coming from me."

"I'll tell him. He'll believe me."

Danny would. If there was anything wrong with this relationship, it was that Danny idealized Gavin. One day, Gavin would fall off Danny's pedestal. No man could continue to breathe comfortably so high up, in such a rarefied atmosphere. Dori only hoped that when the crash came, her son wouldn't be hurt. "Are you having a good time with your cronies?" she asked, leaning against the kitchen wall.

He laughed and the sound produced a tingling rush of pleasure. "Aren't you afraid I've got a woman in the room with me?"

"Not in the least," she answered honestly. "You'd hardly phone here if you did."

"You're too smart for your own good," he chided affectionately. He paused, and Dori's heart began to race. "You're going to San Francisco with us, aren't you?"

"Yes."

"Good." No word had ever sounded more sensuous to Dori.

She straightened quickly, frightened by the intensity of her emotions. "Would you like to talk to Melissa?"

"How's she behaving?"

"As predicted."

Gavin chuckled. "Do you want me to say something?"

Gavin was obviously pleased that his daughter's behavior was running true to form. "No. Danny will undoubtedly list my virtues for hours the next time you have him."

"I'll look forward to that."

"I'll bet." Grinning, Dori set the phone aside and called Melissa, who hurried into the kitchen and grabbed the receiver. Overflowing with enthusiasm, she relayed the events of the day, with Danny motioning dramatically in the background, instructing Melissa to tell Gavin about the goals he'd scored that afternoon. Eventually Danny got a chance to report the great news himself. When the children had finished talking, Dori took the receiver back.

"Have they worn your ear off yet?"

"Just about. By the way, I might be able to catch an early flight out of here on Sunday, after the game."

She hadn't seen Gavin since her date with Tom, and much as she hated to admit it, she wanted to spend some time with him before they went to San Francisco. "Do you want us to pick you up at the airport?"

"If you could."

"I'll see if I can manage it."

Before ending the conversation, Dori wrote down Gavin's flight number and his time of arrival.

Late the following afternoon, the three of them were sitting in the arrivals area at Sea-Tac International. They'd come early, and Dori frequently found herself checking her watch, less out of curiosity about the time than out of an unexpected nervousness. She felt she was behaving almost like a love-struck teenager. Even choosing her outfit had been inordinately difficult; she'd debated between a wool skirt with knee-high black leather boots and something less formal. In the end she chose mauve corduroy pants and a pullover sweater the color of winter wheat.

"Dad's plane just landed." Melissa pointed to the monitor and bounded to her feet.

Dori brushed an imaginary piece of lint from her sweater and cursed herself for being so glad Gavin was home and safe. With the children standing at either side, her hands resting lightly on their shoulders, she forced a strained smile to her lips. A telltale warmth invaded her face and Dori raised a self-conscious hand to brush the hair from her temple. Gavin was the third passenger to appear.

"Dad!" Melissa broke formation and ran to Gavin, hugging him fiercely. Danny followed shyly and offered Gavin his hand to shake. "Welcome back, Mr. Parker," he said politely.

"Thank you, Danny." Gavin shook the boy's hand with all the seriousness of a man closing a million-dollar deal.

"How was the flight?" Dori stepped forward, striving to keep her arms obediently at her sides, battling the impulse to greet him as Melissa had done.

His raincoat was draped over one arm and he carried a small carry-on bag in the other hand. Dark smudges under his eyes told her that he was exhausted. Nonetheless he gave her a warm smile. "The flight was fine."

"I thought you said he'd kiss her," Danny whispered indignantly to Melissa. The two children stood a few feet from Dori and Gavin.

"It's too public...I think," Melissa whispered back and turned accusing eyes on her father.

Arching his brows, Gavin held out an arm to Dori. "We'd better not disappoint them," he murmured, "or we won't hear the end of it for the entire week."

That outstretched arm was all the invitation Dori needed. No step had ever seemed so far—or so close. Relentlessly, Gavin held her gaze as she walked into the shelter of his embrace. His hand slipped around the back of her neck, bringing her closer. Long fingers slid into her hair as his mouth made a slow descent to her parted lips. As the distance lessened, Dori closed her eyes, more eager for this than she had any right to be. Her heart was doing a drumroll and she moistened her suddenly dry lips. She heard Gavin suck in his breath as his mouth claimed hers.

Of their own accord, or so it seemed, her hands moved over the taut muscles of his chest and shoulders until her fingers linked behind his neck. In the next instant, his mouth hardened, his touch firm and experienced. The pressure of his hand at the back of her neck lifted her onto the tips of her toes, forcing the full length of her body close to the unyielding strength of his. The sound of Gavin's bag hitting the floor barely registered on her numbed senses. Nor did she resist when he wrapped both arms around her so tightly that she could hardly breathe. All she could taste, feel, smell, was Gavin. She felt as if she'd come home after a long time away.

He'd kissed her before, but it had never been like this, like a hundred shooting stars blazing a trail across an ebony sky.

Dori struggled not to give in to the magnificent light show, not to respond with everything in her. She had to resist. Otherwise, Gavin would know everything.

Gavin broke the kiss and buried his face in her hair. "That kiss has to be a ten," he muttered thickly.

"A nine," she insisted, her voice weak. "When we get to ten, we're in real trouble."

"Especially if we're at an airport."

Gavin's hold relaxed, but he slipped his hand around her waist, bringing her closer to his side. "Well, kids, are you happy now?"

"You dropped your bag, Mr. Parker." Danny held it out to him and eyed Melissa gleefully. He beamed from ear to ear.

"So I did," Gavin said, taking his carry-on bag. "Thanks for picking it up."

"Dori put a roast in the oven," Melissa informed him, "just in case you were hungry. I told her how starved you are when you get home from these things."

"Your father's tired, Melissa. I'll have you both over for dinner another time."

"I appreciate that," Gavin told Dori, his gaze caressing her. "I *have* been up for the past thirty hours."

A small involuntary smile raised the corners of Dori's mouth. She hadn't been married to Brad all those years without having some idea of the way a man thought and behaved away from home.

Gavin's eyes darkened briefly as if he expected a sarcastic reply. "No comment?"

"No comment," she echoed cheerfully.

"You're not worried about who I was with?"

"I know—or at least I think I do," she amended.

Gavin hesitated, his eyes disbelieving. "You think you do?" he asked.

"Well, not for sure, but I have a pretty good hunch."

"This I've got to hear." His hand tightened around her waist. "Well?"

Both Danny and Melissa looked concerned. They were clearly disappointed that Dori wasn't showing any signs of jealousy. Obviously, they assumed Gavin had been with another woman. Dori doubted it. If he had, he wouldn't be so blatant about it. Nor would he mention it in front of the children.

"I'd guess that you were with some football friends, drinking beer, eating pretzels and playing poker."

The smug expression slowly faded as a puzzled frown drew his brows together. "That's exactly where I was."

Disguising her pride at guessing correctly was nearly impossible. "Honestly, Gavin, it wasn't that hard to figure out. I'm in my thirties. I've been married. I know how a man thinks."

"And men are all alike," he taunted.

"No," she said, trying desperately to keep a straight face. "But I'm beginning to know *you*. When you stop asking me if I'm concerned about who you were with, then I'll worry."

"You think you're pretty smart, don't you?"

"No." She shook her head. "Men I can understand. It's children that baffle me."

He continued to hold her close as they walked down the long concourse. Melissa and Danny skipped ahead.

"Were they a problem this weekend?" Gavin inclined his head toward the two kids.

"Nothing I couldn't handle."

"I have the feeling there's very little you can't handle."

Self-conscious now, Dori looked away. There was so much she didn't know, so much that frightened her. And the main object of her fears was walking right beside her, holding her as if it were the most natural thing in the world—as if he intended to hold on to her for a lifetime. But Dori knew better.

Chapter Seven

The bell of the cable car clanged as Dori, Melissa, Danny and Gavin clung precariously to the side. A low-lying fog was slowly dissipating under the cheerful rays of the early afternoon sun.

"When are we going to Ghiradelli's?" Melissa wanted to know. "I love chocolate."

"Me too," Danny chimed in eagerly.

"Soon," Gavin promised, "but I told Dori we'd see Fisherman's Wharf first."

"Sorry, kids." Although Dori apologized, there was no regret in her voice. The lovely City of Saint Francis was everything she remembered, and more. The steep, narrow streets, brightly painted Victorians, San Francisco Bay and the Golden Gate Bridge. Dori doubted that she'd ever tire of the grace and beauty of this magnificent city.

They'd arrived Thanksgiving Day and gone directly to a plush downtown hotel. Gavin had reserved a large suite with two bedrooms connected to an immense central room. After a leisurely dinner of turkey with all the traditional trimmings, they'd gone to bed, Gavin and Danny in one room, Dori and Melissa in the other, all eager to explore the city the following morning.

After a full day of viewing Golden Gate Park, driving down Lombard Street with its famous ninety-degree curves and strolling through Fisherman's Wharf, they returned to their hotel suite.

Melissa sat in a wing chair and rubbed her sore feet. "I've got an enormous blister," she complained loudly. "I don't think I've ever walked so much in my life. There's nothing I want to do more than watch TV for a while and then go straight to bed." She gave an exaggerated sigh and looked at Danny, who stared back blankly. When he didn't immediately respond, Melissa hissed something at him that Dori couldn't understand, then jabbed him in the ribs with her elbow.

"Oh. Me too," Danny agreed abruptly. "All I want to do is sleep."

"You two will have to go on without us," Melissa continued with a martyred look. "As much as we'd like to join you, it's probably best if we stay here."

Gavin caught Dori's gaze and rolled his eyes. Dori had difficulty containing her own amusement. The two little matchmakers were up to their tricks again. "But we couldn't possibly leave you alone and without dinner," Dori said in a concerned voice.

"I'm not all that hungry." For the first time Danny looked unsure. He'd never gone without dinner in his life and lately his appetite seemed likely to bankrupt her budget. For Danny to offer to go without a meal was the ultimate sacrifice.

"Don't worry about us—we'll order room service," Melissa

said with the casual ease of a seasoned traveler. "You two go on alone. We insist. Right, Danny?"

"Right."

By the time Dori had showered and dressed, Danny and Melissa were poring over the room-service menu like two people who hadn't eaten a decent meal in weeks. Gavin appeared to be taking the children's rather transparent scheme in his stride, but Dori wasn't so confident. They'd had two wonderful days together. Gavin had once lived in San Francisco and he gave them the tour of a lifetime. If he'd hoped that Melissa and Danny would overdose on each other's company, his plan was failing miserably. The two of them had never gotten along better.

After checking the contents of her purse, Dori sat on the end of the bed and slipped on her imported leather pumps. Then she stood and smoothed her skirt. Her pulse was beating madly and she paused to place her hand over her heart and inhale a deep, soothing breath. She felt chilled and warm, excited and apprehensive, all at once. Remembering how unemotional she'd been about their first dinner date only made her fret more. That had been the night of the fights, and she recalled how she hadn't really cared what she wore. Ten minutes before Gavin was due to pick her up, she'd added the final coat of polish to her nails. Tonight, she was as nervous as she'd ever been in her life. Twenty times in as many minutes she'd worried about her dress. This simple green silk dress was her finest, but it wasn't high fashion. Gavin was accustomed to women far more worldly and sophisticated than she could ever hope to be. Bolstering her confidence, Dori put on her gold earrings and freshened her lipstick. With fingers clutching the bathroom sink, she forced a smile to her stiff lips and exhaled a ragged breath. No question, she was falling in love with Gavin Parker. Nothing could be worse. Nothing could be more wonderful, her heart responded.

When she reentered the suite's sitting room, Melissa and Danny were sprawled across the carpet in front of the television. Danny gave her a casual look and glanced back at the screen, but Melissa did an automatic double take.

"Wow!" the young girl murmured, then immediately straightened. Her eyes widened appreciatively. "You're—"

"Lovely." Gavin finished for his daughter, his eyes caressing Dori, roving slowly from her lips to the swell of her breasts and downward.

"Thank you." Dori's voice died to a whisper. She wanted to drown in his eyes. She wanted to be in his arms. A long silence ran between them and Dori looked away, her heart racing.

"Don't worry about us," Melissa said confidently.

"We'll be downstairs if you need anything," Gavin murmured, taking Dori by the elbow.

"Be good, Danny."

"Okay," he answered without glancing up from the television screen.

"And no leaving the room for any reason," she warned.

"What about a fire?"

"You know what we mean," Gavin answered for Dori.

"Don't hurry back on our account," Melissa said, propping up her chin with one hand as she lay sprawled on the carpet. "Danny and I'll probably be asleep before the show's even over."

Danny opened his mouth to protest, but closed it at a fierce glare from Melissa.

Gavin opened the door and Dori threw a smile over her shoulder. "Have fun, you two."

"We will," they chorused.

As the door closed, Dori thought she heard a shout of triumph.

Gavin chuckled and slid a hand around her waist, guiding her to the elevator. "I swear those two have all the finesse of a runaway roller coaster."

"They do seem a bit obvious."

"Just a bit. However, this is one time I don't mind being alone with you." His hand spread across her back, lightly caressing the silk of her dress. Slowly his fingers moved upward to rub her shoulder. His head was so close Dori could feel his breath against her neck. She didn't know what kind of game Gavin was playing, but her heart was a far too willing participant.

At the whirring sound of the approaching elevator, Gavin straightened. The hand at her back directed her inside, and he pushed the appropriate button.

Inside the restaurant, the maître d' led them to a linen-covered table in the middle of the spacious room and held out Dori's chair. Smiling her appreciation, she sat, accepted the menu and scanned the variety of dishes offered. Her mouth felt dry, and judging by the way her nerves were acting, Dori doubted she'd find anything that seemed appetizing.

No sooner were they seated and comfortable than the wine steward approached their table. "Are you Mr. Parker?" he asked.

"Yes." Gavin looked up from his menu.

The man snapped his fingers and a polished silver bucket was delivered to the table. Cradled in a bed of ice was a bottle of French champagne.

"I didn't order this." His brow was creased with lines of bewilderment.

"Yes, sir. This is compliments of Melissa and Danny in room 1423." Deftly he removed the bottle from the silver bucket and held it out for Gavin's inspection. As he read the label, Gavin raised his eyebrows. "An excellent choice," he murmured.

"Indeed," the steward agreed. With impressive dexterity he removed the cork and poured a sample into Gavin's glass. After receiving approval from Gavin, he filled both their glasses and left.

Gavin held up his glass for a toast. "To Melissa and Danny."

"To our children." Dori's answering comment was far more intimate than she'd meant it to be.

The champagne slid smoothly down Dori's throat and eased her tension. She closed her eyes and savored the bubbly tartness. "This is wonderful," she whispered, setting her glass aside. "How did Melissa and Danny know how to order such an exquisite label?"

"They didn't. I have a feeling they simply asked for the best available."

Dori's hand tightened around the stem of her glass. "Oh, my goodness, this must cost a fortune." She felt color flooding her face. "Listen, let me pay half. I'm sure Danny had something to do with this and he knows I love champagne. It's my greatest weakness."

"You're not paying for anything," Gavin insisted with mock sternness. "The champagne is a gift and if you mention it again, you'll offend me."

"But, Gavin, this bottle could cost five hundred dollars and I can't—"

"Are we going to argue?" His voice was low.

Dori felt a throb of excitement at the way he was studying

her. "No," she finally answered. "I'll agree not to argue, but under protest."

"Do you have any other weaknesses I don't know about?" he inquired smoothly.

You! her mind tossed out unexpectedly. Struggling to maintain her composure, she shrugged and dropped her gaze to the bubbling gold liquid. "Bouillabaisse."

Something close to a smile quirked his mouth as he motioned for the waiter and ordered the Provençal fish stew that was cooked with at least eight different types of seafood. In addition, Gavin ordered hearts-of-palm salad. Taking their menus, the waiter left the table and soon afterward the steward returned to replenish their champagne.

Relaxing in her chair, Dori propped her elbows on the table. Already the champagne was going to her head. She felt a warm glow seeping through her.

The bouillabaisse was as good as any Dori had ever tasted; the wine Gavin had ordered with their meal was mellow and smooth.

While they lingered over cups of strong black coffee, Gavin spoke freely about himself for the first time since the night he'd described his marriage. He talked about his position with the computer company and the extensive traveling it sometimes involved. The job was perfect for him because it gave him the freedom to continue broadcasting during the football season. Setting his own hours was a benefit of being part-owner of the firm. He spoke of his goals for the future and his love for his daughter; he spoke of the dreams he had for Melissa.

His look was poignant in a way she'd never expected to see in Gavin. A longing showed there that was deep and intense, a longing for the well-being and future happiness of those he loved. He didn't mention the past or the glories he'd achieved on the football field. Nor did he mention Deirdre.

Every part of Dori was conscious of Gavin, every nerve, every cell. Dori had never expected to feel such a closeness with another human being again. She saw in him a tenderness and a vulnerability he rarely exposed. So often in the past months, just when Dori felt she was beginning to understand Gavin, he'd withdrawn. The fact that he was sharing these confidences with Dori told her he'd come to trust and respect her, and she rejoiced in it.

The waiter approached with a pot of coffee and Dori shook her head.

Gavin glanced at his watch. "Do we dare go back to the suite? We've only been gone two hours."

The way she was feeling, there wasn't any place safe tonight, not if she was with Gavin. She wanted to be in his arms so badly that she was almost anticipating his touch. She cast about for an excuse to stay. "They'd be terribly disappointed if we showed up so soon."

"There's a band playing in the lounge," he said. "Would you care to go dancing?"

"Yes." Her voice trembled slightly with renewed awareness. "I'd like that."

Gavin didn't look for a table when they entered the lounge. A soft, melodious ballad was playing and he led her directly to the dance floor and turned her into his arms.

Dori released a long sigh. She linked her fingers at the back of his neck and pressed the side of her face against the firm line of his jaw. Their bodies were so close that Dori could feel the uneven rhythm of his heartbeat and recognized that her own was just as erratic. They made only the pretense of dancing, holding each other so tightly that for a few seconds breathing was impossible. Dragging air into her lungs, Dori closed her eyes to the fullness of emotion that surged through her. For weeks she'd been fighting her feelings for Gavin. She didn't want to fall in love with him. Now, in the few brief moments since he'd taken her in his arms, Dori knew it was too late. She loved him. Completely and utterly. But admitting her love now would only intimidate him. Her intuition told her that Gavin wasn't ready to accept her feelings or acknowledge his own. Pursuing this tiny spark could well extinguish it before it ever had a chance to flicker and flame.

"Dori." The raw emotion in his voice melted her heart. "Let's get out of here."

"Yes," she whispered.

Gavin led her off the tiny floor, out of the lounge and through the bustling lobby. He hesitated momentarily, apparently undecided about where they should go.

"The children will be in bed," she reminded him softly.

The elevator was empty and just as soon as the heavy doors closed, Gavin wrapped his arms around her.

Yearning shamelessly for his kiss, Dori smiled up at him boldly. She saw his eyes darken with passion as he lowered his head. Leaning toward him, she met his lips with all the eager longing that this evening had evoked. Gavin kissed her with a fierce tenderness until their breaths became mingled gasps and the elevator came to a stop.

Sighing deeply, Gavin tightened his hold, bringing her even closer. "If you kissed me like this every time we entered an elevator, we'd never get off."

"That's what I'm afraid of," she murmured and looked deeply into his eyes.

He was silent for a long moment. "Then perhaps we should

leave now, while we still can." His grip relaxed slightly as they stepped off the elevator.

No light shone from under the door of their suite, but Dori doubted they'd have any real privacy. Undoubtedly Melissa and Danny were just inside the bedroom doors, eager to document the most intimate exchanges between their parents.

Gavin quietly opened the door. The room was dark; what little light there was came from a bright crescent moon that shone in through the windows. They walked into the suite, Gavin's arm around her waist. He turned, closed the door and pressed the full length of her body against it, his gaze holding hers in the pale moonlight.

"I shouldn't kiss you here," he murmured huskily as if he wanted her to refuse.

Dori could find no words to dissuade him—she wanted him so badly. The moment seemed to stretch out. Then, very slowly, she raised her hands to caress the underside of his tense jaw. Her fingertips slid into the dark fullness of his hair and she raised herself onto the tips of her toes to gently place her lips on his. The pressure was so light that their lips merely touched.

Gradually his mouth eased over hers in exquisite exploration, moving delicately from one side of her lips to the other. The complete sensuality of the kiss quivered through Dori. A sigh of breathless wonder slid from the tightening muscles of her throat. The low groan was quickly followed by another as Gavin's mouth rocked over hers in an eruption of passion and desire that was all too new and sudden. She'd thought these feelings, these very sensations, had died with Brad. She wanted Gavin. She couldn't have stopped him if he'd lifted her in his arms and carried her to the bedroom. The realization shocked her.

He stroked the curves of her shoulders as he nibbled at her lips, taking small, sensuous bites. His fingers tangled in her hair, and he slid his mouth over her cheek to her eyes and nose and grazed her jaw. She felt him shudder and held his head close as she took in huge gulps of air. The need to experience the intimate touch of his hands and mouth flowered deep within her. Yet he restrained himself with what Dori believed was great effort.

"If you rate that kiss a ten, then we're in real trouble," he muttered, close to her ear.

"We're in real trouble."

"I thought as much." But he didn't release her.

"Knowing Danny, I'd guess he's probably taken pictures of this little exchange." The delicious languor slowly left her limbs.

"And knowing Melissa, I'd say she undoubtedly lent him the camera." Gradually, his arms relaxed their hold.

"Do you think they'll try to blackmail us?" she asked, hoping to end the evening on a lighter note.

"I doubt it," Gavin whispered. "In any case, I have the perfect defense. I believe we can attribute tonight to expensive champagne and an excellent meal, don't you?"

No, she didn't. But Dori swallowed her argument. She knew that this feeling between them had been there from the time they'd boarded the plane in Seattle. Gavin had wanted to be alone with her tonight, just as she'd longed to be with him. Their kissing was a natural consequence of this awakened discovery.

Deciding that no answer was better than telling a lie, Dori faked an exaggerated yawn and murmured, "I should think about bed. It's been a long day."

"Yes," Gavin agreed far too readily. "And tomorrow will be just as busy."

They parted in the center of the room, going in opposite directions toward their respective rooms. Dori undressed in the dark, not wanting to wake Melissa—if indeed Melissa was asleep. Even if she wasn't, Dori didn't feel up to answering the girl's questions.

Gently lifting back the covers of her twin bed, Dori slipped between the sheets and settled into a comfortable position. She watched the flickering shadows playing on the opposite wall, tormenting herself with doubts and recriminations. Gavin attributed their overwhelming attraction to the champagne. She wondered what he'd say if it happened again. And it would. They'd come too far to go back now.

The following afternoon, Melissa, Danny and Dori sat in front of the television to watch the San Francisco 49ers play the Denver Broncos. Dori wasn't particularly interested in football and knew very little about it. But she'd never before watched a game that Gavin was broadcasting. Now she listened proudly and attentively to his comments, appreciating for the first time his expertise in sports.

Another well-known ex-football player was Gavin's announcing partner and the two exchanged witticisms and bantered freely. During halftime, the television camera crew showed the two men sitting in the broadcast booth. Gavin held up a pad with a note that said, "Hi, Melissa and Danny."

The kids went into peals of delight and Dori looked on happily. This four-day weekend was one she'd never forget. Everything had been perfect—perhaps too perfect.

Gavin came back to the hotel several hours after the end of the game. His broad shoulders were slightly hunched and he rubbed a hand over his eyes. His gaze avoided Dori's as he greeted the children, then sank heavily into a chair.

"You were great!" Danny said with unabashed enthusiasm.

"Yeah, Dad." The pride in Melissa's voice was evident.

"You're just saying that because the 49ers won and you were both rooting for them." Gavin's smile didn't quite reach his eyes.

"Can I get you anything, Gavin?" Dori offered quietly, taking the chair across from him. "You look exhausted."

"I am." His gaze met hers for the first time since he'd returned. The expression that leaped into his eyes made her catch her breath, but just as quickly an invisible shutter fell to hide it. Without a word, he turned his head to the side. "I don't need anything, thanks." The way he said it forced Dori to wonder if he was referring to her. That morning, he'd been cool and efficient, but Dori had attributed his behavior to the football game. Naturally he'd be preoccupied. She hadn't expected him to take her in his arms and wasn't disappointed when he didn't. Or so she told herself.

Melissa sat on the carpet by Gavin's feet. "Danny and I knew you'd be tired so we ordered a pizza. That way, you and Dori can go out again tonight and be alone." The faint stress placed on the last word made Dori blush.

She opened her mouth to protest, then closed it. She certainly wasn't ready for a repeat performance of last night's meal, but she wanted to hear what Gavin thought. His eyes clashed with hers and narrowed fractionally as he challenged her to accept or decline.

"No," Dori protested quickly, her voice low. "I'm sure your dad's much too tired. We'll all have pizza."

"Okay." Melissa shot to her feet, willing to cooperate with

Dori's decision. "Danny and I'll go get it. The pizza place is only a couple of blocks from here."

"I'll go with you," Dori said, not wanting the two children walking the streets by themselves after dark.

A hand stopped her, and Dori turned to find Gavin studying her. His mouth twisted wryly; his eyes were chilling. "What's the matter?" he asked.

She searched his face, wondering about the subtle challenge in his question. "Nothing," she replied smoothly, calmly. "You didn't want to go out, did you?"

"No."

"Then why are you looking at me like I committed some serious faux pas?" Dori inclined her head to one side, not understanding the change in him.

"You're angry because I didn't hold up your name with the kids' this afternoon."

Dori's mouth dropped open in shock. "Of course not! That's crazy." Gavin couldn't believe something that trivial would bother her, could he?

But apparently he did. He released her arm and leaned back in the chair. "Women are all alike. You want attention, and national attention is all the better. Right?"

"Wrong!" She took a step in retreat, stunned by his harshness. She didn't know how to react to Gavin when he was in this mood and judging from the stubborn look on his face, she didn't expect it to change.

Dori's thoughts were prophetic. Gavin seemed withdrawn and unnaturally quiet on the flight home early the next morning. He didn't phone her in the days that followed. During the past month, he'd called her twice and sometimes three times a week. Now there was silence. Even worse was the fact that she found herself waiting for his call. Her own reaction angered her more than Gavin's silence. And yet, Dori thought she understood why he didn't contact her. She also realized that she shouldn't contact him. Maybe he expected her to; maybe he even wanted her to. But Dori wouldn't. She couldn't. Gavin was fighting his feelings for her. He knew that what had happened between them that evening in San Francisco couldn't be blamed on the champagne, and it scared him. He couldn't see her, afraid of what he'd say or do. It was simpler to invent some trumped-up grievance, blame her for some imaginary wrong.

Friday morning, after a week of silence, Dori sat at her desk, staring into space.

"Are you and Gavin going out this weekend?" Sandy asked with a quizzical slant of one delicate brow.

Dori returned her attention to the homeowner's insurance policy on her desk. "Not this weekend."

"Is Gavin announcing another football game?"

"I don't know," she responded without changing her expression.

"Did you two have a fight or something?"

"Or something," Dori muttered dryly.

"Dori." Sandy's eyes became serious. "You haven't ruined this relationship, have you? Gavin Parker is perfect for you. Whatever's happened, make it right. This fish is much too rich and good-looking to throw back. Reel him in very carefully, Dori."

An angry retort trembled on the tip of her tongue, but Dori swallowed it. Not once had she thought of Gavin as a big fish, and she didn't like the cynical suggestion that she should reel him in carefully or risk losing him. Their relationship had never existed on those terms. Neither of them was looking for anything permanent—or at least they hadn't been, not in the beginning.

Dori's mood hadn't improved by the time she got home.

Danny was draped over the sofa, his feet propped up against the back, his head touching the floor. "Hi, Mom."

"Hi." She unwound the scarf from around her neck and unbuttoned her coat. Stuffing her scarf in the sleeve, she reached for a hanger.

"Aren't you going to ask me about school?"

"How was school?" For the first time in years, she didn't care. A long soak in a hot bath interested her far more. This mood infuriated her.

"Good."

Dori closed the closet door. "What's good?"

Danny untangled his arms and legs from the sofa and sat up to stare at her. "School is." He cocked his head and gave her a perplexed look. "You feeling sick?"

It was so easy to stretch the truth. She was sick at heart, disillusioned and filled with doubts. She never wanted to see Gavin Parker again, and yet she was dying for a word from him. Anything. A Christmas card would have elated her, a business card left on her doorstep, a chain letter. Anything. "I'm a little under the weather."

"Do you want me to make dinner tonight?"

"Sure." Her willingness to let Danny loose in the kitchen was a measure of how miserable she felt. This time last week they'd been in San Francisco....

"You *want* me to cook?" Danny was giving her a puzzled look again.

"There might be a microwave dinner in the freezer. You can have that."

"What about you?"

Dori hesitated before heading down the hallway to her room. "I'm not hungry." There wasn't enough chocolate in the world to get her through another week of not hearing from Gavin.

"Not hungry? You must really be sick."

Dori's appetite had always been healthy and Danny was well aware of it. "I must be," she said softly, and went into the bathroom to fill the tub. On impulse she added some bath-oil beads. While the water was running, she stepped into her room to get her pajamas, the faded blue housecoat with the ripped hem and a pair of thick socks.

Just as she was sliding into the fragrant mass of bubbles, Danny knocked anxiously on the bathroom door.

"Go away," she murmured irritably.

Danny hesitated. "But, Mom—"

"Danny, please," she cried. "I don't feel good. Give me a few minutes to soak before hitting me with all your questions." She could hear him shuffling his feet outside the door. "Listen, honey, if there are any cookies left in the cookie jar, they're yours as long as you don't disturb me for thirty minutes. Understand?"

Dori knew she should feel guilty, but she was willing to bend the rules this once if it brought peace and quiet.

"You sure, Mom?"

"Danny, I want to take a nice, hot, uninterrupted bath. Got that?"

He hesitated again. "Okay, Mom."

Dori soaked in the bath until all the bubbles had disappeared and the hot water had turned lukewarm. This lethargy was ridiculous, she decided, nudging up the plug with her big toe. The ends of her curls were wet; after brushing her hair, Dori let it hang limply around her face. The housecoat should have been discarded long ago, but it suited Dori's mood. The socks came up to her knees and she shoved her feet into rabbit-shaped slippers that Danny had given her for Christmas two years before. The slippers had long floppy ears that dragged on the ground and pink powder-puff tails that tickled her ankles. They were easily the most absurd-looking things she owned.

"Hi, Mom…" Danny frowned when she stepped into the living room, concern creasing his face. "You look terrible."

Dori didn't doubt it, with her limp hair, ragged old house-coat and rabbit slippers.

"Mr. Parker's never seen you look so awful."

"He won't, so don't worry."

"But, Mom," Danny protested loudly. "He'll be here any minute."

Chapter Eight

For a wild instant, Dori resisted the panic. "He's not coming." She'd waited all week for him to call and heard nothing. And now he was about to appear on her doorstep, and she didn't want to see him. She couldn't face him, looking and feeling the way she did. In her heart she was pleading with her son to say that Gavin wasn't really coming. "I'm sure Gavin would phone first." He'd better!

"He did, Mom." Danny's expression was one of pure innocence.

"When?" Dori shouted, her voice shaking.

"While you were running your bath. I told him you had a bad day and you wanted to soak."

"Why didn't you *tell* me?" she cried, giving way to alarm.

The doorbell chimed and Dori swung around to glare at it accusingly. Gripping her son by the shoulders, she had the irrational urge to hide behind him. "Get rid of him, Danny. Understand?"

"But, Mom—"

"I don't care what you have to tell him." It occurred to Dori that she must be crazy to make a suggestion like that.

The doorbell continued to ring in short, impatient bursts. Before either mother or son could move, the front door opened and Gavin walked in. "How come your door's open?"

At Danny's guilty look, he scowled. "Don't you know how dangerous that is? Anyone could…" His words faded to a whisper as he stared at Dori. "Has anyone called a doctor? You look terrible."

"So everyone's been telling me," she snapped, clenching her fists. All week she'd been dying for a word or a glance, anything, from Gavin and now that he was here, she wanted to throw him out of her house. Whirling, she stalked into the kitchen. "Go away."

Gavin followed her there and stood, feet braced, as if he expected a confrontation. "I need to talk to you."

Dori opened the refrigerator door and set a carton of eggs on the counter, ignoring him. She wasn't hungry, but scrambling eggs would give her something to concentrate on.

"Did you hear me?" Gavin demanded.

"Yes, but I'm hoping that if I ignore you, you'll go away."

At that moment Danny strolled into the room, pulled out a kitchen chair and sat down. His eager gaze went from his mother to Gavin and again to Dori; they both frowned at him warningly.

"You two want some privacy, right?"

"Right," Gavin answered.

"Before I go, I want you to know, Mr. Parker, that Mom doesn't normally look like…this bad."

"I realize that."

"Well, I was worried because—"

"Danny, please," Dori hissed. "You're doing more harm than good."

His chair scraped against the kitchen floor as he pushed it away from the table. "Don't worry," he said. "I get the picture."

Dori wondered how her son could claim to know what was going on when she didn't have the slightest idea. For that matter, she suspected Gavin didn't, either.

Taking a small bowl from the cupboard, she cracked two eggs against the side.

"How was your week?" Gavin asked.

Dori squeezed her eyes shut and mentally counted to five. "Wonderful."

"Mine too."

"Great." She couldn't hide the sarcasm in her voice.

"I suppose you wondered why I didn't phone," Gavin said next.

Dori already knew, but she wanted to hear it from him. "It crossed my mind once or twice," she said flippantly, as she whipped the eggs with such a vengeance they threatened to slosh out of the small bowl.

"Dori, for heaven's sake, would you turn around and look at me?"

"No!" A limp strand of hair fell across her cheek and she jerked it aside.

"Please." His voice was so soft and caressing that Dori felt her resistance melt away.

With her chin tucked against her collarbone, she winced at a mental image of herself with limp, lifeless hair, a ragged housecoat and silly slippers. She turned toward him, her fingers clutching the counter as she leaned against it for support.

Gavin moved until he stood directly in front of her and placed his hands on her shoulders. Absurd as it was, Dori noticed that his shoes were shined. Worse, they were probably Italian leather, expensive and perfect. He lifted her chin with one finger, but her eyes refused to meet his.

"I've missed you this week," he whispered, and she could feel his gaze on her mouth. It took all Dori's strength not to moisten her lips and invite his kiss. She felt starved for the taste of him. A week had never seemed so long. "A hundred times I picked up the phone to call you," he whispered.

"But you didn't."

"No." He sighed unhappily and slowly shook his head. "Believe it or not, I was afraid."

His unexpected honesty allowed her to meet his gaze openly. "Afraid?"

"Things are getting a little…intense between us, don't you think?" His voice rose with the urgency of his admission.

"And heaven forbid that you have any feelings for a woman in her thirties." She drew a sharp breath and held out a lifeless strand of auburn hair. "A woman who's about to discover her first gray hair, no less."

"Dori, that has nothing to do with it."

"Of course it does," she argued angrily. "If you're going to get involved with anyone, you'd prefer a twenty-five-year-old with a perfect body and flawless skin."

"Would you stop!" He shook her shoulders lightly. "What's the matter with you?"

"Maybe this week has given me time to think. Maybe I know you better than you know yourself. You're absolutely right. You *are* afraid of me and the feelings I can arouse in you, and with good reason. You're attracted to me and it scares you. If it hadn't been for the kids last weekend, who knows what would've happened between us?" At his narrowed look, she took another deep breath and continued her tirade. "Don't try to deny it, Gavin. *I* can figure a few things out for myself—that's the problem when you start seeing a woman whose brain doesn't leak. I know darned well what's going on here. I also know what you're about to suggest."

"I doubt that." His brow furrowed with displeasure.

"It's one of two things," she went on, undaunted.

"Oh?" He took a step in retreat, crossed his arms and leaned against the kitchen table. His eyes were burning her, but Dori ignored the heat.

"Either you want to completely abandon this charade now and never see each other again. This, however, would leave you with a disgruntled daughter who's persistent enough to have you seek out a similar arrangement with another woman. Knowing the way you think, I'd say you probably toyed with the idea for a while. However, since you're here, I'm guessing you've decided another mature woman would only cause you more trouble. You're so irresistible that she's likely to fall in love with you," she said scornfully. "So it's best to deal with the enemy you know—namely me."

His mouth was so tight that white lines appeared at the corners of his lips. "Go on."

"Option number two," she said after a breath. "This one, I'll tell you right now, is completely unacceptable and I'm furious with you for even thinking it."

"What hideous crime have I committed in my thought-life now?" he inquired on a heavy note of sarcasm.

All week the prospect of his "invitation" had been going through her mind. Oh, he'd undoubtedly deny it, but the intention was there; she'd stake a month's salary on it. "You are about to suggest that we both abandon everything we think of as moral to sample marriage."

"Believe me—" he snickered loudly "—marriage is the last thing on my mind."

"I know that. I said *sample*, not actually do it. You were about to suggest that Danny and I move in with you. This, of course, would only be a trial run—a test drive, you'd probably call it—to see if things go smoothly. Then you'd end it when things got complicated or life was disrupted in any way. My advice to you on that one is don't even bother. I'd never agree and I'll think less of you for asking."

"Less than you already do," he finished for her. "But you can rest assured the thought never entered my mind."

Dori could have misjudged him, but she doubted it. "Take a good look at me," she said and held out the sides of her ragged housecoat. Its tattered blue hem dragged on the kitchen floor. "Because what you see is what you get."

Gavin might not have been angry when he arrived, but he was now. "What I can see is that having any kind of rational discussion with you is out of the question."

Lowering her eyes, Dori released a jagged sigh. "As you may have guessed, I'm not the best of company tonight. I...I didn't mean to come at you with my claws showing." She knew she should apologize, but the words stuck in her throat. She wished he'd leave so she could indulge her misery in private.

"I'll admit to having seen you in better moods."

She decided to ignore that. "As I said, it's been a rough week."

A long moment passed before Gaving spoke again and when he did, Dori could tell that he'd gained control of his anger. "There's a Neil Simon play at the 5th Avenue. Do you think you'll feel well enough to go tomorrow night?"

The invitation was so surprising that it stunned her. The muscles of her throat seemed paralyzed, so she merely gave an abrupt nod.

"I'll pick you up around seven-fifteen. Okay?"

Again, all Dori could manage was a nod.

He turned to leave, then paused in the doorway. "Take care of yourself."

"I...I will."

Dori heard the living room door close, and she shuddered in horror. What was the matter with her? She'd come at Gavin like a madwoman. Even now, she didn't know what he'd actually intended to say.

The recriminations and self-doubts remained with her the following afternoon. Perhaps because of them she splurged and had her hair cut and styled, a rare treat. Dori wanted to tell her stylist to do something new and exciting that would look sexy and sophisticated and make five pounds instantly disappear. But she decided not to bother—the woman did hair, not magic.

Dori couldn't recall any other date that had involved so much planning, not even her high school prom. She bought a sleek jumpsuit that came with a fancy title: "Rhapsody in Purple." The label said it was elegant, dynamic and designed for the free-spirited woman, and tonight, those were all the things she wanted to be. Reminding herself that it was the season to be generous and that she deserved some generosity herself, Dori plunked down her credit card, praying the purchase wouldn't take her over her credit limit.

At home, she hung the outfit on the back of her bedroom door and studied it. The soft, pale lavender jumpsuit was simply cut, with long billowy sleeves, and for what she'd paid, it should have been fashioned out of pure gold. The deep V in the back made it the most daring outfit she owned.

Dori had delivered Danny to her parents' house earlier that afternoon, so she was dressed and ready at seven. While she waited for Gavin, she searched the newspaper, looking for an advertisement for the play. He had told her it was a Neil Simon comedy, but he hadn't mentioned which one. A full-page ad announced it: *The Odd Couple.* Dori nearly laughed out loud; the description fit her and Gavin so aptly. She certainly didn't know any odder couple.

Gavin was right on time and did a double take when Dori opened the door.

"Hi," she said almost shyly, holding her head high. Her dangling gold earrings brushed the curve of her shoulders.

"Hello…" Gavin seemed at a loss for words. He let himself into the living room, his gaze never leaving hers. "For a woman who's not twenty-five, you look pretty good."

"I'll take that as a compliment," she said, recalling yesterday's comments. She prided herself on not rising to the bait. Any reaction from Gavin was a plus, and a positive one was worth every penny of the jumpsuit. "You don't look so bad yourself."

He straightened his tie and gave her another of his dazzling smiles. "So my innumerable female companions tell me."

That was another loaded comment best ignored. Dori reached for her handbag, an antique one beaded with a thousand minute pearls. She tucked it under her arm, eager to leave. From past experience, she knew they'd have trouble finding a parking space if they dallied over drinks.

Gavin hesitated as if he expected her at least to offer him something, but she felt suddenly ill-at-ease, anxious to get to the theater and into neutral territory. "We should probably go, don't you think?" she asked flatly.

Gavin frowned and glanced at her hall closet. "What about your coat?" he asked.

"I don't need one." A woman didn't wear "Rhapsody in Purple" with a full-length navy blue coat. This jumpsuit was created for gauzy silk shawls, not wool.

"Dori, don't be ridiculous! It's just above freezing. You can't go outside without a coat."

"I'll be fine," she insisted.

"You'll freeze."

Grudgingly, Dori stomped across the room, yanked open the hall closet and threw on her winter coat. "Satisfied?"

"Yes," he breathed irritably, burying his hands deep in the pockets of his dark overcoat. Dori suspected he was resisting the urge to throttle her.

"I'm ruining my image," she muttered with ill grace, stalking past him and out the front door.

Their seats at the play were excellent and the performers had received enthusiastic reviews. But Dori had trouble concentrating on the characters and the plot. Although Gavin sat beside her, they could've been strangers for all the notice he gave her. He didn't touch her, hold her hand or indicate in any way that he was aware of her closeness. Nor did he laugh at the appropriate times. His mind seemed to be elsewhere; of course, her own concentration wasn't much better.

During the intermission, it became her goal to make him notice her. After all, she'd spent a lot of time, money and effort to attract his attention. And she intended to get it.

Her plan was subtle. When the curtain rose for the second act, Dori crossed her legs and allowed the strap of her sandal to fall loose. With her heel exposed, she pretended to inadvertently nudge his knee. She knew she'd succeeded when he crossed his own legs to avoid her touch. Part two of her plan was to place her hand on the armrest between their seats. Before he was aware of it, she'd managed to curl her fingers around the crook of his elbow. Almost immediately she could feel the tension drain out of him, as though he'd craved her touch, hungered for it. But that couldn't be. If this was how he felt, why hadn't he simply taken her hand? Gavin was anything but shy. This reluctance to touch her shattered her preconceived ideas about him and why he'd asked her out. When he'd admitted the night before that he was frightened, he hadn't been overstating his feelings. The revelation must have been difficult for him and she'd carelessly tossed it back in his face, then hurled her own accusations at him. He wanted to be with her, enjoyed her company—and perhaps he was even falling in love with her. Earlier he'd said he'd missed her that week, and she'd cut him off with her fiery tirade. Now she wanted to groan and cry at her stupidity.

Dori wanted to take him in her arms and humbly ask him to forgive her. She wanted to plead with him to tell her what he'd really come to say. Regret, doubt and uncertainty all collided in her mind, drowning out the performers onstage.

Oh, heavens! Could Gavin have realized that he loved her? Maybe. Even if he wasn't ready to act on his feelings, he had at least reached the point of discussing them. And she'd blown it. She'd taunted him with her outraged presumptions, condemning him before he'd even spoken. Dori closed her eyes at the agony of her own thoughtlessness.

In that moment, when all the doubts crashed together in her mind, Gavin raised his hand and closed it over hers, holding her slender fingers in his warm grasp.

Dori couldn't breathe; she couldn't move. An eternity passed before she could turn her face to him and see for herself the wonder she knew would be waiting for her. What she saw nearly brought her to tears. His eyes were gentle and yielding, his look potent enough to bring her to her knees.

The play ended and they applauded politely only because those around them did. When the audience came to its feet, Gavin and Dori rose, but his hand continued to grip hers.

Dori had never felt such deep communication with another person. If he admitted to being frightened, then so was she. Dori hadn't expected Gavin to come to her so easily. She loved him but had assumed it would take him far longer to acknowledge his feelings.

"I enjoyed the play," he said as he helped her into her coat. His voice was only slightly husky.

"Wonderful." Hers was overwhelmed by emotion. But if he noticed, Gavin gave no indication. It took all Dori had not to throw her arms around his neck and kiss him. She smiled a little, reflecting that if he'd known what she was thinking, Gavin would have been grateful for her restraint.

The drive back to her house was accomplished in a matter of minutes. He pulled to a stop at the curb, but kept his hand on the steering wheel. "Is Danny with his grandparents tonight?"

Dori had the impression that he didn't ask it conversationally but out of a desire to be alone with her. Her heart pounded painfully. "Y-yes."

He looked at her oddly. "Are you feeling sick again?"

"No, I'm fine." Dori cursed the fact that life had to be so complicated. "Would you like to come in for coffee?" They both knew the invitation was a pretense. When Gavin took her in his arms, she didn't want half the neighborhood watching.

The car engine was still running and Gavin made an elaborate show of checking his watch. "Another time," he said. "It's late."

Ten forty-five was not late! If Dori was confused before, it was nothing to the myriad of bewildered emotions that went through her now. "You wanted to say something to me yesterday," she tried again, struggling to sound calm and composed. She forced a smile despite the catch in her voice. "I can't apologize enough for the way I behaved."

"One thing about you, Dori, you're completely unpredictable."

"You did want to tell me something?" she repeated.

"Yes." He paused and she saw the way his fingers tightened around the steering wheel. "As I said, things are getting a little intense between us."

"Yes," she whispered tenderly, her heart in her eyes.

"That's something I hadn't planned on."

"I know." Her throat constricted and she could hardly speak.

"In light of what happened in San Francisco..." He hesitated. "We reached a ten on that last kiss and even you said a ten meant trouble. Heaven only knows where we'd progress from there."

"I remember." Who was he trying to kid? They both knew where they were headed and it wasn't the kitchen. She didn't understand why he was hedging like this.

"Dori," he said, clearing the hoarseness from his throat. "I've been thinking that perhaps we're seeing too much of each other. Maybe it'd be best if we cooled things for a while."

No words could have been more unexpected. All this

time she'd been waiting to hear a profession of love and he'd been trying to tell her he wanted out. To her horror, her eyes filled with stinging tears. Fiercely she blinked them away. She grabbed the door handle in her haste to escape. What a fool she'd been!

"Sure," she managed to stammer without disgracing herself. "Whatever you think." The car door swung open and she clambered out in such a frenzied rush that she was fortunate not to trip. "Thank you for the play. As I said before, it was wonderful." Not waiting for any response, she slammed the car door and hurried toward the house. The sound of his door opening and closing made her suck in a savage breath and battle for control.

"I thought you didn't want any coffee," she said, without turning to face him. The porch light was sure to reveal her tears, which would embarrass them both.

"Dori, listen, I'm sorry. But I need time to sort everything out. Whatever is going on between us is happening too fast. Give me some time…."

From the distance of his voice, Dori guessed he was about halfway up the sidewalk. "I understand." She did, far better than he realized. She'd looked at him with adoring eyes and all the while he'd been trying to come up with some way to dump her—or as he'd probably say, let her down gently. Her eyes blinded by tears, she ripped open her purse and searched for the keys. "Don't worry, you've got all the time in the world," she muttered, clutching the house key between stiff fingers.

"A month. All I want is a month." The pause in his voice revealed his uncertainty.

"Take six," she returned impertinently. "Why stop there—

make it ten." She wanted to laugh, but the noise that erupted from her throat was a dry, pain-filled sob.

"Dori." His shoe scraped sharply against the porch steps and then there was a tentative moment of silence as he stood there, looking up at her. "Are you crying?"

"Who me?" She laughed, sobbing again. "No way! You don't want to see me again? Fine. I'm mature enough to accept that."

"Turn around and let me see your face."

Her chest heaved with the effort of not sobbing openly. She was such a fool.

"Dori, I didn't mean to hurt you."

"I'm not hurt!" she shouted and leaned her forehead against the screen door. Afraid another sob would escape, she covered her mouth with one hand. When she was finally able to catch her breath, she turned to face him. "I'm fine, so please don't feel obligated to stick around. Danny and I'll be just fine."

"Dori—"

"I'm fine!" she insisted again, wiping away her tears. "See?" Without another word, she turned back to the door, inserted the key and let herself in the house.

"Did you have fun with Mr. Parker last night, Mom?" Danny sat at the kitchen table with Dori, who was sipping from a mug of hot coffee. Her mother had phoned earlier to announce that she'd drop Danny off on her way to do some errands.

"The play was great." Dori felt frail and vulnerable but managed to give her son a wan smile. Her thoughts were darker than they'd been since she lost Brad. She'd have to tell Danny that her relationship with Gavin had come to a standstill, but it wasn't going to be easy. "Did you have a good time with Grandma and Grandpa?"

"Yeah, but I'll be glad when you and Mr. Parker get married 'cause I'd rather be a family. Melissa and I could stay alone and I wouldn't have to have a sitter or go to Grandma's every time you want to go out."

"Danny, listen." Dori struggled to maintain an unemotional facade, although she felt as if her heart was breaking. "Mr. Parker and I have decided it would be best if we didn't see each other for a while."

"What?" Danny's mouth dropped open in utter disbelief. "But why? I thought you really liked each other. I thought you might even be talking about marriage. Melissa was sure..." He let the rest drop as if he'd inadvertently divulged a secret.

"No." She lowered her eyes and swallowed hard. There was no choice but to give Gavin exactly what he'd asked for— time. "Gavin isn't ready for that kind of commitment and this is something you and I have to accept."

"But, Mom—"

"Listen," Dori implored, taking his small hand between her own. "You need to promise me that you won't contact Gavin in any way. Sometimes adults need time to think, just like kids do, and we have to respect that. Promise me, Danny. This is important."

He studied her intently, finally nodding. "What about Melissa? Will we be able to see her?"

The two children had become good friends and Dori hated to punish them for their parents' problems. "I'm sure we could make some kind of arrangement to have her over on weekends when Gavin's broadcasting football games." Gavin probably wouldn't mind, as long as he didn't have to see *her*.

"You love him, don't you?"

Dori's smile was wistful. "Gavin Parker is a very special man and loving him is easy. But it won't be the end of the world if we never see him again."

Danny's eyes widened incredulously, as though he found her words completely shocking. "But Mr. Parker was *perfect.*"

"Yes," she agreed, "he met each requirement on your list, but there are lots of other men who will, too."

"Are you going to start looking for another father for me?" Danny rested his chin in the palms of his hands, eyes forlorn.

Immediate protests crowded her mind. "Not right away." Like Gavin, she needed time, but not for the same reasons. For her, it would be a waiting game. In a few weeks, she'd know if her gamble had paid off. Falling for him had been a mistake; he'd warned her often enough. Now she was suffering the consequences.

In the days that followed, Dori was astonished by her own strength of will. It was a struggle, but when thoughts of Gavin invaded her well-defended mind, she cast them aside. He didn't make any effort to get in touch with her and she didn't expect him to. Whatever had happened with Deirdre had hurt him so badly that he might never risk committing himself to another woman. That was his and Melissa's loss… and hers and Danny's.

On Wednesday morning, as Dori stirred hot water into her instant oatmeal, she flipped through the pages of the paper. "Danny," she called over her shoulder. "Hurry, or you'll be late for school."

"Okay, Mom." His muffled voice drifted from his bedroom.

Setting his bowl on the table, Dori leaned against the counter and turned to the society page, looking for the Dear Abby column. At first she didn't recognize the people in the picture on the front page of the city section.

Then her glance fell on Gavin's smiling face and her heart suddenly dropped to her knees. The oxygen became trapped in her lungs, making it painful to breathe. Some unnamed blond-haired beauty who couldn't have been more than twenty-two was grasping his arm and smiling up at Gavin adoringly. Dori knew the look well. Only a few days before she'd gazed at him in exactly the same doting way. She felt a knife twist in her heart as she read the accompanying article, which described the opening of the opera season with a gala performance of Bizet's *Carmen*. So *this* was how Gavin was sorting through his feelings for her. It hadn't taken him long to find a younger woman with flawless skin and a perfect body. *Let him,* her mind shouted angrily. Foolish tears burned her eyes and she blinked them away, refusing to give in to her emotions.

"Mom, what's the matter? You look like you want to hit someone."

"I do?" Hurriedly, she folded the paper. "It's nothing. Okay?"

Danny cocked his head. "Mr. Parker told me that sometimes women act weird. I guess this is one of those times."

"I'm sick of hearing about Mr. Parker." She jerked open the refrigerator and took out bread for her son's lunch. When he didn't respond, she whirled around. "Did you hear me?"

Danny was staring down at his cereal. "Are you going to cry or something?"

"Of course not! Why should I? It's almost Christmas."

His spoon worked furiously, stirring sugar into the

cinnamon-and-raisin-flavored oatmeal. "I don't know, but when your mouth twists up like that, it always means you're upset."

"Thanks," she returned flippantly.

The remainder of the day was as bad as the morning had been. Nothing went right. She mislaid a file. Her thoughts drifted during an important meeting and when Mr. Sandstrom asked her opinion, Dori had no idea what they'd been discussing. Sandy had sent her a sympathetic look and salvaged a potentially embarrassing moment by speaking first. As a thank-you Dori bought her friend lunch, though she couldn't really afford it.

The minute she walked into the house, Dori kicked off her shoes and paused to rub her aching feet. Danny was nowhere to be seen and she draped her coat on the back of a kitchen chair, wondering where he'd gone now. He was supposed to stay inside until she got home. She took a package of hamburger out of the refrigerator, but the prospect of coming up with a decent meal was almost more than she could face.

As she turned, she noticed the telephone. The receiver was off the hook. The cord stretched around the corner and disappeared into the hall closet. Danny. She crossed to the door and pulled it open.

Danny was sitting cross-legged on the floor and at Dori's intrusion, he glanced up, startled, unable to disguise his sudden look of guilt.

"All right, Daniel Robertson, just who are you talking to?"

Chapter Nine

"Oh, hi, Mom," he managed awkwardly, struggling to his feet.

"Who's on the phone?" She repeated her question, but her mind was already whirling with possibilities, all of them unpleasant. If it was Gavin, she was likely to do something stupid, such as grab the receiver and drone in a mechanical-sounding voice that the call had just been disconnected. The memory of his helpful little strategy produced a familiar twinge in her heart. She missed Gavin more than she'd ever thought possible. There was no point in trying to fool herself any longer. She was miserable.

"I'm talking to a girl," Danny admitted, color creeping up his neck at being caught.

"Erica?"

"No." He reluctantly handed her the receiver. "Melissa."

Dori entered the closet, pushing aside their winter coats, and sat on the floor. For the past few days, she'd been cranky with Danny. She hoped this gesture would show him that she regretted being such a grouch.

Amused at his mother's actions, Danny sat next to her and closed the door. Immediately they were surrounded by a friendly darkness. "Hello, Melissa," Dori murmured into the receiver. "How are you?"

"Fine," the thirteen-year-old answered seriously, "I think."

"Why the 'I think' business? It's nearly Christmas and there's lots of stuff going on. A young girl like you shouldn't have a care in the world."

"Yes, I know." Melissa sounded depressed, but Dori didn't know how deeply she should delve into the girl's unhappiness. Where Gavin was concerned—and that included his relationship with his daughter—Dori was particularly vulnerable. She loved Gavin and felt great affection for Melissa.

Danny was whispering furiously from his end of the closet.

"Excuse me a minute, Melissa. It seems Danny has something extremely important to tell me." She placed her palm over the receiver. "Yes, Danny?"

"Melissa's got a mother-daughter fashion thing at her school and she doesn't have anyone to bring."

Dori nodded. "Danny says your school's having a fashion show."

"My Family Studies class is putting it on. I sewed a dress and everything. It's almost as pretty as the outfit you helped me buy. The teacher gave me an A."

"Congratulations. I'm sure you did a good job to have rated such a high grade." Already Dori knew what was coming and she dreaded having to turn the girl down. But with the way things stood between her and Gavin, Dori couldn't very well offer to go.

"I sewed it superbly," Melissa admitted with a charming lack of modesty. "It's the best thing I ever made. Better than the apron, but then I had to take the waistband off four times. I only made one minor mistake on the dress," she continued, her voice gaining volume and speed with each word. "I sewed the zipper in backward, you know, so the tab was on the inside. I thought it was all right, it still went over my head and everything, but I had to take it out and do it again. I was mad at myself for being so dumb." She paused to draw in a giant breath, then hurried on. "Will you come and pretend to be my mother? Please, Dori? Practically everyone has someone coming. Even the other girls who board…"

"Oh, Melissa." Dori's shoulders slumped forward as she sagged against the wall. "Honey, I don't know." Her stomach started churning frantically. She hated to refuse the girl, but Gavin was likely to read something unintended into her acceptance.

"Dori, please, I won't ask anything of you ever again. I need a pretend mother for just one night. For the fashion show."

The soft, pleading quality of the girl's voice was Dori's undoing. She briefly considered suggesting that Melissa ask Lainey, until she recalled the girl's reaction to the blonde. Despite her misgivings, Dori couldn't ignore the yearning in Melissa's request. "I'll do it on two conditions," she agreed cautiously.

"Anything." The girl's voice rose with excitement.

"First, you mustn't tell any of your friends that I'm your mother. That would be wrong. As much as I wish I had a daughter like you, Melissa, I can never be your mother."

"Okay," she agreed, slightly subdued. "What else?"

"I don't want your father to know I've done this." Gavin would be sure to see more in this simple act of kindness than there was. "I'm not asking you to lie to him, but I don't want him assuming the wrong thing. Okay, Melissa?"

"Okay. He won't even need to know because everything's taking place at the school and he never goes there on week-days. And I promise not to tell him."

"Then I guess all I need to know is the date and time."

"Next Monday at seven-thirty. May I talk to Danny again?"

"Sure." Dori handed the receiver back to her son and got awkwardly to her feet, hitting the top of her head on the rod positioned across the small enclosure. "Ouch," she muttered as she gingerly opened the door, seeking a safe passage out.

A few minutes later Danny joined her in the kitchen, where Dori was frying the hamburger. "That was nice of you, Mom."

"I'm happy to do it for Melissa. I'm very fond of her." Gavin loved his daughter—that much Dori didn't doubt—but she hoped he appreciated her, as well.

"Melissa was really worried about the fashion show. I thought it was tough not having a dad, but I guess it's just as bad without a mom."

"I'm sure it is," she replied smoothly. "Now how about if you set the table?"

"What are we having for dinner?"

Dori looked at the sautéing meat and shrugged. "I don't know yet."

"Aw, Mom, is it another one of *those* meals?"

On Friday morning, Dori overslept. Danny woke her almost twenty minutes after her alarm should have gone off.

"Mom," he murmured, rubbing the sleep from his face. "Aren't we supposed to be up? This isn't Saturday, is it?"

Dori took one look at the silent clock radio, gasped and threw back the covers. "Hurry and get dressed! We're late."

Feeling a little like the rabbit in *Alice in Wonderland*, Dori dashed from one room to the next, exclaiming how late they were. Her shower rivaled Danny's thirty-second baths for a new speed record. She brushed her teeth with one hand and blow-dried her hair with the other. The result was hair that looked as if it had been caught in an egg beater and a toothpaste stain on the front of her blouse.

"Should I buy lunch today?" Danny wanted to know, shoving his arms into a sweatshirt and pulling his head through to gaze at her inquisitively.

"Yes." There was no time to fix a sandwich now. "Take some money out of my purse."

Danny returned a minute later with her billfold. "All you've got is a twenty-dollar bill."

"Oh, great." As she slipped her feet into soft leather pumps, her mind raced frantically. "What about your piggy bank?"

"But, Mom…"

"It's a loan, Danny. I'll pay you back later."

"Okay," he agreed with all the charity of an ill-tempered loan shark.

"Hurry up now. I'll get the car out of the garage."

Dori was parked in the driveway, revving the cold engine, when Danny ran through the garage. He slammed the door and climbed into the car.

"I got four dollars."

"Good." She looked over her shoulder as she backed out of the driveway. Traffic was heavy and driving took all her concentration.

"Mom," Danny said after a few minutes. "About that four dollars."

"Danny, good grief, I'll pay you back tonight. Now quit worrying about it." She slowed to a full stop at a traffic light.

"But I'm going to need it! It's almost Christmas and I can't afford to be generous."

Dori paused to think over his words before turning to stare at her son. "Did you hear what you just said?"

"Yeah, I shouldn't have to pay for my own lunch. I want my money back."

"Danny." She gave him an incredulous look. Her son couldn't afford to be generous because it was Christmas? The time of year when love and human goodness were supposed to be at their peak. A low rumbling sound escaped Dori's throat. Then she began to giggle. The giggles burst into full laughter until her whole body shook and she had to hold her side to keep from laughing harder. Still engrossed in the pure irony of his statement, Dori reached over, despite the seat belt, and hugged her son. "Thanks." She giggled. "I needed that."

"It's not that funny," Danny objected, but he was laughing, too. Suddenly he sobered, his hand raised. "Mom, look! It's Mr. Parker. He's in the car right beside us."

Unable to resist, Dori glanced over at the BMW stopped next to her. Her laughter fled as she recognized Gavin. He hadn't seen her and Danny, or if he had, he was purposely looking in the opposite direction. Just when she was wondering what, if anything, she could do, Gavin's eyes met hers. Dori's heart gave a wild leap and began to thump madly as the dark, thoughtful eyes looked straight into hers. Stunned, she recognized an aching tenderness in his face. She saw regret, doubt, even pain. She wanted to smile and assure him she was fine but that she missed him dreadfully. She wanted to ask how he was doing and about that picture in the paper. Ten other flighty, meaningless thoughts came to her all at once, but she didn't have the opportunity to voice even one.

A car horn blared impatiently behind her, and Dori realized the traffic light was green and she was holding up a long line of commuters.

"That *was* Mr. Parker, wasn't it?" Danny said as she stepped on the gas and rushed forward.

"Yes." Her throat felt dry and although earlier there'd been laughter, Dori now felt the compelling need to cry. Swallowing the urge, she took the next right-hand turn for Danny's school. A quick glimpse in her rearview mirror revealed Gavin traveling forward. No wave, no backward look. Perhaps he regretted their relationship, perhaps she'd read him wrong from the start and it hadn't meant a thing. But Dori couldn't allow herself to believe that. She had to trust her instincts. Otherwise it hurt too much.

Saturday and Sunday passed in a blur of vague anticipation. After seeing Gavin on Friday morning, Dori had half expected that he'd call her during the weekend. She should have known better than to second-guess Gavin Parker. He did things his own way. When and if he ever admitted to loving her, she'd never need to doubt again. That was how Gavin was. She knew with absolute certainty that when he truly fell in love, it would be a complete and enduring love, a love to last a lifetime.

The only bright spot in her disappointing weekend was a phone call from Melissa, who wanted to confirm that Dori would attend the Mother-Daughter Fashion Show as she'd promised. During the conversation, the girl casually mentioned that Gavin was in L.A. to broadcast a football game.

Monday evening, Dori dressed in her best professional suit, a charcoal gray two-piece with a white silk shirt. Danny had agreed to submit to the humiliation of having Jody from across the street come to babysit. He was vociferous in letting Dori know that this was a sacrifice on his part and he wanted her to tell Melissa all about his unselfishness.

A light drizzle had begun to fall when Dori pulled into the school parking lot. She was surprised by the large number of cars. Dori had assumed Melissa was exaggerating when she'd declared that she'd be the only girl there without a mother or some other woman as stand-in—a sister, a stepmom, an aunt.

Melissa stood just inside the doorway of the large auditorium, waiting for Dori. A smile brightened her face the moment she caught Dori's eye. Rushing to her side, Melissa gave Dori an excited hug and handed her a program.

"Is this the world-famous creation, designed by the renowned Melissa Parker?" Dori inquired with a proud smile. The corduroy dress was a vivid shade of dark blue.

"Do you like it?" Melissa whirled around, holding out the sides of the skirt in Hollywood fashion. Sheer delight created large dimples in her round cheeks. "I think it turned out so pretty."

"It's wonderful."

Taking her by the arm, Melissa escorted Dori down the middle aisle of folding chairs. "I'm supposed to seat you right here."

"Where are you going?" Dori glanced around her curiously. Only a few women were sitting near the front and it looked as though these seats were reserved.

"Everything's almost ready, so I have to go backstage, but I'll see you later." She started to move away but abruptly changed her mind. "The choral group is singing first. They really aren't very good, but please applaud."

"I will," Dori promised, doing her utmost to maintain a serious expression. "I take it you're not singing."

"Only if I want to offend Ms. Curran."

In spite of herself, Dori chuckled. "Well, break a leg, kid."

Another woman, a day student's mother, was seated next to Dori a few minutes later and they struck up a pleasant conversation. It would've been very easy to pretend Melissa was her daughter, but Dori was careful to explain that she was there as a friend of the Parker family. Even at that, Dori felt she was stretching the truth.

The show began with the introduction of the school staff. Then Dori applauded politely at the end of the first series of songs presented by the choral ensemble. Melissa might not have had a finely tuned musical ear, but her assessment of the group wasn't far off. Nonetheless, the applause was enthusiastic.

Following the musical presentation came the fashion show. Dori straightened in her chair as the announcer, a girl about Melissa's age, stepped toward to the microphone. Obviously nervous, the girl fumbled with her papers and her voice shook as she started to speak.

Melissa in her blue dress was the fourth model. With natural grace, she walked across the stage, then turned once, holding out the skirt with one hand, and paused in front of Dori to display the even stitches of her hem. The mothers loved it and laughed outright.

At the end of the fashion show, the principal, Ms. Curran, approached the front of the room to announce the names of the students who'd made the honor roll for the semester.

"Ladies," the soft voice instructed, "when the name of your daughter—or honorary daughter—is read, would you please come forward to stand with her."

When Melissa's name was called out, the girl came to the

front of the auditorium and cast a pleading glance at Dori. Heart pounding, Dori rose from her seat to stand behind Melissa. She noticed that all the women with honor-roll girls came from the first few rows; this was the reason Melissa had escorted Dori to the front. She wished Melissa had said something earlier. But then, it wouldn't have made any difference.

Dori's smile was proud as she placed her hands on Melissa's shoulders and leaned forward to whisper in her ear. "Daughter or not, I'm extremely proud of you."

Twisting her head, Melissa looked up at Dori, her expression somber. "I wish you were my mother."

"I know," Dori murmured quietly, the emotion building until her throat felt swollen with the effort not to cry. Still, she had to brush a stray tear from her cheek and bite her lip to keep from sobbing out loud.

The final names were read and there was a round of applause. "What now?" Dori whispered.

"I'm supposed to seat you and bring you a cup of tea and some cookies." She led Dori to her seat. "I'll be right back."

"Okay." Dori crossed her legs and, with nothing to do, scanned the program for the fifth time. Her gaze rested on Melissa's name. This child could easily take the place Dori had reserved in her heart for the daughter she'd never had— and never would.

"You enjoyed that little charade, didn't you?" Gavin's voice taunted. Dori turned in shock as he sat down in the vacant chair beside her.

The words ripped through her with the pain of a blunt knife. Her program slipped to the floor and she bent to retrieve it. Fixing a stiff smile on her lips, she straightened, forcing herself to be calm.

"Hello, Gavin," she said with a breathlessness she couldn't control. "What brings you here?"

"My daughter." His emphasis on *my* was obviously intended as a not-so-subtle reminder that she was an intruder.

"Melissa invited me," Dori said in an attempt to explain her presence. "It's a Mother-Daughter Fashion Show." The minute the words were out, Dori knew she'd said the wrong thing.

"You're not her mother," he replied in a remote, impersonal tone.

"No, and I haven't pretended to be."

"That's not how I saw it. Melissa's name was called and you hurried to the front like every other proud mother."

"What was I supposed to do?" she whispered angrily, her hands clenched in her lap. "Sit there with Melissa giving me pleading looks?"

"Yes," he bit back in a low controlled voice. "Did you think that if you maintained a friendship with my daughter we'd eventually resume our relationship? That's not the way it's going to happen. I asked for some time and you're not giving it to me." He paused and raked a hand through his hair. "Your coming here tonight makes things impossible."

A weary sigh came from deep within Dori. Gavin assumed the worst possible explanation for what she'd done. Perhaps he was looking for a reason to hate her and now he had all the excuse he needed.

"I've fended off a lot of women bent on ending my independence," he said harshly, "but you're the best. You know I love my daughter. She's my weakest link."

Unable to bear any more of his sarcasm, Dori stood. "You've got it all wrong, Gavin. Melissa is your strongest point. You're arrogant, egotistical and so stubborn you can't see what's right in front of your face."

"Dori, what's wrong?" Melissa approached her from behind, carefully holding a cup of hot tea in one hand and a small paper plate of cookies in the other.

Dori took the delicate cup and saucer out of Melissa's shaking fingers and handed them to Gavin. If he wanted to play mother, then he could drink the weak tea and eat the stale cookies.

"Daddy…" Melissa choked with surprise and turned stricken eyes to Dori. "I didn't tell him, honest."

"I know," Dori assured her.

"What are you doing here? I didn't tell you about…the tea.… This is supposed to be for mothers and—" The words stumbled over her tongue.

"Sit down," Gavin ordered. "Both of you."

As they seated themselves, he dragged his chair around so that he was facing them. Dori felt like a disobedient child but refused to give in to the sensation. She'd done nothing wrong. Her only motive in attending the fashion show had been kindness; she'd responded to the pleas of a young girl. Dori had come for Melissa's sake alone, and the fact that Gavin was the girl's father had almost deterred her from coming at all—despite what he chose to believe.

"I think you'd better tell me what's going on." His eyes challenged Dori in that chilling way she hated.

"I've already explained the circumstances," she inserted dryly. "However, it seems to me that you've added two and two and come up with five."

"Dad," Melissa demanded with open defiance, clearly taking note of Dori's unapologetic tone, "what are you doing here? This isn't for fathers. You're the only man here."

"The notice came from the school about the fashion show," he explained haltingly, glancing around him. "I have every right to come to my daughter's school any time I please."

"But it doesn't give you the right to say those kinds of things to me," Dori said calmly, and drew together the front of her suit jacket. People sitting nearby were beginning to give them unwanted attention.

Gavin's features hardened and one brow was raised derisively. Without looking at his daughter, he said, "Melissa, get Dori another cup of tea."

"But, Dad—"

"You heard me."

Reluctantly, Melissa rose to her feet. "I'll be back in a couple of minutes." She took a few steps toward the rear of the auditorium, then turned to Dori again. "They have coffee, if you'd prefer that."

"Either one is fine," Dori answered with a smile and a reassuring wink. She probably wouldn't be around to drink it, anyway.

Gavin waited until his daughter was out of earshot. "This whole situation between us has gotten out of hand."

Dori crossed her arms and leaned back in the hard folding chair, suddenly weary.

"We had a nice thing going, but it's over. You broke the rules," he said accusingly. "If you attempt to drag it out, you'll only make it painful for the kids." His voice was harsh with impatience. "I'm seeing someone else now," he explained. "Melissa hasn't met her yet, but she will soon."

Dori drew in a ragged breath and found she couldn't release it. It burned in her lungs until she regained her composure enough to slowly exhale. "I'm sure she will." She didn't know how she could remain so calm when every breath was a struggle and every heartbeat caused her pain. Deep down, Dori had suspected that Gavin would do something like this. "I'm only surprised you waited so long. I scare you to death, Gavin, and you're running as fast as you can in the opposite direction. No doubt you've seen any number of women in the past week—all of them young, blond and gorgeous."

"You think you know me so well." He eyed her coolly. "But you're wrong. I saw what was happening with us and came to my senses in the nick of time."

Dori marveled at her self-control. Even though the whole world felt as if it were dissolving around her, she sat serenely, an expression of apparent indifference on her face. Whatever Gavin might say, she still tried to believe that eventually he'd recognize that he loved her. All she had were her hopes. He was stubborn enough to deny his feelings for her all his life. Dori didn't know what made her think she could succeed where so many others had failed.

"If you expected to shock me with your sudden interest in all these women, you haven't. And despite what you say, I *do* know you."

"You don't know me at all," he said with an angry frown.

"From the beginning, I've found you very easy to read, Gavin Parker." Inside, Dori was convulsed with pain, but she refused to allow him even a glimpse of her private agony. "You love me. You may not have recognized it yet, but someday you will. Date anyone you like, but when you kiss them, it'll be my lips you taste and when they're in your arms, it's *me* you'll long to hold."

"If anyone loves someone around here, it's you." He spoke as though the words were an accusation.

Dori's smile was infinitely sad. "Yes, I'll admit that. I love you and Melissa."

"I told you not to fall in love with me," he said bitterly. "I warned you from the beginning not to smell orange blossoms, but that's all you women seem to think about."

Dori couldn't deny his words. "Yes, you did, and believe me, I was just as shocked as you when I realized I could fall in love with someone so pigheaded, irrational and emotionally scarred." She paused to swallow the ache in her throat. "I don't know and I don't even want to know what Deirdre did to you. That's in the past, but you're still wearing all that emotional pain like...like a shroud."

"I've heard enough." A muscle flexed in his jaw.

Letting her gaze fall, Dori tried to blink back the burning tears. "If you've found someone else who can make you happy, then I wish you the very best. I mean it sincerely, but I doubt you'll ever find that elusive contentment. Goodbye, Gavin. I apologize, I truly do, for ruining a promising agreement. With someone less vulnerable than me, it might have worked."

His gaze refused to meet hers. For all the emotion revealed in his eyes, she could have been talking to a man carved from stone. Without a word he was going to let her go. She'd persisted in hoping that somehow she'd reach him and he'd stop her—but he hadn't.

"You're not leaving, are you?" Melissa spoke from behind them, setting a cup on the seat of the beige metal chair. "I brought your tea."

"I can't stay." Impulsively she hugged the girl and brushed back the thick bangs that hung across Melissa's furrowed brow. "Goodbye." Dori's voice quavered with emotion. She wouldn't see Melissa again. Coming here this evening had been a terrible mistake.

Melissa clung to her, obviously understanding what had happened. "Dori," she begged, "please...don't leave. I promise..."

"Let her go," Gavin barked, causing several heads to turn.

Instantly, Melissa dropped her hands and took a step in retreat. Dori couldn't stand another minute of this. With a forced smile on her face, she hurried out of the auditorium. Once outside, she broke into a half trot, grateful for the cover of darkness. She desperately needed to be alone.

By the time Dori pulled into her garage, the tears were making wet tracks down her face. She turned off the engine and sat with her hands clenching the steering wheel as she fought to control her breathing and stem the flow of emotion.

A glance at her watch assured her that Danny would be in bed and, she hoped, asleep.

The babysitter eyed Dori's red face curiously but didn't ask any questions. "There's a phone message for you on the table," the girl said on her way out the front door.

Dori switched on the kitchen light and smiled absently at the name and number written neatly on the message pad. She reached for the phone and punched out the number, swallowing the painful lump that filled her throat.

He answered on the third ring. "Hi, Tom, it's Dori Robertson, returning your call."

"Hi, Dori," he began awkwardly. "I hope I'm not bothering you."

"No bother." She looked up at the ceiling and rubbed her burning eyes with one hand. "I had a school function to attend for a friend, but I'm home now."

"How are you?"

Dying, her heart answered. "Splendid," she murmured. "Getting ready to do some Christmas shopping. Danny's managed to limit his Christmas list to a mere three hundred items."

"Would you like some company? I mean, I understand if you'd rather not, feeling the way I do about Paula."

"I take it you two haven't managed to patch things up?"

"Not yet," he said with an expressive sigh. "About the shopping—I'd appreciate some advice on gifts and such."

"I'd be happy to go with you, Tom."

"I know you've been seeing a lot of that ex-football player."

"I won't be seeing him anymore." She choked down a sob and quickly covered her mouth.

"How about one night this week?"

"Fine," she said, replacing the receiver after a mumbled goodbye. Leaning against the kitchen wall, Dori made an attempt to regain her composure. She'd known what she was letting herself in for from the beginning. It wouldn't do any good to cry about it now.

She wiped her eyes and looked up to find Danny standing in the doorway, watching her.

"Oh, Mom," he said softly.

Chapter Ten

Danny sat at the kitchen table spreading colored frosting on gingerbread men. His look was thoughtful as he added raisin eyes and three raisin buttons to each.

The timer on the stove went off and Dori automatically reached for the padded oven mitt.

"You know, Mom, I don't like Mr. Parker anymore. Melissa either. I thought she was all right for a girl, but I was wrong."

"The problem is, Danny, we both love them very much and telling ourselves anything else would be lying." For several days Danny had been brooding and thoughtful. They'd had a long talk after the Mother-Daughter Fashion Show, and Dori had explained that they wouldn't be seeing Gavin or Melissa again. Surprisingly, her son had accepted that without argument.

"I don't love anyone who makes my mom sad," he insisted.

"I'm not sad now," she assured him, and it was true, she wasn't. There were regrets, but no tears.

Licking the frosting from his fingers, Danny examined

the "new father" requirement list posted on the refrigerator door. "How long do you think it'll be before we start looking again?"

Dori lifted the cut-out cookies from the sheet with a spatula and tilted her head pensively to one side. "Not long." Gradually, her pain-dulled senses were returning to normal. Dating again would probably be the best thing for her, but there was a problem. She wanted only Gavin. Loved only Gavin.

When she finished sliding the cookies from the sheet, Dori noticed that Danny had removed the requirement list, strawberry magnet and all, and taken a pencil from the drawer. Then he'd carried everything to the table. Dusting her floury hands, she read over his shoulder as his pencil worked furiously across the bottom of the page. "I'm adding something else," he explained needlessly. "I want a new father who won't make my mom cry."

"That's thoughtful, but, Danny, tears can mean different things. There are tears of happiness and tears of frustration, even angry tears. Sometimes crying is good and necessary." She didn't want to explain that the tears were a measure of her love for Gavin. If she hadn't loved him, it wouldn't have hurt so much when they'd stopped seeing each other.

"Mr. Parker wasn't a very good football player, either," Danny complained.

"He was terrific," Dori countered.

"I threw away all the football cards I had of him. And his autograph."

He said it with a brash air of unconcern as though throwing away the cards had been a trivial thing. But Dori knew better. She'd found the whole collection of treasures—the cards, the autograph and the program from the Seahawks football game he and Gavin had attended—in the bottom of his garbage can and rescued them. Later, he'd regret discarding those items. He was hurt and angry now, but he'd recover. Next autumn, he'd be pleased when she returned the memorabilia so he could brag to his new junior-high friends that he had Gavin Parker's autograph.

"While the cookies are cooling, why don't you bring in the mail."

"Sure, Mom."

Usually Dori could count on Danny's good behavior during the month of December, but lately he'd been even more thoughtful, loving and considerate. She was almost beginning to worry about him. Not once had he nagged her about Christmas or his presents. Nor had he continued to pursue the new father business. Until today, he'd said nothing.

The phone rang as Danny barged into the kitchen, tossing the mail on the counter. He grabbed the receiver and answered breathlessly.

A couple of minutes later he turned to Dori. "Mom, guess what? It's Jon. He wants to know if I can come over. He's real excited because his dad's moving back in and they're going to be a real family again."

"That's wonderful. Tell Jon I'm very happy for him." Dori wasn't surprised. From the care with which Tom had gone about choosing Christmas presents for his wife and family, Dori realized how deeply he loved them. He'd never told her why he and his wife had separated, but Dori was genuinely happy to hear they'd settled their problems. Did she dare hope that Gavin would recognize all the love waiting for him and return to her? No man could kiss her and hold her the way he had and then cast her aside without regrets. Paula had her Christmas present and Dori wondered if she'd ever have hers.

"Can I go over? I'll finish decorating the cookies later."

"Don't worry about it. There are only a few from the last batch and I can do those. Go and have a good time."

"Thanks, Mom." He yanked his coat from the closet and blew her a kiss, something he'd taken to doing lately instead of giving her a real kiss.

"You're welcome," she called lightly. "And be home in an hour." The last words were cut off as the back door slammed.

Dori watched Danny's eager escape and sighed. Her son was growing up. She used to look at him and think of Brad, but now she saw that Danny was becoming himself, a unique and separate person.

She reached for the stack of mail, which appeared to consist of bills and a few Christmas cards. She carried everything into the living room, slouched onto the sofa and propped her slippered feet on the coffee table. The first envelope had a return address she didn't immediately recognize and curiously she ripped it open. Instead of a card, there was a personal letter written on notebook paper. Unfolding the page, Dori's gaze slid to the bottom, where she discovered Melissa's signature.

Dori's feet dropped to the floor as she straightened. After the first line, she bit her lip and blinked rapidly.

Dear Dori,

I wanted to write and thank you for coming to the mother-daughter thing. Dad showing up was a real surprise and I hope you believe me when I tell you I didn't say anything to him. Really, I didn't.

Dad explained that I shouldn't bother you anymore

and I won't. That's the hardest part because I really like you. I know Deirdre is my real mother, but I don't think of her as a mother. She's pretty, but I don't think she's really very happy about being a mother. When I think of a mother, I think of someone like you who buys groceries in the Albertson's store. Someone who lets me try on her makeup and perfume even if I use too much. Mothers are special people, and for the first time in my life I got to see one up close. Thank you for showing me how I want to love my kids.

I feel bad that things didn't work out with you and my dad. I feel even worse that Dad says I shouldn't ever bother you again. I don't think I'm even supposed to be writing this letter, but it's only polite to thank you properly. Anyway, Dad refuses to let me talk about you or Danny. He doesn't seem to have time for me right now, but that's okay because I'm pretty mad at him anyhow.

I'd like to think of you as my mother, Dori, but I can't because every time I do, I start to cry. You told me once how much you wanted a daughter. I sure wish I could have been yours.

Your almost daughter,
Melissa

Tears filled Dori's eyes as she refolded the letter and placed it back in the envelope. This was one lesson she hadn't ever counted on learning. This helpless, desolate feeling of grieving for a man incapable of commitment. Yet there was no one to blame but herself. He'd warned her not to fall in love with him. The problem was, he hadn't said anything about loving his daughter and Dori did love Melissa. And now, instead of two people facing Christmas with heavy hearts, there were four.

Gavin Parker could take a flying leap into a cow pasture and the next time she saw him—if she ever saw him again—she'd tell him exactly that. How long would it take him to realize how much she loved him? Let him be angry; she was going to answer Melissa's letter. And maybe in a few months, when it wasn't so painful, she'd visit Melissa at the school and they'd spend the day together.

Dori's gaze rested on the gaily trimmed Christmas tree and the few presents gathered about the base. This was supposed to be the happiest time of the year. Only it wasn't. Not for Danny or Dori. Not this year. The stuffed lion Gavin had won for her sat beside the television, and Dori couldn't resist the impulse to go over and pick it up. Hugging it fiercely, she let the soft fur comfort her.

When the surge of emotion subsided, Dori took out some stationery and wrote a reply to Melissa. Afterward she felt calmer and even a little cheered. Later that night, when Danny was in bed, she reread it to be sure she'd said everything she wanted to say and decided no letter could ever convey all the love in her heart.

Dearest Melissa,

Thank you for your sweet letter. I felt much better after reading it. I know you didn't tell your father about the fashion show, so please don't think I blame you for that.

I'm going to ask you to do something you may not understand right now. It's important that you not be angry with your father; he needs you more than ever. He loves you, Melissa, very much, and you must never doubt that. I care about him, too, but you'll have to love him for both of us. Be patient with him.

Later, after the holidays, if it's all right, I'll come and spend a day with you. Until then, do well in your studies and keep sewing. You show a definite talent for it—especially for stitching hems!

You will always hold a special place in my heart, Melissa, and since I can't be your mother, let me be your friend.

Love,
Dori

Dori was grateful that December was such a busy month. If it had been any other time, she might've fallen prey to even greater doubt and bitterness. Every night of the following week there was an activity she and Danny were expected to attend. But although she was with family and friends, she'd never felt more alone. She felt as if she'd lost a vital part of herself and she had—her heart. She'd given it to Gavin. And now she was caught in this limbo of apathy and indifference. After he'd panicked and run from her love, Dori had thought she could just take up where she'd left off and resume the even pace of her life. Now she was painfully learning that it would be far longer before she found her balance again. But she would, and that was the most important thing.

At the dinner table two days before Christmas, Danny stirred his mashed potatoes with his spoon and cleared his throat, apparently planning to make a weighty pronouncement. "Mom, did you know this is Christmas Eve's eve?"

Dori set her fork aside. "You're right," she said, nodding.

"And since it's so close to Christmas and all, I thought maybe it'd be okay to open one of my presents."

Dori didn't hesitate for an instant. "Not until Christmas morning. Waiting is half the fun."

"Aw, Mom, I hate it. Just one gift. Please."

A stern look silenced him, and he concentrated on slicing his roast beef into bite-size pieces. "Are we going to Grandma and Grandpa's again this year?"

They did every year. Dori wondered why Danny asked when he knew the answer.

"Yes, just like we did last year and the year before that and the year before that and—"

"I get the picture," he mumbled, reaching for his glass of milk. He lifted it to his mouth, then paused, an intense, almost painful look edging its way across his face. "Do you suppose we'll ever see Mr. Parker and Melissa again?"

"I don't know." A sadness invaded her heart, but she managed a strained smile. She hoped. Every minute of every hour she hoped, but she couldn't say that to Danny. "Why do you ask?"

"I don't know." He raised one shoulder in a shrug. "It just doesn't seem right not seeing them."

"I know." Her throat worked convulsively. "It doesn't seem right for me, either."

Danny pushed his plate aside, his meal only half-eaten. "Can I be excused, Mom? I'm not hungry anymore."

Neither was Dori, for that matter. "Sure," she murmured, laying her knife across her own plate.

Danny carried his dishes to the sink and turned back to Dori. "Do you *have* to work tomorrow?"

Dori wasn't too thrilled at the prospect, either. "Just in the morning. If you like, you can stay home by yourself." Danny was old enough to be left alone for a few hours during the day. Usually he preferred company, but on Christmas Eve he'd sleep late and then he could watch television until she got home around eleven-thirty.

"Could I really?" He smiled eagerly. "I'll be good and not have anyone over."

"I know."

The following morning Dori had more than one doubt. Twice she phoned Danny from the office. He assured her he was fine, except that he had to keep answering the phone because Grandma had called three times, too. Dori didn't call after that, but when the office closed, she made it to the employee parking lot and out again in record time. On the drive home, she had to restrain herself from speeding. Waiting at a red light, Dori was convinced she'd done the wrong thing in leaving Danny on his own. He wasn't prepared for this kind of responsibility. True, he was by himself for an hour after school, but this was different. He'd been alone in the house for three and a half hours.

The garage door was open, and with a sigh of relief she drove inside and parked.

"Danny!" she called out, slightly breathless as she walked in the back door. "I'm home. How did everything go?" Hanging her purse in the hall closet, she walked into the living room—and stopped dead. Her heart fell to her knees, rebounded and rocketed into her throat. Gavin was there. In her living room. Dressed casually in slacks and a sweater, he was staring at her with dark, brooding eyes. She looked over at Danny, perched on the ottoman facing Melissa, who sat in the nearby chair.

"Hi, Mom." Danny looked as confused as Dori felt. "I told them it was okay if they came inside. That was the right thing to do, wasn't it?"

"Yes, yes, of course." Her fingers refused to cooperate as

she fiddled with her coat buttons. She was so happy—and so afraid—that her knees gave way and she sank weakly onto the sofa across from Gavin. "This is a..." Her mind went blank.

"Surprise," Melissa finished for her.

A wonderful surprise, her mind threw back. "Yes."

"They brought us Christmas gifts," Danny explained, pointing to the large stack of gaily wrapped presents under the tree.

"Oh." Dori felt as if this wasn't really happening, that somehow she'd wake and find it only a vivid dream. "Thank you. I have yours in the other room."

A hint of a smile touched Gavin's mouth, but his dark eyes studied her like a hawk about to swoop down from the skies to capture its prey. "Were you so sure of me?"

"No, I wasn't sure, but I was hoping."

Their eyes met as he spoke. "Danny and Melissa, why don't you go play a game while I talk to Dori."

"I'm not leaving my mom," Danny declared in a forceful voice. He sprang to his feet defensively and crossed the small room to sit beside his mother.

Shocked by his behavior, Dori stared at him, feeling an odd mixture of pride and disbelief.

A muscle moved in Gavin's rigid jaw when Melissa folded her arms and looked boldly at her father. "I agree with Danny. We should all hear this."

Dori dropped her eyes to keep Gavin from seeing the laughter sparkling there. The kids were obviously going to stay to the end of this, whether they were welcome or not.

Gavin slid to the edge of his seat and raked his hand through his hair in an uncharacteristic gesture of uncertainty.

"I've been doing a lot of thinking about our agreement,"

he began on a note of challenge. "Things didn't exactly work out the way I planned, but—"

"I'm not interested in any more agreements," Dori said honestly and immediately regretted interrupting him. Not for anything would she admit that it hadn't worked because she'd done exactly what he'd warned her not to do. She'd fallen in love with him.

Another long pause followed as he continued to watch her steadily. "I was hoping, Dori, that you'd hear me out before jumping to conclusions." Speaking in front of the children was clearly making him uneasy.

Dori made a limp, apologetic motion with her hand. The living room had never seemed so small, nor Gavin so big. Every nerve in her body was conscious of him and she ached for the feel of his comforting arms. "I'm sorry. I won't interrupt you again."

Gavin ignored her and turned his attention to Danny instead. "Didn't you once tell me that you wrote a requirement list for a new father?"

"Yes." Danny nodded.

"Would you get it for me?"

Danny catapulted from the sofa and into the kitchen. Within seconds he was back, thrusting the list at Gavin. "Here, but I'm not sure why you want to read it. You already know what it says."

"I think Dad might want to apply for the position," Melissa said, her eyes glowing brightly. "Dad and I had a really long talk and he feels bad about what happened and decided—"

"Melissa," he said flatly, "I'd prefer to do my own talking."

"Okay, Dad." She leaned back against the chair with an impatient sigh.

Dori's head was spinning like a satellite gone off its orbit.

Her hands felt both clammy and cold and she clasped them in her lap.

Gavin appeared to be studying the list Danny had given him. "I don't know that I've done such a terrific job in the father department, but—"

"Yes, you have, Dad," Melissa inserted. "You've been really good."

Despite herself, Dori found she had to smile at Melissa and her *reallys*.

"Melissa, please," Gavin barked and paused to smooth the hair he'd rumpled a few minutes earlier. The muscle in his jaw twitched again. "Dori." He said her name with such emotion that her heart throbbed painfully. "I know I don't deserve someone as wonderful as you, but I'd consider it a great honor if you'd consent to marry me."

The words washed over her like warm, soothing water and she closed her eyes at the sudden rush of feeling. "Are...are you saying you love me?" she whispered, unable to make her voice any stronger.

"Yes," he answered curtly.

"This is for *us*—not because of the kids?" She knew that Melissa held a powerful influence on her father. From the beginning, both Melissa and Danny had tried to manipulate them.

"I want to marry you because I've learned that I don't want to live without you." His response was honest and direct.

"Then yes, I'll be your wife." Dori's was just as straightforward.

"Okay, let's set the date. The sooner the better."

If he didn't move to take her in his arms soon, she'd embarrass them both by leaping across the room.

"I'm sorry, Mr. Parker, but you can't marry my mom,"

Danny announced with all the authority of a Supreme Court judge.

"What?" Dori, Melissa and Gavin shouted simultaneously.

Danny eyed all three sternly. "If you read my requirement list for a new father, you'll see there's another requirement down there now."

Gavin's gaze dropped to the paper clenched in his hand.

"You made my mom cry, Mr. Parker, and you might do it again."

A look of pain flashed across Gavin's face. "I realize that, Danny, and I deeply regret any hurt I've caused your mother. If both of you will give me another chance, I promise to make it up to you."

Danny appeared to weigh his words carefully. "So you'll never make her cry again?"

Frowning thoughtfully, Gavin studied the boy in silence. As she watched them, Dori felt a stirring of love and tenderness for her son and for the man who would soon become her husband.

"I hope never to cause your mother any more pain," Gavin muttered, "but I can't promise she won't cry."

"Mom." Danny transferred his attention to Dori. "What do you think?"

"Danny, come on," Melissa said with high-pitched urgency. "Good grief, this is what we all want! Don't blow it now."

Danny fixed his eyes on his mother, unswayed by Melissa's plea. "Well, Mom?"

Dori's gaze met Gavin's and her heart leaped wildly at the tenderness she saw. "Yes, it's what I want." They both stood at the same moment and reached for each other in a spontaneous burst of love and emotion. Gavin caught her in his arms and crushed her against his chest as his hungry mouth came down on hers. With a sigh of longing, Dori received his kiss, glorying in the feel of his arms around her. She knew that coming to her and admitting his love and his need had been difficult, and she thanked him with all the love in her own heart.

Twining her arms around his neck, she held him fiercely. She was vaguely aware of Danny murmuring to Melissa—something about leaving so he didn't have to watch the mushy stuff.

Gavin's arms tightened around her possessively, holding her closer while his hand slid along her spine. "I've missed you so much," he whispered hoarsely against her lips, then kissed her again, harder and longer as if he couldn't possibly get enough of her.

The sensation was so exquisite that Dori felt tears of happiness spring to her eyes and roll unheeded down her cheeks. "Oh, Gavin, what took you so long?"

Drawing back slightly, Gavin inhaled a shuddering breath. "I don't know. I thought it would be so easy to forget you. There's never been a woman in my life who's haunted me the way you have."

Her eyes shone with joyful tears as she smiled mischievously up at him. "Good." What she didn't tell him was that she'd felt the same things.

"Once I'd been in the sunlight, I couldn't go back to the shadows," Gavin said. He buried his face in her hair and breathed in deeply. "I tried," he acknowledged with an ironic laugh. "After Deirdre I didn't want any woman to have this kind of power over me."

"I know."

He shook his head. "How is it you know me so well?"

Smiling happily, she told him, "I guess it comes from loving you so much."

"Everything happened just the way you predicted," he said. "No matter who I kissed, it was your lips I tasted. When I held another woman, I sensed that something was wrong, and I wanted only you."

"Oh, Gavin." She spread tiny kisses over his face. Her lips met his eyes, nose, jaw and finally his eager mouth. She didn't need to be told that these lessons had been difficult ones for Gavin. Surrendering his freedom to a woman had been an arduous battle between his will and his heart. But now he'd find a new freedom in their love for each other. He'd finally come to understand that, and she knew he'd love her with all his strength.

Gently his thumb wiped a tear from the arch of her cheek. "The worst part was seeing you in the car that morning with Danny." Dori heard the remembered pain that made his voice husky. "You were laughing as if you hadn't a care in the world. I saw you and felt something so painful I can't even describe it. You had me so tied up in knots, I was worthless to anyone—and there you were, laughing with Danny as if I meant nothing."

"That's not true," she said. "I was dying inside from wanting you."

"You've got me," he said humbly. "For as long as you want."

"I love you," Dori whispered fervently, laying her trembling hand on his smoothly shaved cheek. "And I can guarantee you that one lifetime won't be enough."

Cradling her face between both his hands, Gavin gazed into her eyes and kissed her with a gentleness that bordered on worship.

* * *

"I told you it'd work," Danny whispered in the kitchen.

"I knew it all along," Melissa agreed with a romantic sigh. "It was obvious from the day we went to the fair. They're perfect together."

"Yeah, your plan worked," Danny agreed.

"We're not through yet." Her voice dropped slightly as if she were divulging a secret.

"But they're getting married," Danny said in low tones. "What more could we want?"

Melissa groaned. "Honestly, Danny, think about it. Four is such a boring number. By next year there should be five."

"Five what?"

"People in our family. Now we've got to convince them to have a baby."

"Hey, good idea," Danny said eagerly. "That'd be great. I'd like a baby brother."

"They'll have a girl first. The second baby will be a boy for you. Okay?"

"I'd rather have the boy first."

"Maybe," Melissa said, obviously feeling generous.

* * * * *

The Courtship of
Carol Sommars

In loving memory of
David Adler, Doug Adler and Bill Stirwalt
Beloved Cousins
Beloved Friends

Special thanks to
Pat Kennedy and her endearing Italian mother,
and Ted Macomber and Bill Hall
for the contribution of their rap music
and all the lessons about living with teenage boys

Chapter One

Carol Sommars swore the entire house shook from her fifteen-year-old son's sound system, which was blasting out his favorite rap song.

I'm the Wizard MC and I'm on the mike
I'm gonna tell you a story that I know you'll like
'Cause my rhymes are kickin', and my beats do flash
When I go to the studio, they pay me cash

"Peter!" Carol screamed from the kitchen, covering her ears. She figured a squad of dive-bombers would've made less of a racket.

Realizing that Peter would never be able to hear her above the din, she marched down the narrow hallway and pounded on his door.

Peter and his best friend, Jim Preston, were sitting on Peter's bed, their heads bobbing in tempo with the music. They both looked shocked to see her.

Peter turned down the volume. "Did you want something, Mom?"

"Boys, please, that music is too loud."

Her son and his friend exchanged a knowing glance, no doubt commenting silently on her advancing age.

"Mom, it wasn't *that* bad, was it?"

Carol met her son's cynical look. "The walls and floors were vibrating."

"Sorry, Mrs. Sommars."

"It's okay, Jim. I just thought I'd save the stemware while I had a chance." Not to mention warding off further hearing loss…

"Mom, can Jim stay for dinner? His dad's got a hot date."

"Not tonight, I'm afraid," Carol said, casting her son's friend an apologetic smile. "I'm teaching my birthing class, but Jim can stay some other evening."

Peter nodded. Then, in an apparent effort not to be out-done by his friend, he added, "My mom goes out on hot dates almost every weekend herself."

Carol did an admirable job of disguising her laugh behind a cough. Oh, sure! The last time she'd gone out had been… she had to think about it…two months ago. And that had been as a favor to a friend. She wasn't interested in remarry-ing. Bruce had died nearly thirteen years earlier, and if she hadn't found another man in that time, she wasn't going to now. Besides, there was a lot to be said for the benefits of living independently.

She closed Peter's bedroom door and braced her shoul-der against the wall as she sighed. A jolt of deafening music brought her upright once more. It was immediately lowered to a respectable level, and she continued back to the kitchen.

At fifteen, Peter was moving into the most awkward teen-age years. Jim, too. Both boys had recently obtained their learner's permits from the Department of Motor Vehicles and were in the same fifth-period driver training class at school.

Checking the time, Carol hurried into the kitchen and turned on the oven before popping two frozen meat pies inside.

"Hey, Mom, can we drive Jim home now?"

The operative word was *we*, which of course, meant Peter would be doing the driving. He was constantly reminding her how much practice he needed if he was going to pass the driving part of the test when he turned sixteen. The fact was, Peter used any excuse he could to get behind the wheel.

"Sure," she said, forcing a smile. These "practice" runs with Peter demanded nerves of steel.

Actually, his driving skill had improved considerably in the last few weeks, but the armrest on the passenger side of the car had permanent indentations. Their first times on the road together had been more hair-raising than a horror movie— another favorite pastime of her son's.

Thanks to Peter, Carol had been spiritually renewed when he'd run the stop sign at Jackson and Bethel. As if to make up for his mistake, he'd slammed on the brakes as soon as they'd cleared the intersection, catapulting them both forward. They'd been saved from injury by their seat belts.

They all clambered into her ten-year-old Ford.

"My dad's going to buy me a truck as soon as I get my license," Jim said, fastening his seat belt. "A red four-by-four with flames painted along the sidewalls."

Peter tossed Carol an accusing glare. With their budget, they'd have to share her cantankerous old sedan for a while. The increase in the car insurance premiums with an additional driver—a male teenage driver—meant frozen meat pies every third night as it was. As far as Carol was concerned, nurses were overworked, underpaid and underappreciated.

"Mom—hide!"

Her heart vaulted into her throat at the panic in her son's voice. "What is it?"

"Melody Wohlford."

"Who?"

"Mom, please, just scoot down a little, would you?"

Still not understanding, she slid down until her eyes were level with the dashboard.

"More," Peter instructed from between clenched teeth. He placed his hand on her shoulder, pushing her down even farther. "I can't let Melody see me driving with my *mother!*"

Carol muttered under her breath and did her best to keep her cool. She exhaled slowly, reminding herself *this, too, shall pass.*

Peter's speed decreased to a mere crawl. He inadvertently poked her in the ribs as he clumsily lowered the window, then draped his left elbow outside. Carol bit her lower lip to prevent a yelp, which probably would've ruined everything for her son.

"Hey, Melody," he said casually, raising his hand.

The soft feminine greeting drifted back to them. "Hello, Peter."

"Melody," Jim said, leaning across the backseat. He spoke in a suave voice Carol hardly recognized.

"Hi, Jimmy," Melody called. "Where you guys off to?"

"I'm driving Jim home."

"Yeah," Jim added, half leaning over Carol, shoving her forward so that her head practically touched her knees. "My dad's ordered me a truck, but it hasn't come in yet."

"Boys," Carol said in a strangled voice. "I can't breathe."

"Just a minute, Mom," Peter muttered under his breath, pressing down on the accelerator and hurrying ahead.

Carol struggled into an upright position, dragging in several deep gulps of oxygen. She was about to deliver a much-needed lecture when Peter pulled into his friend's driveway. Seconds later, the front door banged open.

"James, where have you been? I told you to come directly home after school."

Carol blinked. Since this was the boys' first year of high school and they'd come from different middle schools, Carol had never met Jim's father. Now, however, didn't seem the appropriate moment to leap out and introduce herself.

Alex Preston was so angry with Jim that he barely glanced in their direction. When he did, he dismissed her and Peter without a word. His dark brows lifted derisively over gray eyes as he scowled at his son.

Carol suspected that if Jim hadn't gotten out of the car on his own, Alex would have pulled him through the window.

Carol couldn't help noting that Alex Preston was an imposing man; he had to be easily six-two. His forehead was high and his jaw well-defined. But his eyes were what immediately captured her attention. They held his son's with uncompromising authority.

There was an arrogant set to his mouth that Carol found herself disliking. Normally she didn't make snap judgments, but one look told her she wasn't going to get along with Jim's father, which was unfortunate since the boys had become such fast friends.

Not that it really mattered. Other than an occasional phone conversation, there'd be no reason for them to have any contact with each other.

She didn't know much about the man, other than his

marital status (single—divorced, she assumed) and the fact that he ran some sort of construction company.

"I told you I was going out tonight," Alex was saying. "The least you could've done was have the consideration to let me know where you were. You're lucky I don't ground you for the next ten years."

Jim dropped his head, looking guilty. "Sorry, Dad."

"I'm sorry, Mr. Preston," Peter said.

"It's not your fault."

To his credit, Alex Preston glanced apologetically at Peter and Carol as if to say he regretted this scene.

"It might be a good idea if you hurried home yourself," Alex told her son.

Carol stiffened in the front seat. She felt like jumping out of the car and informing him that they had no intention of staying anyway. "We should leave now," she said to Peter with as much dignity as she could muster.

"Later," Peter called to his friend.

"Later," Jim called back, still looking chagrined.

Peter had reversed the car out of the driveway and was headed toward the house before either of them spoke.

"Did you know Jim was supposed to go home right after school?" Carol asked.

"How could I know something like that?" Peter flared. "I asked him over to listen to my new CD. I didn't know his dad was going to come unglued over it."

"He's just being a parent."

"Maybe, but at least you don't scream at me in front of my friends."

"I try not to."

"I've never seen Mr. Preston blow his cool before. He sure was mad."

"I don't think we should be so hard on him," she said, feeling generous despite her earlier annoyance. Adults needed to stick together. "He was obviously worried."

"But, Mom, Jim's fifteen! You shouldn't have to know where a kid is every minute of the day."

"Wanna bet?"

Peter was diplomatic enough not to respond to that.

By the time they'd arrived at the house and Carol had changed clothes for her class, their dinner was ready.

"Mom," Peter said thoughtfully as she brought a fresh green salad to the table. "You should think about going out more yourself."

"I'm going out tonight."

"I mean on dates and stuff."

"Stuff?" Carol repeated, swallowing a smile.

"You know what I mean." He sighed loudly. "You haven't lost it yet, you know."

Carol wasn't sure she did. But she was fairly certain he meant to compliment her, so she nodded solemnly. "Thanks."

"You don't even need to use Oil of Olay."

She nodded, although she didn't appreciate such close scrutiny of her skin.

"I was looking at your hair and I don't see any gray, and you don't have fat folds or anything."

Carol couldn't help it—she laughed.

"Mom, I'm serious. You could probably pass for thirty."

"Thanks…I think."

"I'm not kidding. Jim's dad is going out with someone who's twenty-one, and Jim told me she's tall and blond and pretty with great big…you know." He cupped his hands over his chest.

Carol sat down at the table. Leaning her elbows on it, she

dangled her fork over her plate. "Are you suggesting I find myself a twenty-one-year-old guy with bulging muscles and compete with Jim's dad?"

"Of course not," Peter said scornfully. "Well, not exactly. I'm just saying you're not over the hill. You could be dating a whole lot more than you do. And you should before…well, before it's too late."

Carol pierced a fork full of lettuce and offered a convenient excuse. "I don't have time to get involved with anyone."

Peter took a bite of his own salad. "If the right guy came along, you'd make time."

"Perhaps."

"Mr. Preston does. Jim says his dad's always busy with work, but he finds time to date lots of women."

"Right, but most of the women he sees are too young to vote." Instantly feeling guilty for the catty remark, Carol shook her head. "That wasn't nice. I apologize."

"I understand," Peter said, sounding mature beyond his years. "The way I see it, though, you need a man."

That was news to her. "Why? I've got you."

"True, but I won't be around much longer, and I hate the thought of you getting old and gray all alone."

"I won't be alone. Grandma will move in with me and the two of us will sit side by side in our rocking chairs and crochet afghans. For entertainment we'll play bingo every Saturday afternoon." Even as she spoke, Carol realized how ridiculous that was.

"Grandma would drive you crazy in three days," Peter said with a know-it-all smile, waving his fork in her direction. "Besides, you'd get fat eating all her homemade pasta."

"Maybe so," Carol agreed, unwilling to argue the point.

"But I have plenty of time before I have to worry about it. Anything can happen in the next few years."

"I'm worried *now*," Peter said. "You're letting your life slip through your fingers like…like the sand in an hourglass."

Carol's eyes connected with her son's. "Have you been watching soap operas again?"

"Mom," Peter cried, "you're not taking me seriously."

"I'm sorry," she said, trying to hide the smile that raised the corners of her mouth. "It's just that my life is full. I'm simply too busy to spend time developing a relationship." One look from her son told her he didn't accept her explanation. "Sweetheart," she told him, setting her fork aside, "you don't need to worry about me. I'm a big girl. When and if I decide to see another man, I promise it'll be someone muscular so you can brag to your friends. Would a wrestler be all right?"

"The least you could've done was get married again," he muttered, his patience clearly strained. "Dad would've wanted that, don't you think?"

Any mention of Peter's father brought with it a feeling of terror and guilt. They'd both been far too young and foolish to get married. They were high school seniors when Carol learned she was pregnant. Given her very traditional Catholic family, marriage had seemed the only option. She'd also believed her love and their baby would change Bruce. For those reasons, Carol had agreed to marry him. But from that point to the moment Bruce had died in a terrible car accident three years later, Carol's life had been a living hell. She'd have to be crazy to even consider remarriage.

"Peter," she said, pointedly glancing at her watch and pushing her plate away. "I'm sorry to end this conversation so abruptly, but I've got to get to class."

"You're just being stubborn, but fine. It's your decision."

Carol didn't have time to argue. She dumped the remainder of her meal in the garbage, rinsed off her plate and stuck it in the dishwasher. She left Peter after giving him instructions to take care of his own dishes, then she hurried into the bathroom.

She refreshed her makeup and ran a brush though her shoulder-length dark hair, then examined her reflection in the mirror.

"Not bad," she muttered, eyeing herself critically. Thirty-four wasn't exactly retirement age.

Releasing her breath, Carol let her shoulders fall. "Who are you kidding?" she said with a depressed sigh. She faced the mirror and glared at her image again. Peter might not think she needed Oil of Olay, but the dew was definitely off the rose.

Tugging at the skin on her cheekbones until it was stretched taut, she squinted at her reflection, trying to remember what she'd looked like at eighteen. Young. Pretty. Stupid.

She wasn't any one of those now. And even if she'd had the opportunity, she wouldn't go back. She'd made plenty of mistakes, but there wasn't a single, solitary thing she'd change about her current life. Although after Peter got his driver's license, she might modify that thought.

No, the only option open to her was the future, and she'd face that, sagging skin and all.

"Hey, Mom." Peter's voice cut into her musings. "Can I invite a friend over tonight?"

Carol opened the bathroom door and frowned at her son. "I can't believe you'd even ask that. You know the rules. No one's allowed here when I'm not home."

"But, Mom," he whined.

"No exceptions."

"You don't trust me, do you?"

"We're not discussing this now. I have a class to teach, and I'm already five minutes behind schedule." She blamed Peter for that. If he hadn't tried to convince her how attractive she was, she wouldn't be late in the first place.

Class went well. They were into the third week of the eight-week course sponsored by Ford Hospital in a suburb of Portland, Oregon. The couples were generally first-time parents, and their eagerness and excitement for the adventure that lay before them filled each session with infectious enthusiasm.

If Carol had known when she was carrying Peter that he was to be her one and only pregnancy, she would've taken time to appreciate it more.

Since she was the last to leave the building, Carol turned off the lights and hauled her material out to her car. The parking lot was well lit, and she hurried through the rain, sliding inside the car. She drew in a deep breath and turned the ignition key. The Ford coughed and objected before roaring to life. Her car had been acting a little funny lately, but it was nothing she could pinpoint. Satisfied that there wasn't anything too terribly wrong, she eased into traffic on the busy street.

It wasn't until she'd stopped for the red light at the first intersection that her car released a series of short pathetic coughs, only this time it really sounded…sick.

"What's wrong?" she cried as the light turned green. Pushing down on the accelerator, she leaped ahead, but it was apparent that the problem, whatever it might be, was serious.

"All right, all right," she said, "I get the message. You need a mechanic and fast." A quick glance down the business-lined thoroughfare revealed there wasn't a single service station in sight.

"Great," she moaned. "How about if I promise not to let Peter behind the wheel for a while. Will that help?"

The ailing car belched loudly and a plume of black smoke engulfed the rear end.

"Okay, so you're not interested in a deal." Turning into the first driveway she happened upon, Carol found herself in a restaurant parking lot. The minute she entered an empty space, the car uttered one last groan and promptly died. And of course she'd left her cell phone charging—at home.

For a full minute Carol just sat here. "You can't do this to me!" Her car disagreed. Climbing out, she walked around it, as if she'd magically discover a cure lying on the ground. The rain was coming down in sheets, and within seconds, she was drenched.

In an act of angry frustration, she kicked a tire, then yelped when the heel of her pump broke off. She wanted to weep.

With no other alternative, she limped into the restaurant, intent on heading for the ladies' room. Once she composed herself, she'd deal with the car and call Peter to tell him she was going to be late.

Alex thought that if his date giggled one more time, he'd have to walk away from the table. Thanks to this woman, he was going slowly insane. He should know by now never to accept a blind date.

The first thing Bambi did when they were seated at the restaurant was to pick up the saltshaker and start discussing the "amazing" qualities of crystal.

It took Alex five minutes to make the connection. The saltshaker was made of crystal.

"I'm crazy about hot tubs," Bambi said, leaning forward to offer him a generous view of her ample breasts.

"They're...hot, all right," Alex murmured, examining the menu without much enthusiasm. His friend—at least someone he *used* to consider a friend—claimed Bambi was every man's dream. Her name should have been his first clue. Once they'd met, he'd learned her given name was Michelle, but she'd started calling herself Bambi because she loved forest animals so much. Animals like deer and chipmunks and hamsters.

Alex didn't have the heart to tell her that in all the years he'd been camping, he had yet to stumble upon a single family of hamsters grazing in a meadow.

When the waitress came to take their order, it took Bambi five minutes to explain how she wanted her salad served. Okay, he was exaggerating. Four minutes. He ordered a steak and asked for it rare.

"I'm on a diet," Bambi said, once the waitress had left.

He smiled benignly.

"Do you think I'm fat, Alex?" she asked.

Her big brown eyes appealed to him to lie if he must. Once more she bunched her full breasts together and leaned toward him. It was more than obvious that she wasn't wearing a bra. He suspected that he was supposed to swoon at the sight.

"You do think I'm fat, don't you?" Bambi asked, pouting prettily.

"No," Alex told her.

"You're just saying that to be nice," she purred, and demurely lowered her lashes against the high arch of her cheek.

Alex smoothed out the linen napkin on his lap, thinking he was getting old. Far too old for someone like Bambi/Michelle. His teenage son might appreciate her finer qualities, but he suspected even James had better sense than that.

"Do you have a hot tub?"

Alex was so caught up in his thoughts, mentally calculating how long it would take to get through dinner so he could drive her home, that he didn't immediately realize she'd directed the question at him.

"I love hot tubs," she reminded him. "I even carry a swimsuit with me just in case my date has a tub. See?" She reached inside her purse and held up the skimpiest piece of material Alex had seen in his entire life. It was all he could do not to grab it out of her hand and shove it back in her purse.

"I don't have a hot tub," he said, making a strenuous effort to remain civil.

"Oh, that poor, pathetic thing," Bambi said, looking past him to the front of the restaurant.

"I beg your pardon?"

Bambi used this opportunity to lean as far forward as possible, drape her breasts over his arm and whisper, "A bag lady just came into the restaurant. She's drenched, and I think she might be hurt because she's limping pretty bad."

Although he really wasn't interested, Alex glanced over his shoulder. The instant his gaze connected with the woman Bambi was referring to, he twisted his chair around for a better view. "That's no bag lady," he said. "I know that girl."

"You do?"

"Yes, she was with my son and his best friend this afternoon. I think she's another friend of theirs." He paused. "She might be in some kind of trouble." He wasn't in the business of rescuing maidens in distress, but someone had to do something. "Will you excuse me a moment?"

"Alex," Bambi cried, reaching out for his arm, stopping him. Half the restaurant turned to stare at them—including the woman at the front. Even from halfway across the room, Alex could feel her eyes on him.

"You can't involve yourself in other people's problems," Bambi insisted.

"She's just a kid." He pulled his arm free.

"Honey, one look at her and I can tell you she's no kid."

Disregarding Bambi's unsought advice, Alex dropped his napkin on the table, stood and walked away.

"Hello, again," he said when he reached his son's friend. Bambi was right about one thing. She looked terrible—nothing like the way she'd looked earlier. Her hair fell in wet tendrils that dripped on her jacket. Her mascara had left black streaks down her face, and she held the heel of her shoe in one hand. "I'm James's dad—we met briefly this afternoon." He held out his hand to her. "Do you remember me?"

"Of course I do," she said stiffly, clearly resenting this intrusion. She glanced longingly at the ladies' room.

"Is something wrong?"

"Wrong?" she echoed. "What could possibly be wrong?"

She thrust out her chin proudly, but he resisted the urge to shake some sense into her. Sarcasm always set his teeth on edge. "I'd like to help if I could."

"I appreciate the offer, but no thanks. Listen, I think you'd better get back to your date." She nodded toward Bambi, and a smile quivered at the corners of her mouth. She had difficulty meeting his eyes.

Briefly Alex wondered what she found so amusing. But then again…he knew.

"I thought she was supposed to be tall," she said next, and it sounded like she was trying not to laugh outright. Alex didn't appreciate her sense of humor, but he wasn't going to respond in kind. She was the one standing there looking like a drowned rat. Not him.

Her brows rose as she studied Bambi. "Actually two out of three isn't bad."

Alex had no idea what she was talking about. His expression must have said as much because she added, "Jim was telling Peter how your date for this evening was tall and blond and had big—"

She stopped abruptly, and Alex could swear she was blushing. A bright pink color started creeping up her neck and into her cheeks. "I'm sorry, that was uncalled for."

Bambi apparently wasn't about to be the center of their conversation while sitting down. She pushed back her chair, joined them near the hostess desk and slipped her arm through Alex's. "Perhaps you'd care to introduce us, Alex darling."

Alex wanted to roll his eyes at the way she referred to him as "darling." They'd barely met. He doubted Bambi knew his last name. He certainly didn't remember hers.

Since he wasn't sure of anyone's name, Alex gestured toward Carol and said, "This is a friend of my son's…."

"Carol Sommars," she supplied.

Alex was surprised. "I didn't know Peter had a sister."

Carol shot him a look. "I'm not his sister. I'm his mother."

Chapter Two

"His mother," Alex echoed, clearly distressed. "But I thought...I assumed when you were with the boys that..."

"She's got to be *way* over thirty!" the blonde with her arm wrapped around Alex's exclaimed, eyeing Carol as possible competition.

Unwilling to be subjected to any debate over her age, Carol politely excused herself and headed blindly toward the ladies' room. The way her luck had been going this evening, it shouldn't be any shock that she'd run into Alex Preston of all people—and his infamous "hot date."

As soon as Carol examined herself in the mirror, she groaned and reached for her purse, hoping to repair the worst of the damage. No wonder Alex had mistaken her for a teenager. She looked like Little Orphan Annie on a bad day.

To add to her consternation, he was waiting for her when she left the restroom.

"Listen," he said apologetically. "We got off to a bad start. Can I do something to help?"

Carol thanked him with a smile. "I appreciate that, but I don't want to ruin your evening. My car broke down and I don't have my cell. I'm just going to call the auto club from here and have them deal with it." She already had the phone number and a quarter in her hand. The pay phone was just outside the restrooms.

"All right." Carol was grateful when he left. She was horrified by the way she'd spoken to him earlier and wanted to apologize—later. Alex had caught her at a bad moment, but he'd made up for it by believing she was Peter's sister. That was almost laughable, but exceptionally flattering.

She finished her call and tried three frustrating times to get through to Peter, but the line was busy. Sitting in the restaurant foyer, she decided to give her son a few more minutes before calling again.

Alex strolled toward her. "Is the auto club coming?"

"They're on their way," she answered cheerfully, flashing him a smile.

"Did you get hold of Peter?"

Her facade melted away. "I tried three times and can't get through. He's probably talking to Melody Wohlford, the love of his life."

"I'll contact James on my cell and have him get in touch with Peter for you. That way, you won't have to worry about it."

"Thank you." She was more gracious this time. "Knowing Peter, he could be on the phone for hours."

Alex stepped away and returned a minute later. "Jim was talking to Peter. Fortunately we have call waiting so I got through to him." He shook his head slightly. "They're doing their algebra homework together, which is probably good because Jim needs all the help he can get."

"In this case it's the blind leading the blind."

Alex grinned, and the mouth she'd found so arrogant and haughty earlier now seemed unusually appealing. His smile was sensual and affable at the same time and Carol liked it a whole lot. It had been a good many years since she'd caught herself staring at a man's mouth. Self-conscious, she dragged her gaze away and looked past him into the restaurant.

Alex glanced uncomfortably at his table, where the other woman was waiting impatiently. "Would you like to join us and have something to eat?" he asked eagerly.

"Oh, no," Carol said, "I couldn't do that."

Alex's gray eyes reached out to hers in blatant appeal. "*Please* join us."

Carol wasn't sure what was going on between Alex and his date, and she was even less sure about putting herself in the middle of it, but... Oh, well, why not?

"All right," she agreed in a tentative voice.

Alex immediately looked grateful. He glanced back at the woman who was glaring at him, clearly displeased that he was paying so much attention to Carol.

However, if her disapproval bothered him, he didn't show it. He led Carol back to the table and motioned for the waitress to bring a menu.

"I'll just have coffee."

As soon as the waitress was gone, Alex introduced the two women. "Bambi, Carol. Carol, Bambi."

"I'm pleased to make your acquaintance," Bambi said formally, holding out her hand. Carol thought she'd never seen longer nails. They were painted a fire engine red and were a good inch in length.

"Alex and I have sons the same age," Carol explained. Her

coffee arrived, and she quickly took a sip to disguise her uneasiness.

"Eat your dinner, Alex," Bambi instructed. "There's no need to let our evening be ruined by Carol's problems."

"Yes, please," Carol said hurriedly. "By all means, don't let me keep you from your meal."

Alex reached for the steak knife. "Is Peter trying out for track this year?"

"He wouldn't miss it. I'm positive that's the only reason he's managed to keep his grades up. He knows the minute he gets a D, he's off the team. Who knows what'll happen next year when he takes chemistry."

"Jim's decided to take chemistry his junior year, too."

"I took chemistry," Bambi told them. "They made us look inside a worm."

"That's biology," Carol said kindly.

"Oh, maybe it was."

"I need to apologize for the way I blew up this afternoon," Alex continued. "I felt bad about it afterward. Yelling at Jim in front of his friends was not the thing to do. It's just that there are times my son frustrates me no end."

"Don't worry about it. I feel the same way about Peter when he does something I've specifically asked him not to do." Feeling guilty for excluding Bambi from the conversation, Carol turned toward her and asked, "Do you have children?"

"Heavens, no. I'm not even married."

"Children can be extremely wonderful and extremely frustrating," Carol advised Bambi, who seemed far more interested in gazing lovingly at Alex.

"Jim only has one chore around the house during the week," Alex went on to say. "He's supposed to take out the garbage. Every week it's the same thing. Garbage starts stacking up against the side of the refrigerator until it's as high as the cabinets, and Jim doesn't even notice. I end up having to plead with him to take it out."

"And two days later he does it, right? Peter's the same."

Alex leaned forward and braced his forearms against the table, pushing his untouched steak aside. "Last week, I didn't say a word, wanting to see how long it would take him to notice. Only when something began to stink did he so much as—"

"Pass the salt," Bambi said, stretching her arm between Carol and Alex and reaching for it herself. She shook it over her salad with a vengeance, then slammed it down on the table.

Apparently Alex felt contrite for having ignored his date. He motioned toward her salad. "Bambi's on a diet."

"I am not fat!" Bambi cried. "You said so yourself."

"I...no, I didn't mean to imply that you *needed* to be on a diet, I was just...making small talk."

"Well, if you don't mind, I'd prefer it if you didn't discuss my eating habits."

"Where's the protein?" Carol asked, examining Bambi's plate of greens. "You should be having some protein—eggs, lean meat, that sort of thing."

"Who are you?" Bambi flared. "Jenny Craig?"

"You're right, I'm sorry. It's just that I'm a nurse, and I work with pregnant women, and nutrition is such an important part of pregnancy that—"

"Are you suggesting I'm pregnant?"

"Oh, no, not in the least." Every time Carol opened her mouth, it seemed she made an even worse mess of the situation. "Look, I think the auto club might need some help finding me. If you'll both excuse me, I'll wait outside."

"You should," Bambi said pointedly. "You're over thirty, so you can take care of yourself."

Carol couldn't get away fast enough. The rain was coming down so hard it was jitterbugging across the asphalt parking lot. Standing just inside the restaurant doorway, Carol buried her hands in her pockets and shivered. She hadn't been there more than a few minutes when Alex joined her.

Before she could say anything, he thrust his hands in his own pockets, sighed and said, "I gave her money for a taxi home."

Carol wasn't sure how to respond. "I hope it wasn't on account of me."

"No." He gave her another of his warm sensual smiles. "It was a blind date. I should've known better than to let myself get talked into it."

"I went out on one a while ago, and it was a disaster, too." It got worse the longer she was single. Her friends seemed to believe that since she'd been alone for so many years, she should be willing to lower her standards. "How long have you been single?" she asked Alex.

"Two years. What about you?"

"Thirteen."

He turned to face her. "That's a long time."

"So Peter keeps telling me. According to him, I'm about to lose it and need to act fast. I haven't figured out precisely what *it* is, but I have a good idea."

"Jim keeps telling me the same thing. Between him and Barney—that's the guy who arranged this date—they're driving me crazy."

"I know what you mean. My brother's wife calls me at least

once a week and reads me ads from the personal columns. She's now progressed to the Internet, as well. The one she picked out last week really got me. It was something like— Male, thirty-five, dull and insecure, seeks exciting, wealthy female any age who's willing to love too much. Likes string cheese and popcorn. If you can do *Sudoku for Dummies,* I'm the man for you."

"Maybe we should introduce him to Bambi."

They laughed together, and it felt natural.

"Give me your car keys," Alex said suddenly. "I'll check it out and if it's something minor, I might be able to fix it."

"I don't think it is. When the engine died, it sounded pretty final." Nevertheless, she handed him her key ring and stood under the shelter while Alex ran across the parking lot to test her car. She stood on her tiptoes and watched him raise the hood, disappear under it for a few minutes and then close it and come running back to her.

"I think you're right," he said, rubbing the black grease from his hands with a white handkerchief.

"Excuse us, please," a soft feminine voice purred from behind Carol. Bambi slithered past them, her arm looped through that of a much older gentleman. She cast Carol a dirty look and smiled softly in Alex's direction before turning her attention to her most recent admirer. "Now, what were you saying about your hot tub?"

The two were barely out of earshot when Alex started to chuckle. "It didn't take her long, did it?"

"I really am sorry," Carol felt obliged to say. "I feel terrible…as though I personally ruined your evening."

"No," he countered. "On the contrary, you saved me. By the time you arrived, I was trying to figure out how long my patience was going to hold out. I had the distinct impression that before the evening was over I was going to be fighting her off."

Carol laughed. It didn't require much imagination to see Bambi in the role of aggressor. Come to think of it, Carol had dealt with a handful of Bambi's male counterparts over the years.

The rain had diminished and it was drizzling when the auto club van arrived. Alex walked the driver to Carol's car, and together the two men tried to determine what was wrong with her faithful Ford. They decided that whatever the problem was, it couldn't be fixed then and there and that the best thing to do was call a tow truck.

Carol agreed and signed on the dotted line.

"I'll give you a lift home," Alex volunteered.

"Thanks." She was already in his debt; one more thing wouldn't matter.

Within minutes, they were sitting inside Alex's car with the heater running full blast. Carol ran her hands up and down her arms to warm them.

"You're cold."

"I'll be fine in a minute. If I wasn't such a slave to fashion," she said with self-deprecating humor, "I would've worn something heavier than this cotton jacket. But it's the same pale green as my slacks and they go so well together."

"You sound just like Jim. It was forty degrees yesterday morning, and he insisted on wearing a shirt from last summer."

They smiled at each other, and Carol was conscious of how close they were in the snug confines of Alex's sports car. Her dark eyes met his warm gray ones. Without warning, the laughter faded from Alex's lips, and he studied her face. After viewing the damage earlier, Carol knew her hair hung in springy ringlets that resembled a pad used to scrub pots and pans. She'd done the best she could, brushing it away from her face and securing it at the base of her neck with a wide barrette she'd found in the bottom of her purse. Now she was certain the tail that erupted from her nape must be sticking straight out.

A small lump lodged in her throat, as though she'd tried to swallow a pill without water. "You never did get your dinner, did you?" she asked hastily.

"Don't worry about it."

"Listen, I owe you. Please...stop somewhere and let me treat you. It's after nine—you must be starved." She glanced at her watch and felt a blush heat her cheeks. It'd been longer than she could recall since a man had unsettled her quite this much.

"Don't worry about it," he said again. "I'm a big boy. I'll make myself a sandwich once I get home."

"But—"

"If you insist, you can have me over to eat sometime. All right? When it comes to dinner, Jim and I share the duties. A good home-cooked meal would be welcome."

Carol didn't have any choice but to agree, and she did so by nodding her damp head briskly until she realized she was watering the inside of his car. "Oh, sure, I'd like that." She considered saying that she came from a large Italian family and was an excellent cook, but that would sound too much like the personal ads her sister-in-law, Paula, insisted on reading to her.

"You *do* cook?"

"Oh, yes." Once more she held her tongue. Whereas a few moments earlier she'd been cold, now she felt uncomfortably warm. Her hands were clammy and her stomach was filled with what seemed like a swarm of bees.

They chatted amicably on the rest of the drive to her house. When Alex pulled into her driveway, she turned and smiled at him, her hand on her door handle. "I'm really grateful for all your help."

"No problem."

"And…I'm sorry about what happened with Bambi."

"I'm not," he said, then chuckled. "I'll give you a call later, all right? To check on your car…."

The question seemed to hang between them, heavy with implication. It was the "all right" that told her he was referring to something beyond the state of her car.

"Okay," she said almost flippantly, feeling more than a little light-headed.

"So, tell me about this man who brings color back to my little girl's cheeks," Angelina Pasquale said to Carol as she carried a steaming plate of spaghetti to the table.

Carol's mother didn't know how to cook for three or four; it was twelve or fifteen servings for each and every Sunday dinner. Her two older sisters lived in California now, and only Tony and Carol and their families came religiously for Sunday dinner. Her mother, however, continued to cook as if two or three additional families might walk in unannounced for the evening meal.

"Mama, Alex Preston and I just met last week."

"That's not what Peter said." The older woman wiped her hands on the large apron tied around her thick waist. Her dark hair, streaked with gray, was tucked into a neat bun. She wore a small gold crucifix that had been given to her by Carol's father forty-two years earlier.

Carol brought the long loaves of hot bread from the oven. "Alex is Jim's father. You remember Peter's friend, don't you?"

"He's not Italian."

"I don't know what he is. Preston might be an English name."

"English," Angelina said as if she was spitting out dirty dishwater. "You gonna marry a non-Italian again?"

"Mama," Carol said, silently laughing, "Alex helped me when my car broke down. I owe him dinner, and I insisted on taking him out to repay him. We're not stopping off at the church to get married on the way."

"I bet he's not even Catholic."

"Mama," Carol cried. "I haven't the faintest clue where he attends church."

"You taking a man to dinner instead of cooking for him is bad enough. But not even knowing if he's Catholic is asking for trouble." She raised her eyes as if pleading for patience in dealing with her youngest daughter; when she lowered her gaze, they fell to Carol's feet. She folded her hands in prayer-like fashion. "You wear pointed-toe shoes for this man?"

"I didn't wear these for Alex. I happen to like them—they're in style."

"They're gonna deform your feet. One day, you'll trip and end up facedown in the gutter like your cousin Celeste."

"Mama, I'm not going to end up in a gutter."

"Your cousin Celeste told her mother the same thing, and we both know what happened to her. She had to marry a foot doctor."

"Mama, please don't worry about my shoes."

"Okay, but don't let anyone say your mama didn't warn you."

Carol had to leave the room to keep from laughing. Her mother was the delight of her life. She drove Carol crazy with her loony advice, but Carol knew it was deeply rooted in love.

"Carol," Angelina said, surveying the table, "tell everyone dinner's ready."

Peter was in the living room with his younger cousins, who were watching the Dodgers play Kansas City in a hotly contested baseball game.

"Dinner's on the table, guys."

"Just a minute, Mom. It's the bottom of the eighth, with two out." Peter's intense gaze didn't waver from the screen. "Besides, Uncle Tony and Aunt Paula aren't back from shopping yet."

"They'll eat later." Carol's brother Tony and his wife had escaped for the afternoon to Clackamas Town Center, a large shopping mall south of Portland, and they weren't expected back until much later.

"Just a few more minutes," Peter pleaded.

"Mama made zabaglione," Carol said.

The television went off in a flash, and four children rushed into the dining room, taking their places at the table like a rampaging herd of buffalo. Peter was the oldest by six years, which gave him an air of superiority over his cousins.

Sunday dinner at her mother's was tradition. They were a close-knit family and helped one another without question. Her brother had lent her his second car while hers was being repaired. Carol didn't know what she'd do without him. She'd have her own car back in a few days, but Tony's generosity had certainly made her life easier.

Mama treasured these times with her children and grandchildren, generously offering her love, her support and her pasta. Being close to her family was what had gotten Carol through the difficult years following Bruce's death. Her parents had been wonderful, helping her while she worked her way through college and the nursing program, caring for Peter when she couldn't and introducing her to a long list of nice Italian men. But after three years of dealing with Bruce's mental and physical abuse, she wasn't interested. The scars from her marriage ran deep.

"I'll say grace now," Angelina said. They all bowed their heads and closed their eyes.

No one needed any encouragement to dig into the spaghetti drenched in a sauce that was like no other. Carol's mother was a fabulous cook. She insisted on making everything from scratch, and she'd personally trained each one of her three daughters.

"So, Peter," his grandmother said, tearing off a thick piece from the loaf of hot bread. "What do you think of your mother marrying this Englishman?"

"Aw, Grandma, it's not like that. Mr. Preston called and Mom's treating him to dinner 'cause he gave her a ride home. I don't think it's any big deal."

"That was what she said when she met your father. 'Ma,' she told me, 'it's just dinner.' The next thing I know, she's standing at the altar with this non-Italian and six months later the priest was baptizing you."

"Ma! Please," Carol cried, embarrassed at the way her mother spoke so freely—although by now she should be used to it.

"Preston." Her mother muttered the name again, chewing it along with her bread. "I could accept the man if he had a name like Prestoni. Carol Prestoni has a good Italian ring to it…but Preston. Bah."

Peter and Carol exchanged smiles.

"He's real nice, Grandma."

Angelina expertly wove the long strands of spaghetti around the tines of her fork. "Your mama deserves to meet a nice man. If you say he's okay, then I have to take your word for it."

"Mama, it's only one dinner." Carol wished she'd never said anything to her mother. Alex had called the night before, and although he sounded a little disappointed that she wouldn't be making the meal herself, he'd agreed to let her repay the favor with dinner at a local restaurant Monday night. Her big mistake was mentioning it to her mother. Carol usually didn't say anything to her family when she was going out on a date. But for some reason, unknown even to herself, she'd mentioned Alex as soon as she'd walked in the door after church Sunday morning.

"What color eyes does this man have?"

"Gray," Carol answered and poured herself a glass of ice water.

Peter turned to his mother. "How'd you remember that?"

"I...I just recall they were...that color." Carol felt her cheeks flush. She concentrated on her meal, but when she looked up, she saw her mother watching her closely. "His eyes are sort of striking," she said, mildly irritated by the attention her mother and her son were lavishing on her.

"I never noticed," Peter said.

"A boy wouldn't," Angelina told him, "but your mother, well, she looks at such things."

That wasn't entirely true, but Carol wasn't about to claim otherwise.

As soon as they were finished with the meal, Carol's mother brought out the zabaglione, a rich sherry-flavored

Italian custard thick with eggs. Angelina promptly dished up six bowls.

"Mama, zabaglione's high in fat and filled with cholesterol." Since her father's death from a heart attack five years earlier, Carol worried about her mother's health, although she wasn't sure her concern was appreciated.

"So zabaglione's got cholesterol."

"But, Mama, cholesterol clogs the veins. It could kill you."

"If I can't eat zabaglione, then I might as well be dead."

Smiling wasn't what Carol should have done, but she couldn't help it.

When the dishes were washed and the kitchen counters cleaned, Carol and her mother sat in the living room. Angelina rocked in the chair her mother's mother had brought from Italy seventy years earlier. Never one for idle hands, she picked up her crocheting.

It was a rare treat to have these moments alone with her mother, and Carol sat on the sofa, feet tucked under her, head back and eyes closed.

"When am I gonna meet this Englishman of yours?"

"Mama," Carol said with a sigh, opening her eyes, "you're making me sorry I ever mentioned Alex."

"You didn't need to tell me about him. I would have asked because the minute you walked in the house I could see a look in your eyes. It's time, my *bambina*. Peter is growing and soon you'll be alone."

"I…I'm looking forward to that."

Her mother discredited that comment with a shake of her head. "You need a husband, one who will give you more children and bring a sparkle to your eyes."

Carol's heart started thundering inside her chest. "I…I don't think I'll ever remarry, Mama."

"Bah!" the older woman said. A few minutes later, she murmured something in Italian that Carol could only partially understand, but it was enough to make her blush hotly. Her mother was telling her there were things about a man that she shouldn't be so quick to forget.

The soft Italian words brought a vivid image to Carol's mind—an image of Alex holding her in his arms, gazing down at her, making love to her. It shocked her so much that she quickly made her excuses, collected Peter and drove home.

Her pulse rate hadn't decreased by the time she arrived back at her own small house. Her mother was putting too much emphasis on her dinner date with Alex…far more than necessary or appropriate.

As soon as Peter went over to a neighbor's to play video games, Carol reached for the phone. When voice mail kicked in on the fourth ring, she immediately hung up.

On second thought, this was better, she decided, and dialed again, planning to leave a message. "You're a coward," she muttered as she pushed down the buttons.

Once more the recorded message acknowledged her call. She waited for the greeting, followed by a long beep.

"Hello…Alex, this is Carol…Carol Sommars. About our dinner date Monday night…I'm sorry, but I'm going to have to cancel. Something…has come up. I apologize that thisis-suchshortnotice. Bye." The last words tumbled together in her haste to finish.

Her face was flushed, and sweat had beaded on her upper lip as she hung up the phone. With her hand on the receiver, she slowly expelled her breath.

Her mother was right. Alex Preston was the one man who could bring the light back into her eyes, and she'd never been more frightened in her life.

Chapter Three

Carol's hand remained closed around the telephone receiver as she heaved in a giant breath. She'd just completed the most cowardly act of her life.

Regretting her actions, she punched out Alex's phone number again, and listened to the recorded message a third time while tapping her foot. At the beep, she paused, then blurted out, "I hope you understand…I mean…oh…never mind." With that, she replaced the receiver, pressed her hand over her brow, more certain than ever that she'd just made a world-class idiot of herself.

Half an hour later, Carol was sorting through the dirty clothes in the laundry room when Peter came barreling into the house.

He paused in the doorway, watching her neatly organize several loads. "Hey, Mom, where's the TV guide?"

"By the television?" she suggested, more concerned about making sure his jeans' pockets were empty before putting them in the washer.

"Funny, Mom, real funny. Why would anyone put it there?"

Carol paused, holding a pair of dirty jeans to her chest. "Because that's where it belongs?" she said hopefully.

"Yeah, but when's the last time anyone found it there?"

Not bothering to answer, she dumped his jeans in the washing machine. "Did you look on the coffee table?"

"It's not there. It isn't by the chair, either."

"What are you so keen to watch, anyway? Shouldn't you be doing your homework?"

"I don't have any...well, I do, but it's a snap."

Carol threw another pair of jeans into the churning water. "If it's so easy, do it now."

"I can't until Jim gets home."

At the mention of Alex's son, Carol hesitated. "I...see."

"Besides, it's time for wrestling, but I don't know what channel it's on."

"Wrestling?" Carol cried. "When did you become interested in *that?*"

"Jim introduced me to it. I know it looks phony and stuff, but I get a kick out of those guys pounding on each other and the crazy things they say."

Carol turned and leaned against the washer, crossing her arms. "Personally I'd rather you did your homework first, and if there's any time left over you can watch television."

"Of course you'd prefer that," Peter said. "You're a mom— you're supposed to think that way. But I'm a kid, and I'd much rather watch Mr. Muscles take on Jack Beanstalk."

Carol considered her son's argument for less than two seconds. "Do your homework."

Peter sighed, his shoulders sagging. "I was afraid you'd say that." Reluctantly he headed toward his bedroom.

It was still light out, and with the wash taken care of, Carol ventured into the backyard, surveying her neatly edged flower beds. Besides perennials, she grew Italian parsley, basil and thyme and a few other herbs in the ceramic pots that bordered her patio. One of these days she was going to dig up a section of her lawn and plant an honest-to-goodness garden.

"Mom…" Peter was shouting her name from inside the house.

She turned, prepared to answer her son, when she saw Alex walk out the back door toward her. Her heart did a somersault, then vaulted into her throat and stayed there for an uncomfortable moment.

"Hello, Alex," she managed to say, suspecting that her face had the look of a cornered mouse. She would gladly have given six months' mortgage payments to remove her messages from his voice mail. It wasn't easy to stand there calmly and not run for the fence.

"Hello, Carol." He walked toward her, his gaze holding hers.

He sounded so…relaxed, but his eyes were a different story. They were like the eyes of an eagle, sharp and intent. They'd zeroed in on her as though he was about to swoop down for the kill.

For her part, Carol was a wreck. Her hands were clenched so tightly at her sides that her fingers ached. "What can I do for you?" she asked, embarrassed by the way her voice pitched and heaved with the simple question.

A brief smile flickered at the edges of Alex's mouth. "You mean you don't know?"

"No…well, I can guess, but I think it would be best if you just came out and said it." She took a couple of steps toward him, feeling extraordinarily brave for having done so.

"Will you offer me a cup of coffee?" Alex asked instead.

The man was full of surprises. Just when she was convinced he was about to berate her for behaving like an utter fool, he casually suggested she make coffee. Perhaps he often confronted emotionally insecure women who left him nonsensical messages.

"Coffee? Of course...come in." Pleased to have something to occupy her hands, Carol hurried into the kitchen. Once she'd added the grounds to the filter and filled the coffeemaker with water, she turned and leaned against the counter, hoping to look poised. She did an admirable job, if she did say so herself—at least for the first few minutes. After all, she'd spent the last thirteen years on her own. She wasn't a dimwit, although she'd gone out of her way to give him that impression, and she hadn't even been trying. That disconcerted her more than anything.

"No, I don't understand," Alex said. He opened her cupboard and took down two ceramic mugs.

"Understand what?" Carol decided playing dumb might help. It had worked with Bambi, and who was to say it wouldn't with her? However, she had the distinct notion that if she suggested they try out a hot tub, Alex would be more than willing.

"I want to know why you won't have dinner with me."

Carol was completely out of her element. She dealt with pregnancy and birth, soon-to-be mothers and terrified fathers, and she did so without a pause. But faced with one handsome single father, she was a worthless mass of frazzled nerves. Fearing her knees might give out on her, she walked over to the table, pulled out a chair and slumped into it. "I didn't exactly say I wouldn't go out with you."

"Then what did you say?"

She lowered her gaze, unable to meet his. "That…something came up."

"I see." He twisted the chair around and straddled it. The coffeemaker gurgled behind her. Normally she didn't even notice it, but now it seemed as loud as the roar of a jet plane.

"Then we'll reschedule. Tuesday evening at six?"

"I…I have a class… I teach a birthing class to expectant parents on Tuesday evenings." Now that was brilliant! Who else would attend those classes? But it was an honest excuse. "That's where I'd been when my car broke down in the parking lot of the restaurant where I met you…last Tuesday… remember?"

"The night I helped you," Alex reminded her. "As I recall, you claimed you wanted to repay me. Fact is, you insisted on it. You said I'd missed my dinner because of you and that you'd like to make it up to me. At first it was going to be a home-cooked meal, but that was quickly reduced to meeting at a restaurant in separate cars, and now you're canceling altogether."

"I…did appreciate your help."

"Is there something about me that bothers you? Do I have bad breath?"

"Of course not."

"Dandruff?"

"No."

"Then what is it?"

"Nothing," she cried. She couldn't very well explain that their one meeting had jolted to life a part of her that had lain dormant for years. To say Alex Preston unsettled her was an understatement. She hadn't stopped thinking about him from the moment he'd dropped her off at the house. Every thought that entered her mind was linked to those few minutes they'd spent alone in his car. She was an adult, a professional, but he made her forget everything—except him. In thinking about it, Carol supposed it was because she'd married so young and been widowed shortly afterward. It was as though she didn't know how to behave with a man, but that wasn't entirely true, either. For the past several years, she'd dated numerous times. Nothing serious of course, but friendly outings with "safe" men. One second with Alex, and she'd known instantly that an evening with him could send her secure, tranquil world into a tailspin.

"Wednesday then?"

Carol looked warily across the kitchen, wanting to weep with frustration. She might as well be a good sport about it and give in. Alex wasn't going to let her off the hook without a fuss.

"All right," she said, and for emphasis, nodded. "I'll see you Wednesday evening."

"Fine." Alex stood and twisted the chair back around. "I'll pick you up at seven." He sent her one of his smiles and was gone before the coffee finished brewing.

Once she was alone, Carol placed her hands over her face, feeling the sudden urge to cry. Closing her eyes, however, was a mistake, because the minute she did, her mother's whispered words, reminding her of how good lovemaking could be, saturated her thoughts. That subject was the last thing Carol wanted to think about, especially when the man she wanted to be making love with was the one who had so recently left her kitchen.

Abruptly she stood and poured herself a cup of coffee. It didn't help to realize that her fingers were shaking. What was so terrific about men and sex, anyway? Nothing that *she* could remember. She'd been initiated in the backseat of a car at eighteen with the boy she was crazy in love with. Or the boy she *thought* she was in love with. More likely it had been hormones on the rampage for both of them.

After she'd learned she was pregnant, Carol was never convinced Bruce had truly wanted to marry her. Faced with her hotheaded father and older brother, he'd clearly regarded marriage as the more favorable option.

In the last of her three years with Bruce, he'd been drunk more than he was sober—abusive more than he was considerate. Lovemaking had become a nightmare for her. Feeling violated and vaguely sick to her stomach, she would curl up afterward and lie awake the rest of the night. Then Bruce had died, and mingled with the grief and horror had been an almost giddy sense of relief.

"I don't want a man in my life," she said forcefully.

Peter was strolling down the hallway to his room and stuck his head around the doorway. "Did you say something?"

"Ah..." Carol wanted to swallow her tongue. "Nothing important."

"You look nice," Peter told Carol on Wednesday when she finished with her makeup.

"Thanks," she said, smiling at him. Her attitude toward this evening out with Alex had improved now that she'd had time to sort through her confused emotions. Jim's father was a nice guy, and to be honest, Carol didn't know what had made her react the way she did on Sunday. She was a mature adult, and there was nothing to fear. It wasn't as though she was going to fall into bed with the man simply because she was attracted to him. They'd have the dinner she owed him and that would be the end of it.

But, as much as she would've liked to deny it, Alex was special. For the first time since she could remember, she was physically attracted to a man. And what was wrong with that? It only went to prove that she was a normal, healthy woman. In fact, she should be grateful to Alex for helping her realize just how healthy she was.

"Where's Mr. Preston taking you?" Peter asked, plopping himself down on the edge of the tub.

"Actually I'm taking him, and I thought we'd go to Jake's." Jake's was a well-known and well-loved Portland restaurant renowned for its Cajun dishes.

"You're taking Mr. Preston to Jake's?" Peter cried, his voice shrill with envy. "Are you bringing me back anything?"

"No." As it was, she was stretching her budget for the meal.

"But, Mom—Jake's? You know that's my favorite restaurant in the whole world." He made it sound as though he were a global traveler and connoisseur of fine dining.

"I'll take you there on your birthday." The way she had every year since he was ten.

"But that's another five months," Peter grumbled.

She gave him what she referred to as her "Mother Look," which generally silenced him.

"All right, all right," he muttered. "I'll eat frozen pot pie for the third time in a week. Don't worry about me."

"I won't."

Peter sighed with feeling. "You go ahead and enjoy your *étouffée*."

"I'm sure I will." She generally ordered the shrimp dish, which was a popular item on the menu.

Peter continued to study her, his expression revealing mild surprise. "Gee, Mom, don't you have a heart anymore? I used to be able to get you with guilt, but you hardly bat an eyelash anymore."

"Of course I've got a heart. Unfortunately I don't have the wallet to support it."

Peter seemed about to speak again, but the doorbell chimed and he rushed out of the tiny bathroom to answer it as though something dire would happen if Alex was kept waiting more than a few seconds.

Expelling a sigh, Carol surveyed her appearance in the mirror one last time, confident that she looked her best. With a prepared smile on her face, she headed for the living room.

The instant she appeared, Alex's gaze rushed to hers. The impact of seeing him again was immediate. It was difficult to take her eyes off him. Instead, she found herself thinking that his build suggested finely honed muscles. He was tall, his shoulders were wide and his chest solid. Carol thought he was incredibly good-looking in his pin-striped suit. His face was weathered from working out of doors, his features bronzed by the sun.

So much for the best-laid plans, Carol mused, shaking from the inside out. She'd planned this evening down to the smallest detail. They would have dinner, during which Carol would subtly inform him that she wasn't interested in anything more than a casual friendship, then he'd take her home, and that would be the end of it. Five seconds after she'd walked into the living room, she was thinking about silk sheets and long, slow, heart-melting kisses.

Her mother was responsible for this. Her outrageous, wonderful mother and the softly murmured Italian words that reminded Carol she was still young and it was time to live and love again. She was alive, all right. From the top of her head to the bottom of her feet, she was *alive*.

"Hello, Carol."

"Alex."

"Mom's taking you to Jake's," Peter muttered, not bothering to hide his envy. "She can't afford to bring me anything, but that's okay."

"Peter," she chastised, doubting Alex had heard him.

"Are you ready?"

She nodded, taking an additional moment to gather her composure while she reached for her jacket and purse. Glancing at her son, she felt obliged to say, "You know the rules. I'll call you later."

"You don't need to phone," he said, making a show of rolling his eyes as if to suggest she was going overboard on this parental thing.

"We'll be back early."

Alex cupped her elbow as he directed her to the door. "Not too early," he amended.

By the time they were outside, Carol had bridled her fears. Her years of medical training contributed to her skill at presenting a calm, composed front. And really, there wasn't a reason in the world she should panic....

They talked amicably on the drive into downtown Portland, commenting on such ordinary subjects as the weather, when her car would be fixed and the approach of summer, which they both dreaded because the boys would be constantly underfoot.

Alex managed to find parking on the street, which was a feat in its own right. He opened her car door and took her hand, which he didn't release.

Since Carol had made a reservation, they were immediately

seated in a high-backed polished wood booth and greeted by their waiter, who brought them a wine list and recited the specials of the day.

"Jim tells me you're buying him a truck," Carol said conversationally when they'd placed their order.

"So he'd like to believe."

Carol hesitated. "You mean you aren't?"

"Not to the best of my knowledge," Alex admitted, grinning.

Once more, Carol found herself fascinated by his smile. She found herself wondering how his mouth would feel on hers. As quickly as the thought entered her mind, she discarded it.

"According to Jim it's going to be the latest model, red with flames decorating the sidewalls."

"The boy likes to dream," Alex said, leaning back. "If he drives any vehicle during the next two years, it'll be because he's impressed me with his grades and his maturity."

"Oh, Alex," Carol said with a sigh, "you don't know how relieved I am to hear that. For weeks, Peter's been making me feel as though I'm an abusive mother because I'm not buying him a car—or, better yet, a truck. Time and time again he's told me that *you're* buying one for Jim and how sharing the Ford with me could damage his self-esteem, which might result in long-term counseling."

Alex laughed outright. "By the way," he added, "Jim isn't Jim anymore, he's James."

"James?"

"Right. He noticed that his learner's permit listed his name as James Preston, and he's insisting everyone call him that. Actually, I think he came up with the idea after I spoke to him about driving and his level of maturity. Apparently, James is more mature-sounding than Jim."

"Apparently," Carol returned, smiling. "Well, at least if Peter does end up having to go to a counselor, he'll have company."

Their wine arrived and they both commented on its delicious flavor and talked about the quality of Walla Walla area wineries.

Their meal came soon after. The steaming *étouffée* was placed before her, and she didn't experience the slightest bit of guilt when she tasted the first bite. It was as delicious as she remembered.

"Have you been a nurse long?" Alex asked, when their conversation lagged.

"Eight years. I returned to school after my husband was killed, and nursing was a natural for me. I was forever putting Band-Aids on my dolls and treating everyone from my dog to my tolerant mother."

"Next time I have a cold, I'll know who to call," Alex teased.

"Oh, good. And when I'm ready to put the addition on the house, I'll contact you," Carol told him.

They both laughed.

The evening wasn't nearly as difficult as Carol had feared. Alex was easy to talk to, and with the boys as common ground, there was never a lack of subject matter. Before Carol was aware of it, it was nearly ten.

"Oh, dear," she said, sliding from the booth. "I told Peter I'd check in with him. Excuse me a minute."

"Sure," Alex said, standing himself.

Carol was in the foyer on her cell, waiting for Peter to

answer when she looked over and saw that Alex was using his own cell phone.

"Hello."

"Peter, it's Mom."

"Mom, you said you were going to phone," he said, sounding offended. "Do you know what time it is? When you say you're going to phone you usually do. James is worried, too. Where have you guys been?"

"Jake's—you knew that."

"All this time?"

"Yes. I'm sorry, sweetheart, the evening got away from us."

"Uh-huh," Peter said and paused. "So you like Mr. Preston?"

Carol hedged. "He's very nice," she murmured.

"Do you think you'll go out with him again? What did you guys talk about? Just how long does it take to eat dinner, anyway?"

"Peter, this isn't the time or place to be having this discussion."

"Were there any leftovers?"

"None."

Her son sighed as if he'd actually been counting on her to bring home her untouched dinner—a reward for the supreme sacrifice of having to eat chicken pot pie, which just happened to be one of his favorites.

"When will you be home? I mean, you don't have to rush on my account or anything, but you'd never let *me* stay out this late on a weeknight."

"I'll be back before eleven," she promised, ignoring his comment about the lateness of the hour. Sometimes Peter forgot who was the adult and who was the child.

"You *do* like Mr. Preston, don't you?" His tone was too smug for comfort.

"Peter," she moaned. "I'll talk to you later." She was about to replace the receiver when she heard him call her name. "What is it now?" she said sharply, impatiently.

He hesitated, apparently taken aback by her brusqueness. "Nothing, I just wanted to tell you to wake me up when you get home, all right?"

"All right," she said, feeling guilty.

She met Alex back at their table. "Everything okay at home?" he asked.

"Couldn't be better." There was no need to inform Alex of the inquisition Peter had attempted. "What about Jim—James?"

"He's surviving."

"I suppose we should think about getting home," Carol suggested, eager now to leave. The evening had flown by. At some point during dinner, her guard had slipped and she'd begun to enjoy his company. There'd been none of the terrible tension that had plagued her earlier.

"I suppose you're right," Alex said with enough reluctance to alarm her. He'd obviously enjoyed their time as much as she had.

They had a small disagreement over the check, which Alex refused to let her take. He silenced her protests by reminding her that she owed him a home-cooked meal and he wasn't accepting any substitutes. After a couple of glasses of wine and a good dinner, Carol was too mellow to put up much of an argument.

"Just don't let Peter know," she said as they walked toward the car. Alex held her hand, and it seemed far too natural, but she didn't object.

"Why?"

"If Peter discovers you paid, he'll want to know why I didn't bring anything home for him."

Alex grinned as he unlocked his car door and held it open. He rested his hand on the curve of her shoulder. "You *will* make me that dinner sometime, won't you?"

Before she realized what she was doing, Carol found herself nodding. She hadn't had a chance to compose herself by the time he'd walked around the front of the car and joined her.

Neither of them spoke on the drive back to her house. Carol's mind was filled with the things she'd planned to tell him. The things she'd carefully thought out beforehand— about what a nice time she'd had, and how she hoped they'd stay in touch and what a good boy Jim—James—was and how Alex was doing a wonderful job raising him. But the trite, rehearsed words refused to come.

Alex pulled into her driveway and turned off the engine. The living room was dark and the curtains drawn. The only illumination was the dim light on her front porch. When Alex turned to face her, Carol's heart exploded with dread and wonder. His look was warm, eager enough to make her blood run hot…and then immediately cold.

"I had a good time tonight." He spoke first.

"I did, too." How weak she sounded, how tentative…

"I'd like to see you again."

They were the words she'd feared—and longed for. The deep restlessness she'd experienced since the night her car had broken down reverberated within her, echoing through the empty years she'd spent alone.

"Carol?"

"I…don't know." She tried to remind herself of what her

life had been like with Bruce. The tireless lies, the crazy brushes with danger as though he were courting death. The anger and impatience, the pain that gnawed at her soul. She thought of the wall she'd so meticulously constructed around her heart. A wall years thick and so high no man had ever been able to breach it. "I...don't think so."

"Why not? I don't understand."

Words could never explain her fear.

"Let me revise my statement," Alex said. "I *need* to see you again."

"Why?" she cried. "This was only supposed to be one night...to thank you for your help. I can't give you any more...I just can't and..." Her breath scattered, and her lungs burned within her chest. She couldn't deny the things he made her feel.

"Carol," he said softly. "There's no reason to be afraid."

But there was. Except he wouldn't understand.

He reached up and placed his calloused palm against her cheek.

Carol flinched and quickly shut her eyes. "No...please, I have to go inside...Peter's waiting for me." She grabbed the door handle, and it was all she could do not to escape from the car and rush into the house.

"Wait," he said huskily, removing his hand from her face. "I didn't mean to frighten you."

She nodded, opening her eyes, and her startled gaze collided with his. She watched as he slowly appraised her, taking in her flushed face and the rapid rise and fall of her breasts. He frowned.

"You're trembling."

"I'm fine...really. Thank you for tonight. I had a marvelous time."

His hand settled over hers. "You'll see me again."

It wasn't until she was safely inside her living room and her heart was back to normal that Carol realized his parting words had been a statement of fact.

Chapter Four

"So, Dad, how did dinner go with Mrs. Sommars?" James asked as he poured himself a huge bowl of cornflakes. He added enough sugar to make eating it worth his while, then for extra measure added a couple of teaspoons more.

Alex cupped his steaming mug of coffee as he considered his son's question. "Dinner went fine." It was afterward that stayed in his mind. Someone had hurt Carol and hurt her badly. He'd hardly touched her and she'd trembled. Her dark brown eyes had clouded, and she couldn't seem to get out of his car fast enough. The crazy part was, Alex felt convinced she was attracted to him. He knew something else—she didn't want to be.

They'd spent hours talking over dinner, and it had seemed as though only a few moments had passed. There was no need for pretense between them. She didn't pretend to be anything she wasn't, and he was free to be himself as well. They were simply two single parents who had a lot in common. After two years of dealing with the singles scene, Alex found Carol a refreshing change. He found her allur-

ingly beautiful and at the same time shockingly innocent.
During the course of their evening, she'd argued with him
over politics, surprised him with her wit and challenged
his opinions. In those few hours, Alex learned that this in-
triguing widow was a charming study in contrasts, and he
couldn't wait to see her again.

"Mrs. Sommars is a neat lady," James said, claiming the
kitchen chair across from his father. "She's a little weird,
though."

Alex looked up from his coffee. "How's that?"

"She listens to opera," James explained between bites.
"Sings it, too—" he planted his elbows on the tabletop, leaned
forward and whispered "—in Italian."

"Whoa." Alex was impressed.

"At the top of her voice. Peter told me she won't let him
play his rap CDs nearly as loud as she does her operas."

"The injustice of it all."

James ignored his sarcasm. "Peter was telling me his grandmother's a real kick, too. She says things like 'Eat your vegetables or I'm calling my uncle Vito in Jersey City.'"

Alex laughed, glanced at his watch and reluctantly got to
his feet. He finished the last of his coffee, then set the mug
in the sink. "Do you have your lunch money?"

"Dad, I'm not a kid anymore. You don't have to ask me
stuff like that."

"Do you?" Alex pressed.

James stood and reached inside his hip pocket. His eyes
widened. "I...guess I left it in my room."

"Don't forget your driver's permit, either."

"Dad!"

Alex held up both hands. "Sorry."

He was all the way to the front door when James's shout stopped him.

"Don't forget to pick me up from track practice, all right?"

Alex pointed his finger at his son and calmly said, "I'll be there."

"Hey, Dad."

"What now?" Alex complained.

James shrugged and leaned his shoulder against the door leading into the kitchen. "In case you're interested, Mrs. Sommars will be there, too."

Alex was interested. Very interested.

He left the house and climbed inside his work van, sitting in the driver's seat with his hands on the steering wheel. He mulled over the events of the night before. He'd dated several women recently. Beautiful women, intelligent women, wealthy women. A couple of them had come on hot and heavy. But not one had appealed to him as strongly as this widow with the dark, frightened eyes and the soft, delectable mouth.

A deep part of him yearned to stroke away the pain she held on to so tightly, whatever its source. He longed to watch the anxiety fade from her eyes when she settled into his arms. He wanted her to feel secure enough with him to relax. The urge to hold her and kiss her was strong, but he doubted Carol would let him.

"Okay, Peggy, bear down...push...as hard as you can," Carol urged the young mother-to-be, clutching her hand. Peggy did as Carol asked, gritting her teeth, arching forward and lifting her head off the hospital pillow. She gave it everything she had, whimpering softly with the intensity of the labor pain. When the contraction had passed, Peggy's head fell back and she took in several deep breaths.

"You're doing a good job," Carol said, patting her shoulder.

"How much longer before my baby's born?"

"Soon," Carol assured her. "The doctor's on his way now."

The woman's eyes drifted closed. "Where's Danny? I need Danny."

"He'll be back in a minute." Carol had sent her patient's husband out for a much-needed coffee.

"I'm so glad you're here."

Carol smiled. "I'm glad I'm here, too."

"Danny wants a son so much."

"I'm sure he'll be just as happy with a little girl."

Peggy smiled, but that quickly faded as another contraction started. She reached for Carol's hand, her face marked by the long hours she'd struggled to give birth. Carol had spent the past hour with her. She preferred it when they weren't so busy and she could dedicate herself to one patient. But for more days than she cared to remember, the hospital's five labor rooms had been full, and she spent her time racing from one to the other.

Peggy groaned, staring at a focal point on the wall. The technique was one Carol taught in her classes. Concentrating on a set object helped the mother remember and practice the breathing techniques.

"You're doing just fine," Carol said softly. "Take a deep breath now and let it out slowly."

"I can't do it anymore...I can't," Peggy cried. "Where's Danny? Why's he taking so long?"

"He'll be back any second." Now that her patient was in

the final stages of labor, the pains were stronger and closer together.

Danny walked into the room, looking pale and anxious… and so very young. He moved to the side of the bed and reached for his wife's hand, holding it to his cheek. He seemed as relieved as Peggy when the contraction eased.

Dr. Adams, old and wise and a hospital institution, sauntered into the room, hands in his pockets, smiling. "So, Peggy, it looks like we're going to finally have that baby."

Peggy grinned sheepishly. "I told Dr. Adams yesterday I was sure I was going to be pregnant until Christmas. I didn't think this baby ever wanted to be born!"

Phil Adams gave his instructions to Carol, and within a few minutes the medical team had assembled. From that point on, everything happened exactly as it should. Before another hour had passed, a squalling Danny, Jr., was placed in his father's arms.

"Peggy…oh, Peggy, a son." Tears of joy rained down the young man's face as he sobbed unabashedly, holding his son close.

Although Carol witnessed scenes such as this day in and day out, the thrill of helping to bring a tiny being into the world never left her.

When her shift was over, she showered and changed clothes, conscious of the time. She had to pick Peter up from track practice on her way home, and she didn't want to keep him waiting, although she was the one likely to be twiddling her thumbs.

The first thing Carol noticed when she pulled into the school parking lot was a van with Preston Construction printed in large black letters on the side. Alex. She drew in a shaky breath, determined to be friendly but reserved. After the way she'd escaped from his car the night before, it was doubtful he'd want anything to do with her, anyway.

The fact was, she couldn't blame him. She wasn't sure what had come over her. Then again, she did know...and she didn't want to dwell on it.

She parked a safe distance away, praying that either Peter would be finished soon and they could leave or that Alex wouldn't notice her arrival. She lowered the window to let in the warm breeze, then turned off the ignition and reached for a magazine, burying her face in its pages. For five minutes nothing happened.

When the driver's side of the van opened, Carol realized her luck wasn't going to hold. She did her best to concentrate on a recipe for stuffed pork chops and pretend she hadn't seen Alex approach her. When she glanced up, he was standing beside her car. Their eyes met for what seemed the longest moment of her life.

"Hello again." He leaned forward and rested his hands on her window.

"Hello, Alex."

"Nice day, isn't it?"

"Lovely." It wasn't only his smile that intrigued her, but his eyes. Their color was like a cool mist rising off a pond. Would this attraction she felt never diminish, never stop? Three brief encounters, and she was already so tied up in knots she couldn't think clearly.

"How was your day?" His eyes were relentless, searching for answers she couldn't give him to questions she didn't want him to ask.

She glanced away. "Good. How about yours?"

"Fine." He rubbed a hand along the back of his neck. "I was going to call you later."

"Oh?"

"To see if you'd like to attend the Home Show with me next Friday night. I thought we could have dinner afterward."

Carol opened her mouth to refuse, but he stopped her, laying his finger across her lips, silencing her. The instant his hand touched her, the warm, dizzy feeling began. As implausible, as preposterous as it seemed, a deep physical sensation flooded her body. And all he'd done was lightly press his finger to her lips!

"Don't say no," Alex said, his voice husky.

She couldn't, at least not then. "I...I'll have to check my schedule."

"You can tell me tomorrow."

She nodded, although it was an effort.

"Good...I'll talk to you then."

It wasn't until he'd removed his finger, sliding it across her moist lips, that Carol breathed again.

"What do you mean you can't pick me up from track?" Peter complained the next morning. "How else am I supposed to get home? Walk?"

"From track practice, of all things." She added an extra oatmeal cookie to his lunch because, despite everything, she felt guilty about asking him to find another way home. She was such a coward.

"Mom, coach works us hard—you know that. I was so stiff last night I could barely move. Remember?"

Regretfully, Carol did. A third cookie went into the brown-paper sack.

"What's more important than picking me up?"

Escaping a man. If only Alex hadn't been so gentle. Carol had lain awake half the night, not knowing what was wrong with her or how to deal with it. This thing with Alex, whatever it was, perplexed and bewildered her. For most of her life, Carol had given and received countless hugs and kisses—from relatives, from friends. Touching and being touched were a natural part of her personality. But all Alex had done was press his finger to her lips, and her response...her response still left her stunned.

As she lay in bed, recalling each detail of their brief exchange, her body had reacted again. He didn't even need to be in the same room with her! Alone, in the wee hours of the morning, she was consumed by the need to be loved by him.

She woke with the alarm, in a cold sweat, trembling and frightened, convinced that she'd be a fool to let a man have that kind of power a second time.

"Mom," Peter said impatiently. "I asked you a question."

"Sorry," she said. "What was it you wanted to know?"

"I asked why you aren't going to be at track this afternoon. It's a simple question."

Intuitively Carol knew she wouldn't be able to escape Alex, and she'd be a bigger fool than she already was even to try.

She sighed. "I'll be there," she said, and handed him his lunch.

Peter stood frozen, studying her. "Are you sure you're not coming down with a fever?"

If only he knew...

When Carol pulled into the school parking lot later that same day, she saw Alex's van in the same space as the day before. Only this time he was standing outside, one foot braced against it, fingers tucked in his pockets. His jeans hugged his hips and fit tight across his thighs. He wore a checked work shirt with the sleeves rolled up past his elbows.

When she appeared, he lowered his foot and straightened, his movement leisurely and confident.

It was all Carol could do to slow down and park her car next to his. To avoid being placed at a disadvantage, she opened her door and climbed out.

"Good afternoon," she said, smiling so brightly her mouth felt as though it would crack.

"Hello again."

A lock of his dark hair fell over his forehead, and he threaded his fingers through its thickness, pushing it away from his face.

His gaze tugged at hers until their eyes met briefly, intently.

"It's warmer today than it was yesterday," she said conversationally.

"Yes, it is."

Carol lowered her eyes to his chest, thinking she'd be safe if she practiced what she preached. Find a focal point and concentrate. Only it didn't work as well in situations like this. Instead of saying what had been on her mind most of the day, she became aware of the pattern of his breathing, and how the rhythm of her own had changed, grown faster and more erratic.

"Have you decided?"

Her eyes rushed to his. "About…"

"Going to the home show with me."

She wished it could be the way it had been in the restaurant. There was something about being with a crowd that relaxed her. She hadn't felt intimidated.

"I…don't think seeing each other is such a good idea. It'd

be best if we…stayed friends. I can foresee all kinds of problems if we started dating, can't you?"

"The Home Show's going to cause problems?"

"No…our seeing each other will."

"Why?"

"The boys—"

"Couldn't care less. If anything, they approve. I don't
understand why there'd be any problems. I like you and you
like me—we've got a lot in common. We have fun together.
Where's the problem in that?"

Carol couldn't very well explain that when he touched her,
even lightly, tiny atoms exploded inside her. Whenever they
were within ten feet of each other, the air crackled with sensuality that grew more intense with each encounter. Surely he
could feel it, too. Surely he was aware of it.

Carol held a hand to her brow, not knowing how to answer
him. If she pointed out the obvious, she'd sound like a fool,
but she couldn't deny it, either.

"I…just don't think our seeing each other is a good idea,"
she repeated stubbornly.

"I do," he countered. "In fact, it appeals to me more every
minute."

"Oh, Alex, please don't do this."

Other cars were filling the parking lot, and the two of
them had quickly become the center of attention. Carol
glanced around self-consciously, praying he'd accept her re-
fusal and leave it at that. She should've known better.

"Come in here," Alex said, opening the side panel to
his van. He stepped inside and offered her his hand. She
joined him before she had time to determine the wisdom
of doing so.

Alex closed the door. "Now, where were we…ah, yes. You'd decided you don't want to go out with me again."

That wasn't quite accurate, but she wasn't going to argue. She'd rarely wanted anything more than to continue seeing him, but she wasn't ready. Yet…Bruce had been dead for thirteen years. If she wasn't ready by now, she never would be. The knowledge hit her hard, like an unexpected blow, and her eyes flew to his.

"Carol?" He moved toward her. The walls of the van seemed to close in around her. She could smell the scent of his after-shave and the not unpleasant effects of the day's labor. She could feel the heat coming off his body.

Emotion thickened the air, and the need that washed through her was primitive.

She backed as far as she could against the orderly rows of tools and supplies stacked on the shelves. Alex towered above her, studying her with such tenderness and concern that she had to repress the urge to weep.

"Are you claustrophobic?"

She shook her head.

His eyes settled on her mouth, and Carol felt her body's reaction. She unconsciously held her breath so long that when she released it, it burned her chest. If she hadn't been so frightened, she would have marveled at what was happening between them, enjoyed the sensations.

Gently Alex whisked back a strand of hair from her face. At his touch, Carol took a deep breath, but he seemed to gain confidence when she didn't flinch away from him. He cupped her cheek.

Her eyes momentarily drifted shut, and she laid her own hand over his.

"I'm going to kiss you."

She knew it and was unwilling to dredge up the determination to stop him.

His hands slipped to her shoulders as he slowly drew her forward. She considered ending this now. At the least amount of resistance, he would have released her; she didn't doubt that for a second. But it was as if this moment had been pre-ordained.

At first all he did was press his lips to hers. That was enough, more than enough. Her fingers curled into his shirt as he swept his mouth over hers.

She whimpered when he paused.

He sighed.

Her breathing was shallow.

His was harsh.

He hesitated and lifted his head, eyes wide and shocked, his brow creased with a frown. Whatever he'd decided, he didn't share, letting her draw her own conclusions.

Her hands were braced against his chest when he sought her mouth again. This time, the force of his kiss tilted back her head as he fused their lips together, giving her no choice but to respond. The heat, hot enough to scorch them both, intensified.

He kissed and held her, and her lungs forgot it was necessary to breathe. Her heart forgot to beat. Her soul refused to remember the lonely, barren years.

From somewhere far, far away, Carol heard voices. Her ears shut out the sound, not wanting anything or anyone to destroy this precious time.

Alex groaned, not to communicate pleasure but frustration. Carol didn't understand. Nor did she comprehend what was happening when he released her gradually, pushing himself away. He turned and called, "The door's locked."

"The door?" she echoed. It wasn't until then that she realized Alex was talking to the boys. Peter and Jim were standing outside the van, wanting in. She'd been so involved with Alex that she hadn't even heard her own son calling her name.

"Please open that door," she said, astonished by how composed she sounded. The trembling hadn't started yet, but it would soon, and the faster she made her escape, the better.

"I will in just a minute." He turned back to her and placed his hands on her shoulders. "You're going with me next Friday night. Okay?"

"No…"

He cradled her face with his hands and kissed her once more, forcefully.

She gasped with shock and pleasure.

"I'm not going to argue with you, Carol. We've got something good between us, and I'm not about to let you run away from it."

Standing stock-still, all she could do was nod.

He kissed the tip of her nose, then turned again and slid open the van door.

"What are you doing with Mrs. Sommars?" Jim demanded. "I've been standing out here for the past five minutes."

"Hi, Mom," Peter said, studying her through narrowed eyes. "Everyone else has gone home. Did you know you left your keys in the ignition?"

"I…Mr. Preston was showing me his…van." She was sure her face was as red as a fire truck, and she dared not meet her son's eyes for fear he'd know she'd just been kissed. Good heavens, he probably already did.

"Are you all right?" Peter asked her.

"Sure. Why?" Stepping down onto the pavement she felt

as graceful as a hippo. James climbed in when she'd climbed out; she and Peter walked over to her car.

"I think you might be coming down with something," Peter said as he automatically sat in the driver's seat, assuming he'd be doing the honors. He snapped the seat belt into place. "There were three cookies in my lunch, and no sandwich."

"There were?" Carol distinctly remembered spreading peanut butter on the bologna slices—Peter's favorite sandwich. She must have left it on the kitchen countertop.

"Not to worry, I traded off two of the cookies." He adjusted the rearview mirror and turned the key. He was about to pull out of the parking space when a huge smile erupted on his face. "I'm glad you and Mr. Preston are getting along so well," he said.

Alex sat at his cluttered desk with his hands clasped behind his head, staring aimlessly into space. He'd finally kissed her. He felt like a kid again. A slow, easy smile spread across his face, a smile so full, his cheeks ached. What a kiss it had been. Seductive enough to satisfy him until he could see her again. He was going to kiss her then, too. He could hardly wait.

The intercom buzzed. "Mr. Powers is here."

Alex's smile brightened. "Send him in." He stood and held out his hand to Barney, his best friend. They'd been in college together, roommates their senior year, and had been close ever since. Barney was a rare kind of friend, one who'd seen him through the bad times and the good times and been there for both in equal measure.

"Alex, great to see you." He helped himself to a butterscotch candy from the bowl on the edge of the desk and sat down. "How you doing?"

"Fine." It was on the tip of his tongue to tell Barney about Carol, but everything was so new, he didn't know if he could find the words to explain what he was feeling.

"I've decided to forgive you."

Alex arched his eyebrows. "For what?"

"Bambi. She said you dumped her at the restaurant."

"Oh, that. It wouldn't have worked, anyway."

"Why not?" Barney said, unwrapping the candy and popping it in his mouth.

"I don't have a hot tub."

"She claimed you left with another woman. A bag lady?"

Alex chuckled. "Not exactly."

"Well, you needn't worry, because ol' Barn has met Ms. Right and is willing to share the spoils."

"Barn, listen…"

Barney raised his hand, stopping him. "She's perfect. I swear to you she's bright, beautiful and buxom. The three *b*'s—who could ask for anything more?"

"As I recall, that's what you told me about Bambi," Alex countered, amused by his friend's attempts to find him a wife. It wouldn't be quite as humorous if Barney could stay married himself. In the past fifteen years, his friend had gone through three wives. Each of them bright, beautiful and buxom.

They might've been the best of friends, but when it came to women, their tastes were as dissimilar as could be. Barney went for breasts, whereas Alex was far more interested in brains.

"You're going to let me introduce her, aren't you? I mean, the least you can do is meet Babette."

"No, thanks." The guy had an obsession with *B*-words, Alex thought. The next woman would probably be named Brandy. Or Barbie.

"You won't even have a drink with her?"

"Sorry, not interested."

Barney leaned back and crossed his legs, sucking on the butterscotch candy for a few seconds before he spoke. "She was first runner-up for Miss Oregon several years back. Does that tell you anything?"

"Sure," Alex said, reaching for a candy himself. "She looks terrific in a swimsuit and is interested in world peace."

Barney slowly shook his head. "I don't understand it. I thought you were ready to get back into dating."

"I am."

"Listen, buddy, take a tip from me. Play the field, sample the riches available, then settle down. I'm happier when I'm married, and you will be, too. Frankly, with your looks and money, I don't think you'll have much of a problem. There are plenty of willing prospects out there. Only I notice you aren't doing anything to meet one."

"I don't have to, with you around. You're worse than a matchmaker."

Barney ignored that. "It's time, Alex. You said so yourself. Just how long are you going to wait? Gloria's been gone two years now. She wouldn't have wanted this."

"I know." At the mention of his late wife, Alex felt a twinge of pain. Time had healed the worst of it, but he'd always remember the agony of watching the woman he loved die.

"You want me to give you Babette's phone number?" his friend asked gently.

Alex shook his head. "Don't bother to introduce me to any more of your women friends."

Barney's mouth sagged open. "But you just admitted I was right, that it's time to get out there and—"

"Remember the bag lady Bambi was telling you about?"

Alex asked, interrupting his friend before he could deliver the entire five-minute lecture.

"Yeah, what about her?"

"I'm going to marry her."

Chapter Five

"You know, Mom, I like Mr. Preston," Peter announced over dinner as though this was a secret he'd been waiting to share.

"He seems very nice," Carol agreed, reaching for a slice of tomato. She didn't want to say anything more to encourage this topic, so she changed it. "How was school?"

"Fine. James was telling me about all the neat things him and his dad do together, like camping and fishing and stuff like that."

"Your uncle Tony takes you with him."

"Not camping or fishing and besides, it's not the same," Peter murmured. "Uncle Tony's my *uncle*."

Carol paused, her fork over the plump red tomato. "Now, that was profound."

"You don't know what I mean, do you?"

"I guess not," Carol said.

"Going camping with Mr. Preston would be like having a dad."

"How's that?" She took a bite of her roast, then braced her elbows on the tabletop.

"You know."

"No, I don't."

Peter lapsed into silence as he mulled over his thoughts. "I guess what I'm trying to say is that James and I talked it over and we decided we'd like it if the two of you got married."

Carol was so shocked by her son's statement that she stopped eating. Peter was staring at her intently, waiting for some sign or reaction.

"Well?" he pressed. "Is it going to happen? I can tell you like each other."

Chewing furiously, Carol waved her fork at her son, letting it speak for her. The meat, which had been so tender a moment before, took on the quality of leather. The faster she chewed, the more there seemed to be.

"You may think I'm still a kid and I don't know much," Peter continued, "but it didn't take James and me long to figure out what was going on inside his dad's van."

The piece of meat finally slid down Carol's throat. She blinked, uncertain if she could speak normally.

Peter was grinning from ear to ear. "I wish you could've seen your face when Mr. Preston opened the door of the van." Peter didn't bother to disguise his amusement. "If I hadn't been arguing with James, I would've started laughing right then."

"Arguing with James?" Those three words were all she could force past her lips. From the moment the two boys had met on the first day of high school, they'd been the best of friends. In all the months since September, Carol couldn't remember them disagreeing even once.

"We had an argument when we couldn't get his dad to

open the van," Peter admitted, his mouth twitching. "Your face was so red, and you had this stunned look, like an alien had hauled you inside his spaceship." Peter's deepening voice vibrated with humor.

"Peter," she demanded, furiously spearing another piece of meat. "What did you argue about?"

"We argued over what his father was doing with you in that van. What kind of son would I be if I didn't defend your…honor?"

"What did James say?"

Peter shrugged. "That his dad wouldn't do anything you didn't want him to."

"*Those* were fighting words?"

Peter shrugged again. "It was the way he said them."

"I see."

Peter scooped himself a second helping of the scalloped potatoes. "Getting back to the marriage part. What do you think?"

"That you need to finish your peas and carrots."

Peter's eyes rushed to hers, but only for a moment. Then he grinned. "Oh, I get it—you want me to mind my own business. Right?"

"Exactly."

"But think about it, Mom. Promise me you'll at least do that much. Meeting Mr. Preston could be the greatest thing that's ever happened to us."

"And when you're finished with your dinner, I want you to stack the dirty dishes in the dishwasher," Carol said without a pause. She ate the last bite of her roast, although it tasted more like rubber.

"Every time I mention Mr. Preston, are you going to give me another job to do?"

Her son was a quick study, Carol would grant him that.

"But you *are* going to see him again, aren't you?" he asked hopefully.

"The garbage should be taken out, and I noticed that the front flower beds should be weeded. I know you worked out there last Saturday, but—"

"All right, all right," Peter cried, throwing his hands in the air. "Enough—I get the message."

"I certainly hope so," she said and got up to carry her plate to the sink.

Carol waited until Peter was busy with his homework and the dishes were done before she snuck into the kitchen and turned off the light. Then she called Alex. She wasn't sure what she'd do if James answered.

"Hello."

"Alex?" She cupped her hand over the receiver and kept her eye on the doorway in case Peter strolled past.

"I can't talk long. Listen, did James happen to have a heart-to-heart discussion with you about...us?"

"Not exactly. He said something about the two of them having a talk about you and me. Why?"

"That's what I'm talking about," she whispered, ignoring his question. "Over dinner Peter threw a grenade at my feet."

"He did *what?*"

"It's a figure of speech—don't interrupt me. He said the two of them argued when you didn't open the van door and afterward decided it would be just great if the two of us... that's you and me...got *married*." She could barely get the words past the growing lump in her throat.

"Now that you mention it, James did say something along those lines."

Carol pressed her back to the kitchen wall, suddenly needing its support. "How can you be so casual about this?" she burst out.

"Casual?"

"My son announced that he knew what was going on inside the van and that I should've seen my face and that fishing and camping with you would be like having a father." She paused long enough to draw in a breath.

"Carol?"

"And then when I try to calmly warn you what these two are plotting, you make it sound like...I don't know...like we're discussing basketball or something."

"Carol, slow down, I can barely understand you."

"Of course you can't understand me—I'm upset!"

"Listen, this is clearly disturbing you. We need to talk about it. Can you meet me for lunch tomorrow?"

"I'm working tomorrow. And can't go out for lunch, for heaven's sake—I'm a nurse."

"Okay, I'll meet you in the hospital cafeteria at noon."

Just then Peter strolled nonchalantly into the kitchen. He stood in the doorway, turned on the light and stared curiously at his mother.

"Sure, Mama, whatever you say," Carol said brightly—too brightly.

"Mama?" Alex echoed chuckling. "Okay, I get the picture. I'll see you tomorrow at noon."

Agreeing to meet Alex at the hospital was a mistake. Carol should have realized it immediately, but she'd been so concerned with the shocking news Peter had delivered over dinner that she didn't stop to consider what could happen once she was spotted with Alex in the gossip-rich cafeteria at Ford Memorial.

"Sorry I'm late," Carol murmured as she joined him at a table for two, sliding her orange tray across from his. A couple of nurses from surgery walked past, glanced at Alex, then at Carol, and then back at Alex. Carol offered her peers a weak smile. Once she returned to the obstetrics ward, she was in for an inquisition that could teach the Spaniards a lesson.

"I haven't been here long." Alex grinned and reached for his ham sandwich. "How much time do you have?"

Carol checked her watch. "Forty-five minutes."

He opened a carton of milk. "All right. Do you want to tell me what upset you so much about last night?"

"I already did."

"Refresh my memory."

Carol released a slow sigh. Several more of her friends had seen her and Alex, including Janice Mandle, her partner in the birthing classes. By this time, the probing stares being sent their way were rattling Carol's shaky composure. "Apparently James and Peter have come to some sort of agreement... about you and me."

"I see." Humor flashed through his eyes like a distant light.

"Alex," she cried. "This is serious. We've gone out to dinner *once,* and our sons are talking about where the four of us are going to spend our honeymoon."

"And that bothers you?"

"Of course it does! And it should bother you, too. They already have expectations about how our relationship's going to develop. I don't think it's a healthy situation, and furthermore, they know about next Friday." She took a bite of her turkey sandwich and picked up her coffee.

"You mean that we're going to the Home Show?"

Carol nodded. "Yes, but I think we should forget the whole thing. We're looking at potential trouble here, and I for one have enough problems in my life without dealing with the guilt of not giving my son a father to take him fishing." She breathed deeply, then added, "My brother doesn't camp or fish. Actually no one in our family does."

Alex held his sandwich in front of his mouth. He frowned, his eyes studying hers, before he lowered his hands to the plate. "I beg your pardon?"

Carol shook her head, losing patience. "Never mind."

"No," he said after a thoughtful pause. "Explain to me what taking Peter fishing has to do with us seeing each other Friday night and your brother Tony who doesn't camp and hunt."

"Fish," Carol corrected, "although he doesn't hunt, either."

"That part makes sense."

Curious stares seemed to come at Carol from every corner of the room. Alex had finished his sandwich, and Carol wasn't interested in eating any more of hers.

"Do you want to go outside?" she suggested.

"Sure."

Once they'd disposed of their trays, Carol led him onto the hospital grounds. The weather had been beautiful for April. It wouldn't last much longer. The rains would return soon, and the "Rose City" would blossom into the floral bouquet of the Pacific Northwest.

With her hands in the front pockets of her uniform, Carol strolled in the sunshine, leading them away from the building and toward the parking lot. She saw his van in the second row and turned abruptly in the opposite direction. That construction van would be nothing but a source of embarrassment to her now.

"There's a pond over this way." With its surrounding green lawns, it offered relative privacy.

An arched bridge stretched between its banks, and goldfish swam in the cold water. Sunlight rippled across the pond, illuminating half, while the other half remained in enigmatic shadow. In some ways, Carol felt her budding relationship with Alex was like sun and shadow. When she was with him, she felt as though she was stepping into the light, that he drew her away from the shade. But the light was brilliant and discomfiting, and it illuminated the darkest corners of her loneliness, revealing all the imperfections she hadn't noticed while standing numbly in the shadows.

Although gentle, Alex had taught her painful lessons. Until she met him, she hadn't realized how hungry she was to discover love in a man's arms. The emptiness inside her seemed to echo when she was with him. The years hadn't lessened the pain her marriage had brought into her life, but seemed to have intensified her self-doubts. She was more hesitant and uncertain now than she'd been the year following Bruce's death.

With his hand on her elbow, Alex guided her to a park bench. Once they were seated, he reached for her hand, lacing their fingers together.

"I don't want you to worry about the boys," he said.

She nodded and lowered her eyes. She couldn't help being worried, but Alex didn't understand her fears and revealed no distress of his own. That being the case, she couldn't dwell on the issue.

He raised her fingers to his mouth. "I suppose what I'm about to say is going to frighten you even more."

"Alex...no."

"Shh, it needs to be said." He placed his finger across her

lips to silence her, and who could blame him, she mused. It had worked so well the first time. "The boys are going to come to their own conclusions," he continued, "and that's fine, they would anyway. For Peter to talk so openly with you about our relationship is a compliment. Apparently he felt comfortable enough to do so, and that reflects well on the kind of mother you are."

Carol hadn't considered it in those terms, but he was right. She and Peter were close.

"Now, about you and me," Alex went on, "we're both adults."

But Carol felt less mature than an adolescent when it came to Alex. She trembled every time she thought of him, and that was far more often than she would've liked. When he touched and kissed her, her hormones went berserk, and her heart seemed to go into spasms. No wonder she was frightened by the things Alex made her experience.

"I like you, and I'm fairly confident you like me."

She agreed with a sharp nod, knowing it wouldn't do any good to deny it.

"The fact is, I like everything about you, and that feeling increases whenever we're together. Now, if it happens that this attraction between us continues, then so be it. Wonderful. Great. It would be a big mistake for us to allow two teenage boys to dictate our relationship. Agreed?"

Once more, Carol nodded.

"Good." He stood, bringing her with him. "Now we both have to get back to work." Tucking her hand in the crook of his arm, he strode back toward the parking lot, pausing when he came to his van. He opened the door, then turned to face her.

"It seems to me we should seal our agreement."

"Seal it? I don't understand." But she did…. His wonderful, mist-gray eyes were spelling out exactly what he meant.

He caressed her cheek, then traced the outline of her lips. Whatever it was about his touch that sent her heart into such chaos, Carol couldn't understand. She reacted by instinct, drawing his finger between her lips, touching it with the tip of her tongue. The impact of her action showed in his eyes with devastating clarity.

He leaned forward and slipped his finger aside, replacing it with his mouth. His kiss was exquisitely slow and wildly erotic.

When he broke away they were both shaking. Carol stared up at him, her breath ragged, her lips parted and eager.

"I've got to get back to work…." she whispered.

"I know," Alex said. But he didn't make any effort to leave.

Instead he angled his head and dropped tiny kisses on her neck, then her ear, taking the lobe in his mouth before trailing his lips in heart-stopping increments back to hers. She was ready for him this time, more than ready.

The sound of a car door slamming somewhere in the distance abruptly returned them to the real world. Carol leaped back, her eyes startled, her breathing harsh and uneven. She smoothed her hands down the front of her uniform, as though whisking away wrinkles. She'd been kissing him like a lover and in broad daylight! To her chagrin, Alex didn't look at all dismayed by what had happened between them, just pleased.

"I wish you hadn't done that," she said, knowing he wasn't the only one to blame—but at the moment, the most convenient.

"Oh, baby, I don't regret a thing."

She folded her arms over her chest. "I've got to get back inside." But she had to wait until the flush of desire had left her face and her body had stopped trembling.

"It seems to me," Alex said with a smile of supreme confidence, "that if kissing you is this good, then when we finally make love it'll be downright dangerous." With that, he climbed into the driver's seat, closed the door and started the engine.

"You didn't call me," Carol's mother complained the following Friday evening. "All week I waited for you to phone and tell me about your date with the non-Italian."

"I'm sorry, Mama," Carol said, glancing at the kitchen clock. Alex was due to pick her up for the Home Show in ten minutes. Peter was staying overnight at a friend's, and she was running behind schedule as it was. The last thing she wanted to do was argue with her mother.

"You *should* be sorry. I could have died this week and you wouldn't have known. Your uncle in Jersey City would've had to call you and tell you your mother was dead."

"Mama, Peter started track this week, and we've gotten home late every single night."

"So don't keep me in suspense. Tell me."

Carol paused. "About what?"

"Your date with that Englishman. Did he take you to bed?"

"Mama!" Sometimes the things her mother said actually shocked Carol. "Of course not."

"It's a shame. Are you seeing him again? But don't wear those shoes with the pointed toes or he'll think you're a loose woman. And to be on the safe side, don't mention your cousin Celeste."

"Mama, I can't talk now. Alex will be here any minute—

we're going to the Home Show. His company has a booth there, and it'd be impolite to keep him waiting."

"Do you think he'll convert?"

"Mama, I'm not marrying Alex."

"Maybe not," her mother said with a breathless sigh, "but then again, who knows?"

The doorbell chimed, and Carol, who'd been dreading this evening from the moment she'd agreed to it, was flooded with a sense of relief.

"Bye, Mama."

Angelina said her farewells and added something about bringing Alex over to try her pasta. Carol was putting down the receiver by the time her mother had finished issuing her advice.

The doorbell rang again as Carol hurried into the living room. She rushed to open the door. "I'm sorry it took me so long to answer. My mother was on the phone."

"Did she give you any advice?" Alex teased.

"Just a little. She said it might not be a good idea if I mentioned my cousin Celeste."

"Who?"

"Never mind." Carol laughed a little nervously. Alex looked too good to be true, and the warm, open appreciation in his eyes did wonders for her self-esteem.

"You were worth the wait."

Carol could feel the blush in her cheeks. She wasn't used to having men compliment her, although her family was free with praise and always had been. This was different, however. Alex wasn't family.

His eyes compelled her forward, and she stepped toward him without question, then halted abruptly, realizing she'd very nearly walked into his arms.

"I'll…get my purse." She turned away, but his hand at her shoulder turned her back.

"Not yet."

"Alex…I don't think we should—"

But that was all the protest she was allowed. She closed her eyes as he ran his hand through her hair, then directed her mouth to his with tender restraint. He kissed her lightly at first, until she was pliant and willing in his arms….

When he pulled away from her, she slowly, languorously, opened her eyes to meet his.

"Don't look at me like that," he groaned. "Come on, let's get out of here before we end up doing something we're not ready to deal with yet."

"What?" Carol asked, blinking, still too dazed to think coherently.

"I think you know the answer to that."

They were in Alex's car before either of them spoke again. "If it's okay with you, I've got to stop at the office and pick up some more brochures," Alex said. "We're running low already."

"Of course it's okay," Carol told him. It was a good thing she was sitting down because her legs seemed too weak to support her. She was sure her face was flushed, and she'd rarely felt this shaky.

Her mind became her enemy as Alex headed toward the freeway. Try as she might, she couldn't stop thinking about how he'd felt against her. So strong and warm. A thin sheen of perspiration moistened her upper lip, and she swiped at it, eager to dispel the image that refused to leave her mind.

"How far is your office?" Carol asked after several strained minutes had passed. Alex seemed unusually quiet himself.

"Another quarter of an hour."

Not knowing how else to resume the conversation, she dropped it after that.

"Peter's staying with Dale tonight?" he finally asked.

"Yes. James, too?"

"Yes."

That was followed by ten more minutes of silence. Then Alex exited the freeway.

Carol curled her fingers around the armrest when he stopped at the first red light. The district was an industrial area and well lit.

As soon as he pulled into a side street, she saw his company sign. She'd never asked about his business and was impressed when she saw a small fleet of trucks and vans neatly parked in rows outside. He was apparently far more successful than she'd assumed.

Unlocking the door, Alex let her precede him inside. He flicked a switch, and light immediately flooded the office. One entire wall was lined with filing cabinets. Three desks, holding computers, divided the room. Carol didn't have time to give the room more than a fleeting glance as Alex directed her past the first desk and into another large office. She saw his name on the door.

The room was cluttered. The top of his desk looked as if a cyclone had hit it.

"The brochures are around here someplace," he muttered, picking up a file on a corner of the credenza. "Help yourself to a butterscotch candy."

"Thanks." As Carol reached for one, her gaze fell on the two framed photographs hidden behind a stack of computer printouts. The top of a woman's head showed on one of the photos, but that was all she could see. The second one was of James.

"I've got to get organized one of these days," Alex was saying.

Curious, Carol moved toward the credenza and the two photographs. "Who's this?" She asked, lifting the picture of the woman. She was beautiful. Blond. Blue-eyed. Wholesome. Judging by the hairstyle and clothes, the picture had been taken several years earlier.

Alex paused. "That's Gloria."

"She was your wife?"

Alex nodded, pulled out the high-backed cushioned chair and sank into it. "She died two years ago. Cancer."

It was all Carol could do to hold on to the picture. The pain in his voice stabbed through her.

"I...I thought you were divorced."

"No," Alex said quietly.

Carol continued to study the beautiful woman in the photo. "You loved her, didn't you?"

"So much that when the time came, I wanted to die with her. Yes, I loved her."

With shaking hands, Carol replaced the photograph. Her back was to Alex, and she briefly closed her eyes. She made a rigorous effort to smile when she turned to face him again.

He frowned. "What's wrong?"

"Nothing," she said breezily.

"You look pale all of a sudden. I thought you knew.... I assumed James or Peter had told you."

"No—neither of them mentioned it."

"I'm sorry if this comes as a shock."

"There's no reason to apologize."

Alex nodded, sighed and reached for her hand, pulling her down into his lap. "I figured you'd understand better than most what it is to lose someone you desperately love."

Chapter Six

"Gloria had problems when James was born," Alex began. His hold on Carol's waist tightened almost painfully, but she was sure he wasn't aware of it. "The doctors said there wouldn't be any more children."

"Alex, please, there's no need to tell me this."

"There is," he said. "I want you to know. It's important to me...."

Carol closed her eyes and pressed her forehead against the side of his head. She knew intuitively that he didn't often speak of his late wife, and that he found it difficult to do so now.

Alex wove his fingers into her hair. "In the years after Jim's birth, Gloria's health was never good, but the doctors couldn't put their finger on what was wrong. She was weak and tired a lot of the time. It wasn't until Jim was in junior high that we learned she had leukemia—myelocytic leukemia, one of the most difficult forms to treat." He paused and drew in an unsteady breath.

"Alex," she pleaded, her hands framing his face. "Don't,

please—this is obviously so painful for you." But the moment
her eyes met his, she knew nothing she said or did would stop
him. She sensed that only sharing it now, with her, would
lessen the trauma of his memories.

"We did all the usual things—the chemotherapy, the other
drugs—but none of it helped, and she grew steadily worse.
Later, when it was clear that nothing else could be done, we
opted for a bone-marrow transplant. Her sister and mother
flew in from New York, and her sister was the better match.
But…that didn't work, either."

Carol stroked his cheek, yearning to do anything she could
to lessen the pain.

He hesitated and drew in a quavering breath. "She suffered
so much. That was the worst for me to deal with. I was her
husband, and I'd sworn to love and protect her, and there
wasn't a thing I could do…not a single, solitary thing."

Tears moistened Carol's eyes, and she struggled to keep
them at bay.

Alex's voice remained firm and controlled, but Carol
recognized the pain he was experiencing. "I didn't know
what courage was until I watched Gloria die," he whispered. He closed his eyes. "The last three weeks of her life,
it was obvious she wasn't going to make it. Finally she fell
into a coma and was put on a respirator. The doctors knew
she'd never come out of it and so did the nurses. I could
see them emotionally removing themselves, and I couldn't
bear it. I became a crazy man, refusing to leave her side,
letting no one care for her but me. I held on to her hand
and silently willed her to live with every breath I took. I
honestly believe I kept her alive by the sheer force of my
will. I was afraid to leave her, afraid that when I did, she'd
slip silently into death. Eventually that was exactly what

happened. I left her because Jim needed me and because I knew that at some point I'd have to leave. I sat in the hospital waiting room with my son, telling him about his mother, and suddenly a pain, an intense stabbing pain, shot through me—" he hesitated and gave a ragged sigh "—and in that instant, I knew she was gone. I've never felt anything like it. A few minutes later, a nurse came for me. I can remember that scene so vividly—my mind's played it back so many times.

"I stood up and Jim stood with me, and I brought my son as close to my side as I could, looked the nurse in the eye and said, 'She's gone, isn't she?' The nurse nodded and Jim started to cry and I just stood there, dazed and numb. I don't remember walking back to Gloria's room, but somehow I found myself there. I lifted her into my arms and held her and told her how sorry I was that I'd been so stubborn and selfish, keeping her with me those three weeks, refusing to let her die. I told her how I would much rather have been with her, how I'd wanted to hold her hand as she stepped from one life into the next."

By now Carol was weeping softly, unabashedly.

Alex's fingers stroked her hair. "I didn't mean for you to cry," he whispered, and his regret seemed genuine. "You would have liked her."

Carol had felt the same way from the first moment she'd seen Gloria's photograph. Nodding, she hid her face in the strong curve of his neck.

"Carol," he whispered, caressing her back, "look at me."

She sniffled and shook her head, unwilling to let him witness the strength of her emotion. It was one thing to sit on his lap, and entirely another to look him in the eye after he'd shared such a deep and personal part of himself.

His lips grazed the line of her jaw.

"No," she cried softly, her protest faint and nearly inaudible, "don't touch me...not now." He'd come through hell, suffered the torment of losing his wife, and he needed Carol. He was asking for her. But her comfort could only be second-best.

"Yes," he countered, lifting her head so he could look at her. Against her will, against her better judgment, her gaze met his. His eyes were filled with such hunger that she all but gasped. Again and again, they roamed her face, no doubt taking in the moisture that glistened on her cheeks, the way her lips trembled and the staggering need she felt to comfort him. Even if that comfort was brief, temporary, a momentary solace.

"I'm sorry I upset you." He wove his fingers into her hair and directed her lips to his. His mouth was warm and moist and gentle. No one had ever touched her with such tenderness and care. No kiss had ever affected her so deeply. No kiss had ever shown her such matchless beauty.

Tears rained down Carol's face. Sliding her fingers through his hair, she held him close. He was solid and muscular and full of strength. His touch had filled the hollowness of her life and, she prayed, had helped to ease his own terrible loneliness.

"Carol," he breathed, sounding both stunned and dismayed, "what is it? What's wrong?"

"Nothing," she whispered. "Everything."

"I'm sorry...so sorry," he said in a low voice.

Confused and uncertain, Carol turned to face him. "You are? Why?"

"For rushing you. For thinking of my own needs instead of yours."

"No..." She shook her head, incapable of expressing what she felt.

"Are you going to be all right?"

She nodded, still too shaken to speak.

He placed his hands on the curve of her shoulder and kissed the crown of her head. "Thank you."

"For what?" Reluctantly her eyes slid to his.

"For listening, for being here when I needed you."

All she could manage in response was a tremulous smile.

For the rest of the evening, Alex was a perfect gentleman. He escorted her to the Home Show, where they spent several hours wandering from one display to another, discussing the ideas and products represented. They strolled hand in hand, laughing, talking, debating ideas. Carol was more talkative than usual; it helped disguise her uneasiness. She told him about her plan to dig up a portion of her back lawn and turn it into an herb garden. At least when she was talking, her nerve endings weren't left uncovered and she didn't have to deal with what had happened a few hours before...

After they'd toured the Home Show, Alex took her out to eat at a local Greek restaurant. By that time of the evening, Carol should have been famished, since they were having dinner so late. But whatever appetite she'd had was long gone.

When Alex dropped her off at the house, he kissed her good-night, but if he was expecting an invitation to come inside, he didn't receive one.

Hours later, she lay staring at the ceiling, while shadows of the trees outside her window frolicked around the light fixture like dancing harem girls. Glaring at the clock radio, Carol punched her pillow several times and twisted around so she lay on her stomach, her arms cradling her head. She *should* be sleepy. Exhausted. Drained after a long, trying week. Her job took its toll in energy, and normally by Friday night, Carol collapsed the moment she got into bed, waking refreshed Saturday morning.

She would've liked to convince herself that Alex had nothing to do with this restless, trapped feeling. She tried to analyze what was bothering her so much. It wasn't as though Alex had never kissed her before this evening. The impact he had on her senses shouldn't come as any surprise. She'd known from the first night they'd met that Alex had the power to expose a kaleidoscope of emotions within her. With him, she felt exhilarated, excited, frightened, reborn.

Perhaps it was the shock of passion he'd brought to life when he'd kissed her. No, she mused, frowning, she'd yearned for him to do exactly that even before they'd arrived at his office.

Squeezing her eyes closed, she tried to force her body to relax. She longed to snap her fingers and drift magically into the warm escape of slumber. It was what she wanted, what she needed. Maybe in the morning, she'd be able to put everything into perspective.

Closing her eyes, however, proved to be a mistake. Instead of being engulfed by peace, she was confronted with the image of Alex's tormented features as he told her about Gloria. *I figured you'd understand better than most what it is to lose someone you desperately love.*

Carol's eyes flew open. Fresh tears pooled at the edges as her sobs took control. She'd loved Bruce. She'd hated Bruce.

Her life ended with his death and her life had begun again.

It was the end; it was the beginning.

There hadn't been tears when he'd died—not at first but

later. Plenty of tears, some of profound sadness, and others that spoke of regrets. But there was something more. A release. Bruce had died, and at the same moment, she and Peter had been set free from the prison of his sickness and his abuse.

The tears burned her face as she sobbed quietly, caught in the horror of those few short years of marriage.

Bruce shouldn't have died. He was too young to have wasted his life. Knowing he'd been drunk and with another woman hadn't helped her deal with the emotions surrounding his untimely death.

I figured you'd understand better than most what it is to lose someone you desperately love. Only Carol didn't know. Bruce had destroyed the love she'd felt for him long before his death. He'd ravaged all trust and violated any vestiges of respect. She'd never known love the way Alex had, never shared such a deep and personal commitment with anyone— not the kind Alex had shared with Gloria, not the kind her mother had with her father.

And Carol felt guilty. Guilty. Perhaps if she'd been a better wife, a better mother, Bruce would have stopped drinking. If she'd been more desirable, more inventive in the kitchen, a perfect housekeeper. Instead she felt guilty. It might not be rational or reasonable but it was how she felt.

"Well?" Peter asked as he let himself in the front door the next morning. He dumped his sleeping bag on the kitchen floor, walked over to Carol and dutifully kissed her cheek.

"Well, what?" Carol said, helping herself to a second cup of coffee. She didn't dare look in the mirror, suspecting there were dark smudges under her eyes. At most, she'd slept two hours all night.

"How did things go with Mr. Preston?"

Carol let the steam rising from her coffee mug revive her. "You never told me James's mother had died."

"I didn't? She had leukemia."

"So I heard," Carol muttered. She wasn't angry with her son, and Alex's being a widower shouldn't make a whole lot of difference, but for reasons she was only beginning to understand, it did.

"James said it took his dad a long time to get over his mother's death."

Carol felt her throat muscles tighten. He wasn't over her, not really.

"James keeps a picture of her in his room. She was real pretty."

Carol nodded, remembering the bright blue eyes smiling back at her from the framed photograph in Alex's office. Gloria's warmth and beauty were obvious.

"I thought we'd work in the backyard this morning," Carol said, as a means of changing the subject.

"Aw, Mom," Peter groaned. "You know I hate yard work."

"But if we tackle everything now, it won't overwhelm us next month."

"Are you going to plant a bunch of silly flowers again? I don't get it. Every year you spend a fortune on that stuff. If you added it all up, I bet you could buy a sports car with the money."

"Buy who a sports car?" she challenged, arms akimbo.

"All right, all right." Peter clearly didn't want to argue. "Just tell me what I have to do."

Peter's attitude could use an overhaul, but Carol wasn't in the best of moods herself. Working with the earth, thrusting her fingers deep into the rich soil, was basic to her nature and never more than now.

The sun was out when Carol, dressed in her oldest pair of jeans and a University of Oregon sweatshirt, knelt in front of her precious flower beds. She'd tied a red bandanna around her head, knotting it at the back.

Peter brought his portable CD player outside and plugged it into the electrical outlet on the patio. Next, he arranged an assortment of CDs in neat piles.

Carol glanced over her shoulder and groaned inwardly. She was about to be serenaded with music that came with words she found practically impossible to understand. Although maybe that was a blessing…

"Just a minute," Peter yelled and started running toward the kitchen.

That was funny. Carol hadn't even heard the phone ring. Ignoring her son, she knelt down, wiping her wrist under her nose. The heat was already making her perspire. Bending forward, she dug with the trowel, cultivating the soil and clearing away a winter's accumulation of weeds.

"Morning."

At the sound of Alex's voice, Carol twisted around to confront him. "Alex," she whispered. "What are you doing here?"

"I came to see you."

"Why?"

He joined her, kneeling beside her on the lush, green grass. His eyes were as eager as if it had been weeks since he'd seen her instead of a few hours.

"What are you doing here?" she demanded again, digging more vigorously than necessary. She didn't want to have this conversation. It was too soon. She hadn't fully recovered from their last encounter and was already facing another one.

"I couldn't stay away," he said, his voice harsh and husky at once, and tinged with a hint of anger as if the lack of control bothered him. "You were upset last night, and we both ignored it instead of talking about it the way we should have."

"You were imagining things," she said, offering him a false smile.

"No, I wasn't. I felt guilty, too."

"Guilty?" she cried. "Whatever for?"

"Because I told you about Gloria and didn't ask about your husband. It would've been the perfect time for you to tell me."

Carol's stomach lurched. "That was a long time ago...and best forgotten."

"But you loved him and were saddened by his death, and I should've realized that talking about Gloria would be especially painful for you. I should have been more sensitive."

She shut her eyes. "There's no reason to feel guilty. You talked openly and honestly, and I appreciated knowing about your wife."

"Maybe so," Alex conceded, "but I frightened you, and now you're feeling confused."

"Nothing could be further from the truth." She continued to work, dragging the trowel through the damp soil.

Alex chuckled softly. He gripped her shoulders and turned her toward him as he scanned her features. "You shouldn't lie, Carol Sommars. Because you blush every time you do."

"That's ridiculous." As if on cue, she felt her cheeks grow pink. Carol groaned inwardly, furious with Alex and even more so with herself.

"No, it isn't ridiculous." He paused, and his mouth quivered as he studied her. "You're doing it now."

"Where are the boys?"

Alex's chuckle deepened. "Don't try changing the subject—it isn't going to work."

"Alex, please."

"Hey, Mom, you'll never guess what!"

Grateful for the distraction, Carol dragged her eyes away from Alex and turned to her son, who stood on the patio, looking exceptionally pleased.

"What is it, Peter?"

"James and Mr. Preston brought over one of those fancy, heavy-duty tillers. They're going to dig up that garden space you've been talking about for the past two summers."

Carol's gaze flew back to Alex's, full of unspoken questions.

"You said something last night about wanting to grow an herb garden, didn't you?"

"Yes, but why...I mean, you don't have to do this." She felt flustered and surprised and overwhelmed that he'd take a casual comment seriously and go out of his way to see that her wish was fulfilled.

"Of course I don't have to, but I want to. Peter and James and I are your willing servants, isn't that right, boys?" Neither bothered to answer, being far more interested in sorting through the CDs Peter had set out.

Two hours later, Carol had been delegated to the kitchen by all three men, who claimed she was a world-class nuisance.

"Mom," Peter said, "do something constructive like make lunch. You're in the way here."

Slightly taken aback by her son's assessment of her role, Carol muttered under her breath and did as he asked. Her ego suffered further when James sent his friend a grateful glance. Even Alex seemed pleased to have her out from under their capable feet.

Twenty minutes later, Alex entered the kitchen. He paused when he saw her stacking sandwiches on a platter. He walked over to her, slipped his arms around her waist and nuzzled her neck.

"Alex," she protested in a fierce whisper, "the boys will see you."

"So?"

"So, what they're thinking is bad enough without you adding fuel to the fire."

"They're too busy to care."

"I care!"

His growl was low as he slid his hand from her navel up her midriff. "I know."

"If you don't stop I'll…I'll…I'm not sure what I'll do—but it won't be pleasant." Her threat was an empty one, and Alex knew it as well as she did. She was trembling the way she always did when he touched her. The more intimate the caress, the more she shivered.

"I told the boys I was coming inside to pester you, and I'm nothing if not a man of my word," Alex informed her, clearly relishing her shyness.

"Alex…"

"Don't say it," he murmured. "I already know—this isn't the time or the place. I agree, but I don't have to like it." Slowly and with great reluctance, he released her.

Carol was aware of every nuance of this man. He made the most innocent caress sweet with sensations. His touch only created a need for more. Much more.

Once he'd released her, Carol sighed with relief—or was it regret? She no longer had any idea. She carried the platter of sandwiches to the table and brought out a pitcher of fresh lemonade.

Alex pulled out a chair and sat down. "I like watching you move," he whispered. "I like touching you even more."

"Alex...please don't. You're making me blush."

He laughed lightly. "I like that, too. Being with you makes me feel alive again. I hadn't realized how...desensitized I'd become to life. The first time we kissed I discovered what I'd been missing. All those arranged dates, all those wasted evenings—and all that time you were right under my nose and I didn't even know it."

"I...I think I'll put out two kinds of chips," Carol said, completely unsettled by the way he spoke so openly, so frankly.

"You're beautiful." His eyes were dark, filled with the promise of things to come. "So beautiful..."

"Alex, please." She leaned against the counter, overwhelmed by his words.

"I can't help it. I feel as though I've been granted a second chance at life. Tell me I'm not behaving like an idiot. Tell me you feel it, too."

She did feel everything he did, more profoundly than she dared let him know. "We've both been alone too long," she said. "People in situations like ours must think these kinds of thoughts all the time."

Her comment didn't please him. He frowned and slowly stood. "You may find this difficult to believe, Carol, but there hasn't been anyone since Gloria who made me feel the things you do. And trust me, there've been plenty who tried."

Gulping, Carol whirled around and made busy work opening a bag of potato chips.

Alex joined her, leaning against the counter and facing her

so she couldn't ignore him. "You, on the other hand, don't even need to touch me to make me respond. You might not want to admit it, but it's the same for you."

"When you decide to pester someone, you don't do it by half measures, do you?" she muttered.

"Admit it, Carol."

"I..."

He slid his lips across hers. "Are you ready to admit it yet?"

"No, I—"

He bent forward and kissed her again.

Carol's knees buckled and she swayed toward him.

Alex instantly reached for her. Without question, without protest, Carol fell into his arms, so hungry for his touch, she felt as if she were on fire.

The sound of someone clearing his throat was followed by, "Hey, we're not interrupting anything, are we?" Peter was standing just inside the kitchen. "In case you two haven't noticed, it's lunchtime."

Chapter Seven

Alex pressed one knee down on the green and stretched out his putter, judging the distance to the hole with a sharp eye. He'd been playing golf with Barney every Sunday afternoon for years.

"So when do I get to meet this female dynamo?" Barney asked after Alex had successfully completed the shot.

"I don't know yet," Alex said as he retrieved his golf ball. He inserted the putter back inside his bag before striding toward the cart.

"What do you mean, you don't know?" Barney echoed. "What's with you and this woman? I swear you've been a different man since you met her. You stare off into space with this goofy look on your face. I talk to you and you don't hear me, and when I ask you about her, you get defensive."

"I'm not defensive, I'm in love."

"Alex, buddy, listen to the voice of experience. You're not in love, you're in lust. I recognize that gleam in your eye. Ten to one you haven't slept with her yet. So I recommend that you get her in the sack and be done with it before you end up doing something foolish."

Alex's gaze fired briefly as he looked at his friend. How did Barney know the progress of his relationship with Carol?

"I have every intention of sleeping with her. Only I plan to be doing that every night for the rest of my life. Carol's not the type of woman to have a fling, and I refuse to insult her by suggesting one."

Barney stared at Alex as if seeing him for the first time. "I don't think I ever realized what an old-fashioned guy you are. Apparently you haven't noticed, but the world's become a lot more casual. Our clothes are casual, our conversations are casual and yes, even our sex is casual. In case you hadn't heard, you don't have to marry a woman to take her to bed."

"Continue in this vein," Alex said, "and you're going to become a casual friend."

Barney rolled his eyes dramatically. "See what I mean?"

If three wives hadn't been able to change Barney's attitude, Alex doubted he could, either. "As I recall, the last time we had this conversation," Alex reminded him, "you said settling down was the thing to do. I'm only following your advice."

"But not yet," Barney said. "You haven't played the field enough. There are riches out there—" he gestured with his hands "—female gold nuggets just waiting to be picked up, then set gently back in place for the next treasure-hunter."

"You mean like Bambi and what was the name of the other one? Barbie?"

"Stop being clever," Barney snickered. "I have your best interests at heart, and frankly I'm concerned. Two years after Gloria's gone, you suddenly announce it's time to start dating again. Man, I was jumping up and down for joy. Then you go out with a grand total of ten different women—most of them only once—and calmly inform me you've met *the one*. You plan to marry her, just like that, and you haven't even slept with her yet. How are you going to find out if you're sexually compatible?"

"We're compatible, trust me."

"You may think so now, but *bingo*, once she's got a wedding band, it's a totally different story."

"Stop worrying, would you?" Alex eased his golf cart into his assigned space. From the day he'd decided to look for another wife, Barney had been a constant source of amusement. The problem was, his most hilarious moments had come in the form of women his friend had insisted he meet.

"But, Alex, I *am* worried about you," Barney muttered as he lifted his clubs from the back of the cart. "You don't know women the way I do. They're scheming, conniving, money-hungry, and how they get their clutches into you is by marriage. Don't be so eager to march up the aisle with Carol. I don't want you to go through what I have."

After three wives, three divorces and child support payments for two separate families, Barney was speaking from experience—of a particularly negative sort.

"Gloria was special," his longtime friend said. "You're not going to find another one like her. So if it's those qualities that attract you to Carol, look again. You may only be seeing what you want to see."

"You wanna yell?" Angelina Pasquale shouted from the doorway of the kitchen into the living room where her grandchildren were squabbling. "Then let's have a contest. But remember—I've been doing it longer. They can hear me all the way in Jersey City."

Peter and his younger cousins ceased their shouting match,

and with a nod of her head, Angelina returned to the kitchen, satisfied that a single threat from her was enough to bring about peace that would last through the afternoon.

Carol was busy slicing tomatoes for the salad, and her sister-in-law, Paula, was spreading garlic butter on thick slices of French bread.

The sauce was warming on the stove, and the water for the long strands of fresh pasta was just starting to boil. The pungent scent of basil and thyme circled the kitchen like smoke from a campfire. From Carol's earliest memory, her mother had cooked a pot of spaghetti sauce every Saturday evening. The unused portion from Sunday's dinner was served in a variety of ways during the week. Leftover pot roast became something delectable with her mother's sauce over top. And chicken with Mama's sauce rivaled even the Cajun chicken at Jake's restaurant.

"So, Carol," her mother began, wiping her hands on the ever-present apron. She took a large wooden spoon and stirred the kettle of simmering sauce. "I suppose your English friend thinks good spaghetti sauce comes from a jar," she said disparagingly. This was her way of letting Carol know the time had come to invite Alex and his son to Sunday dinner.

"Mama, Alex plays golf on Sundays."

"Every Sunday?"

Carol nodded.

"That's because he's never tasted my sauce." Angelina shook her head as though to suggest Alex had wasted much of his life walking from green to green when he could've been having dinner at her house.

Adding serving utensils to the salad, Carol set the wooden bowl on the dining room table.

Tony, Carol's brother, sauntered into the kitchen and

slipped his arms around Paula's waist. "How much longer until dinner? The natives are getting restless."

"Eleven minutes," Angelina answered promptly. She tasted the end of the wooden spoon and nodded in approval.

Carol returned to the kitchen and noticed that her mother was watching her under the guise of waiting for the water to boil. The question Carol had expected all day finally came.

"You gonna marry this non-Italian?" her mother asked, then added the noodles, stirring with enough energy to create a whirlpool in the large stainless-steel pot.

"Mama," Carol cried. "I barely know Alex. We've only gone out a handful of times."

"Ah, but your eyes are telling me something different."

"The only thing my eyes are interested in is some of that garlic bread Paula's making," Carol said, hoping to divert her mother's attention from the subject of Alex.

"Here." Her sister-in-law handed her a slice. "But it's no substitute for a man." Paula turned her head to press a quick kiss on her husband's cheek.

Tony's hands slipped further around Paula's waist as he whispered in his wife's ear. From the way her sister-in-law's face flooded with warm color, Carol didn't need much of an imagination to guess what Tony had said.

Carol looked away. She wasn't embarrassed by the earthy exchange between her brother and his wife; instead, she felt a peculiar twinge of envy. The realization shocked her. In all the years she'd been alone, Carol had never once longed for a pair of arms to hold her or for a man to whisper suggestive comments in her ear. Those intimacies were reserved for the happily married members of her family.

Yet, here she was, standing in the middle of her mother's kitchen, yearning for Alex to stroll up behind her, circle her waist and whisper promises in her ear. The image was so vivid that she hurried into the living room to escape it.

It wasn't until later, when the dishes were washed, that Carol had a chance to sort through her thoughts. Tony and Peter were puttering around in the garage. Paula was playing a game of Yahtzee with the younger children. And Angelina was rocking in her chair, nimble fingers working delicate yarn into a sweater for her smallest grandchild.

"So are you gonna tell your mama what's troubling you?" she asked Carol out of the blue.

"Nothing's wrong," Carol fibbed. She couldn't discuss what she didn't understand. For the first time, she felt distanced from the love and laughter that was so much a part of Sunday dinner with her family. For years she'd clung to the life she'd built for herself and her son. These few, short weeks with Alex had changed everything.

Alex had discovered all her weaknesses and used them to his own advantage. Digging up the earth for her herb garden was a good example. She could've asked her brother to do it for her. Eventually she probably would have. But Tony did so much to help her already that she didn't want to burden him with another request. It wasn't as if tilling part of the backyard was essential. But one casual mention to Alex, and next thing she knew, there was freshly tilled earth waiting for basil and Italian parsley where before there'd been lawn.

"You like this man, don't you?"

Carol responded with a tiny nod of her head.

A slow, easy smile rose from her mother's mouth to her eyes. "I thought so. You got the look."

"The look?"

"Of a woman falling in love. Don't fight it so hard, my

bambina. It's time you met a man who brings color to your cheeks and a smile to your lips."

But Carol wasn't smiling. She felt confused and ambivalent. She was crazy about Alex; she prayed she'd never see him again. She couldn't picture her life with him; she couldn't picture her life without him.

"I lit a candle in church for you," her mother whispered. "And said a special prayer to St. Rita."

"Mama…"

"God and I had a good talk, and He told me it's predestined."

"What's predestined?"

"You and this non-Italian," her mother replied calmly.

"Mama, that doesn't make the least bit of sense. For years you've been telling me to marry a rich old man with one foot in the grave and the other on a banana peel. You said everyone loves a rich widow."

"Keep looking for the rich old man, but when you find him, introduce him to me. With any luck his first wife made spaghetti sauce with tomato soup and he'll worship at my feet."

Carol couldn't keep from smiling. She wasn't so sure about her mother lighting candles on her behalf or deciding that marrying Alex was predestined, but from experience she'd learned there wasn't any point in arguing.

Tony, Paula and their two children left around five. Usually Carol headed for home around the same time, but this afternoon she lingered. The 1940s war movie on television held Peter's attention, and her eyes drifted to it now and again.

It wasn't until she felt the moisture on her cheeks that she realized she was crying.

Doing what she could to wipe away the tears so as not

to attract attention to herself, she focused on the television screen. Her mother was right; she was falling in love, head over heels in love, and it was frightening her to death.

Silently Angelina set her knitting aside and joined Carol on the sofa. Without a word, she thrust a tissue into Carol's hand. Then she wrapped her arm around her daughter's shoulders and pressed her head tenderly to her generous bosom. Gently patting Carol's back, Angelina whispered soothing words of love and encouragement in a language Carol could only partially understand.

Alex didn't see Carol again until Monday afternoon when he pulled into the high school parking lot. He angled his van in front of the track, four spaces down from her car. He waited a couple of minutes, hoping she'd come and see him of her own free will. He should've known better. The woman wasn't willing to give an inch.

Deciding to act just as nonchalant, Alex opened his door, walked over to the six-foot-high chain-link fence and pretended to be watching the various groups participate in field events. Neither James nor Peter was trying out for any of those positions on the team.

Then he walked casually toward Carol, who was determined, it seemed, to ignore him, hiding behind the pages of a women's magazine.

"Hello, Carol," he said after a decent interval.

"Oh—Alex." She held the magazine rigidly in place.

"Mind if I join you?"

"Not at all." The hesitation was long enough to imply that she would indeed mind. Regardless, he opened the passenger door and slid inside her car. Only then did Carol bother to close the magazine and set it down.

By now, Alex told himself, he should be accustomed to her aloof attitude toward him. It was like this nearly every time they were together. She'd never shown any real pleasure at seeing him. He had to break through those chilly barriers each and every encounter. The strangest part was that he knew she was as strongly attracted to him as he was to her. And not just in the physical sense. Their lives were like matching bookends, he thought.

"Did you have a good day?" he asked politely.

She nodded and glanced away, as though she thought that sharing even a small part of her life with him was akin to admitting she enjoyed his company.

"I suppose it would be too much to hope that you missed me the last couple of days?" he asked.

"Yes."

Alex was almost embarrassed by the way his heart raced. "You missed me," he repeated, feeling like a kid who'd been granted free rein in a candy store.

"No," Carol said, clearly disconcerted. "I meant it would be too much to hope I did."

"Oh." The woman sure knew how to deflate his pride.

"It really was thoughtful of you to dig up that area in my backyard on Saturday. I'm grateful, Alex."

Crossing his arms, Alex leaned against the back of the seat and tried to conceal his injured pride with a lazy shrug. "It was no trouble." Especially since the two boys had done most of the work, leaving him free to "pester" Carol in the kitchen. With everything in him, he wished they were back in that kitchen now. He wanted her in his arms the way she'd been on Saturday afternoon, her lips moist and swollen with his kisses, her eyes dark with passion.

"The boys will be out any minute," Carol said, studying the empty field.

Alex guessed this was his cue to leave her car, but he wasn't taking the hint. When it came to Carol Sommars, he was learning that his two greatest allies were James and Peter.

It was time to play his ace.

Alex waited until the last possible minute. Both boys had walked onto the parking lot, their hair damp from a recent shower. They were chatting and joking and in a good mood. Climbing out of Carol's car, Alex leaned against the fender in a relaxed pose.

"Peter, did you say something about wanting to go camping?" he said, casting Carol a defiant look. "James and I were thinking of heading for the Washington coastline this coming weekend and thought you and your mother might like to go with us."

"We are?" James asked, delighted and surprised.

Peter's eyes widened with excitement. "Camping? You're inviting Mom and me to go camping?"

At the mention of the word *camping,* Carol opened her car door and vaulted out. Her eyes narrowed on Alex as if to declare a foul and charge him a penalty.

"Are you two free this weekend?" Alex asked with a practiced look of innocence, formally extending the invitation. The ball was in her court, and he was interested in seeing how she volleyed this one.

"Yes," Peter shouted. "We're interested."

"No," Carol said at the same moment. "We already have plans."

"We do?" her son moaned. "Come on, Mom, Mr. Preston just offered to take us camping with him and James. What could possibly be more important than that?"

"I wanted to paint the living room."

"What? Paint the living room? I don't believe it." Peter slapped his hands against his thighs and threw back his head. "You know how I feel about camping," he whined.

"Give your mother time to think it over," Alex urged, confident that Carol would change her mind or that Peter would do it for her. "We can talk about it tomorrow evening."

James gave Peter the okay signal, and feeling extraordinarily proud of himself, Alex led the way to his van, handing his son the keys.

"You're going to let me drive?" James asked, sounding more than a little stunned. "Voluntarily?"

"Count your blessings, boy, and drive."

"Yes, sir!"

Carol was furious with Alex. He'd played a faultless game, and she had to congratulate him on his fine closing move. All day she'd primed herself for the way she was going to act when she saw him again. She'd allowed their relationship to progress much further than she'd ever intended, and it was time to cool things down.

With her mother lighting candles in church and having heart-to-heart talks with God, things had gotten completely out of hand. Angelina barely complained anymore that Alex wasn't Catholic, and worse, not Italian. It was as if those two prerequisites no longer mattered.

What Carol hadn't figured on was the rush of adrenaline she'd experienced when Alex pulled into the school parking lot. She swore her heart raced faster than any of the runners on the track. She'd needed every ounce of determination she possessed not to toss aside the magazine she'd planted in the car and run to him, bury her face in his chest and ask him to explain what was happening to her.

Apparently Alex had read her perfectly. He didn't appear at all concerned about her lack of welcome. That hadn't even fazed him. All the arguments she'd amassed had been for naught. Then at the last possible minute he'd introduced the subject of this camping trip, in what she had to admire was a brilliant move. Her chain of resistance was only as strong as the weakest link. And her weakest link was Peter.

Grudgingly she had to admire Alex.

"Mom," Peter cried, restless as a first grader in the seat beside her. "We're going to talk about it, aren't we?"

"About the camping trip?"

"It's the chance of a lifetime. The Washington coast—I've heard it's fabulous—"

"We've got plans."

"To paint the living room? We could do that any old time!"

"Peter, please."

He was silent for a minute or so. The he asked, "Do you remember when I was eleven?"

Here it comes, Carol mused darkly. "I remember," she muttered, knowing it would've been too much to expect him not to drag up the lowest point of her life as a mother.

"We were going camping then, too, remember?"

He said *remember* as though it was a dirty word, one that would get him into trouble.

"You promised me an overnight camping trip and signed us up for an outing through the Y? But when we went to the meeting you got cold feet."

"Peter, they gave us a list of stuff we were supposed to bring, and not only did I not have half the things on the list, I didn't even know what they were."

"You could have asked," Peter cried.

"It was more than that."

"Just because we were going to hike at our own pace? They said we'd get a map. We could've found the camp, Mom, I know we could have."

Carol had had visions of wandering through the woods for days on end with nothing more than a piece of paper that said she should head east—and she had the world's worst sense of direction. If she could get lost in a shopping mall, how would she ever find her way through dense forest?

"That wasn't the worst part," Peter murmured. "Right there in the middle of the meeting you leaned over and asked me what it would cost to buy your way out of the trip."

"You said you wouldn't leave for anything less than a laser tag set," Carol said, tormented by the unfairness of it all. The toy had been popular and expensive at the time and had cost her a pretty penny. But her son had conveniently forgotten that.

"I feel like I sold my soul that day," Peter said with a deep sigh.

"Peter, honestly!"

"It wasn't until then that I realized how much I was missing by not having a dad."

The kid was perfecting the art of guilt.

"Now, once again," he argued, "I have the rare opportunity to experience the great out-of-doors, and it's like a nightmare happening all over again. My own mother's going to pull the rug out from under my feet."

Carol stopped at a red light and pretended to play a violin. "This could warp your young mind for years to come."

"It just might," Peter said, completely serious.

"Twenty years from now, when they lock those prison doors

behind you, you can cry out that it's all my fault. If only I'd taken you camping with Alex and James Preston, then the entire course of your life would have been different."

A short pause followed her statement.

"Sarcasm doesn't suit you, Mother."

Peter was right, of course, but Carol was getting desperate. At the rate this day was going, she'd end up spending Saturday night in front of a campfire, fighting off mosquitoes and the threat of wild beasts.

Because she felt guilty, despite every effort not to, Carol cooked Peter his favorite chicken-fried steak dinner, complete with gravy and mashed potatoes.

After the dishes had been cleared and Peter was supposed to be doing his homework, Carol found him talking on the phone, whispering frantically. It wasn't hard to guess that her son was discussing strategies with James. The three of them were clearly in cahoots against her.

Carol waited until Peter was in bed before she marched into the kitchen and righteously punched out Alex's phone number. She'd barely given him a chance to answer before she laid into him with both barrels.

"That was a rotten thing to do!"

"What?" he asked, feigning innocence.

"You know darn well what I'm talking about. Peter's pulled every trick in the book from the moment you mentioned this stupid camping trip."

"Are you going to come or is this war?"

"It's war right now, *Mister* Preston."

"Good. Does the victor get spoils? Because I'm telling you, Carol Sommars, I intend to win."

"Oh, Alex," she said with a sigh, leaning against the wall.

She slid all the way down to the floor, wanting to weep with frustration. "How could you do this to me?"

"Easy. I got the idea when you told me it was too much to hope that you'd miss me."

"But I don't know anything about camping. To me, roughing it is going without valet service."

"It'll be fun, trust me."

Trusting Alex wasn't at the top of her priority list at the moment. He'd pulled a fast one on her, and she wasn't going to let him do it again.

"Is Peter sleeping?" Alex asked softly.

"If he isn't, he should be." She didn't understand where this conversation was heading.

"James is asleep, too," he said. "After the cold shoulder you gave me this afternoon, I need something to warm my blood."

"Try a hot water bottle."

"It won't work. Keep the door unlocked and I'll be right over."

"Absolutely not. Alex Preston, listen to me, I'm not dressed for company and—"

It was too late. He'd already disconnected.

Chapter Eight

Standing in front of her locked screen door, Carol had no intention of letting Alex inside her home. It was nearly eleven, and they both had to work in the morning. When his car pulled into the driveway, she braced her feet apart and stiffened her back. She should be furious with him. Should be nothing; she *was* furious!

But when Alex climbed out of his car, he stood in her driveway for a moment, facing the house. Facing her. The porch light was dim, just bright enough to outline his handsome features.

With his hands in his pockets, he continued to stand there, staring at her. But that seemed such an inadequate way to describe the intensity of his gaze as his eyes locked with her own. Not a muscle moved in the hard, chiseled line of his jaw, and his eyes feasted on her with undisguised hunger. Even from the distance that separated them, Carol saw that his wonderful gray eyes had darkened with need.

He wanted her.

Heaven help her, despite all her arguments to the contrary, she wanted him, too.

Before he'd marched two steps toward her, Carol had un-locked the screen door and held it open for him.

"I'm not going camping," she announced, her voice scarcely audible. Her lips felt dry and her hands moist. Once she'd stated her position, her breath escaped with a ragged sigh. She thought of ranting at him, calling him a coward and a cheat to use her own son against her the way he had, but not a word made it from her mind to her lips.

Alex turned and shut the front door.

The only light was a single lamp on the other side of the room.

They didn't move, didn't breathe.

"I'm not going to force you to go camping," Alex whispered. "In fact, I…" He paused as he lowered his eyes to her lips, and whatever he intended to say trailed into nothingness.

Carol felt his eyes on her as keenly as she had his mouth.

In an effort to break this unnatural spell, she closed her eyes.

"Carol?"

She couldn't have answered him had her life depended on it. Her back was pressed to the door, and she flattened her hands against it.

Not once during her marriage had Carol felt as she did at that moment. So…needy. So empty.

He came to her in a single, unbroken movement, his mouth descending on hers. Carol wound her arms around him and leaned into his solid strength, craving it as never before. Again and again and again he kissed her.

"Alex." She tore her lips from his. "Alex," she breathed again, almost panting. "Something's wrong…."

She could feel his breath against her neck and his fingers

in her hair, directing her mouth back to his, kissing her with such heat, Carol thought she'd disintegrate.

Her tears came in earnest then, a great profusion that had been building inside her for years. Long, lonely, barren years.

With the tears came pain, pain so intense she could hardly breathe. Agony spilled from her heart. The trauma that had been buried within her stormed out in a torrent of tears that she could no more stop than she could control.

Huge sobs shook her shoulders, giant hiccupping sobs that she felt all the way to her toes. Sobs that depleted her strength. Her breathing was ragged as she stumbled toward the edge of hysteria.

Alex was speaking to her in soft, reassuring whispers, but Carol couldn't hear him. It didn't matter what he said. Nothing mattered.

She clutched his shirt tighter and tighter. Soon there were no more tears to shed, no more emotion to be spent. Alex continued to hold her. He slid his arms all the way around her, and although she couldn't understand what he was saying, his voice was gentle.

Once the desperate crying had started to subside, Carol drew in giant gulps of air in a futile effort to gain control of herself.

Slowly Alex guided her to the sofa and sat her down, then gathered her in his arms and held her tenderly.

Time lost meaning to Carol until she heard the clock chime midnight. Until then she was satisfied with being held in Alex's arms. He asked no questions, demanded no explanations. He simply held her, offering comfort and consolation.

This newfound contentment in his arms was all too short-lived, however. Acute embarrassment stole through the stillness, and fresh tears stung Carol's eyes. Her mind, her thoughts, her memories were steeped in emotions too strong to bear.

"I...I'll make some coffee," she whispered, unwinding her arms from him, feeling she had to escape.

"Forget the coffee."

She broke away and got shakily to her feet. Before he could stop her, she hurried into the kitchen and supported herself against the counter, not sure if she could perform the uncomplicated task of making a pot of coffee.

Alex followed her into the darkened room. He placed one hand on her shoulder and gently turned her around, so she had no choice but to face him. "I want to talk about what happened."

"No...please." She leveled her eyes at the floor.

"We *need* to talk."

"No." She shook her head emphatically. "Not now. Please not now."

A long, desperate moment passed before he gently kissed the crown of her head. "Fine," he whispered. "Not now. But soon. Very soon."

Carol doubted she could ever discuss what had happened between them, but she didn't have the strength or the courage to say so. That would only have invited argument.

"I...I think you should go."

His nod was reluctant. "Will you be all right?"

"Yes." A bold-faced lie if ever there was one. She would never be the same again. She was mortified to the very marrow of her bones by her behavior. How could she ever see him again? And then the pain, the memories came rushing back...

No, she wouldn't be all right, but she'd pretend she was, the same way she'd been pretending from the moment she married Bruce.

The message waiting for Alex when he returned to his office the following afternoon didn't come as any surprise. His secretary handed him the yellow slip, and the instant he saw Carol's name, he knew. She was working late that evening and asked if he could pick up Peter from track and drop him off at the house.

The little coward! He sat at his desk, leaned back in his chair and frowned. He hadn't wanted to leave her the night before. Hadn't wanted to walk out of her kitchen without being assured she was all right. Carol, however, had made it clear that she wanted him to leave. Equally apparent was the fact that his being there had only added to her distress. Whatever Carol was facing, whatever ghost she'd encountered, was ugly and traumatic.

So he'd left. But he hadn't stopped thinking about her all day. The thought of her had filled every waking minute.

Even now, hours later, he could remember in vivid detail the way she'd started to unfold and blossom right before his eyes. Because of him. For him.

His frown deepened. She'd never talked about her marriage. Alex assumed it had to be the source of her anguish, but he didn't know why. He didn't even know her late husband's name. Questions bombarded him, and he cursed the lack of answers.

And now, his sweet coward had gone into hiding.

"Will you talk to her, Mr. Preston?" Peter begged as he climbed inside the van in the school parking lot. "Mom's never gone camping, and I think she'd probably like it if she gave it half a chance."

"I'll talk to her," Alex promised.

Peter sighed with relief. "Good."

Sounding both confident and proud, James said, "My dad can be persuasive when he wants to be."

Alex intended to be *very* persuasive.

"I tried to reason with Mom this morning, and you know what she said?" Peter's changing voice pitched between two octaves.

"What?"

"She said she didn't want to talk about it. Doesn't that sound just like a woman? And I thought Melody Wohlford was hard to understand."

Alex stifled a chuckle. "I'll tell you boys what I'm going to do. We'll pick up hamburgers on the way home, and I'll drop you both off at my house. Then I'll drive over to your place, Peter, and wait for your mother there."

"Great idea," James said, nodding his approval.

"But while I'm gone, I want you boys to do your homework."

"Sure."

"Yeah, sure," James echoed. "Just do whatever it takes to convince Mrs. Sommars to come on our camping trip."

"I'll do everything I can," Alex said.

Carol let herself in the front door, drained from a long, taxing day at the hospital and exhausted from the sleepless night that had preceded it. That morning, she'd been tempted to phone in sick, but with two nurses already out due to illness, there wasn't anyone to replace her. So she'd gone to work feeling emotionally and physically hungover.

"Peter, I'm home," she called. "Peter?"

Silence. Walking into the kitchen, she deposited her purse on the counter and hurried toward her son's bedroom. She'd contacted Alex and asked that he bring Peter home, with instructions to phone back if he couldn't. She hadn't heard from him, so she'd assumed he'd pick up her son and drop him off at the house.

Peter's room was empty, his bed unmade. An array of clean and dirty clothes littered his floor. Everything was normal there.

This was what she got for trying to avoid Alex, Carol mused, chastising herself. Peter was probably still waiting at the high school track, wondering where she could possibly be.

Sighing, she hurried back into the kitchen and reached for her purse. She had to get him his own cell phone, she decided—it would help in situations like this.

The doorbell rang as she walked through the living room. Impatiently she jerked open the door and her eyes collided with Alex's. She gasped.

"Hello again," he said in the warm, husky way that never failed to affect her. "I didn't mean to startle you."

"You didn't." He had, but she wasn't about to admit it. "Apparently you didn't get my message…. Peter must still be at the school."

"No. He's at my house with James."

"Oh." That hardly expressed the instant dread she felt. They were alone, and there was no escape, at least not by the most convenient means—Peter.

Alex stepped into the house and for the first time, she noticed he was carrying a white paper bag. Her gaze settled on it and she frowned.

"Two Big Macs, fries and shakes," he explained.

"For whom?"

Alex arched his eyebrows. "Us."

"Oh…" He honestly expected her to sit down and eat with him? It would be impossible. "I'm not hungry."

"I am—very hungry. If you don't want to eat, that's fine. I will, and while I'm downing my dinner, we can talk."

It wouldn't do any good to argue, and Carol knew it. Without another word, she turned and walked to the kitchen. Alex followed her, and his movements, as smooth and agile as always, sounded thunderous behind her. She was aware of everything about him. When he walked, when he breathed, when he moved.

His eyes seemed to bore holes in her back, but she ignored the impulse to turn and face him. She couldn't bear to look him in the eye. The memory of what had happened the night before made her cheeks flame.

"How are you?" he asked in that husky, caring way of his.

"Fine," she answered cheerfully. "And you?"

"Not so good."

"Oh." Her heart was pounding, clamoring in her ears. "I'm…sorry to hear that."

"You should be, since you're the cause."

"Me? I'm…sure you're mistaken." She got two plates from the cupboard and set them on the table.

As she stepped past him, Alex grabbed her hand. "I don't want to play word games with you. We've come too far for that…and we're going a lot further."

Unable to listen to his words, she closed her eyes.

"Look at me, Carol."

She couldn't do it. She lowered her head, eyes still shut.

"There's no need to be embarrassed."

Naturally he could afford to be generous. He wasn't the one who'd dissolved in a frenzy of violent tears and emotion. She was just grateful that Peter had slept through the whole episode.

"We need to talk."

"No…" she cried and broke away. "Couldn't you have ignored what happened? Why do you have to drag it up now?" she demanded. "Do you enjoy embarrassing me like this? Do you get a kick out of seeing me miserable?" She paused, breathless, her chest heaving. "Please, just go away and leave me alone."

Her fierce words gave birth to a brief, tense silence.

Grasping her chin between his thumb and forefinger, Alex lifted her head. Fresh emotion filled her chest, knotting in her throat as her eyes slid reluctantly to his.

"I don't know what happened last night," he said. "At least not entirely." His voice was gruff, angry, emotional. "All I know is that I've never felt closer to anyone than I did to you—and I've never felt more helpless. But we've got something special, Carol, and I refuse to let you throw it away. Understand?"

She bit her lower lip, sniffled, then slowly nodded.

The tension eased from Alex, and he reached for her, gently taking her in his arms. She went without question, hiding her face against his neck.

Long, lazy moments passed before he spoke. "I want you to tell me about your marriage."

"No!" she cried and frantically shook her head.

He was silent again, and she could feel him withdrawing from her—or maybe she was the one withdrawing. She wanted to ask him to be patient with her, to give her breathing room, time to analyze what was happening between them.

Just when she was ready to speak, she felt him relax. He chuckled softly, his warm breath mussing her hair. "All right, I'll strike a bargain with you. If you go camping with me this weekend, I'll drop the subject—not forever, mind you, but until you're comfortable enough to talk about it."

Carol raised her head, her eyes meeting his. "You've got a black heart, Alex Preston."

He chuckled and kissed the tip of her nose. "When it comes to courting you, I've learned I need one."

"I can't believe I'm doing this," Carol muttered as she headed up the steep trail into the trees. The surf pounded the Washington beach far below. But directly in front of her was a narrow path that led straight into the rain forest.

"We don't have to wait for you guys, do we?" James whined. He and Peter were obviously eager to do some exploring on their own.

Carol was about to launch into a long list of cautions when Alex spoke. "Feel free," he told the two boys. "Carol and I will be back at camp in time for dinner. We'll expect you to be there then."

"Great!"

"All *right.*"

Within minutes both boys were out of sight, and Carol resumed the increasingly difficult climb. A mountain goat would've had trouble maneuvering this path, she told herself.

"You're doing fine," Alex said behind her. Breathless from the physical exertion required by the steep incline, Carol paused and took a couple of minutes to breathe deeply.

"I love it when you get all hot and sweaty for me."

"Will you stop," she cried, embarrassed and yet amused by his words.

"Never."

To complicate things, Alex moved with grace and skill, even while carrying a backpack. So far, he hadn't even worked up a sweat. Carol, on the other hand, was panting. She hadn't realized how out of shape she was until now.

"The view had better be worth all this effort," she said with a moan five minutes later. The muscles in her calves were beginning to protest, and her heart was pounding so hard it echoed in her ears.

To make matters worse, she'd worn the worst possible combination of clothes. Not knowing what to expect weather-wise, she'd donned heavy boots, jeans and a thick sweatshirt, plus a jacket. Her head was covered with a bright pink cap her mother had knitted for her last Christmas. Should they happen upon a snowstorm, Carol was prepared.

"It's worth the climb," Alex promised. "Do you want me to lead?"

"No way," she said, dismissing his offer. "I'd never be able to keep up with you."

A little while later, Carol staggered into a clearing. She stopped abruptly, astonished by the beauty that surrounded her. The forest she'd just left was dense with a variety of evergreens. Huge limbs were draped with mossy green blankets that hung down so far they touched the spongy ground. Moss-coated stumps dotted the area, some sprouting large white mushroom caps. Wildflowers carpeted the earth and a gentle breeze drifted through the meadow and, catching her breath, Carol removed her hat in a form of worship.

"You're right," she murmured. "This is wonderful...I feel

like I'm standing in a cathedral…this makes me want to pray."

"This isn't what I wanted you to see," Alex said, resting his hand on the curve of her shoulder.

"It isn't?" she whispered in disbelief. "You mean there's something better than this?"

"Follow me."

Carol pulled off her jacket, stuffed her hat into one of the pockets and tied the sleeves around her waist. Eagerly she trailed Alex along the winding narrow pathway.

"There's a freshwater cove about a mile from here," he explained, turning back to look at her. "Are you up to the trek?"

"I think so." She felt invigorated. More than that, she felt elated. *Alive.*

"You're being a good sport about all this," Alex said, smiling at her.

"I knew I was going to be okay when I saw that you'd pitched the tents close to the public restrooms. I'm not comfortable unless I'm near something that goes flush in the night."

Alex laughed. They hiked for another twenty minutes and eventually came to the edge of a cliff that fell sharply into the water. The view of bright green waves, contrasted by brilliant blue skies, was beautiful enough to bring tears to Carol's eyes. The park department had set up a chain-link fence along the edge, as well as a rough-hewn bench that had been carved out of an old tree trunk.

Alex gestured for her to sit down. Spreading her coat on the bench, Carol sat down and gazed out at the vista before her.

"You hungry?"

"Starving."

"I thought you would be." He slipped off his pack and set it in front of them. Then he unfastened the zipper and removed a folded plastic bag that resembled the ones Carol used to line her garbage cans.

"What's that?" she asked.

"A garbage bag."

"Oh." Well, that was what it looked like.

Next, he took out a whistle, which he held up for her inspection. "A whistle," he announced unnecessarily. Finally he found what he was searching for and placed a thick chocolate bar and two apples on the bench.

"Without appearing completely stupid," Carol said, biting into her apple, "may I ask why you hauled a garbage bag all the way up here?"

"In case we get lost."

"What?" she cried in alarm. She'd assumed Alex knew his way back to their campsite. He'd certainly implied as much.

"Even the best of hikers have been known to get lost. This is just a precaution."

"When…I mean, I thought you were experienced."

He wiggled his eyebrows suggestively. "I am."

"Alex, this is no time to joke."

"I'm not joking. The garbage bag, the whistle and the chocolate are all part of the hug-a-tree program."

"Hug-a-tree?"

"It's a way of preparing children, or anyone else for that matter, in case they get lost in the woods. The idea is to stay in one place—to literally hug a tree. The garbage bag is for warmth. If you slip inside it, feet first, and crouch down, gathering the opening around your neck, you can keep warm in near-freezing temperatures. It weighs practically nothing.

The whistle aids rescuers in locating whoever's lost, and the reason for the candy is obvious."

"Do you mean to tell me we're chowing down on our limited food rations?" Carol bit into her apple again before Alex could change his mind and take it away from her.

"Indeed we are, but then we're practically within sight of the campground, so I don't think we're in any danger of getting lost."

"Good." Too ravenous to care, Carol peeled the paper from the chocolate bar and took a generous bite.

"I was waiting for that," Alex murmured, setting aside his apple.

Carol paused, the candy bar in front of her mouth. "Why?"

"So I could kiss you and taste the chocolate on your lips." He reached for her, and his mouth found hers with such need, such hunger, that Carol groaned. Alex hadn't touched her in days, patiently giving her time to determine the boundaries of their relationship. Now she was starving for him, eager for his kiss, his touch.

His kiss was slow, so slow and deliberate. When he lifted his head Carol moaned and sagged against him.

"You taste sweet," he whispered, tugging at her lower lip with his teeth. "Even sweeter than I expected. Even sweeter than chocolate."

Chapter Nine

Her sleeping bag and air mattress didn't look as comfortable as a bed at the Hilton, but they appeared adequate, Carol decided later that night. At least Alex had enough equipment for the four of them. All Carol and Peter owned was one GI Joe sleeping bag, decorated with little green army men, and Carol wasn't particularly excited about having to sleep in that.

They'd hiked and explored most of the afternoon. By the time everything was cleared away after dinner, dusk had settled over Salt Creek Park. Carol was out of energy, but Peter and James insisted they couldn't officially call it camping unless everyone sat around the campfire, toasted marshmallows and sang silly songs. And so a lengthy songfest had ensued.

Carol was yawning when she crawled inside the small tent she was sharing with Peter. Alex and James's larger tent was pitched next to theirs. By the dim light of the lantern hanging from the middle of the tent, Carol undressed, cleaned her face and then slipped into the sleeping bag.

"Is it safe yet?" Peter yelled impatiently from outside the tent.

"Safe and sound," Carol returned. She'd just finished zipping up the bag when Peter pulled back the flap and stuck his head in.

Smiling, he withdrew, and she heard him whisper something to James about how unreasonable women could be. Carol didn't know what she'd done that could be considered unreasonable, and she was too drained to ask.

"Good night, everyone," Carol called out when Peter dimmed the lantern.

There was a mixed chorus of "good nights." Content, she rolled onto her stomach and closed her eyes.

Within minutes Carol was fast asleep.

"Carol."

She woke sometime later as her name was whispered close to her ear. Jerking her head up, she saw Alex kneeling just inside the tent, fully dressed. A shaft of moonlight showed her that he'd pressed his finger to his lips, indicating she should be quiet.

"What is it?"

"I want to show you something."

"Now?"

He grinned at her lack of enthusiasm and nodded.

"It can't wait until morning?" she said, yawning.

"It'll be gone by morning," he whispered. "Get dressed and meet me in five minutes."

She couldn't understand what was so important that she couldn't see it by the light of day.

"If you're not out here in five minutes," he warned in a husky voice from outside her tent, "I'm coming in after you."

Carol grumbled as she scurried around looking for her clothes. It was difficult to pull on her jeans in the cramped space, but with a few acrobatic moves, she managed. Before she crawled out, she tapped Peter's shoulder and told him she'd be back in a few minutes.

Peter didn't seem to care one way or the other.

Alex was waiting for her. His lazy smile wrapped its way around her heart and squeezed tight. For all her moaning and complaining about this camping trip, Carol was having a wonderful time.

"This had better be good," she warned and ingloriously yawned.

"It is," he promised. He held a flashlight and a blanket in one hand and reached for hers with the other. Then he led her toward the beach. Although she was wearing her jacket, the wind made her shiver. Alex must have noticed, because he slid his arm around her shoulder and drew her closer.

"Where are we going?" She found herself whispering, not sure why.

"To a rock."

"A rock," she repeated, incredulous. "You woke me from a sound sleep so I could see a *rock*?"

"Not see, sit on one."

"I couldn't do this at noon in the warm sun?" she muttered, laughing at him.

"Not if you're going to look at the stars."

Carol's step faltered. "Do you mean to tell me you rousted me from a warm, cozy sleeping bag in the middle of the night to show me a few stars? The very same stars I could see from my own bedroom window?"

Alex chuckled. "Are you always this testy when you just wake up?"

"Always," she told him. Yawning again, she covered her mouth with one hand.

Although the campsite was only a few feet away, it was completely hidden behind a clump of trees. Carol could hear the ocean—presumably at the bottom of some nearby cliff—but she couldn't see it.

"I suppose I should choose a tree now. Which one looks the friendliest to you?" Carol asked.

"A tree? Whatever for?"

"To hug. Didn't you tell me this afternoon that if I ever get lost in the woods a tree is my friend? If we get separated, there's no way I'd ever find my way back to camp."

Alex dropped a kiss on her head. "I won't let you out of my sight for a minute, I promise."

"The last time I trusted a guy, I was eighteen and I was pregnant three weeks later." She meant it as a joke, but once the words were out they seemed to hang in the air between them.

"You were only eighteen when you got married?"

Carol nodded, pulled her hand free from his and shoved it in the pocket of her jacket. She could feel herself withdrawing from him. She drew inside herself a little more.

They walked in silence for several minutes.

Suddenly Alex aimed the flashlight at the ground and paused. "This way."

"Over there?" Carol asked. She squinted but couldn't see any rock.

"Just follow me," Alex said. "And no more wisecracks about what happened the last time you listened to a guy. I'm not your first husband, and it would serve us both well if you remembered that." His words were light, teasing, but they sent Carol reeling.

He reached for her hand, lacing his fingers through hers. She could almost hear the litany of questions in Alex's mind. He wanted her to tell him about Bruce. But no one fully knew what a nightmare her marriage had been. Not even her mother. And Carol wasn't about to drag out all the pain for Alex to examine.

Within a couple of minutes, Alex had located "his" rock. At first Carol thought it looked like all the other rocks, silhouetted against the beach.

He climbed up the side, obviously familiar with its shape and size, then offered Carol his hand. Once they were perched on top, he spread out the blanket and motioned for her to sit down.

Carol did and pulled her knees under her chin.

Alex settled down beside her. "Now," he said, pointing toward the heavens, "can you see *that* outside your bedroom window?"

Having forgotten the purpose of this outing, Carol cast her gaze toward the dark sky, then straightened in wonder and surprise. The sky was so heavy with stars—hundreds, no, thousands of them—that it seemed to sag down and touch the earth. "Oh, Alex," she breathed.

"Worth waking up for?" he asked.

"Well worth it," she said, thanking him with a smile.

"I thought you'd think so." His returning smile flew straight into her heart.

She'd been struck by so much extraordinary beauty in such a short while that she felt almost overwhelmed. Turning her head slightly, she smiled again at this man who had opened her eyes to life, to beauty, to love and whispered fervently, "Thank you, Alex."

"For what?"

"For the hike in the rain forest, for the view of the cove, for ignoring my complaints and showing me the stars, for... everything." For coming into her life. For leading her by the hand. For being so patient with her.

"You're welcome."

Lost in the magic, Carol closed her eyes and inhaled the fragrant scent of the wind, the ocean and the night. Rarely had she experienced this kind of contentment and uncomplicated happiness.

When the breeze came, the trees whispered, and the sound combined with the crashing of the surf below. The scents of pine and sea drifted over her. Throwing back her head, Carol tried to take it all in.

"I don't think I appreciated how truly beautiful you are until now," Alex murmured. His face was carved in severe but sensual lines, and his eyes had darkened with emotion.

Carol turned, and when she did, he brushed back the curls from her cheek. His hand lingered on her face, and Carol covered it with her own, closing her eyes at all the sensations that accompanied his touch.

He brought his free hand to her hair, which he threaded through his fingers as though the texture was pure silk. He traced her lower lip with his finger. Unable to resist, Carol circled it with the tip of her tongue....

Time seemed to stand still as Alex's eyes sought and held hers.

He kissed her, and it was excruciatingly slow. Exquisitely slow.

He pressed warm kisses in the hollow of her neck and slipped his hands inside her jacket, circling her waist and bringing her closer. "The things you do to me," he said in a low voice.

"The things I do to *you?*" She rested her forehead against his own. "They can't compare to what you do—have always done—to me."

His lips twitched with the beginnings of a smile, and Carol leaned forward just enough to kiss him again.

Under her jacket Alex slid his hands up her back. He stopped abruptly, went still and tore his mouth from hers.

"What's wrong?" Carol asked, lifting her head. Her hands were on his shoulders.

"You're not wearing a bra, are you?"

"No. You said I had only five minutes to dress, so I hurried."

His eyes burned into hers, then moved lower to the snap of her jeans. "Did you...take any other shortcuts?"

"Wanna find out?"

He shook his head wildly. "I...I promised myself when you agreed to go camping that I'd do everything I could to keep my hands off you." Although she was still in his arms, Carol had to strain to hear him.

"I think that was a wise decision," she murmured, looking up at him. Alex's expression was filled with surprise. An inner happiness she'd banished from her life so long ago she hadn't known it was missing pulsed through her now.

When he finally released her, Carol was so weak with longing that she clung to him, breathing deeply.

"Carol," he said, watching her closely as she shifted positions. She climbed onto his lap, wrapped her legs around his waist and threw her arms around his neck.

"Oh...Carol." Alex moaned and closed his eyes.

"Shhh," she whispered, kissing him deeply. He didn't speak again for a long, long time. Neither did she...

Thursday afternoon, with a stethoscope around her neck, Carol walked down the hospital corridor to the nurses' station. Her steps were brisk and her heart heavy. She hadn't talked to Alex since late Sunday, when he'd dropped Peter and her at the house after their camping trip. There could be any number of excellent reasons why he hadn't called or stopped by. Maybe he was simply too busy; that made sense. Maybe he didn't want to see her again; perhaps he'd decided to start dating other women. Younger women. Prettier women. He was certainly handsome enough. Perhaps aliens had captured him, and he was trapped in some spaceship circling uncharted universes.

Whatever the reason, it translated into one glaring, inescapable fact. She hadn't seen or heard from Alex in four days. However, she reminded herself, she didn't need a man to make her happy. She didn't need a relationship.

"There's a call for you on line one," Betty Mills told her. "Want me to take a message?"

"Did the person give a name?"

"Alex Preston. He sounds sexy, too," Betty added in a succulent voice. "I don't suppose he's that handsome guy you were having lunch with a little while ago."

Carol's heart slammed against her ribs—first with alarm and then with relief. She'd done everything she could to ignore the gaping hole in her life without Alex there. All it would've taken was a phone call—she could have contacted him. She could've asked Peter to talk to James. She could've driven over to his house. But she'd done none of those things.

"Carol? Do you want me to take a message or not?" Betty asked.

"No, I'll get it."

Betty laughed. "I would, too, if I were you." With that, she turned and marched away.

Carol moved to the nurses' station and was grateful no one else was around to overhear her conversation. "This is Carol Sommars," she said as professionally as she could manage.

"Carol, it's Alex."

His words burned in her ears. "Hello, Alex," she said, hoping she didn't sound terribly stiff. Her pulse broke into a wild, absurd rhythm at his voice, and despite her best efforts, a warm sense of happiness settled over her.

"I'm sorry to call you at the hospital, but I haven't been able to reach you at home for the past few nights."

"I've been busy." Busy trying to escape the loneliness. Busy ignoring questions she didn't want to answer. Busy hiding.

"Yes, I know," Alex said impatiently. "Are you avoiding me?"

"I…I thought you…if you want the truth, I assumed you'd decided not to see me again."

"Not *see* you," he repeated loudly. "Are you crazy? I'm nuts about you."

"Oh." Her mouth trembled, but whether it was from irritation or sheer blessed relief, Carol didn't know. If he was nuts about her, why had he neglected her all week? Why hadn't he at least left her a message?

"You honestly haven't figured out how I feel about you yet?"

"You haven't been at the school in the past few days, and since I didn't hear from you it made sense—to me, anyway—that you wanted to cool things down, and I don't blame you. Things are getting much too hot and much too…well, fast, and personally I thought that…well, that it was for the best."

"You thought *what?*" he demanded, his voice exploding over the wire. "When I get home the first thing I'm going to do is kiss some sense into you."

"When you get home?"

"I'm in Houston."

"Texas?"

"Is there any other?"

Carol didn't know. "What are you doing there?"

"Wishing I was in Portland, mostly. A friend of mine, another contractor, is involved in a huge project here and ran into problems. There must've been five messages from him when we returned from the camping trip. He needed some help right away."

"What about James? He isn't with you, is he?"

"He's staying with another friend of mine. I've probably mentioned him before. His name is Barney."

Vaguely Carol *did* remember either Alex or James mentioning the man, but she couldn't remember where or when she'd heard it. "How…long will you be gone?" She hated the way her voice fell, the way it made her need for him all too evident.

"Another week at least."

Her heart catapulted to her feet, then gradually righted itself. "A *week?*"

"I don't like it any better than you do. I can't believe how much I miss you. How much I needed to hear your voice."

Carol felt that, too, only she hadn't been willing to admit it, even to herself.

There was a slight commotion on Alex's end of the line and when it cleared, he said, "I'll try to call you again, but we're working day and night and this is the first real break I've had in three days. I'm glad I got through to you."

Her grip tightened on the receiver. "I'm glad, too."

"I have to go. Bye, Carol. I'll see you Thursday or so of next week."

"Goodbye, Alex...and thanks for phoning." She was about to hang up when she realized there was something else she had to say. She cried his name, desperate to catch him before he hung up.

"I'm here. What is it?"

"Alex," she said, sighing with relief. "I've...I want you to know I...I've missed you, too."

The sound of his chuckle was as warm and melodious as a hundred-voice choir. "It's not much, but it's something. Keep next Thursday open for me, okay?"

"You've got yourself a date."

Tuesday evening of the following week, Carol was teaching her birthing class. Ten couples were sprawled on big pillows in front of her as she led them through a series of exercises. She enjoyed this work almost as much as she did her daytime job at the hospital. She and Janice Mandle each taught part of the class, with Carol handling the first half.

"Everyone's doing exceptionally well tonight," Carol said, praising the teams. "Okay, partners, I have a question for you. I want you to tell me, in number of seconds, how long you think a typical labor pain lasts."

"Thirty seconds," one young man shouted out.

"Longer," Carol said.

"Sixty seconds," yelled another.

Carol shook her head.

"Ninety?"

"You don't sound too sure about that," Carol said, smiling. "Let's stick with ninety seconds. That's a nice round number, although in the final stages of labor it's not unusual for a contraction to last much longer."

The pregnant women eyed each other warily.

"All right, partners, I want you to show me your biceps. Tighten them as hard as you can. Good. Good," she said, surveying the room, watching as several of the men brought up their fists until the muscles of their upper arms bulged. "Make it as tight and as painful as you can," she continued. Most of the men were gritting their teeth.

"Very good," she went on to say. "Now, hold that until I tell you to relax." She walked to the other side of the room. "As far back as 1913, some doctors and midwives recognized that fear and tension could interfere with the birthing process. Even then they believed that deep breathing exercises and relaxation could aid labor." She paused to glance at her watch. "That's fifteen seconds."

The look of astonishment that crossed the men's faces was downright comical.

"Keep those muscles tightly clenched," Carol instructed. She strolled around the room, chatting amiably as the men held their arms as tight as possible. Some were already showing the strain.

"Thirty seconds," she announced.

Her words were followed by a low groan. Carol couldn't help smiling. She hated to admit how much she enjoyed their discomfort, but this exercise was an excellent illustration of the realities of labor, especially for the men. The smile remained on her lips as the door in the back of the room opened to admit a latecomer. Carol opened her mouth to welcome the person, but the words didn't reach her lips.

There, framed inside the door, stood Alex Preston.

Chapter Ten

Carol stared at Alex. Alex stared at Carol.

The room went completely still; the air felt heavy, and the quiet seemed eerie, unnatural. It wasn't until Carol realized that several taut faces were gazing up at her anxiously that she pulled her attention away from Alex and back to her class.

"Now, where were we?" she asked, flustered and nervous.

"Ninety seconds," one of the men shouted.

"Oh. Right." She glanced at her watch and nodded. "Ninety seconds."

The relief could be felt all the way across the room.

A few minutes later Carol dismissed everyone for a fifteen-minute break. Janice strolled over to Carol and eyed the back of the room, where Alex was patiently waiting. He was leaning against the back wall, his ankles crossed and his thumbs hooked in the belt loop of his jeans.

"He's gorgeous."

Carol felt too distracted and tongue-tied to respond, although her thoughts had been traveling along those same lines. Alex was the sexiest man Carol had ever known. Unabashedly wonderful, too.

"He's…been out of town," she said, her eyes magnetically drawn to Alex's.

Janice draped her arm across Carol's shoulders. "Since your portion of tonight's class is finished, why don't you go ahead and leave?"

"I couldn't." Carol tore her eyes from Alex long enough to study her co-teacher. They were a team, and although they'd divided the class into two distinct sections, they stayed and lent each other emotional support.

"Yes, you can. I insist. Only…"

"Only what?" Carol pressed.

"Only promise me that if another gorgeous guy walks in off the street and looks at me like he's looking at you, you'll return the favor."

"Of course," Carol answered automatically.

Janice's voice fell to a whisper. "Good. Then we'll consider this our little secret."

Carol frowned. "I don't understand—what do you mean, our little secret?"

"Well, if my husband found out about this agreement, there could be problems."

Carol laughed. Janice was happily married and had been for fifteen years.

"If I were you I wouldn't be hanging around here talking," Janice murmured, giving Carol a small shove. "Don't keep him waiting any longer."

"Okay…thanks." Feeling unaccountably shy, Carol retrieved her purse and her briefcase and walked toward Alex. With each step that drew her nearer, her heart felt lighter. By the time she made her way to the back of the room, she felt nearly airborne.

He straightened, his eyes warm and caressing. "Hello."

"Hi."

"Peter told me you were teaching tonight and where. I hope you don't mind that I dropped in unexpectedly."

"I don't mind." *Mind?* Her heart was soaring with gladness. She could've flown without an airplane. No, she didn't mind that he'd dropped in—not in the least.

For the longest moment all they did was gaze at each other like starry-eyed lovers.

A noise at the front of the room distracted Carol. She glanced over her shoulder and saw several couples watching them with undisguised curiosity.

"Janice said she'd finish up here, and I could…should leave now."

Alex grinned, and with that, Carol could feel whole sections of the sturdy wall around her heart start to crumble. This man's smile was nothing short of lethal.

"Remind me to thank her later," Alex said. He removed the briefcase from her unresisting fingers and opened the door, letting her precede him outside.

They hadn't taken two steps out the door when Alex paused. Carol felt his hesitation and stopped, turning to face him. That was when she knew Alex was going to kiss her. It didn't matter that they were standing in front of a public building. It didn't matter that it was still light enough for any number of passersby to see them. It didn't matter that they were both respected professionals.

Alex scooped her into his arms and with a lavish sigh lowered his head and covered her lips in the sweetest, wildest kiss of her life.

"I've missed you," he whispered. "The hours felt like years, the days like decades."

Carol felt tears in the corners of her eyes. She hadn't thought about how empty her life had felt without him, how bleak and alone she was with him away. Now it poured out of her in a litany of sighs and kisses. "I…I missed you, too—so much."

For years she'd been content in her own secure world, the one she'd created for herself and her son. The borders had been narrow, confining, but she'd made peace with herself and found serenity. Then she'd met Alex, and he'd forced her to notice how cramped and limited her existence was. Not only that, he'd pointed toward the horizon, to a new land of shared dreams.

When Alex spoke again, his voice was heavy with need. "Come on, let's get out of here."

She nodded and followed him to his car, ready to abandon her own with little more than a second thought.

He unlocked the passenger door, then turned to face her. His eyes were dancing with excitement. "Let's dispense with formalities and elope. Now. Tonight. This minute."

The words hit her hard. She blinked at the unexpectedness of his suggestion, prepared to laugh it off as a joke.

But Alex was serious. He looked as shocked as Carol felt, but she noted that the idea had begun to gain momentum. The mischievous spark in his eyes was gone, replaced by a solemn look.

"I love you, Carol. I love you so much that my buddy in Texas practically threw me on the plane and told me to get home before I died of it. He said he'd never seen anyone more lovesick and made me promise we'd name one of our children after him."

The mention of a child was like a right cross to the jaw after his punch to her solar plexus, and she flinched involuntarily.

Alex set his hands on her shoulders, and a smile touched his eyes and then his mouth. He smiled so endearingly that all of Carol's arguments fled like dust in a whirlwind.

"Say something."

"Ah…my car's parked over there." She pointed in the general vicinity of her Ford. Her throat was so tight she could hardly speak.

He laughed and hugged her. "I know this is sudden for you. I'm a fool not to have done it properly. I swear I'll do it again over champagne and give you a diamond so large you'll sink in a swimming pool, but I can't keep the way I feel inside anymore."

"Alex…"

He silenced her with a swift kiss. "Believe me, blurting out a proposal like this is as much of a surprise to me as it is to you. I had no idea I was going to ask you tonight. The entire flight home I was trying to figure out how I could make it as romantic as possible. The last thing I expected to do was impulsively shout it out in a parking lot. But something happened tonight." He reached for her limp hands and brought them to his lips, then kissed her knuckles with reverence. "When I walked into your class and saw you with all those pregnant women, I was hit with the most powerful shock of my life." His voice grew quiet. "All of a sudden, my mind conjured up the image of you pregnant with our child, and I swear it was all I could do not to break down and weep." He paused long enough to run his fingers through his hair. "Children, Carol…our children." He closed his eyes and sighed deeply.

Carol felt frozen. The chill worked its way from her heart,

the icy circles growing larger and more encompassing until the cold extended down her arms and legs and into her fingers and toes.

"I know this is abrupt, and I'm probably ruining the moment, but say something," Alex urged. "Anything."

Carol's mind refused to function properly. Panic was closing in, panic and a hundred misgivings. "I...don't know what to tell you."

Alex threw back his head and laughed. "I don't blame you. All right," he said, his eyes flashing, "repeat after me. I, Carol Sommars." He glanced expectantly at her.

"I...Carol Sommars..."

"Am crazy in love with Alex Preston." He waited for her to echo his words.

"Am crazy in love with Alex Preston."

"Good," he whispered and leaned forward just enough to brush his mouth over hers. His arms slipped around her, locking at the small of her back and dragging her unresistingly toward him. "You know, the best part about those babies is going to be making them."

A blush rose up her neck, coloring her cheeks with what she felt sure was a highly uncomplimentary shade of pink. Her eyes darted away from his.

"Now all you need to do is say *yes*," Alex said.

"I can't. I...don't know." To her horror, she started to sob, not with the restrained tears of a confused woman, but the harsh mournful cries of one in anguish.

Alex had apparently expected anything but tears. "Carol? What's wrong? What did I say?" He wrapped his arms around her and brought her head to his shoulder.

Carol wanted to resist his touch, but she so desperately needed it that she buried her face in the curve of his neck and wept. Alex's arms were warm and safe, his hands gentle. She did love him. Somewhere between his rescue the night her car broke down and the camping trip, her well-guarded heart had succumbed to his appeal. But falling in love was one thing; marriage and children were something else entirely.

"Come on," Alex finally said. He opened the car door for her.

"Where are we going?" she asked, sniffling.

"My house. James won't be home yet, and we can talk without being disturbed."

Carol wasn't sure what more he could say, but she agreed with a nod of her head and climbed inside. He closed the door for her, then paused and ran a hand over his eyes, slumping wearily.

Neither of them said much during the ten-minute drive. He helped her out of his car, then unlocked the front door to his house. His suitcases had been haphazardly dumped on the living room carpet. When he saw Carol looking at them, he said simply, "I was in a hurry to find you." He led the way into the kitchen and started making a pot of coffee.

Carol pulled out a stool at the counter and seated herself. His kitchen—in fact, his home—wasn't at all what she expected. A woman's touch could be seen and felt in every room. The kitchen was yellow and cheery. What remained of the evening light shone through the window above the sink, sending warm shadows across the polished tile floor. Matching ceramic canisters lined the counter, along with a row of well-used cookbooks.

"Okay, Carol, tell me what's on your mind," Alex urged, facing her from behind the tile counter. Even then Carol wasn't safe from his magnetism.

"That's the problem," she said, swallowing hard. "I don't *know* what's on my mind. I'm so confused...."

"I realize my proposal came out of the blue, but once you think about it, you'll understand how perfect we are for each other. Surely you've thought about it yourself."

"No," she said quickly, and for emphasis, shook her head. "I hadn't...not once. Marriage hadn't occurred to me."

"I see." He raised his right hand to rub his eyes again.

Carol knew he must be exhausted and was immediately overcome with remorse. She *did* love Alex, although admitting it—to herself as much as to him—had sapped her strength.

"What do you want to do?" he asked softly.

"I'm not sure," she whispered, staring down at her hands, which were tightly clenched in her lap.

"Would some time help?"

She nodded eagerly.

"How long?"

"A year. Several months. At the very least, three or four weeks."

"How about two weeks?" Alex suggested.

"Two weeks," she echoed feebly. That wasn't nearly enough. She couldn't possibly reach such an important decision in so little time, especially when there were other factors to consider. Before she could voice a single excuse, Alex pressed his finger to her lips.

"If you can't decide in that length of time, then I doubt you ever will."

A protest came and went in a single breath. There were so many concerns he hadn't mentioned—like their sons!

She was about to bring this up when Alex said, "I don't

think we should draw the boys into this until we know our own minds. The last thing we need is pressure from them."

Carol agreed completely.

The coffee had finished perking, and Alex poured them each a cup. "How about dinner Friday night? Just the two of us." At her hesitation, he added, "I'll give you the rest of this week to sort through your thoughts, and if you still have any questions or doubts by Friday, we can discuss them then."

"But not a final decision?" Carol murmured, uneasy with the time limitation. He'd said two weeks, and she was going to need every minute to make up her mind.

Carol woke around three with her stomach in painful knots. She lay on her side and at a breath-stopping cramp, she tucked her knees under her chin. A wave of nausea hit her hard, and she couldn't stifle a groan. Despite her flu shot last fall, maybe she'd caught one of the new strains that emerged every year.

She lay perfectly still in the fervent hope that this would ward off her growing need to vomit. It didn't work, and a moment later she was racing for the bathroom.

Afterward, sitting on the floor, her elbows on the edge of the toilet, she breathed deeply.

"Are you all right?" Peter asked from behind her.

"I will be. I just need a couple more minutes."

"What's wrong?" Peter asked. He handed her a warm washcloth, following that with a cup of water.

"The flu, I guess."

He helped her to her feet and walked her back to her bedroom. "I appreciate the help, Peter, but it would be better if you went back to bed. I'll be fine by morning."

"I'll call work for you and tell them you're too sick to come in."

She shook her head. "No...I'll need to talk to them myself." Her son dutifully arranged the blankets around her, giving her a worried look before he slipped out of her bedroom.

Peter must have turned off her alarm because the next thing Carol knew it was eight-thirty. The house was eerily silent.

Sitting up, she waited for an attack of nausea. It didn't come. She'd slept without waking even once. She was astonished that she hadn't heard Peter roaming about. He was usually as noisy as a herd of rampaging buffalo. Perhaps he'd overslept as well.

In case he had, she threw the sheets back, sat on the edge of the bed and shoved her feet into slippers before wandering into the kitchen. The minute she stepped inside, it was obvious that her son had been up and about. A box of cold cereal stood in the middle of the kitchen table, along with a bowl half-filled with milk and crusts from several pieces of toast.

Posted on the refrigerator door was a note from Peter, informing her that he'd phoned the hospital and talked to her supervisor, who'd said Carol didn't need to worry about coming in. He proudly added that he'd made his own lunch and that he'd find a ride home from track practice, so she should stay in bed and drink lots of fluids. In a brief postscript he casually mentioned that he'd also called Grandma Pasquale.

Carol's groan had little to do with the way she was feeling. All she needed was her mother, bless her heart, hovering over her and driving her slowly but surely crazy. No sooner had the thought formed in her mind than the doorbell chimed, followed by a key turning in the lock and the front door flying open. Her mother burst into the house as though Carol lay on her deathbed.

"Carol," she cried, walking through the living room. "What are you doing out of bed?"

"I'm feeling much better, Mama."

"You look terrible. Get back in bed before the undertaker gets wind of how you look."

"Ma, please, I'm just a little under the weather."

"That's what my uncle Giuseppe said when he had the flu, God rest his soul. His wife never even got the chicken stewed, he went that fast." She pressed her hands together, raised her eyes to the ceiling and murmured a silent prayer.

"Peter shouldn't have phoned you," Carol grumbled. She certainly didn't need her mother fussing at her bedside, spooning chicken soup down her throat every time she opened her mouth.

"Peter did the right thing. He's a good boy."

At the moment Carol considered that point debatable.

"Now back to bed before you get a dizzy spell." Her mother made a shooing motion with her hands.

Mumbling under her breath, Carol did as Angelina insisted. Not because she felt especially ill, but because arguing required too much energy. Carol might as well try to talk her mother into using canned spaghetti sauce as convince her she wasn't on her deathbed.

Once Carol was lying down, Angelina dragged the rocking chair into her bedroom and sat down. Before another minute had passed, she was busy with her knitting. Several balls of yarn were lying at her feet in case she wanted to start a second or third project in the next few hours.

"According to Peter you were sick in the middle of the night," Angelina said. Eyes narrowed, she studied Carol, as if staring would reveal the exact nature of her daughter's illness. She shook her head, then paused to count the neat row of stitches before glancing back at Carol, clearly expecting an answer.

"It must've been something I ate for dinner," she suggested lamely.

"Peter said you were looking at parts of a toilet no one should see that close up."

Her teenage son certainly had a way with words. "I'm feeling better," she said weakly.

"Your face is paler than bleached sheets. Uncle Giuseppe has more color than you, and he's been in his grave for thirty years."

Carol leaned back against the pillows and closed her eyes. She might be able to fool just about anyone else, but her mother knew her too well.

Several tense minutes passed. Angelina said not a word, patient to a fault. Yes, her mother knew; Carol was sure of it. She kept her eyes closed, afraid that another searching look would reveal everything. Oh, what the heck, Angelina would find out sooner or later.

"Alex asked me to marry him last night." Carol tried to keep her voice even, but it shook noticeably.

"Ah," her mother said, nodding. "That explains everything. From the time you were a little girl, you got an upset stomach whenever something troubled you, although why you should be troubled when this man tells you he loves you is a whole other question."

Carol didn't need to hear stories from her childhood to recognize the truth.

"So what did you say to him?"

"Nothing," she whispered.

"This man brings color to your cheeks and a smile to your eyes and you said *nothing?*"

"I...need time to think," Carol cried. "This is an important decision.... I've got more than myself and my own life to consider. Alex has a son and I have a son.... It isn't as simple as it sounds."

Her mother shook her head. Her rocker was going ninety miles an hour, and Carol was positive the older woman's thoughts were churning at equal speed.

"Don't be angry with me, Mama," she whispered. "I'm so frightened."

Angelina stopped abruptly and set her knitting aside. She reached for Carol's hands, holding them gently. A soft smile lit her eyes. "You'll make the right decision."

"How can you be so sure? I've been wrong about so many things—I've made so many mistakes in my life. I don't trust my own judgment anymore."

"Follow your heart," Angelina urged. "It won't lead you wrong."

But it would. She'd followed her heart when she married Bruce, convinced their love would see them through every difficulty. The marriage had been a disaster from the honeymoon on, growing more painful and more difficult with each passing day. The horror of those years with Bruce had shredded her heart and drained away all her self-confidence. She'd offered her husband everything she had to give, relinquished her pride and self-respect—and to what end? Bruce hadn't appreciated her sacrifices. He hadn't cherished her love, but turned it into something cheap and expendable.

"Whatever you decide will be right," her mother said once again. "I know it will be."

Carol closed her eyes to mull over her mother's confidence in her, which she was sure was completely unfounded. Angelina seemed to trust Carol's judgment more than Carol did herself.

A few minutes later, her mother started to sing softly, and her sweet, melodious voice harmonized with the clicking of the needles.

The next thing Carol knew, it was early afternoon and she could smell chicken soup simmering in the kitchen.

Angelina had left a brief note for her that was filled with warmth and encouragement. Feeling much better, Carol helped herself to a bowl of the broth and noodles and leisurely enjoyed her first nourishment of the day.

By the time Peter slammed into the house several hours later, she was almost back to normal.

"Mom," he said rushing into the room. His face was flushed and his eyes bright. It looked as though he'd run all the way home. His chest was heaving as he dropped his books on the table, then tried to catch his breath, arms waving excitedly.

"What is it?" Carol asked, amused by the sight her son made.

"Why didn't you *say* anything?" he demanded, kissing both her cheeks the way her mother did whenever she was exceptionally pleased. "This is great, Mom, really great! Now we can go fishing and camping and hiking all the time."

"Say anything about what?" she asked in bewilderment. "And what's this about fishing?"

"Marrying Mr. Preston."

Carol was half out of her seat before she even realized she'd moved. "Who told you…who so much as mentioned it was a possibility?"

"A possibility?" Peter repeated. "I thought it was a done deal. At least that's what James said."

"James told you?"

Peter gave her a perplexed look. "Who else? He told me about it first thing when I got to school this morning." He studied her, his expression cautious. "Hey, Mom, don't look so upset—I'm sorry if you were keeping it a secret. Don't worry, James and I think it's a great idea. I've always wanted a brother, and having one who's my best friend is even better."

Carol was so outraged she could barely talk. "H-he had no business saying a word!" she stammered.

"Who? James?"

"Not James. Alex." If he thought he'd use the boys to influence her decision, he had another think coming.

Carol marched into her bedroom, throwing on a pair of jeans and an old sweatshirt. Then she hurried into the living room without bothering to run a brush through her tousled hair.

"Where are you going?" Peter demanded. He'd ladeled himself a bowl of soup and was following her around the house like a puppy while she searched for her purse and car keys.

"Out," Carol stormed.

"Looking like that?" He sounded aghast.

Carol whirled around, hands on her hips, and glared at him.

Peter raised one hand. "Sorry. Only please don't let Mr. Preston see you, all right?"

"Why not?"

Peter raised his shoulder in a shrug. "If he gets a look at you, he might withdraw his proposal. Honestly, Mom, this is the best thing that's happened to us in years. Don't go ruining it."

Chapter Eleven

James answered the door, and a smile automatically came to his lips when he saw it was Carol. Then his eyes narrowed as though he wasn't sure it was her, after all. Carol realized he was probably taken aback by her appearance. Normally she was well-dressed and well-groomed, but what Alex had done—had tried to do—demanded swift and decisive action. She didn't feel it was necessary to wear makeup for this confrontation.

"Where is he?" Carol asked through gritted teeth.

"Who? Dad?" James frowned. "He's watching the news." The teenager pointed toward the family room, which was adjacent to the kitchen.

Without waiting for James to escort her inside, Carol burst past him, intent on giving Alex a piece of her mind. She was furious. More than furious. If he'd honestly believed that involving the boys would affect her decision, then he knew absolutely nothing about her. In fact, he knew so little, they had no business even considering marriage.

She refused to be pressured, tricked, cajoled or anything

else, and before this day was over Alex would recognize that very clearly indeed.

"Carol?" Alex met her halfway into the kitchen. His eyes softened perceptibly as he reached for her.

Carol stopped just short of his embrace. "How dare you," she snapped.

"How dare I?" Alex repeated. His eyes widened with surprise, but he remained infuriatingly calm. "Would you elaborate, please, because I'm afraid I have no idea what you're talking about."

"Oh, yes, you do."

"Dad?" James ventured into the kitchen, giving Carol a wide berth. "Something must really be wrong," the boy said, and then his voice dropped to a whisper as he pointed to Carol's feet. "Mrs. Sommars is wearing two different shoes."

Carol's gaze shot downward, and she mentally groaned. But if either of the Preston men thought they'd throw her off her guard by pointing out that she'd worn a blue tennis shoe on her right foot and a hot-pink slipper on her left, then she had news for them both.

"I have the feeling Mrs. Sommars was in a hurry to talk to me," Alex explained. The smile that quivered at the corners of his mouth did little to quell her brewing temper.

James nodded. "Do you want me to get lost for a few minutes?"

"That might be a good plan," Alex replied.

James exchanged a knowing look with his father before discreetly vacating the room. As soon as Carol heard James's bedroom door close, she put her hands on her hips, determined to confront Alex.

"How dare you bring the boys into this," she flared.

"Into what?" Alex walked over to the coffeepot and got

two mugs. He held one up to her, but she refused the offer with a shake of her head. "I'm sorry, Carol, but I don't know what you're talking about."

Jabbing her index finger at him, she took several steps toward him. "Don't give me that, Alex Preston. You know very well what I mean. We agreed to wait, and you saw an advantage and without any compunction, you took it! Did you really think dragging Peter and James into this would help? How could you be so foolish?" Her voice shook, but her eyes were as steady as she could make them.

"I didn't mention the possibility of our getting married to James, and I certainly didn't say anything to Peter." He leaned against the kitchen counter and returned her disbelieving glare with maddening composure.

Angrily Carol threw back her head. "I don't believe you."

His eyes hardened but he didn't argue with her. "Ask James then. If he heard that I'd proposed to you, the information didn't come from me."

"You don't expect me to believe that, do you?" she cried, not nearly as confident as she'd been earlier. The aggression had gone out of her voice, and she lowered her hands to her sides, less certain with each minute. The ground that supported her outrage started to shift and crumble.

"I told you I wouldn't bring the boys into this," he reminded her smoothly. "And I didn't." He looked over his shoulder and shouted for James, who opened his bedroom door immediately. Carol didn't doubt for an instant that he'd had his ear pressed to it the entire time they'd been talking.

With his hands in his jean pockets, James strolled casually into the room. "Yes, Dad?"

"Do you want to tell me about it?"

"About what?" James wore a look of complete innocence.

"Apparently you said something to Peter about the relationship between Mrs. Sommars and me. I want to know what it was and where you found out about it." Alex hadn't so much as raised his voice, but Carol recognized that he expected the truth and wouldn't let up until he got it.

"Oh…that," James muttered. "I sort of overheard you saying something to Uncle Barn."

"Uncle Barn?" Carol asked.

"A good friend of mine. He's the one I was telling you about who kept Jim while I was out of town."

"Call me *James*," his son reminded him.

Alex lifted both hands. "Sorry."

"Anyway," James went on to say, "you were on the phone last night talking to him about the basketball game tonight, and I heard you say that you'd *asked* Carol—Mrs. Sommars. I'm not stupid, Dad. I knew you were talking about the two of you getting married, and I thought that Peter and I had a right to know. You should've said something to us first, don't you think?"

"For starters, this whole marriage business is up in the air—when and if anything's decided, you two boys will be the first to find out."

"What do you mean, the wedding's up in the air?" This piece of information obviously took James by surprise. "Why? What's the holdup? Peter and I think it's a great idea. We'd like it if you two got married. It'd be nice to have a woman around the house. For one thing, your cooking could use some help. But if you married Mrs. Sommars—"

"James," Alex broke in, "I think it's time for you to go back to your room before Carol decides she wants nothing more to do with the likes of us."

James looked affronted, but without further questions, he pivoted and marched back into his bedroom.

Alex waited until his son was out of sight. He sighed loudly and rammed his fingers through his hair. "I'm sorry, Carol. I had no idea James overheard my conversation with Barney. I thought he was asleep, but I should've been more careful."

"I…understand," Carol whispered, mollified.

"Contrary to what James just said," Alex continued, the line of his mouth tight and unyielding, "I don't want to marry you for your cooking skills. I couldn't care less if you never cooked again. I love you, and I'm hoping we can make a good life together."

James tossed open his bedroom door and stuck out his head. "Peter says she's as good a cook as his grandmother. She's—"

Alex sent his son a look hot enough to melt tar.

James quickly withdrew his head and just as quickly closed his door.

"I'll talk to Peter and explain the mix-up, if you'd like," Alex offered.

"No…I'll say something to him." Suddenly self-conscious, Carol swung her arms at her sides and retreated a couple of steps. "I suppose I should get home…."

"You were sick last night?" Alex asked, his expression concerned. "James told me when I picked him up after school. I would gladly have given Peter a ride, but he'd apparently found another way because he was gone before James could find him."

"Peter decided to run home."

"But you *had* been ill?"

She nodded. "I…must've caught a twenty-four-hour bug." Her eyes darted around the room. She felt so foolish, standing there with her hair a tangled mess, wearing the oldest clothes she owned, not to mention mismatched shoes.

"You're feeling better today?"

"A lot better. Thank you." She was slowly but surely edging toward the front door. The sooner she escaped, the better it would be for everyone involved. If Alex was merciful, he'd never mention this visit again.

She was all the way across the living room and had just reached the front door, when Alex appeared behind her. As she whirled around, he flattened his hands on either side of her head.

"Have you come to a decision?" he asked softly. His gaze dropped to her mouth. "Do you need any help?"

"The only thing I've managed to come up with is the flu," she murmured in a feeble attempt at humor. Alex wasn't amused, however, and she rushed to add, "Obviously you want to know which way I'm leaning, but I haven't had time to give your proposal much thought. I will, I promise I will... soon." She realized she was chattering, but couldn't seem to stop. "We're still on for Friday night, aren't we? We can discuss it then and—"

The doorbell chimed, frightening Carol out of her wits. She gasped and automatically catapulted herself into Alex's arms. He apparently didn't need an excuse to hold her close. When he released her several awkward seconds later, he smiled at her, then kissed the tip of her upturned nose.

"That'll be Barney now. It's time the two of you met."

"*That* was Carol Sommars?" Barney asked for the third time. He scratched his jaw and continued to frown. "No wonder Bambi mistook her for a bag lady. I'm sorry, man, you're my best friend and we've been buddies for a lot of years, but I've got to tell you, you can do better than that."

Chuckling, Alex dismissed his friend's statement and walked into the family room. If he lived to be a hundred, he'd never forget Carol's mortified look as she bolted from the house.

Barney certainly hadn't helped the situation any. Doing his best to keep a straight face, Alex had introduced the two. Barney's eyes had widened and his mouth had slowly dropped open in disbelief. It took a moment before he had the presence of mind to step forward and accept Carol's outstretched hand. Barney had mumbled that it was a pleasure to finally meet her, but his eyes had said something else entirely.

"Trust me," Alex felt obliged to explain, "she doesn't always look like that."

Barney stalked over to the refrigerator and opened it. He stared inside for a long time before he reached for a cold beer. "What time do the Trail Blazers play?"

Alex checked his watch. Both he and Barney were keen fans of Portland's professional basketball team. The team had been doing well this year and were in the first round of the play-offs. "Seven."

"So," Barney said, making himself comfortable in the overstuffed chair. He crossed his legs and took a long swig of beer. "What happened to her foot?" he asked casually. "Did she sprain it?"

"Whose foot?"

"Carol's," Barney said, casting Alex a questioning glance. "She was wearing a slipper—you mean you didn't notice? Did she twist her ankle?"

"Nah," James answered for Alex, wandering into the family room holding a bag of pretzels. He plopped himself down on the sofa, resting his legs on the coffee table. "Peter says she does weird stuff like that all the time. Once she wore his swimming goggles in the shower."

Barney raised his eyebrows. "Should I ask why?"

"It made sense—sort of—when Peter explained it. His mother had gone to one of those cosmetics stores and they put some fancy makeup on her eyes, and she didn't want to ruin it when she took a shower, so she wore Peter's rubber goggles."

"Why didn't she just take a bath?" Barney asked. He threw Alex a look that suggested his friend have his head examined.

"She couldn't take a bath because the faucet was broken," James said, "and her brother hadn't gotten around to fixing it yet."

"That makes sense," Alex said in Carol's defense.

Barney rolled his eyes and tipped the beer bottle to his lips.

To his credit, Barney didn't say anything else about Carol until James was out of the room. "You're really serious about *this* woman?" His question implied that Alex had introduced Barney to the wrong one, and that the whole meeting was a setup to some kind of joke that was to follow.

"I'm totally serious. I told you I asked her to marry me—I can't get any more serious than that."

"And she's *thinking* about it?" Barney asked mockingly. Being the true friend he was, Barn clearly couldn't understand why Carol hadn't instantly leaped at Alex's offer.

To be honest, Alex wondered the same thing himself. True, he'd blurted out his proposal in a parking lot. He still had trouble believing he'd done anything so crazy. As a contractor, he'd sold himself and his company hundreds of times. He'd prepared bids and presented them with polish and professionalism. He always had solid arguments that made his proposals sound attractive and intelligent. Carol deserved nothing less.

But something had happened to him when he'd visited her birthing class. Something enigmatic and profound. Even now he had to struggle not to get choked up when he thought about it.

After nearly two weeks in Texas, Alex had been starved for the sight of her, and he'd barely noticed the others in the class. In retrospect, he was sure his reaction could be attributed to seeing all those soon-to-be mothers.

In fifteen years Alex hadn't given babies more than a passing thought. He had a son and was grateful for that. He might have suffered a twinge of regret when he learned there'd be no more children, but he'd been more concerned about his wife's well-being than the fact that they wouldn't be adding to their family.

Then he'd watched Carol with those pregnant couples, and the desire for another child, a daughter, had suddenly overwhelmed him. He'd decided while he was in Texas that he loved Carol and wanted to marry her, but the idea of starting a family of their own hadn't so much as crossed his mind. But why not? They were both young enough and healthy enough to raise a houseful of children.

He'd been standing at the back of her class, waiting for her, when it happened. Out of nowhere, yet as clear as anything he'd ever seen or felt, Alex saw Carol pregnant with a child. *His* child. He'd realized at the time that this—he used the word *vision* for lack of a better one—was probably due to physical and emotional exhaustion. Wanting to hold on to the image as long as he could, he'd closed his eyes. He'd pictured her.... Her breasts were full, and when she smiled at him, her eyes had a radiance that couldn't be described. She'd taken his hand and settled it on her protruding stomach. In his fantasy he'd felt their child move.

This fantasy was what had prompted the abrupt marriage proposal. He wanted to kick himself now. If he'd taken her in his arms, kissed her and said all the things she deserved to hear, things might have gone differently. He hadn't meant to rush her, hadn't meant to be so pushy, but once he'd realized how resistant she was to the idea, he'd panicked. The two-week ultimatum was unfair. He'd tell her that on Friday night when they went out for dinner.

Then again, maybe he wouldn't. He'd wait to hear what she was thinking, which way she was leaning, before he put his foot any farther down his throat.

Then he began to smile. Perhaps it wasn't too late for a proper proposal, after all.

"Alex?"

His name seemed to be coming from some distance away.

"What?" he asked, pulling himself out of his thoughts.

"The game's started," Barney said. "Don't you want to see it?" He peered closely at Alex. "Is something wrong with you?"

Yes, something *was* wrong, and there was only one cure. Carol Sommars.

Carol dressed carefully for her dinner date with Alex Friday evening. After going through her closet and laying half of everything she owned across the bed, she chose a demure, high-necked dress of soft pink that buttoned down the front. That seemed safe enough, especially with a shawl.

She'd hardly ever felt this awkward. Trying to make her decision, she'd swayed back and forth all week. One day she'd decide she would be a fool *not* to marry him, and the next, she'd been equally convinced she'd be crazy to trust a man a second time.

Marrying Alex meant relinquishing her independence. It meant placing herself and her son at the mercy of another human being. Memories of her marriage to Bruce swiped at her viciously, and whenever she contemplated sharing her well-ordered life with another man, she broke into a cold sweat.

Years ago, someone had told her it took a hell of a man to replace no man. It wasn't until Carol graduated from college with her nursing degree and was completely on her own that she fully understood that statement. Her life was good, too good to tamper with, and yet…

Her thoughts were more confused than ever when the doorbell chimed. She paused, took a calming breath and headed across the room.

"Hello, Alex," she said, smiling stiffly.

"Carol."

He looked gorgeous in a three-piece suit. Her eyes took him in, and she felt some of the tension leave her muscles. It was when she met his eyes that she realized he was chuckling.

"We're going to dinner," he said, nodding at her dress, "not a baptism."

She blinked, not sure she understood.

"If that collar went any higher up your neck, it'd reach your nose."

"I…I was removing temptation," she said, embarrassed by the blush that heated her face.

"Honey, at this rate, the only thing we'll be removing is that dress."

Carol decided the best thing to do was ignore his remark. "Did you say where we're going for dinner?"

"No," he answered cryptically, and his warm eyes caressed her with maddening purposefulness. "I didn't. It's a surprise."

"Oh." After all the time they'd been together, after all the moments she'd spent in his arms, after all the dreams she'd had about Alex, she shouldn't feel this uncomfortable. But her heart was galloping, her hands felt damp, her breath was coming in soft gasps—and they hadn't even left her house yet.

"Are you ready?"

It was a question he shouldn't have asked. *No*, her mind screamed. *Yes*, her heart insisted. "I guess so," her lips answered.

Alex led her outside and held open his car door.

"It was thoughtful of you to drop the boys at the theater. Personally I don't think they were that keen on seeing a Disney movie," she said, slipping inside his car.

"Too bad. I gave them a choice of things to do this evening."

"Attending a kids' movie on the other side of town or being set adrift in the Columbia River without paddles probably isn't their idea of a choice."

Alex chuckled. "I don't want anyone disturbing us tonight."

Their eyes met. Alex's were hot and hazy and so suggestive, Carol's heart skipped a beat. For sanity's sake, she looked away.

"I hope you like steak."

"I love it."

"The champagne's cooling."

"You must've ordered in advance," she murmured, having difficulty finding something to do with her hands. Her fingers itched to touch him...*needed* to touch him. A need that only confused her more.

"I...hope you explained to Barney—your friend—that I...that I don't normally look the way I did the evening we met. When I got home and saw myself in the mirror...well, I could just imagine what he must've thought." Carol cursed the madness that had sent her rushing out of her house that evening to confront Alex.

"Barney understood."

"Oh, good."

A couple of minutes later, Alex turned into his own driveway. Carol looked at him, somewhat surprised. "Did you forget something?"

"No," he said.

A moment later, he let her into the house. She paused in the doorway, and her heart gave a sudden, sharp lurch. They weren't going to any restaurant. Alex had always planned to bring her back to his house.

The drapes were drawn, and the lights had been lowered. Carol saw that the dining room table was set with crystal and china. Two tapered candles stood in the middle of the table, waiting to be lit.

Alex went over to the stereo and pushed a single button. Immediately the room was drenched with the plaintive sound of violins.

Carol was still trying to assimilate what was happening when he walked over to the table and lit the candles. Tiny flames sent a golden glow shimmering across the pristine white cloth.

"Shall we?" Alex said, holding out his hands.

Carol was too numb to reply. He took the lacy shawl from her shoulders and draped it over the back of the sofa. Then he pulled her purse from her unresisting fingers and set it next to the shawl. When he'd finished, he turned and eased her into his arms.

Their bodies came gently together, and a shudder went through her. She wasn't a complete fool—she knew what Alex was planning. She lowered her eyelids. Despite her doubts and fears, she wanted this, too.

For a moment, she battled the feeling, then with a deep sigh, she surrendered.

Alex wrapped his arms around her. "Oh, baby," he whispered in her ear. "You feel so good."

She emptied her lungs of air as his hands slid down her back, to her waist.

There was music, such beautiful music, and then Carol realized they were supposed to be dancing. She rested her fingertips on his shoulders as his mouth moved toward hers. Carol sighed. Alex's breath was moist and warm, his hands gentle as they pressed her closer and closer.

When he kissed her, the moment of anticipation ended, and Carol felt a tremendous surge of relief. He groaned. She groaned. He leaned back and began to unfasten the buttons at her throat.

That all too brief pause helped Carol collect her scattered senses. "Alex," she whispered, "what are you doing?"

"Undressing you."

"Why?" she asked breathlessly, knowing what a stupid question it was.

"Why?" he repeated with amusement. "Because we're going to make love."

Her pulse went wild.

"I love you," he said. "You love me. Right?"

"Oh…yes."

"Good." He kissed her again, so passionately she could hardly resist—and yet she had to. She broke away from him with what little strength she still possessed.

"Alex…please don't."

"Tonight's a new beginning for us. I'm crazy in love with you. I need you so much I can't think straight anymore."

"You brought me here to make love to me, didn't you?"

"You mean it wasn't obvious?" he asked as he nibbled kisses along the side of her neck.

"Why now? Why not that night on the Washington coast…? Why tonight?"

"Carol, do we need to go through this evaluation?"

"I have to know," she cried, pushing herself away from him. Her hands trembled, and it was with some difficulty that she rebuttoned her dress. "The truth, Alex. I want the truth."

"All right," he murmured. "I thought…I believed that if we made love, it would help you decide you wanted to marry me."

Carol felt as though he'd tossed a bucket of ice water in her face. She raised her hand to her pounding heart. "Oh, no…" she whispered. "Not again."

"Carol? What's wrong?"

"Bruce did this to me, too…pressured me into giving in to him…then he hated me…punished me…." Blindly she reached for her purse and shawl, then headed for the front door.

Alex caught up with her before she made it outside. His hand clasped her shoulder as he turned her to face him. By then she was sobbing, her whole body trembling with terror. Stark terror—stark memories.

Alex took one look at her and hauled her into his arms. "Carol." He threaded his fingers through her hair. "It's all right, it's all right. I would *never* have forced you."

Chapter Twelve

All Carol could do was cry, and the pile of used tissues was mounting. Alex tried to comfort her, to help her, but everything he did seemed to make matters worse. One thing he'd immediately recognized—she didn't want him to touch her.

She'd curled herself up on his sofa and covered her face as she wept. She wouldn't talk to him. She wouldn't look at him. The only comprehensible statement she'd made in the last fifteen minutes had been a demand that he take her home.

Fear knotted his stomach. He had the inexplicable feeling that if he did as she asked, he'd never see her again. He had tonight and only tonight to repair the trust he'd unwittingly destroyed.

"Carol, I'm sorry." He must have told her that twenty times. It was true enough. Everything he tried to do with this woman was wrong. Tonight was the perfect example. For days he'd been searching for a way to prove to Carol how much he loved her and how right they were for each other.

This evening had seemed the perfect place and time. He'd

planned it all—the music, champagne, the carefully worded proposal, the diamond ring.

He'd thought that if everything went well, they'd make love, and afterward, they could discuss the details of their wedding and their lives. He wanted her in his bed, and although it was more than a little arrogant of him, he didn't think he'd have any problem getting her there.

He'd also come to the conclusion that once they made love, she'd be convinced that they belonged together, and their marriage would naturally follow.

At first, his plan had worked flawlessly. Carol had walked into the house, seen that the table was set and the candles ready to light. She'd looked at him with those huge eyes of hers and given him a seductive smile. Then, with barely a pause, she'd waltzed into his arms.

From there everything had gone downhill.

One minute he was kissing her, marveling at the power she had over his body, and the next, she was cold and trembling, demanding answers that should've been obvious.

"Would you like some coffee?" he asked her gently for the second—or was it the third?—time. Although his arms ached with the need to hold her, he resisted.

"No," she whispered. "I want to go home."

"We need to talk first."

"Not now. I *need* to go home." She rubbed her face and plucked a clean tissue from the nearby box. Apparently she'd regained her resolve because she stood, wrapped her shawl around her, and stumbled to the door. "If you won't drive me, then I'll walk."

Alex heard the desperation in her voice and was helpless to do anything other than what she asked. As he stood, the regret swept through him. If there was anything he could do to ease her pain, he would've done it. If there were any words he could have uttered to comfort her, he would've said them gladly. But all she wanted him to do was take her back to her own home. Back to her own bed. Her own life.

Who did he think he was? Some Don Juan who could sweep this beautiful, sensitive woman into his bed and make love to her? He felt sick to his stomach at the way he'd plotted, the way he'd planned to use her body against her, to exploit the attraction between them to serve his own ends.

Now he was losing her, and there wasn't anyone he could blame but himself. He'd known his chances weren't good the night he'd asked her to marry him. He'd hoped to see joy in her eyes when he suggested it. He'd longed to see happiness on her face. He'd wanted Carol to hurl herself into his arms, excited and overcome with emotion.

He should've known he'd been watching too many old movies.

He'd asked Carol to marry him, and none of the things he'd hoped for had happened. Instead, her eyes had reflected fear. And tonight...tonight he'd witnessed stark terror.

Alex was astute enough to realize the problem lay in Carol's brief marriage. Whatever had gone on had left deep emotional scars. Even when he'd felt the closest to her, Alex had learned very little about her relationship with her late husband. She'd let tidbits of information drop now and then, but every time she did, Alex had the feeling she'd regretted it.

On her way out the door, Carol grabbed a handful of fresh tissues, and with nothing more to say, Alex led the way to his car.

He opened the passenger door, noticing how she avoided any possibility of their accidentally touching as she climbed inside.

The tension inside the car made the air almost too thick to breathe. He could hardly stand it and he wondered how she could.

When he braked at a stop sign, he decided to make one last effort.

"Carol, please, how many times do I have to tell you how sorry I am? I made a mistake. I behaved like a jerk. Tell me what you want me to do, because I'll do it. Anything you say. I love you! You've got to believe I'd never intentionally do anything to hurt you."

His pleas were met with more of the same strained, intolerable silence.

In frustration he pressed his foot to the gas, and they shot ahead. The seat belts were all that kept them from slamming forward with the car.

The fiercest argument of their courtship now ensued, and the crazy part was, neither of them uttered a word. Every once in a while, Alex could hear Carol drag a breath through her lungs, and he knew she was doing everything in her power not to cry. Each tear she shed, each sob she inhaled, felt like a knife wound.

He was losing her, and there wasn't a thing he could do about it. It wouldn't be so tragic if he didn't care for her so much. After Gloria's death, Alex had never truly believed he'd fall in love again. Even when he'd made the decision to remarry, he hadn't expected to find the depth of emotion he'd experienced with Carol.

And now it might be too late.

"Hey, Mom, did you and Mr. Preston have a fight or something?" Peter asked the following morning.

"W-why do you ask?"

Peter popped two frozen waffles in the toaster, then stood guard over them as though he expected Carol to snatch them out of his hands.

"I don't know. Mr. Preston was acting strange last night when he picked us up from the movie."

"Strange?"

"Sad. Mr. Preston's usually loads of fun. I like him, I mean, he's about the neatest adult I know. He doesn't treat me like I'm a kid, and he likes the same things I like and—I don't know—I just think he's an all-around great guy. Fact is, Mom, men don't come much better than James's dad."

"He is...nice, isn't he?" she agreed. She tightened her fingers around the handle of her coffee mug and looked anywhere but at her son.

Peter leaned toward her and squinted. "Have you been crying?"

"Don't be silly," she said lightly, trying to make a joke out of it.

"Your eyes are all puffy and red like you have an allergy or something."

"Pollen sometimes affects me that way." Which was the truth. It just didn't happen to be affecting her eyes at that particular moment.

The waffles popped up, and Peter grabbed them, muttering under his breath when he burned his fingers. He spread a thin layer of butter on them and followed that with a puddle of syrup. Once that task was complete, he added two more waffles to the toaster, then sat across the table from Carol.

"I kind of thought you and Mr. Preston might've had a fight," Peter said, obviously feeling it was safe to probe some more. "That would've been too bad because on the way to the movie he was telling us that he wanted to make this dinner the most romantic night of your life. Was it?"

"He...tried."

"How did the Baked Alaska taste?"

"The Baked Alaska?" Carol made a nondescript gesture. "Oh...it was great."

"Mr. Preston made everything himself. Right down to the salad dressing. James told me he'd been shopping for days. It would've been terrible if you'd had a fight and ruined it.... You love Mr. Preston, don't you?" Peter asked earnestly.

Carol closed her eyes to the emotion assaulting her from all sides. She would be lying if she didn't admit it. And her heart refused to let her lie. But no one seemed to understand that love wasn't a cure-all. She'd loved Bruce, too—or thought she did—and look where that had gotten her.

"Yes," she whispered. She'd averted her gaze, but she could hear Peter's sigh of relief.

"I knew you did," he said cheerfully, slicing into his waffle. "I told James you were wild about his dad and that whatever happened at dinner would be okay in the morning."

"I'm sure you're right," Carol murmured.

An hour later, Carol was working in the garden space Alex had tilled for her several weeks earlier. She was cultivating the soil, preparing it to plant several different herbs that afternoon. She'd done her homework and discovered a wide variety that grew well in the moist climate of the Pacific Northwest.

Her back was to the kitchen, and she hadn't heard the doorbell. Nor was there the usual commotion that occurred whenever Peter let someone in.

Yet without a doubt, she knew Alex was standing in the

doorway watching her. She felt his presence in the same way she experienced his absence.

Running her forearm across her damp brow, she leaned back and removed her gloves. "I know what you want to say," she said, "and I think it would be best if we just dropped the whole issue."

"Unfortunately that's a luxury neither of us can afford."

"I knew you were going to say that," she sighed, awkwardly struggling to an upright position. The knees of her jeans were caked with mud and the sweat was pouring down her flushed face.

There'd probably been only two other times in her life when she'd looked worse, and Alex had seen her on both occasions.

With the cultivator gripped tightly in her fist, she walked over to the patio and sank down on a deck chair. "All right, say what you have to say."

Alex grinned. "Such resignation!"

"I'd rather be working in my garden."

"I know." He flexed his hands a couple of times. "I suppose I should start at the beginning."

"Oh, Alex, this isn't necessary, it really isn't. I overreacted last night. So, you made a mistake—you're only human and I forgive you. Your intentions weren't exactly honorable, but given the circumstances they were understandable. You wanted to take me into your bed and afterward make an honest woman of me." She made quotation marks with her fingers around the words *honest woman.* "Right?"

"Something like that," he mumbled. Although of course the issue was much more complicated than that....

"The thing is, I've been made an honest woman once and

it was the biggest mistake of my life. I'm not planning to repeat it."

"What was your husband's name?" Alex asked without preamble.

"Bruce...why?"

"Do you realize you've never told me?"

She shrugged; she never talked about Bruce if possible.

"Tell me about him, Carol," Alex pleaded, "tell me everything. Start with the minute you noticed each other and then lead me through your relationship to the day you buried him."

"I can't see how that would solve anything."

"Tell me, Carol."

"No." She jumped to her feet, her heart in a panic. "There's nothing to say."

"Then why do you close up tight anytime someone mentions him?"

"Because!" She paced the patio. Stopping abruptly, she whirled around and glared at him, angry all over again. "All right, you want to know? I'll tell you. We were teenagers—young, stupid, naive. We made out in the back seat of a car... and when I got pregnant with Peter we got married. Bruce died three years later in a car accident."

An eternity passed before Alex spoke again. "That's just a summary. Tell me what *really* happened in those three years you were married." His voice was soft and insistent.

Her chest constricted painfully. Would nothing satisfy him short of blood? How could she ever hope to describe three years of living in hell? She couldn't, and she didn't even want to try.

Alex wouldn't understand, and nothing she could ever say

would help him. What purpose would it serve to dredge up all that misery? None that she could see.

Slowly she lowered herself onto the deck chair again, trying to still her churning thoughts, to nullify the agonizing memories. The pain was so distinct, so acute, that she opted for the only sane solution. She backed away.

Alex reached for her hand, holding it loosely. "I know this is difficult."

He didn't know *how* difficult.

"Bruce and I were married a long time ago. Suffice it to say that the marriage wasn't a good one. We were much too young...and Bruce had...problems." She bit her lip, not willing to continue. "I don't want to drag up the past. I don't see how it would do any good."

"Carol, please."

"No," she said sharply. "I'm not about to dissect a marriage that ended thirteen years ago simply because *you're* curious."

"We *need* to talk about it," he insisted.

"Why? Because I get a little panicky when you start pressuring me into bed? Trust me, any woman who's gone through what I did would react the same way. You know the old saying—once burned, twice shy." She tried to make light of it and failed. Miserably.

For the longest time Alex said nothing. He did nothing. He stared into the distance, and Carol couldn't tell where his thoughts were taking him.

"I never expected to fall in love again," he said.

Carol frowned at the self-derision in his words.

"Gloria knew I would, but then she always did know me better than I knew myself." He paused for a moment, and he gave a sad, bitter smile. "I'll never forget the last time we were able to talk. The next day she slipped into a coma, and soon afterward, she died. She knew she was dying and had accepted it. The hospital staff knew it was only a matter of time. But I couldn't let go of her. I had such faith that God would save her from this illness. Such unquestionable trust. He did, of course, but not the way I wanted."

"Alex…" Tears were beginning to blur her vision. She didn't want to hear about Gloria and the wonderful marriage he'd had with her. The contrast was too painful. Too bleak.

"Gloria took my hand and raised her eyes to mine and thanked me for staying at her side to the very end. She apologized because she'd been ill. Can you imagine anyone doing that?"

"No." Carol's voice was the faintest of whispers.

"Then she told me God would send another woman into my life, someone healthy and whole who'd love me the way I deserved to be loved. Someone who'd share my success and who'd love our son as much as she did." He paused and smiled again, but it was the same sad smile. "Trust me, this was the last thing I wanted to hear from my wife. First of all, I was in denial, and I refused to believe she was dying, and second, nothing could have convinced me I'd ever love another woman as much as I loved Gloria."

Carol shut her eyes tightly and took deep breaths to keep from weeping openly.

"She told me that when I met this other woman and decided to marry her, I shouldn't feel guilty for having fallen in love again. She must've known that would be something powerful I'd be dealing with later. She squeezed my fingers— she was so weak, and yet, so strong. And wise, so very wise. Within a few hours she was gone from me forever." He rubbed his eyes and hesitated before continuing. "I didn't believe her.

I didn't think it would be possible to love anyone as much as I loved her.

"Then I met you, and before I knew it, I was falling in love all over again." Once more he brought a weary hand to his face. His expression was blank, his eyes unrevealing. "And again I'm relinquishing the woman I love." He paused. "I'll give you the two weeks to make your decision, Carol. In fact, I'll make it easy for you. I won't call or contact you until the seventh—that's exactly two weeks from the day we talked about it. You can tell me your decision then. All right?"

"All right," she agreed, feeling numb.

Slowly he nodded, then stood and walked out of her house.

"The way I see it," Peter said, holding a red Delicious apple in one hand and staring at his mother, "James's dad can adopt me."

Carol felt the fleeting pain that tore through her every time Peter not-so-casually mentioned Alex's name. He seemed to plan these times with precision. Just when she least expected it. Just when she was sure she knew her own mind. Just when she was feeling overly confident. Then *pow*, right between the eyes, Peter would toss some remark carefully chosen for its effect. It was generally preceded by some bit of information about Alex or a comment about how wonderful life would be when they were one big, happy family.

"I'd have to marry Alex first, and I'm not sure that's going to happen," she said reproachfully. One challenging look defied him to contradict her.

"Well, it makes sense, doesn't it? *If* you marry him, naturally." Peter took a huge bite of the apple. Juice dribbled down his chin, and he wiped it away with the back of his hand. "I haven't heard from Dad's family in years, and they wouldn't even care if someone adopted me. That way we could all have the same last name. Peter Preston has a cool sound to it, don't you think?"

"Peter," she groaned, frustrated and angered by the way he turned a deaf ear to everything she said. "If this is another tactic to manipulate me into marrying Alex so you can go fishing, then I want you to know right now that I don't appreciate it."

She was under enough pressure—mainly from herself—and she didn't need her son applying any more.

"But, Mom, think about how good our lives would be if you married Mr. Preston. He's rich—"

"I've heard all of this conversation that I want to. Now sit down and eat your dinner." She dished up the crispy fried pork chop and a serving of rice and broccoli, and set the plate on the table.

"You're not eating?" Peter asked, looking mildly disappointed. "This is the third night you've skipped dinner this week."

Carol's appetite had been nil for the entire two weeks. "No time. I've got to get ready for class."

"When will these sessions be over?"

"Two more weeks," she said, walking into her bedroom. *Two weeks* seemed to be the magical time period of late. Alex had given her two weeks to decide if she'd accept his proposal. Two weeks that were up today. He'd granted her the breathing space she needed to come to a sensible decision. Only "sensible" was the last thing Carol felt. It shouldn't be this difficult. She wondered why she had so many doubts if she loved Alex—which she did. But Carol knew the answer to that.

Alex's marriage had been wonderful.

Hers had been a disaster.

He was hoping to repeat what he'd shared with Gloria.

She wanted to avoid the pain Bruce had brought into her life.

"Mom...phone."

Carol froze. She'd been on tenterhooks waiting for Alex to contact her. All day she'd felt a growing sense of dread. She'd expected Alex to come strolling out from behind every closed door, to suddenly appear when she least expected him.

The last thing she'd figured he'd do was phone.

With one shoe on, she hobbled over to her nightstand and picked up the phone, wondering what she was going to say.

"Hello."

"Carol, it's your mother."

"Hello, Ma, what can I do for you?" Relief must have been evident in her voice.

Angelina Pasquale said, "I was in church this morning, lighting a candle to St. Rita, when something happened to my heart."

"Did you see your doctor?" Carol's own heart abruptly switched gears. Her greatest fear was losing her mother to heart disease the way she'd lost her father.

"Why should I see a doctor?" her mother protested. "I was talking to God—in my heart—and God was telling me I should have a talk with my daughter Carol, who's deciding if she's going to marry this rich non-Italian or walk away from the best thing since the invention of padded insoles."

"Mama, I've got a class—I don't have time to talk."

"You've seen Alex?"

"Not...yet."

"What are you going to tell him?"

Her mother was being as difficult as Peter. Everyone

wanted to make up her mind for her. Everyone knew what she should do. Everyone except Carol.

"You know he's not Catholic, don't you?" she told her mother, who had once considered that an all-important factor in choosing a husband. Religion and an equally vital question—whether her potential husband was allergic to tomatoes.

Her mother snickered. "I know he's not Catholic! But don't worry, I've got that all worked out with God."

"Mama, I'm sorry, but I have to leave now or I'll be late for my class."

"So be late for once in your life. Who's it gonna hurt? All day I waited, all day I said to myself, my *bambina's* going to call and tell me she's going to marry again. I want to do the cooking myself, you tell him that."

"Mama, what are you talking about?"

"At the wedding. No caterers, understand? I got the menu all planned. We'll serve—"

"Ma, please."

It took Carol another five minutes to extricate herself from the conversation. Glancing at her watch, she groaned. Rushing from room to room, she grabbed her purse, her other shoe and her briefcase. She paused on her way out the door to kiss Peter on the cheek and remind him to do his homework. Then she jumped in the car, still wearing only one shoe.

Her breathing was labored by the time she raced through traffic and pulled into the parking lot at the community center where the birthing classes were held.

She'd piled everything she needed in her arms, including her umbrella, when she realized she'd left her lecture notes at the house.

"Damn," she muttered. She took two steps before she remembered she was carrying her shoe.

"It might help if you put that on instead of holding it in your arms."

Carol froze. She whirled around, angry and upset, directing all her emotion at Alex. "This is *your* fault," she said, dropping her shoe to the ground and positioning it with her toe until she could slip her foot inside. "First, Peter's on my case, and now my mother's claiming she received a message directly from God and that He's worked out a deal with her, since you're not Catholic, and frankly, Alex—don't you dare laugh." She finished with a huge breath. "I swear, if you laugh I wouldn't marry you if you were the last living male in the state of Oregon."

"I'm sorry," he said, holding up both hands.

"I should hope so. You don't know what I've been through this past week."

"Your two weeks are up, Carol."

"You don't need to tell me that. I know."

"You've decided?"

Her eyes shut, and she nodded slowly. "I have," she whispered.

Chapter Thirteen

"Before you tell me what you've decided," Alex said, moving toward Carol, his eyes a smoky gray, "let me hold you."

"Hold me?" she echoed meekly. Alex looked one-hundred-percent male, and the lazy smile he wore was potent enough to tear through her defenses.

"I'm going to do much more than simply hold you, my love," he whispered, inching his way toward her.

"Here? In a parking lot?"

Alex chuckled and slipped his arms around her waist, tugging her closer. Carol had no resistance left in her. She'd been so lonely, so lost, without him. So confused.

His mouth brushed hers. Much too briefly. Much too lightly.

Carol didn't want him to be gentle. Not when she was this hungry for his touch. Her lips parted in a firm and wanting kiss. Alex sighed his pleasure and she clung to him, needing him.

When they drew apart, she rested her forehead against his.

"Okay," Alex said, his breath warm and heavy. "Tell me. I'm ready now."

"Oh, Alex," she murmured, and her throat constricted with ready tears. "I can't decide. I've tried and tried and tried, and the only thing I really know is I need more time."

"Time," he repeated. Briefly he closed his eyes. His shoulders sagged with defeat. "You need more time. How much? A week? A month? Six months? Would a year fit into your schedule?" He broke away from her and rubbed his hand along the back of his neck. "If you haven't made up your mind by now, my guess is you never will. I love you, Carol, but you're driving me insane with this waiting."

"Can't you see things from my point of view?" she protested.

"No, I can't," he said. "I'm grateful for this time we've had, because it's taught me something I hadn't been willing to recognize before. I'm lonely. I want someone in my life—someone permanent. I want you as my wife. I *need* you as my wife. But if you don't want what I'm offering, then I should cut my losses and look elsewhere."

A strangled cry erupted from her lips. He was being so unfair, pressuring her like this. Everything had to be decided in *his* time frame, without any allowance for doubts or questions. Something broke in Carol. Control. It was all about control. She couldn't—wouldn't—allow another man to control her the way Bruce had.

"I think you're right, Alex," she finally said. "Find yourself someone else."

The shock of her words hit him like a blow to the head. He actually flinched, but all the while his piercing eyes continued to hold hers. Carol saw the regret and the pain flash through his burning gaze. Then he buried his hands in his pockets, turned and marched away.

It was all Carol could do not to run after him, but she knew that if she did she'd be giving up her self-respect.

Janice Mandle stuck her head out the door and scanned the parking lot. She looked relieved when she saw Carol, and waved.

Carol waved back. Although she wanted nothing more than to be alone, she didn't have any choice but to teach her class.

Janice called, mentioning the time.

Still Carol couldn't seem to tear her gaze from Alex, holding on to him for as long as she could. He made her feel things she'd never known she was capable of experiencing. When he kissed her, she felt hot and quivery, as though she'd just awakened from a long, deep sleep. Spending time with him was fun and exciting. There'd been adventures waiting to happen with this man. Whole new worlds in the making. Yet something was holding her back. Something powerful. She wanted everything Alex was offering, and at the same time her freedom was too precious, too important.

Carol didn't see Alex again until the end of the week, when the boys were participating in the district track meet. James was running in the four-hundred- and eight-hundred-meter races, and Peter was scheduled for the 1500-meter. On their own, the two friends had decided to choose events in which they weren't competing together. Carol had been impressed with their insight into each other's competitive personalities.

Carol's mother had decided to attend the meet with her. Angelina was as excited as a kid at the circus. They'd just settled themselves in the bleachers when out of the corner of her eye, Carol saw Alex. Since they both had sons involved in track, she knew avoiding him would be nearly impossible, but she hadn't expected to see him quite so soon. Although, in retrospect, she should've realized he'd be attending this important meet.

Preparing herself, she sat stiffly on the bleachers as Alex strolled past. Instantly her heart started to thunder. His friend was with him, the one she'd met briefly—Barney or Bernie... Barney, she decided. Her hands were tightly clenched in her lap, and she was prepared to exchange polite greetings.

To her consternation, Alex didn't so much as look in her direction. Carol knew it would've been nearly impossible for him to have missed seeing her. If he'd wanted to hurt her, he'd done so—easily.

"So when does the man running with the torch come out?" Angelina asked.

"That's in the Olympics, Mama," Carol answered, her voice weak.

Her mother turned to look in Carol's direction, and her frown deepened. "What's the matter with you?" she demanded. "You look as white as bleached flour."

"It's nothing."

"What is it?" Angelina asked stubbornly.

"Alex...just walked past us."

"Not *the* Alex?"

Carol nodded. Before she could stop her mother, Angelina rose to her feet and reached for Carol's binoculars. "Where is he? I want to get a good look at this man who broke my daughter's heart."

"Ma, please, let's not get into that again." The way her mother had defended her had touched Carol's heart, although

Angelina hadn't wasted any time berating her daughter's foolishness, either. She'd spent most of Sunday muttering at Carol in Italian. Carol wasn't fluent enough to understand everything, but she got the gist of it. Angelina thought Carol was a first-class fool to let a man like Alex slip through her fingers.

"I want one look at this Alex," Angelina insisted. She raised the binoculars to her face and twisted the dials until she had them focused correctly. "I'm gonna give this man the eye. Now tell me where he's sitting."

Carol knew it would be easier to bend a tire iron than persuade her mother to remove the binoculars and sit down before she made a scene.

"He's on your left, about halfway up the bleachers. He's wearing a pale blue sweater," she muttered. If he glanced in her direction, she'd be mortified. Heaven only knew what interpretation he'd put on her mother glaring at him through a set of field glasses, giving him what she so quaintly called "the eye."

Her mother had apparently found him, because she started speaking in Italian. Only this time her comments were perfectly understandable. She was using succulent, suggestive phrases about Alex's sexual talents and how he'd bring Carol pleasure in bed.

"Ma, *please,*" Carol wailed. "You're embarrassing me."

Angelina sat down and put the glasses on her lap. She began muttering in Italian again, leaning her head close to Carol.

"Ma!" she cried, distressed by the vivid language her mother was using. "You should have your mouth washed out with soap."

Angelina folded her hands and stared at the sky. "Such beautiful *bambinos* you'd have with this man."

Carol closed her eyes at the image of more children—hers and Alex's. Emotion rocked through her.

Her mother took the opportunity to make a few more succinct remarks, but Carol did her best to ignore them. It seemed as if the track meet wasn't ever going to begin. Carol was convinced she'd have to spend the afternoon listening to her mother whispering in her ear. Just when she couldn't endure it any longer, the kids involved in the hurdle events walked over to the starting line. They shook their arms at their sides and did a couple of stretching exercises. Carol was so grateful to have her mother's attention on the field that it was all she could do not to rush out and kiss the coach.

The four-hundred-meter race followed several hurdle events. Carol watched James through the binoculars as he approached the starting line. He looked confident and eager. As they were taking their positions, he glanced into the stands and cocked his head just slightly, acknowledging his father's presence. When his gaze slid to Carol, his eyes sobered before he smiled.

At the gun, the eight boys leapt forward. Carol immediately vaulted to her feet and began shouting at the top of her lungs.

James crossed the finish line and placed second. Carol's heart felt as though it would burst with pride. Without conscious thought her gaze flew to Alex, and she saw that he looked equally pleased by his son's performance. He must have sensed her watching him because he turned his head slightly and their eyes met. He held on to hers for just a moment, and then with obvious reluctance looked away.

Carol sagged onto her seat.

"So who is this boy you scream for like a son?" her mother demanded.

"James Preston—the boy who finished second."

"So that was Alex's son?" Angelina asked slowly, as she took the binoculars and lifted them to her eyes once more. She was apparently satisfied with what she saw, because she grinned. "He's a fine-looking boy, but he's a little on the thin side. He needs my spaghetti to put some meat on those bones."

Carol didn't comment. She *did* love James like a son. That realization forced a lump into her throat. And her heart— her poor, unsuspecting heart—was fluttering hard enough to take flight and leave her body behind.

Feeling someone's eyes on her, she glanced over her shoulder. Instantly Alex turned away. Carol's hands began to tremble, and all he'd done was look in her direction....

James raced again shortly afterward, placing third in the eight-hundred-meter. For a high school sophomore, he was showing a lot of potential, Carol mused, feeling very proud of him.

When her own son approached the starting line for his race, Carol felt as nervous as she ever had in her life....

Since the 1500-meter meant almost four long turns around the track, it didn't have the immediacy of the previous races. By the time Peter was entering the final lap, Carol and her mother were on their feet, shouting their encouragement. Carol in English. Angelina in Italian. From a distance, Carol heard a loud male voice joining theirs. Alex.

When Peter crossed the finish line in a solid third position, Carol heaved a sigh of pride and relief. Tears dampened her lashes, and she raised her hands to her mouth. Both the first-

and second-place winners were seniors. As a sophomore, Peter had done exceptionally well.

Again, without any conscious decision on her part, Carol found herself turning to look at Alex. This time he was waiting for her, and they exchanged the faintest of smiles. Sad smiles. Lonely smiles. Proud smiles.

Carol's shoulders drooped with defeat. It was as if the worlds of two fools were about to collide.

He was pushy. She was stubborn.

He wanted a wife. She wanted time.

He refused to wait. She refused to give in.

Still their eyes held, each unwilling to pull away. So many concerns weighed on Carol's heart. But memories, too—good memories. She remembered how they'd strolled through the lush green foliage of the Washington rain forest. Alex had linked his fingers with hers, and nothing had ever felt more right. That same night they'd sat by the campfire and sung with the boys, and fed each other roasted marshmallows.

The memories glided straight to Carol's heart.

"Carol?"

Dragging her gaze away from Alex, Carol turned to her mother.

"It's time to leave," Angelina said, glancing into the stands toward Alex and his friend. "Didn't you notice? The stadium's almost empty, and weren't we supposed to meet Peter?"

"Yes..." Carol murmured, "we were...we are."

Peter and James strolled out of the locker room and onto the field together, each carrying a sports bag and a stack of school books. Judging by their damp hair, they'd just gotten out of the shower.

Carol and her mother were waiting where Peter had suggested. It seemed important to keep them as far away from the school building as possible for fear any of his friends would realize he had a family.

Alex didn't seem to be anywhere nearby, and for that Carol was grateful. And even if it made no sense, she was also regretful. She wanted to be as close to him as she could. And yet she'd happily move to the Arctic Circle to escape him. Her thoughts and desires were in direct contrast and growing more muddled every second.

Peter and James parted company about halfway across the field. Before they went their separate ways, they exchanged a brief nod, apparently having agreed or decided upon something. Whatever it was, Peter didn't mention it.

He seemed unusually quiet on the ride home. Carol didn't question her son until they'd dropped her mother off. "What's bothering you?"

"Nothing." But he kept his gaze focused straight ahead.

"You sure?"

His left shoulder rose and fell in an indecisive shrug.

"I see."

"Mr. Preston was at the meet today. Did you see him?"

"Ah…" Carol hedged. There was no reason to lie. "Yeah. He was sitting with his friend."

"Mr. Powers and Mr. Preston are good friends. They met in college."

Carol wasn't sure what significance, if any, that bit of information held.

"According to James, Mr. Powers's been single for the past couple years, and he dates beautiful women all the time. He's the one who arranged all those hot dates for James's dad… and he's doing it again."

"That's none of our business." Her heart reacted to that, but what else could she expect? She was in love with the man.

However, it wasn't as if Alex hadn't warned her; he'd said that if she wasn't willing to accept what he was offering, it was time to cut his losses and look elsewhere. She just hadn't expected him to start so soon.

"James was telling me his dad's been going out every night this week."

"Peter," she said softly, "I think it would be best if we made it a rule not to discuss Alex or his dating practices. You know, and, I hope, have accepted, the fact that the relationship between James's dad and me is over…by mutual agreement."

"But, Mom, you really love this guy!"

She arched her eyebrows at that.

"You try to fool me, but I can see how miserable you've been all week. And Mr. Preston's been just as unhappy, James says, and we both think he's going to do something stupid on the rebound, like marry this Babette girl."

"Peter, I thought I just said I don't want to talk about this."

"Fine," he muttered, crossing his arms and beginning to sulk. Five minutes passed before he sighed heavily. "Babette's a singer. In a band. She's not like the run-of-the-mill bimbos Barney usually meets. Mom, you've got to *do* something. Fast. This woman is real competition."

"Peter!" she cried.

"All right. All right." He raised both hands in surrender. "I won't say another word."

That proved to be a slight exaggeration. Peter had ways of letting Carol know what was going on between Alex and his newfound friend without ever having to mention either name.

Saturday, after playing basketball with James in the local park, Peter returned home, hot and sweaty. He walked straight to the refrigerator and took out a cold can of soda, taking the first swallows while standing in front of the open refrigerator.

Carol had her sewing machine set up on the kitchen table. Pins pressed between her lips, she waved her hand, instructing her son to close the door.

"Oh, sorry," Peter muttered. He did as she asked, then wiped his face. "Ever hear of a thirty-six-year-old man falling head over heels in love with a twenty-three-year-old woman?" Peter asked disdainfully.

Stepping on a nail couldn't have been more painful—or more direct—than her son's question. "No. Can't say that I have," she said, so flustered she sewed a seam that was so crooked she'd have to immediately take it out. With disgust, she tossed the blouse aside, and when her son had left the room, she trembled and buried her face in her hands.

On Sunday morning, Peter had stayed in church a few extra minutes after Mass, walking up to the altar. When he joined Carol in the vestibule, she placed her hand on his shoulder and studied him carefully. She'd never seen her son quite so serious.

"What's on your mind, honey?"

He gave her another of his one-shoulder rolls. "I thought if Grandma could talk to God, then I'd try it, too. While I was up there, I lit a candle to St. Rita."

Carol didn't respond.

After that, she and her son drove over to her mother's house. The tears started when she was in the kitchen helping Angelina with dinner. It surprised Carol, because she had nothing to cry about—not really. But that didn't seem to matter. Soon the tears were flowing from her eyes so hard and fast that they were dripping from her chin and running down her neck.

Standing at the sink washing vegetables helped hide the fact that she was weeping, but that wouldn't last long. Soon someone would see she was crying and want to know why. She tried desperately to stop, but to no avail. If anything, her efforts only made her cry more.

She must've made more noise than she realized, because when she turned to reach for a hand towel to wipe her face, she found her mother and her sister-in-law both staring at her.

Her mother was murmuring something to Paula in Italian, which was interesting since the other woman didn't understand a word of the language. But Carol understood each and every one. Her mother was telling Paula that Carol looked like a woman who was in danger of losing the man she loved.

With her arm around Carol's shoulders, Angelina led her into her bedroom. Whenever Carol was ill as a little girl, her mother had always brought her to her own bed and taken care of her there.

Without resistance, Carol let her mother lead her through the house. By now the tears had become soft sobs. Everyone in the living room stopped whatever they were doing and stared at her. Angelina fended off questions and directed Carol to her bed, pulling back the blankets. Sniffling, Carol lay down. The sheets felt cool against her cheeks, and she closed her eyes. Soon she was asleep.

She woke an hour later and sat bolt upright. Suddenly she knew what she had to do. Sitting on the edge of the bed, she held her hands to her face and breathed in deep, steadying breaths. This wasn't going to be easy.

Her family was still busy in the living room. The conversation came to an abrupt halt when Carol moved into the room. She picked up her purse, avoiding their curious eyes.

"I…have to go out for a while. I don't know when I'll be back."

Angelina and Peter walked to the front door with her, both looking anxious.

"Where are you going?" her son asked.

She smiled softly, kissed his cheek and said, "St. Rita must have heard your prayers."

Her mother folded her hands and raised her eyes to heaven, her expression ecstatic. Peter, on the other hand, blinked, his gaze uncertain. Then understanding apparently dawned, and with a shout, he threw his arms around Carol's neck.

Chapter Fourteen

A lex was in the kitchen fixing himself a sandwich when the doorbell chimed. From experience, he knew better than to answer it before James did. Leaning against the counter, Alex waited until his son had vaulted from the family room couch, passed him and raced toward the front door.

Alex supposed he should show some interest in his unannounced guest, but frankly he didn't care—unless it was one stubborn Italian woman, and the chances of that were more remote than his likelihood of winning the lottery.

"Dad," James yelled. "Come quick!"

Muttering under his breath, Alex dropped his turkey sandwich on the plate and headed toward the living room. He was halfway through the door when he jerked his head up in surprise. It was Carol. Through a fog of disbelief, he saw her, dressed in a navy skirt and white silk blouse under a rose-colored sweater.

At least the woman resembled Carol. His eyes must be playing tricks on him, because he was sure this woman standing inside his home was the very one who'd been occupying his thoughts every minute of every hour for days on end.

"Hello, Alex," she said softly.

It sounded like her. Or could it be that he needed her so badly that his troubled mind had conjured up her image?

"Aren't you going to say anything?" James demanded. "This is Carol, Dad, Carol! Are you just going to stand there?"

"Hello," he finally said, having some trouble getting his mouth and tongue to work simultaneously.

"*Hello?* That's it? You aren't saying anything more than that?" James asked, clearly distressed.

"How are you?" Carol asked him, and he noticed that her voice was husky and filled with emotion.

Someday he'd tell her how the best foreman he ever hoped to find had threatened to walk off the job if Alex's foul mood didn't improve. Someday he'd let her know he hadn't eaten a decent meal or slept through an entire night since they'd parted. Someday he'd tell her he would gladly have given a king's ransom to make her his wife. In time, he *would* tell her all that, but for now, all he wanted to do was enjoy the luxury of looking at her.

"Carol just asked you a question. You should answer her," James pointed out.

"I'm fine."

"I'm glad," she whispered.

"How are you?" He managed to dredge up the polite inquiry.

"Not so good."

"Not so good?" he echoed.

She straightened her shoulders, and her eyes held his as she seemed to be preparing herself to speak. "Do you…are you in love with her, because if you are, I'll…I'll understand and get out of your life right now, but I have to know that much before I say anything else."

"In love with her?" Alex felt like an echo. "With whom?"

"Babette...the singer you've been dating."

James cleared his throat, and, looking anxious, glanced at his father. "I...you two obviously need time alone. I'll leave now."

"James, *what* is Carol talking about?"

His son wore an injured look, as if to suggest Alex was doing him a terrible injustice by suspecting he had anything to do with Carol's belief that he was seeing Babette.

"James?" He made his son's name sound like a threat.

"Well," the boy admitted with some reluctance, "Mrs. Sommars might've gotten the impression that you were dating someone else, from...from something I said to Peter. But I'm sure whatever I said was very nebulous." When Alex glared at him, James continued. "All right, all right, Peter and I got to talking things over, and the two of us agreed you guys were wasting a whole lot of time arguing over nothing.

"Mrs. Sommars is way, way better than any of the other women you've dated. Sometimes she dresses a little funny, but I don't mind. I know Peter would really like a dad, and he says you're better than anyone his mom's ever dated. So when Uncle Barn started pressuring you to date that Babette, we... Peter and I, came up with the idea of...you know..."

"I don't know," Alex said sternly, lacing his words with steel. "Exactly what did you say to Carol?"

"I didn't," James was quick to inform him. "Peter did all the talking, and he just casually let it drop that you were dating again and..."

"And had fallen head over heels in love with someone else," Carol supplied.

"In the space of less than a week?" Alex demanded. Did she really think his love was so fickle he could forget her in a few short days? He'd only retreated to fortify himself with ideas before he approached her again.

"You said it was time to cut your losses and look elsewhere," she reminded him.

"You didn't believe that, did you?"

"Yes…I thought you must've done it, especially when Peter started telling me about you and…the singer. What else was I supposed to believe?"

"I'll just go to my room now," James inserted smoothly. "You two go ahead and talk without having to worry about a kid hanging around." He quickly disappeared, leaving only the two of them.

"I'm not in love with anyone else, Carol," Alex said, his eyes holding hers. "If you came because you were afraid I was seeing another woman, then rest assured it isn't true. I'll talk to James later and make sure this sort of thing doesn't ever happen again."

"It won't be necessary."

"It won't?" he asked, frowning. They stood across the room from each other, neither of them making any effort to bridge the distance. The way Alex felt, they might as well have been standing on opposite ends of a football field…playing for opposing teams.

Her eyes drifted shut, and she seemed to be gathering her courage. When she spoke, her voice was low and trembling. "Don't be angry with James…"

"He had no right to involve himself in our business."

"It worked, Alex. It…worked. When I believed I was losing you, when I thought of you with another woman in your arms, I…I wanted to die. I think maybe I did, just a little, because I realized how much I love you and what a fool I've been to think I could go on without you. I needed time, I *demanded* time, and you wouldn't give it to me..."

"I was wrong—I understood that later."

"No," she countered, "you were right. I would never have made up my mind because...because of what happened in my marriage. With Bruce."

The whole world seemed to go still as comprehension flooded Alex's soul. "Are you saying...does this mean you're willing to marry me?" he asked, barely able to believe what she was saying. Barely able to trust himself to stay where he was a second longer.

Alex didn't know who moved first, not that it mattered. All that did matter was Carol in his arms, kissing him with a hunger that seemed to consume them both.

"Yes...yes, I'll marry you," she cried between kisses. "When? Oh, Alex, I'm so anxious to be your wife."

Alex stifled the sudden urge to laugh, and the equally powerful urge to weep. He buried his face in the soft curve of her neck and swallowed hard before dragging several deep breaths through his lungs. He slid his hands into her hair as he brought his mouth to hers, exploring her lips in all the ways he'd dreamed of doing for so many sleepless nights.

Her purse fell to the floor, and she wound her arms around him, moved against him, whispering over and over how much she loved him.

"I missed you so much," he told her as he lifted her from the carpet and carried her across the room. He was so famished for her love that he doubted he'd ever be satisfied.

"I thought I'd never kiss you again," she moaned. "I couldn't bear the thought of not having you in my life."

Alex made his way to the sofa, throwing himself on the

cushions, keeping her in his lap. He stroked her hair as he gazed into her beautiful dark eyes. Unable to resist, he kissed her again.

When they drew apart, Alex rested his forehead against hers and closed his eyes, luxuriating in the warm sensations inside him. He didn't want to talk, didn't want to do anything but hold her and love her.

"Alex," she whispered. "You asked me about Bruce, and I didn't tell you. I was wrong to hold back, wrong not to explain before."

"It's all right, my..."

She gently stroked his face. "For both our sakes, I need to tell you."

"You're sure?"

She didn't *look* sure, but she nodded, and when she started speaking, her voice trembled with pain. "I was incredibly young and naive when I met Bruce. He was the most fun-loving, daring boy I'd ever dated. The crazy things he did excited me, but deep in my heart I know I'd never have married him if I hadn't gotten pregnant with Peter."

Alex kissed her brow and continued to stroke her hair.

"Although Bruce seemed willing enough to marry me," she began, "I don't know how much pressure my father applied." Her voice was gaining strength as she spoke. "It was a bad situation that grew worse after Peter was born. That was when Bruce started drinking heavily and drifted from one job to another. Each month he seemed to be more depressed and more angry. He claimed I'd trapped him and he was going to make sure I paid for what I did." She closed her eyes and he heard her sigh. "I did pay, and so did Peter. My life became a nightmare."

Alex had suspected things were bad for her, but he'd no idea how ugly. "Did he beat you, Carol?"

Her eyes remained closed, and she nodded. "When Bruce drank, the demon inside him would give rise to fits of jealousy, fear, depression and hatred. The more he drank, the more the anger came out in violent episodes. There were times I thought that if I didn't escape, he'd kill me."

"Didn't your family know? Surely they guessed?"

"I hardly ever got to see them. Bruce didn't approve of me visiting my family. In retrospect, I realize he was afraid of my father. Had Dad or Tony known what was happening, they would've taken matters into their own hands. I must have realized it, too, because I never told them, never said a word for fear of involving them. It was more than that.... I was too humiliated. I didn't want anyone to know about the terrible problems we were having, so I didn't say anything—not even to my mother."

"But surely there was someone?"

"Once…once Bruce punched me so hard he dislocated my jaw, and I had to see a doctor. She refused to believe all my bruises were due to a fall. She tried to help me, tried to get me to press charges against him, but I didn't dare. I was terrified of what Bruce would do to Peter."

"Oh, Carol." The anger Alex was experiencing was so profound that he clenched his fists. The idea of someone beating this warm, vibrant woman filled him with impotent rage.

"I'd lost any respect I ever had for Bruce shortly after we were married. Over the next three years I lost respect for myself. What kind of woman allows a man to abuse her mentally and physically, day after day, week after week, year after year? There must've been something terribly wrong with me. In ways I can't even begin to understand, all the hurtful, hateful things Bruce accused me of began to seem valid."

"Oh, Carol…" Alex's chest heaved with the weight of her pain.

"Then Bruce didn't come home one night. It wasn't unusual. I knew he'd come back when he was ready, probably in a foul mood. That was what I'd braced myself for when the police officer came to tell me Bruce had been killed in an accident. I remember I stared up at the man and didn't say anything. I didn't feel anything.

"I was hanging clothes on the line, and I thanked him for letting me know and returned to the backyard. I didn't phone anyone, I didn't even cry."

"You were in shock."

"I suppose, but later when I was able to cry and grieve, mingled with all the pain was an overwhelming sense of relief."

"No one could blame you for that, my love," Alex said, wanting with everything in him to wipe away the memories of those years with her husband.

"Now…now do you understand why I couldn't tell you about Bruce?" she asked. "Your marriage to Gloria was so wonderful—it's what a marriage was meant to be. When she died, your love and James's love surrounded her. When Bruce died—" she hesitated, and her lips were trembling "—he was with another woman. It was the final rejection, the final humiliation." She drew in a ragged breath and turned, her eyes burning into his. "I don't know what kind of wife I'll be to you, Alex. Over the years I've thought about those three nightmarish years and I've wondered what would've happened had I done things differently. Maybe the fault *was* my own…maybe Bruce was right all along, and if I'd only been a better woman, he wouldn't have needed to drink. If I'd done things differently, he might've been happy."

"Carol, you don't truly believe that, do you?"

"I…I don't know anymore."

"Oh, love, my sweet, sweet love. You've got to realize that any problems Bruce had were of his own making. The reasons for his misery lay within himself. Nothing you could ever have done would've been enough." He cupped her face in his hands. "Do you understand what I'm saying?"

"I…I can't make myself fully believe that, and yet I know it's true. But Alex…this time I want everything to be right." Her eyes were clouded and uncertain, as if she suspected he'd be angry with her.

"It will be," he promised her, and there wasn't a single doubt in his heart.

Carol awoke when dawn silently slipped through the lush drapes of the honeymoon suite. She closed her eyes and sighed, replete, sated, unbelievably happy. Deliriously happy.

From the moment Carol had agreed to become Alex's wife to this very morning, exactly one month had passed. One month. It hardly seemed possible.

In one month, they'd planned, arranged and staged a large wedding, complete with reception, dinner and dance.

True to her word, Carol's mother had prepared a reception dinner that couldn't have been surpassed. Angelina had started dragging out her biggest pots and pans the Sunday afternoon she brought Alex back to the house to introduce him to the family.

Last week, Carol's sisters and their families had all arrived.

The wedding became a celebration of love, a family reunion, a blending of families, all at once.

At the reception, Alex had surprised her with the honeymoon trip to Hawaii. The boys were mildly put out that they hadn't been included. Hawaii would have been the perfect place to "check out chicks," as Peter put it. To appease them, Alex promised a family vacation over the Thanksgiving holiday. Peter and James had promptly started talking about a Mexican cruise.

Carol smiled as she savored memories of her wedding day. Peter and James had circulated proudly among the guests, accepting full credit for getting their parents together.

Alex stirred and rolled onto his side, slipping his hand around her waist and tucking his body against hers as naturally as if they'd been married three years instead of three marvelous days.

Carol had been crazy in love with Alex before she married him, but the depth of emotion that filled her after the wedding ceremony made what she'd experienced earlier seem weak by comparison.

Never had she been more in love. Never had she felt so desirable. Just as she'd known it would be, Alex's lovemaking was gentle and unselfish while at the same time fierce and demanding. Thinking of how often and well he'd loved her in the last few days was enough to increase the tempo of her heart.

"Good morning," she whispered, as Alex turned to face her.

"Good morning."

Their eyes met and spoke in silent messages.

He was telling her he loved her. She was saying she loved him back. He was saying he needed her. She echoed that need.

Alex kissed her again, lightly, his lips as weightless as the creeping sunlight.

"Oh, love," he whispered reverently, spreading moist kisses over her face. "I don't think I'll ever get tired of making love with you."

"I certainly hope not." She smiled at him, brushing a stray curl from his brow. She fought back the ready tears that his love brought so easily to the surface. But it would've been impossible to restrain them. Alex didn't understand her tears, and Carol could find no way to explain.

He tenderly wiped the moisture from her face and kissed her eyes. "I can't bear to see you cry. Please tell me if there's anything I can do…."

"Oh, no…" After all the times they'd made love, learned and explored each other's bodies in the past three days, he still couldn't completely accept her tears, fearing he was the cause. Once again, Carol tried to make him understand. "I…I didn't realize making love could be so wonderful…so good."

Alex momentarily closed his eyes, his look full of chagrin and something else she couldn't name. "We didn't take any precautions last night."

His words triggered a slow easy smile. "I know, and I'm glad."

"Why? I thought we decided to wait a few months before we even considered starting a family.

"What do you think your chances of getting pregnant are?" he asked after several minutes of kissing and touching.

She smiled again. "About a hundred percent."

The room went quiet. When Alex spoke, his voice was strangled. "How would you feel about that?"

"Unbelievably happy. I want your child, Alex."

His mouth found hers again for a kiss that grew wilder and wilder. Nestling her head against his strong shoulder, Carol sighed. She felt happier than she'd ever imagined possible. Happy with her husband, her family, herself.

Epilogue

After all the years Carol had worked as an obstetrical nurse, after all the birthing classes she'd taught, she should be able to recognize a contraction. Still, she wasn't a hundred percent sure and had delayed contacting Alex until she was several hours into labor.

Resting her hands on her distended abdomen, she rubbed it gently, taking in several relaxing breaths. Twins! She and Alex were having *twins*. He felt as excited, as ecstatic, as she did. Maybe even more so… Everything was ready for their babies. The nursery was furnished with two cradles, each with a different mobile hanging above it, and Alex had painted a mural, a forest scene, on the wall for his daughters. All their little sweaters and sleepers were stacked in twin dressers he'd lovingly refinished.

Carol took another deep breath as the next pain struck. Then, knowing she shouldn't delay much longer, she reached for the phone and called Alex at the office.

"Yes," he cried impatiently. This last week he'd been as nervous as…a father-to-be.

"It's Carol."

She heard his soft intake of breath. "Are you all right?"

"I'm fine."

"You wouldn't be calling me at the office if you were fine," he countered sharply. "Is something going on that I should know about?"

"Not really. At least not yet, but I think it might be a good idea if you took the rest of the afternoon off and came home."

"Now?"

"If you're in the middle of a project, I can wait," she assured him, but she hoped he'd be home soon, otherwise she was going to end up driving herself to the hospital.

"I'm not worried about *me*," he said. "Are the babies coming now? Oh, Carol, I don't know if I'm prepared for this."

"Don't worry. I am."

Alex expelled his breath forcefully. "I'll be there in ten minutes."

"Alex," she cried. "Don't speed."

She used the time before his arrival to make some phone calls, then collected her purse and her small suitcase—packed several weeks ago. Finally, she sank into her favorite chair, counting the minutes between contractions.

From a block away, Carol could hear the roar of his truck as he sped toward the house. The squealing of brakes was followed by the truck door slamming. Seconds afterward, Alex vaulted into the house, breathless and pale.

She didn't get up from her chair; instead, Carol held out both hands to him. "Settle down, big daddy."

He flew to her side and knelt in front of her, clasping her hands in his. It took him a moment to compose himself.

"This is it, isn't it? We're in labor?" he asked when he'd found his voice.

"We're in labor," Carol told him and stroked his hair.

"How can you be so calm about this?"

She smiled and bent forward to brush her lips over his. "One of us has to be."

"I know…I know…you need me to be strong for you now, but look at me," he said, holding out his hands for her inspection. "I'm shaking." Gently he laid those same shaking hands on Carol's abdomen, and when he glanced up at her, his eyes were bright with unshed tears. "I love these babies—our daughters—so much. I can't believe how lucky I am. And now that they're about to be born, I feel so humble, so unworthy."

"Oh, Alex…"

"I guess we'd better go. Is there anything we need to do first?"

"No. I've phoned my mother and the doctor, and my suitcase is by the door." She made an effort to disguise the intensity of her next contraction by closing her eyes and breathing slowly and deeply until it passed. When she opened her eyes, she discovered Alex watching her intently. If possible, he looked paler than he had before.

"Are you going to be all right?" she asked.

"I…I don't know. I love our babies, but I love you more than anything. I can't stand to see you in pain. I—"

His words were interrupted by the sound of another car pulling into the driveway and two doors slamming. James burst into the house first, followed by Peter, both looking as excited as if it were Christmas morning.

"What are you two doing home from school?" Carol demanded.

"We heard you were in labor. You don't think we'd miss this, do you?"

"You heard?" Carol echoed. "How? From whom?"

The two boys eyed each other. "We've got our sources," James said.

This wasn't the time or place to question them. "All right, we won't discuss it now. James, take care of your father. Peter, load up the car. I think it might be best if you drove me yourself. James, bring your father—he's in no condition to drive."

Their sons leaped into action. "Come on, Dad, we're going to have a couple of babies," James said, urging his father toward the late-model sedan the two boys shared.

By the time they got to Ford Memorial, Carol's pains had increased dramatically. She was wheeled to the labor room while James and Peter were left to fend for themselves in the waiting room.

Alex was more composed by now, more in control. He smiled shyly and took her hand, clutching it between both of his. "How are you doing?"

"Alex, I'm going to be fine and so are our daughters."

Janice Mandle came bustling in, looking pleased. "Okay, we all ready for this special delivery?" she asked.

"Ready," Carol said, nodding firmly.

"Ready," Alex echoed.

With Janice's help and Alex's love, Carol made it through her next contractions. As she was being taken into the delivery room, Alex walked beside her. The pains were coming faster, but she managed to smile up at him.

"Don't worry," she whispered.

"I love you," he whispered back. He reached for her hand again and they met, palm to palm, heart to heart.

* * *

"Grandma, can I have seconds on the zabaglione?" James called from the large family kitchen.

Angelina Pasquale's smile widened and her eyes met those of her daughter. "I told you my cooking would put some meat on his bones."

"That you did, Mama," Carol said, exchanging a private smile with her husband. She and the babies had been home for a week. Royalty couldn't have been treated better. James and Peter were crazy about their sisters, and so far the only tasks allotted Carol had been diaper-changing and breastfeeding. She was well aware that the novelty would wear off, but she didn't expect it to be too soon. Angie and Alison had stolen two teenage hearts without even trying.

"I brought you some tea," Alex said, sliding onto the sofa beside her. His eyes were filled with love. From the moment Carol was brought to the delivery room, the light in Alex's eyes hadn't changed. It was filled with an indescribable tenderness. As she gave birth, his hand had gripped hers and when their two perfect identical daughters were born, there'd been tears in both parents' eyes. Tears of joy. Tears of gratitude. They'd each been granted so much more than they'd ever dreamed. New life. New love. A new appreciation for all the good things in store for them and their combined families.

The soft lilting words of an Italian lullaby drifted toward Carol and Alex. Eyes closed, Carol's mother rocked in her chair, a sleeping infant cradled in each arm. The words were familiar to Carol; she'd heard her mother sing them to her as a child.

When she'd finished, Angelina Pasquale murmured a soft, emotional prayer.

"What did she say?" Alex asked, leaning close to Carol.

A smile tugged at the edges of Carol's mouth. Her fingers were twined with Alex's and she raised his knuckles to her lips and kissed them gently. "She was thanking St. Rita for a job well done."

* * * * *

Welcome to Cedar Cove—
a small town with a big heart!

Guess what? I'm falling in love! With Mack McAfee.

My baby daughter, Noelle, and I have been living next door to Mack since the spring. I'm still a little wary about our relationship, because I haven't always made good decisions when it comes to men. My baby's father, David Rhodes, is testament to *that*.

Come by sometime for a glass of iced tea. Oh, and maybe Mack can join us…

Mary Jo Wyse

Make time for friends.
Make time for Debbie Macomber.

M259_1022EP

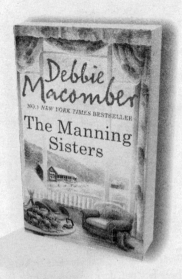
M242_TMS

Join the Manning family for weddings to remember!

Jamie Warren's biological clock is ticking. There is one hope—her tall, dark, gorgeous best friend Rich Manning. Much to her surprise he says he'll help, but has one unexpected condition—they're legally married before the baby is born...

Paul's wife recently passed away, leaving him devastated. So when Diane's sister Leah arrives every night to take care of the dinner she saves him from the verge of collapse. Will grief be allowed to turn to happiness?

Make time for friends.
Make time for Debbie Macomber.

www.mirabooks.co.uk

Sometimes, where you think you're going isn't where you end up...

Bethanne Hamlin has her life all mapped out. Until her ex-husband, Grant, suggests they reconcile—now Bethanne's facing a turn in the road. So, when her former mother-in-law, Ruth, suggests a road trip she jumps at the chance to escape… As they pull away from Blossom Street, Bethanne's daughter Annie decides she's joining this trip of a lifetime—proving to her one-time boyfriend that she can live a brilliant life without him!

Standing at their own personal crossroads, sharing secrets and confronting fears, this journey could change three women's lives forever.

If you had one wish this Christmas...

Make time for friends.
Make time for Debbie Macomber.

www.mirabooks.co.uk

MIRA®

The mark of a good book

At MIRA we're proud of the books we publish, that's why whenever you see the MIRA star on one of our books, you can be assured of its quality and our dedication to bringing you the best books. From romance to crime to those that ask, "What would you do?" Whatever you're in the mood for and however you want to read it, we've got the book for you!

Visit **www.mirabooks.co.uk** and let us help you choose your next book.

★ **Read** extracts from our recently published titles

★ **Enter** competitions and prize draws to win signed books and more

★ **Watch** video clips of interviews and readings with our authors

★ **Download** our reading guides for your book group

★ **Sign up** to our newsletter to get helpful recommendations and **exclusive discounts** on books you might like to read next

www.mirabooks.co.uk